Happily Never After

Heart Springs
Book One

Paisley Nash

This book is a love letter to the dreamers… the ones who grew up wishing on stars, eyelashes, and birthday candles, waiting to be chosen, seen, loved for all that they are.
And for the ones who showed up later, the quiet kind of love that stays, healing the hurts they didn't cause.
This is for every broken beginning rewritten by a braver, softer kind of love. For every rainbow that came after the storm.
Keep wishing, keep dreaming, keep chasing your happily ever after, however it may look.

"Happily ever after isn't a finish line, it isn't a paradise, and it isn't a phenomenon that makes all your dreams come true. Happily ever after is about finding happiness within yourself and holding on to it through any storm that comes your way."

-Chris Colfer

Content Warning

PTSD(military)
Adoption
Death of a parent (heart attack, not on page, but recalled)
Death of a parent during child birth (not on page)
Foster care
Drunk driving deaths (off page)
Drugs and alcohol use (alcohol on page, drugs not)
Abuse of a child (not on page, just discussed)
Celiac, including but not limited to: flare ups (vomiting, illness, etc)
Graphic/explicit sexual content
A fire on page (no death or loss)

Dear Nashland

Please Read Before Diving In

Thank you so much for reading Happily Never After! I am so appreciative of each and every one of you!

If you've ever read a book from my other pen name, Bex Dawn, you know I love a long, angsty, tragic story with an HEA. I love the depth I can create with writing. I love making characters feel real, their stories tangible. That in mind, she is on the moderately longer side, but to me, she's worth every heartbreaking and healing moment!

Also, there is a slight suspense plot line that isn't fully solved in this book as it continues on throughout the series. It doesn't change anything for these characters or their HEA! Please be warned, it's not fully solved in this book.

Happily Never After is a slow burn, spicy romance with enemies to lovers elements, a man learning to become a father AND his road to adoption (keep in mind, he does not have the child for the entire book as the stages of him getting custody are a heavy topic)

This story contains a social worker but she is not on Kade's case when they get together. I did a lot of research, spoke to many people in the applicable fields, and took care when writing this book. It's been through Alphas, Betas, Sensitivity Readers, and an editing team. However, it is still a work of fiction, and liberties have been taken.

I hope you enjoy every banter rich and angsty, loved up moment!

*Looking for others to chat with about HNA? There's a spoiler thread pinned in my reader group, **<u>Nashland</u>***

*If you notice a trigger I didn't catch, please feel free to DM on Insta-gram(fastest), email my PA Taylor **(<u>paisleynashauthor.pa@gmail.com</u>)** or through my reader group!*

Thank you again!
Paisley

*Check out the Spotify playlist that made me sob way too many times while writing this book! Enjoy, Nashland and **Welcome to Heart Springs!***

PROLOGUE

Fuck Forever and Fuck Happily Ever Afters

I'VE LOVED MARLEE MAY Parker since I was six years old. She was the prettiest thing I'd ever seen, and she wouldn't pay me a lick of attention. So, I pulled her pigtails. The moment I locked my gray eyes with her baby blues as she drove her tiny little fist directly into my nose, she owned me.

Hook.

Line.

Sinker.

When blood was spouting down my chubby cheeks as she whined and cradled her hand, I was smiling. Smiling because I knew, even back then, that I'd found her.

My true love.

The one who completed me just like my mama completed my dad. Just like Grammy did Grandad, and so on. Gravity wavered. I felt my feet shift from under me. My world rocked—*literally*.

And then, I fainted.

Turns out I don't do well with blood.

But I do a hell of a lot better than Marlee does. She screamed at the top of her lungs for the police, claiming there'd been an attack, and a *stupid boy* was dying. We were both put in a time out.

Marlee cried big, giant crocodile tears. All I wanted was to hug her. To wipe them away. To make her smile. So, from my spot in time out next to her, I tugged her into my arms, vowing to make it all better.

She kneed me in the nuts.

I told her I loved her.

She told me to *fudge off.*

Not much has changed in the last seventeen years, and yet *everything* has changed. And it's about to change again—for the better.

So much better.

I grin to myself as my thumb runs over the edge of the dainty gold band nestled around my neck along with my dog tags. Six more months. That's all I need before my life, *our life*, can finally begin.

"Seriously, man?" Griffin barks, shoving the back of my head roughly. I bat his hand away with a smirk. "If you're hellbent on spending your time with your head up your ass, might as well daydream about pussy instead of wedding bells."

My eyes narrow on the big bastard. "Don't talk about her—"

"Pussy?" He smirks, crossing his thick arms over his equally thick chest. His army green pulls taut, and it only serves to further piss me off. "I bet pretty little Marlee May has a pretty tight p—"

And those are the only words he gets out before I'm on him.

Our limbs are a blur as we grapple for dominance. My fist collides with his sharp jaw, and pain immediately lances up my arm, but I don't stop. No one talks about Marlee like that. No one.

He chuckles deeply, his chest rattling beneath me as I finally get him on his back. Sterling grins up at me as my arm arcs, ready to make his dumbass bleed.

"There he is," he rumbles, Tennessee accent thick. My brows furrow, my breaths coming in heaving pants as I freeze. "Glad to see you haven't lost your balls completely. You're gonna need 'em."

I exhale roughly, my hand dropping to my side. "What's that supposed to mean?"

"You got fat." He grunts as he heaves upward, tossing me to the side.

I jump to my feet and roll my eyes as I offer him my hand to help him get up. He reaches to accept, but at the last second, I yank my hand away, leaving him to collide heavily with the floor.

"Sorry." I shrug, dropping back down onto my bunk with a chuckle. "Must be too *fat* to help your big ass up."

"You're such a fuckin' prick." Griffin shoots me a glare and jumps to his feet with more grace than he should possess.

He tries to run a hand through his hair but grimaces when he remembers he's now bald—a gift from me and the other guys in our squad yesterday. We gave him a little trim while he slept, stealing our retribution where we could.

I snicker to myself.

"Yeah, yeah, laugh it up, asshole." He eyes my thick dark brown hair. Even with my military cut, it's still a lot. "While you can," he mutters ominously.

I scoff and bend down to re-tie my boots. Nothing but perfection. Always. "What did you mean before?"

He waits for me to finish lacing up and the silence grates on my nerves. Griffin's never quiet, so whatever it is, it can't be good. I swallow thickly, preparing myself as I meet his steely gaze.

"We're shipping out."

My spine snaps straight as dread pools in my gut. "When?"

His jaw ticks. "Three days from now. Big aid mission." He stands and leans forward, giving my shoulder a firm squeeze. "Time will pass quickly, and before you know it, you'll be in South Dakota, on one knee, finally giving away that ring around your neck—just wait."

I look up into my Staff Sergeant's eyes. A man I've known for nearly three and a half years. A man I respect. He's more than my best friend; he's family.

Despite all the shit he's seen in the last decade, he's still good. More than that, he's honest. If he says we'll be back for me to make it home in time, I trust him.

"Thank you, Sir." He glares at me. I grin wider. "Now fuck off so I can check in on my girl."

He shakes his head and steps back, letting his heavily tattooed arm drop to his side. His gaze snags on the newest letter sitting on my pillow.

"Still think you deserve better than her," he mutters but I ignore him, tossing a middle finger in the air.

His comments are nothing new. None of the guys like Marlee, but I don't care. I love her.

"Fuck off," I grumble. "And get out."

"Don't get cum on the fucking floor!" he shouts, letting the heavy door slam behind him.

A bark of laughter slips from my lips as I fall onto my back to get comfortable. If this letter is what I think it is, I make no promises.

Smiling, I gently slip the folded piece of paper from the bent and stained envelope. I'd expect nothing less when they've traveled over five-thousand miles, sometimes farther, depending on where I'm at, and while it sucks being so far from home, I've known this was coming for a long time.

It's been the plan for as long as I can remember.

Work on the farm, get good grades, graduate, join the military, and honor my country. Have a pack of kids and be beyond fucking happy.

I made promises to my girl. Promises I intend to keep.

Four years apart. Together forever.

Happily ever after.

The ring. The wedding. The white picket fence. All the fucking babies I can get her to give me. I want a whole house full of them. I want loud mornings with my family and quiet nights with my wife. Crying and crappy diapers. I want the whole goddamned package.

Don't realize I'm smiling till it falls. Normally, she writes about home, about my family and how she's loving college. But that's not what this letter's about…

Not at *fucking* all.

I jackknife up to a seated position, and the room spins.

Air stalls in my lungs as I finish the shorter than normal letter, already knowing the second I'm done reading, my life will change forever.

Forever.

Four years and then forever.

That's what she said. What she promised.

But as I read the last word, finding my entire world crumbling beneath my feet, I know without a shadow of a doubt that Marlee May Parker is a motherfucking *liar*, because she's no longer promising me forever.

"I want a big life, Kade. Cities, adventure, the world. Something more than a dusty town and a farm that smells like hay, horse shit, and honey. You dream small, and I can't shrink myself to fit it. I don't want this. I don't want you. I can't do this anymore. I don't love you."

The paper slips from my fingers, fluttering gently in the air, like a delicate feather on the wind, instead of a death knell in my entire relationship.

Fuck… in my world.

Nausea swells rapidly in my throat, and I swallow it down, refusing to give way to the emotions battering against my insides.

Not yet.

Not right now.

Instead, I slowly push to my feet and roll my shoulders back. I inhale once, hold it for ten beats, then exhale, releasing every aching pain and desire to scream, *to fucking rage*, out with it.

Not yet.

Not right now.

It takes me less than five minutes to make it to the administrative building and even less time to barge into my C.O.'s office. He's probably pissed, and I'm more than likely about to get my ass reamed but I don't care.

I don't care about anything.

Not even as the words that will once again change my life slip from my lips without pause.

"I'd like to extend my contract, Sir. I'm no longer going home."

Fuck forever and fuck happily ever after's.

Chapter One

WiFi Strong, Life Weak

9 YEARS LATER

Fuck is that?

An incessant buzzing noise tries to pull me from my dreamless sleep. I ignore it, willing it to shut the fuck up. Hold my breath, head pounding as the seconds tick by.

When it finally stops, I exhale roughly, shoving my face deeper into my pillow, and pray for darkness to find me again.

Half a minute later, it starts up again.

"Goddammit!" I snap, shoving upright in my bed.

My world spins, blurry vision straining against the burning light spilling in from my window. I squeeze my eyes shut, breathing deeply. My head pounds, and my right eye twitches so rapidly, I seriously consider taking a knife to it.

The laminate floor is cold under my feet. I really need a rug. But getting a rug means going out, means shopping and buying things for this shithole of an apartment, and if I do that…

Shaking my head, I spear my fingers through my hair, getting caught up in the tangles halfway through.

My phone buzzes, and I yank the fuckin' thing from my nightstand. The charger releases with a jerk, and the rickety, hand-me-down end table wobbles precariously. My brow arches as I eye the ancient wood for a moment, wondering if this will be the day it finally gives out.

It sways once, twice, before settling with a creak. Could just fix it, but again, fixing reeks of permanence, and the only thing I want permanently in this life is a good buzz and some fucking silence.

The vibrating device in my palm assures me that the latter is nothing more than a pipe dream, but the bottle of Jack on my floor murmurs that not all dreams are lost.

I snatch it up and flick the partially screwed-on cap off before tipping it back for a deep swallow. The lukewarm liquid burns its way down my throat, through my veins, my lungs, before settling heavily in my empty gut.

It's enough to wake me up, but I take another drink for good measure before dropping it onto the nightstand. The thing groans from the weight—the sound mimicking exactly how I feel.

My eyes slide across the outdated studio apartment I live in. Walls that were once covered in white floral wallpaper are now tinged a questionable yellow, telling a long tale of smoke-filled nights and sweaty days. The floors are those wooden tiles from the seventies that remind you of exactly two things: your grandma and Dahmer.

And they are, in fact, from the seventies.

Originally built for my landlord's son after college, the above-garage apartment is small, simple, and barely functional. The furniture is an eclectic mash-up of things she no longer wanted, crap he left behind, and stuff my family forced me to take.

Basically, it's a shithole.

Agnes Whittaker, the property owner, is the oldest person in town, and like Agnes, this place is on its last leg. But it's got four walls, a roof, and a stellar internet signal that I'd never be able to get back in Heart Springs, so it's home.

I roll my neck, relishing the way the tight muscles stretch and tug. Lift my right arm, feeling every bone and joint pop with the movement. Jaw ticking, teeth grinding, I slowly repeat the process on my left side. My peck burns worse than the liquor, screaming at me to stop.

I don't.

Can't.

I have to feel it—it reminds me why I'm here. And like it always does, the thought clouds my vision like some sort of fucked-up rose-colored glasses, making me see my home with fresh eyes.

Accepting eyes.

With a grunt, I wrap my fingers tightly around my vibrating phone and stomp toward my desk, dodging heaps of laundry left over from my recent work trip. My bare foot catches on the jerry-rigged internet cable that leads from the only window to my computer setup. Stumbling, I catch myself on my desk seconds before my already pounding skull collides with it.

My eyes slice over the notifications rapidly pinging across my wall of monitors, and my stomach sinks. I missed a meeting with my team, and my boss is pissed.

Like to say it's unlike me to sleep in late, but that'd make me a liar. I may be many things these days—a shitty son, bad friend, messy son-of-bitch, grumpy fucker who drinks too much to combat the demons in his soul, but a liar is something I'm *not.*

Despite the slight buzz burning through me, it takes me no time at all to get the most important issues handled before I switch over to emails that have accumulated over the last week I spent on a protection detail out of state.

102 Unread Messages

"Hell with this," I mutter. I'll hear shit for it later, but that's future me's problem.

Sober me.

Leaning over my keyboard, I type out an away notice in the chat and set my computer to sleep. I can't stand to be inside this place for one more minute. I feel like the walls are closing in on me.

Foregoing a shirt, I snatch my phone and head for the door. My eyes slide across the bottle of Jack.

I pause for less than a second before muttering, "Fuck it."

Best way to spend the anniversary of the worst day of my life? Drunk.

Sweat beads down the center of my chest as I push myself harder than I have in weeks. Harder than I should. My back arches as I press the weights high above me, feeding off the ache burning through my muscles.

I lower the barbell with control, ignoring the sharp pull in my shoulder. The pain's buried beneath layers of damage, scar tissue, and memories I don't want to touch. It begs me to stop.

But I don't.

Even if I wish I could.

I'm somewhere around my twelfth set when a god-awful noise cuts through Metallica's "Enter Sandman." The sudden blare of a different song jars me mid-rep, and my arms give out, turning to limp pasta before I can catch myself. The bar drops toward my chest, and I twist hard to the right, barely dodging it. Plates crash to the concrete on either side, loud as hell.

Grunting, I sit up and shoot a glare at the speaker hanging in the corner. It's old, crackles when the volume's too high, and likes to switch over to Agnes's talk radio at random. But it's loyal.

Until now.

"What the fuck is that?" I bark, blinking at my phone as some pop-girl bullshit blares through the speaker like a traitor.

My brows crash together when I try to place the song but come up blank. The chick is repeatedly singing the words "*shake it off*" at an octave that makes my teeth ache. After she circles through the same set of lyrics for the third time, the room falls silent for a split second before my playlist kicks back on. As soon as Metallica fills my ears, my shoulders drop in relief.

I move to reset the barbell, but the moment I touch it, the same song blasts again. With a snarl, my head snaps toward the old stereo across the room, only to notice my phone lighting up and rattling with vibrations across the workbench.

I gape at the device, slowly realizing the random song isn't just a song—it's a ringtone.

And it's coming from my phone.

"Fucking kill me," I mutter, shaking my head as I yank the aux cord from the boombox.

The screen lights up with a horribly filtered photo of my younger sister, Hazel, except someone's edited it to make her look like a man.

"Colby." I sigh with a small, reluctant chuckle, instantly knowing which one of my twin sisters is behind the prank.

But the laugh doesn't stick.

The weight of the inevitable conversation presses in, thick and unwanted, wrapping around my chest like a vice.

Blowing out a slow breath, I drop onto the bench, and swipe to answer, bracing for impact. "What?"

"Where have you been?" she shouts, her pitch oddly reminiscent of the song still echoing around in my brain. "I've been calling you for days. I could have been dying, Kade! You do realize that, right?"

I roll my eyes. "Clearly, you're alive. More than that, you're well enough to scream at me, so things can't be that bad." Waving a dismissive hand through the air, I add, "Silver linings, and all that shit. What do you need, Hazy?"

"You need to come home, Kade," she demands. "You didn't even call—today of all days."

Today of all days.

Like it's just any other date. A casual reminder that this is the day our dad died.

The day everything cracked wide open.

When I don't immediately respond, she tacks on, "Mom really misses you."

Guilt washes over me, fast and hard. The words *I know she does*, almost fall from my lips right alongside, *I miss her, too*. But I choke them down like I always do.

I wish I had the strength to show up for the people who need me, but I don't. I can't.

"I just saw her a few weeks ago."

"You popped into town for an hour before rushing off, claiming you had to work."

"I did have to work." Annoyed as hell, I stomp to the nearest wall and promptly bang my head against the dilapidated wood. "Besides, if mom misses me so much, she can call me."

Hazel scoffs. "Or you can pick your big, man-child of an ass up off your dirty leather throne, and leave that dumpster fire you call a house. You can take a shower, because we all know you smell like actual shit right now. Then you can put on some real clothes, touch some fucking grass, and *come home*, Kade. It's not that hard. Just get in your truck and drive the thirty miles it takes to do the right thing. It's time."

"Who the hell was that and where is my baby sister?" I ask, my stomach twisting at the accuracy of her words. "And I don't smell."

I lift my arm, smelling my bare pit and cringe.

I might smell a little bit.

"One, I'm hardly your baby sister. I'm only eleven months younger than you."

"Semantics." My lip tips up in a smirk. "You'll always be my baby sister."

"And two," she continues, ignoring me. "Stop trying to change the subject. You forget how well I know you, Kade William Archer. You forget that you were once my best friend."

The ache in the pit of my stomach spreads to my heart. *Once my best friend.* I know we're older, and there's a world of differences between us now, but the stark realization that so much has changed in the last decade hits harder than I expected.

Hazel and I *were* best friends.

Like she said, we were born just eleven months apart—Irish twins. With Gemma a few years ahead and completely disinterested in the farm life we were raised to embrace, the daily grind often fell on us. Colby and Clementine, the actual twins in our family, were way too young to be helpful. Hazel and I picked up the slack, but it never felt like work when we were side by side. We were inseparable.

Now, I can't recall a single detail about her life beyond what I knew back when we were kids.

Fuck.

I drag my fingers through my beard, contemplating the words I should, but can't, say. After a long pause, the best I can come up with is a gruff, "What's your point?"

"The point is, you need to get over your shit and step the hell up!"

"Step up?" I snap. "What the fuck does that mean?"

I did step up. I served my fucking country. I nearly *died* for it. And I did all that after spending over a decade working my ass off on my family's farm. Early mornings before school, late nights after homework. Sunup to sundown when I wasn't in school.

I broke my back for Honey Bea Farm—and for what? It's nothing but dirt and bad memories.

"It means, *prickhole*, that it's time for you to get over whatever issues you have with us and help out. The farm is going to shit. Mom is struggling to handle things by herself, and I can only do so much."

My spine snaps straight. "What do you mean the farm is going to shit?"

"Exactly what it sounds like!"

I shake my head, tugging on my hair that apparently fell out of its weird updo somewhere between upstairs and here. "That doesn't make any sense." I say the words, more to myself than anything, but she hears me just the same.

"Are you seriously that dense? It's just mom and I running the entire operation now that Dad's gone. What did you expect? Money is tight, which means the ranch hands have no incentive to stick around. Things are changing, especially with that new—"

"What about Ridge?" I interrupt, my heart slamming against my rib cage as the need to run so fucking far away from this conversation fills my veins.

Guilt is eating me alive with every brutal word she tacks on, but all I can see are sunflower fields, and white picket fences. All I can *hear* is the sound of Dad laughing as he chases the twins around the yard, while Mom cheers him on from the porch.

"Hell, Kade. You're so damn detached from our lives, it's not even funny," Hazel mutters, sounding exhausted and so much older than a moment ago. "Clearly, you lost more than Marlee when you shipped off to God knows where and forgot all about your family."

I freeze.

She goes silent.

Everything goes still.

"Holy shit!" my sister cries, immediately backpedaling, but it's too late. "I'm so sorry, K—"

I hang up.

She calls again.

I send her to voicemail.

Again and again. Unmoving, I stand in the middle of Mrs. Whittaker's shitty garage, beneath her shitty apartment, filled with shitty things, and I feel *shitty*.

It's not the mention of Marlee that guts me. Not really. I mourned that love story—and the way it ended—a long-ass time ago.

It's everything that came *after*.

The choices I made because of it.

The years I spent away and who I lost while I was gone.

That's what keeps me up at night.

I gained so damn much when I decided to become a Ranger, but I don't know if it'll ever outweigh everything I lost.

When the phone pings repeatedly from incoming texts, everything turns back on, like pressing *play* on an old black-and-white film. The screen glitches, the lines dance hazily, the soundtrack clicks on with an annoying sound.

Suddenly, birds are chirping, Mrs. Whittaker is yelling at her yappy Chihuahua, and my world is slotting into place around me. I tune it all out like I always do, going back into the perfectly crafted, quiet box of nothingness I choose to exist in as I glance at my phone.

Hazy: I'm so fucking sorry.

Hazy: I didn't mean it.

Hazy: Okay. I meant it.

Hazy: But I'm still sorry.

Hazy: You know what, Kade? Get over yourself. Your a dick, and you know it.

*Kade: You're**

Feeling spiteful, I tap out a quick response I know will piss her off. Then I snag the Jack and head upstairs to my apartment.

"I didn't take you for a Swifty."

I snap my head down, finding Agnes standing at the foot of the outdoor stairs that lead to my place, and cock a brow in confusion.

She hikes a thumb over her shoulder, pointing to the garage. "The music."

I shake my head slowly, still not getting it. She plants her hands on her narrow hips, the thin blue material of her outfit that does nothing to hide her… *form*…swaying with the movement.

With a grimace, I look elsewhere. It's not her fault. I'm sure if I was a ninety-something-year-old woman living alone in the middle of nowhere, I'd burn my bras too.

"You know," she calls, her voice shaking with the exertion of yelling up at me. "*Hate, hate, hate,*" she sings—at least, I think that's what she's doing. My mouth gapes open as I watch my ancient landlord sway her busted hips side to side, her muumuu unable to contain all her assets. "*Shake, shake, shake—*"

I slam a hand up in the air between us and back into my place. My head snaps side to side so quickly, I get whiplash.

"No, Agnes!" I shout. "No. Don't shake anything. Just—" I break off, running a trembling hand through my hair. "I can see *everything*," I whisper-hiss, thoroughly destroyed, inside and out.

She freezes, narrowing her eyes at me. "Are you gawkin' at my tits, boy?"

"What?" I shout, hands going up in frustration. "Oh, my god! This can't be my fucking life."

She clicks her tongue. "Don't be so damn dramatic."

I see the moment she decides to further traumatize me, and I internally die a little more. Smirking, Mrs. Whittaker reaches her hands up and slowly unbuttons the first hook on her weird dress.

"I haven't seen any lady friends around here in a long while. If you're that hard up to see some flesh, all ya had to do was ask."

"I'm leaving," I state, taking another step away as revulsion fills me so fast, my cock does something it's never done before—disappears inside my body like a goddamn turtle hiding in its shell. "You're nuts. I'm moving out."

She plants her tiny, bony foot on the bottom step and waggles her bushy gray brows as she works the third button open, revealing a patch of aged skin. I shudder.

"Come on, Kade. You know what they say. Once you lay a gray, you never—"

"Jesus Christ, Agnes!" I shout, jolting backward into my apartment. "Leave me alone so I can die in peace, you old bat!"

The door slams just as her raucous laughter kicks up, adding insult to injury.

"One of these days, boy, I'm sending you a hooker! A real good one, too!"

A shiver racks through my body, and I hear her stomp back down the driveway while singing the words to a song that will forever haunt my dreams.

Bringing the bottle to my lips, I take a long, burning swallow, then collapse onto my tattered couch and close my eyes.

This day can't possibly get any worse.

CHAPTER TWO

ONE CORNFIELD FROM A BREAKDOWN

"WHERE THE HELL AM I?" I mutter, turning down Fleetwood Mac so I concentrate on the maze of winding country roads.

The GPS in my temporary lease chirps, rerouting for the fifth time, and I barely resist the urge to toss it into a ditch. I'm one wrong turn away from needing a search party.

I bump up the heat, rubbing my arms against the chill creeping in. The black satin tank top I threw on this morning is too small, clinging to me like a bad hangover and doing absolutely nothing to keep me warm.

I'd hoped to find my favorite sweater before leaving, but it's probably buried somewhere in the mess of half-unpacked moving boxes back at my tiny new rental. Instead, all I could find was a black suit I thrifted back in New York, the tank, and some sky-high heels, since the pants are way too long.

The outfit's not my style in the least, but it's my first house visit at my new job, and I'm making a futile attempt at professionalism.

A sudden chime blasts through the car's Bluetooth system, making me jump.

The oversized dash screen lights up with a picture of my best friend, Abigail Murphy, and me in footy pajamas—beyond drunk and surrounded by snacks.

Fairest Feral Witch of Them All flashes in bold letters, and I grin, a pang of homesickness twisting my gut as I answer.

"Please tell me you haven't been murdered by a local with a pitchfork already."

"I mean… the odds are narrowing," I mutter, glancing nervously at a crooked mailbox I definitely passed ten minutes ago. "I think my GPS is gaslighting me."

She laughs, and I can practically see her curled up on her Brooklyn couch, messy, dark bun perched atop her head, snacking on something I'm sad I can't eat.

"I take it you're lost?"

"I'm not lost." *I'm super lost.* "I'm just… aggressively rerouting."

"To where, exactly?"

"I'm heading to a house in Wildwood, a little town twenty minutes away from Heart Springs. The case is new, started off with someone named Ethel, but her appendix burst last night and now she's on emergency leave. I'm stepping in until she's back since I don't have any cases of my own yet."

"Look at you," she coos. "You've been at your new job less than a week, and you're already putting out fires all by yourself."

Her words twist something in my gut. I'd be lying if I said I wasn't nervous as hell about doing this home assessment alone. Back in New York, we never went anywhere without a partner—it wasn't safe.

But Summit County's office is way smaller, and they simply don't have the resources for protocol like that.

"I don't know about putting out any fires." I sigh. "Ethel only had a few days on the case, and since everything is so rural here, she seems to have been struggling to gather intake info. The file's practically empty."

She clicks her tongue. "And your boss passed that off to you without any help?"

"He said, and I quote, '*Just get eyes on the place, document, assess. We'll go from there.*' Then told me good luck with this long, solemn look that freaked me out."

Abby claps with glee, the sound so loud through my speakers that I wince.

"Please, oh, please tell me your boss is hot as hell. Like, silver daddy in slacks energy. Tell me he had that whole *I will protect thee and rearrange your insides* look." She sucks in a breath. "Lie if you have to. I won't know."

I groan, dragging a hand through my hair. "Abby. He's like seventy, smells like arthritis cream, and I'm pretty sure I saw a cane in his office."

"I could get into impact play," she murmurs.

"Okay, I'm hanging up now."

"No! Don't leave me!" she cries pitifully. "I'm already withering away without you."

I scoff, but a smile tugs at my lips. "Can we stop talking about my boss now? I'm nervous as it is."

"I guess." She sighs. "Why are you nervous? You've been a social worker for years. You've dealt with some really hard shit and survived."

"These families… they don't have a Safe Haven like we did in the city. There aren't any backup teams, established protocols, or fully staffed departments. It's just a team of, like, ten at most. And sometimes, the difference between a child slipping through the cracks or finding a future is one exhausted caseworker who's willing to show up anyway."

A beat of silence passes before she says, "That was so hot." She moans. "Say it again, but *slower*."

I laugh, easing up a little as the fields roll by in waves of green and gold. Cows. Barns. A tractor that looks older than America. There's even a dog lying in the middle of a dirt road.

It's absurd.

And yet, part of me exhales at the sight of it. Something buried deep tugs loose—nostalgia wrapped in hard, beautiful memories.

It's been a long time since I've spent any time in the country, but I've always loved it.

The quiet, and stillness. The way everything smells like grass and dirt and possibilities. Like Ms. Robin's back porch when the sun was going down and the crickets were just starting to sing.

But, that was years ago, and since then, I've changed. Maybe I'm not cut out for country roads or tiny towns anymore.

"Did I fuck up, Abbs?" I swallow roughly. "What if I can't handle this?"

"By *this*, do you mean your new job, the adventure of a lifetime, or the real reason you moved to the middle of nowhere, South Dakota?"

"All of the above," I choke out.

Abby tuts. "This is your path, Georgia. I know it in my soul. Good things are coming."

I don't answer. Not right away. Because I want to believe her. I want to believe that this leap wasn't a mistake. That trading the tight-knit, well-oiled machine of Safe Haven for Summit County was brave, not stupid.

That I didn't ruin my life by selling most of my possessions and flying halfway across the country to start over in a tiny town, sight unseen, with nothing but a binder of questions, an autoimmune disorder, a suitcase filled with baggage, and a heart full of dreams.

Unfortunately, only time will tell.

For now, I have to get my mind right and focus on what's right in front of me—the future of a tiny little girl who just lost her parents, and the man who's supposed to heal her through her grief.

The click of my blinker fills the silent car at a four-way stop, but no one's around, so I grab the file and scan it again.

Aurora Grace Vernal.

Eight months old, and she's already lost everyone who's ever loved her. She was in a car accident with her parents a week ago. Her mom and dad were pronounced dead at the scene, and Aurora is now in the pediatric intensive care unit at the only hospital in Summit County—Rydell General—over an hour away.

I haven't had time to ascertain the extent of her injuries, but Ethel noted she's recovering well.

The rest of the file's pretty much blank. The number for a probate attorney who filed the parents' will, and the letter of intent stating the guardian. But the attorney is on vacation, so there's no copy of the letter yet, just the guardian's name, age, and a rural address.

Kade William Archer. Thirty-One.

Nothing else. That's all I have to go by. That, and my boss's order to evaluate the guardian and his home and inform him of the mediation set one week from today.

For all I know, Ethel will be back by then, and I'll be off the case, but that doesn't take away the weight of my job today.

"Are you alright?" Abby asks, as if she can tell I'm spiraling from hundreds of miles away. "Do you need me to send you a picture of my boobs?"

I scoff, smiling, and finally make my turn. "No, thanks. I've seen them enough to last a lifetime."

She laughs but quickly sobers. "Seriously. What's going on?"

"Honestly? I don't know." I grip the wheel tighter.

I know I can handle the job. I was trained for this. I studied, prepared, got the damn degree, and passed the licensing exams. Then, I studied again to transfer my license to South Dakota. I know the rules, the assessments, the legal protocols.

But I didn't train for this *feeling*. And no matter how many bad things you see, it never gets easier.

Neither does the weight of deciding whether a baby ends up in the arms of a stranger with no history. Not when you know that if you get it wrong, it won't just be a mark on a file, it'll shape someone's entire life.

Something I can relate to all too well.

"I'm not used to being on my own in this," I admit. "Back at Safe Haven, we had a process, support, and backup. People I could go to if something didn't sit right."

"You had a village."

"Exactly," I whisper.

She's quiet for a long moment, and I keep my eyes on the road, refusing to let myself unravel. Instead, I take the next turn, jaw tight, and glance at the GPS again. My chest stutters with quiet relief when I see the mile countdown flash—two minutes away.

"Hey, Georgia?"

"Yeah?"

"Don't forget… you're not alone just because you're far away."

And there it is.

The reason I refuse to let go of Abigail Murphy, even when my broken brain tells me to run before I lose her, too.

My eyes sting, and I blink fast, like that'll help. Like I can shove the emotion back down where it belongs, but an undeniable sniffle slips free. A reflex.

Abby's quiet voice cuts through the car, sharp with suspicion. "Wait. Are you… are you actually crying?"

I suck in a breath. "No."

"Oh, my God! You are." Her voice climbs an octave. "You never cry! What the hell? I'm officially worried. Come home. Or, no—better yet, I'm coming to South—"

"I'm here, gotta go!" I jab at the *end* button on my steering wheel.

"Don't you dare die!" she yells just as the call cuts out.

I let out a long, uneven exhale, my fingers trembling slightly as they drop from the wheel. My chest feels tight, heart thudding like I just ran a mile instead of having an existential crisis in a car so silent, it feels like I'm emotionally unraveling inside a padded cell.

"You have arrived," the GPS with a robotic, British accent, announces.

"Thank fuck," I murmur, just as a dilapidated, off-white structure tucked between overgrown fields and crooked laundry lines comes into view. I flick on my blinker and ease into the nonexistent driveway, pulling up next to a beat-up station wagon.

The second I park, the front door creaks open with the kind of haunted house groan that makes my spine lock straight.

My arm hairs stand at attention.

This is happening. Like, *right now.*

"Shit," I choke out, wiping my clammy palms on my slacks as I check my reflection in the rearview and immediately regret it.

My eyeliner is smudged, and my skin is pale. I look like a business-casual vampire trying to blend in at a tractor pull.

"Okay, Georgia. Game face." I slap my cheeks and fix my liner while muttering my mantra. "You're a twenty-nine year old badass bitch. You're not that lonely kid anymore. You can do this. There are way scarier things waiting for you in this podunk town than—"

"Who the balls are you talking to?" a raspy voice calls out, slicing through the air like a warning shot as my car rocks side to side.

My eyes snap to the yard in front of me just in time to see a tiny, elderly woman in a faded blue nightgown glaring at me like I just insulted her begonias. Her wild gray curls defy gravity, and her hands are planted firmly on her hips, elbows sharp as scythes.

And I... *I may be in danger.*

The car rocks again.

I jam the window button aggressively, my temper fully engaged.

"Are you seriously kicking my tire?" I snap, mentally calculating if there's any possibility she has a shotgun tucked under her muumuu.

As if in slow motion, we both watch her bony knee arc back before shooting forward with impressive speed. She's got on a pair of cowboy boots a few sizes too big, and when her foot collides with my tire, I realize they must be steel-toed.

"What are you doing?" I cry, my eyes wide. She does it again, and I quickly shove the door open. This is a lawsuit waiting to happen. "Stop it! You're going to hurt yourself!"

The woman huffs and scowls, squaring her narrow shoulders. "It ain't my safety you should be concerned with, girly."

My jaw unhinges, my hands flapping uselessly.

"Are you..." What the hell is happening right now? "Are you *threatening* me?"

She shrugs and picks at her nail with a knitting needle. I have no idea where it came from. "Dunno. Does it *feel* like a threat?"

Okaaay.

So, she's nuts.

I run an agitated hand through my red curls as I scan the property like a prank show crew might pop out of the tumbleweeds. How did this become my life? Two weeks ago, I was sitting in a five-star café eating gluten-free macarons.

"Where the hell did I wind up?" I whisper to the universe at large, not expecting an answer.

"You wound the hell up on my land," she sasses with all the attitude of a petulant teenager. "And you ain't supposed to be here, so get gone!"

My eyes squeeze shut, and my head falls back. I'm suddenly tired. Really fucking tired.

Something cold and metallic presses against my bicep, dangerously close to my boob. I wince. Not because it hurts, but because I already know what I'll see when I open my eyes, and I'm not mentally prepared to fight an old lady today.

Exhaling slowly, I meet the woman's eyes. They're so blue, they're nearly clear, and it dawns on me that she might not be able to see all that well. Without breaking eye contact, I flick the knitting needle away and step back, crossing my arms.

"Look," I say gently, but not weakly. "My name is Georgia Walker. I'm with the Department of Child and Family Services."

Her eyes narrow. "You don't look like no government worker. You look like one of those dominatrix gals off late-night cable."

I blink. "I... *what*?"

She squints harder. "That get-up. Those heels. That car. And all that black? *Mm-hm*. Real *Fifty Shades*."

Oh, *God*.

"I'm here," I enunciate, "on official business. I'm conducting a wellness check at this address. I'm trying to locate Kade Archer."

At the name, her whole body goes taut. Her knitting needle lowers.

"And what's a city girl like you want with Kade?" she snaps, immediately suspicious. "He didn't do nothin' wrong."

"That's not what I'm implying."

"Suits always say that." She pokes the needle toward my chest, this time indenting my push-up bra. "You a tax collector?"

"No."

"In a cult?"

"No."

"Do you sell timeshares?"

"Hell no."

"You're one of those sexy surprise-gram things, aren't ya? Lord knows he needs to get laid. Maybe you're here for his birthday?" Her bushy brows drop. "No, real early for that." She snaps her fingers, chuckling. "Late Valentine's gift."

I gape. "What?"

"You don't have to play coy, sugar. I've read about folks like you." She bites her lip, her glossy dentures pressing into the thin flesh, and leans in, dropping her voice. "Tell me what kind of kinks he has. I've been dyin' to know."

I physically choke on air, and the world around me sort of spins.

Am I high right now?

"I'm right, ain't I?" The woman cackles, shoving me playfully. "Teach me some moves. There's this man down at the bar—"

"I am *not* a stripper," I whisper-hiss. "Or a dancer-gram thing. I'm not here for Mr. Archer like *that*—I'm here for—I'm from…" Holy shit. I can't even speak. I take a deep breath and let it out. "Do you know where Kade Archer is, ma'am?"

"Of course, I do. Boy's been grumpy as a goat in a snowstorm lately. I figured he just needed a good woman. Or at least a flexible one." She stretches out her arms. "I offered, but I'm not as limber as I used to be."

Oh. My. God.

"Head down that gravel path back there, 'bout a quarter mile," she says, nodding toward a barely visible dirt track behind the house. "He's in the apartment over the garage. Looks like a meth den, but the man inside is hotter than a whore in church."

"I think it's *sweating* like a—"

"Stop stallin', girly," she interrupts with a clap. "Put those slutty little heels to work!"

I back up slowly and drop into my car without turning around. I'm pretty sure she's two seconds from slapping my ass and saying *attaboy*.

Just as I'm pulling away, she calls, "Tell him you're a gift from Agnes! Maybe he'll mow my weeds!"

I'm still confused when I pull up to the building *Agnes* indicated. This time, I park next to a much nicer truck, but the house—if one can even call it that—is substantially worse than the front residence.

Brows furrowed, I slide from the car and snag my blazer and work bag from the passenger side. Glancing in the tinted car windows, I check my reflection, adjusting the sleeves to cover my tattoos.

My eyes rake over the dilapidated garage and apartment unit above it. The stairs look sturdy, recently built, but the rest of the place is holding on by a thread.

Like the front house, the once-white walls are stained with dirt and age, the peeling paint barely clinging to the siding. Rust streaks down from the gutters, and the windows are more grime than glass. I do a quick loop around the place, finding the back just the same and note that the only entrance to the apartment is the set of stairs out front. I quickly jot down my findings, forcing myself to stay objective.

I know better than anyone that a house doesn't tell the whole story. I've seen mothers love their children with every breath in their bodies while fighting to survive in shelters. I've helped babies find stability when their parents weren't fit to provide it.

Poverty doesn't equate to neglect. Peeling paint doesn't mean a child isn't cherished, and a fresh coat won't fix what's broken beneath the surface.

But sometimes, it does.

Sometimes the state of a house mirrors the state of its occupants. The mess, the decay… they're not always just symptoms of hard times. They can be signs of something worse. And I've seen that, too.

Families who tried their best, but it wasn't enough.

That's why I'm here.

Not to judge, but to *see*.

And right now, all I see is a building that's barely holding itself together. Of course, the cherry-red vintage truck out front is pristine. Because why bother fixing up the house when you can show off a shiny testament to misplaced priorities?

I shift my bag to one hand and grip the railing, taking the stairs cautiously. My heart slams against my ribs, but I ignore the annoying organ and plaster a professional, kind smile on my face. The platform at the top doesn't so much as wobble in the wind, and I thank every single star I've ever wished on that I'm not about to fall to my death.

With a steadying breath, I knock, counting each second that passes as I wait.

And wait.

I eye the truck and check my watch. It's just after one in the afternoon. If he's not here, maybe he's working. Though, judging by the state of the apartment, I'm not exactly envisioning a boardroom exec. Something more blue-collar, make-your-own-hours, type.

Raising my fist, I knock harder this time. Seconds later, a loud bang, followed by a clatter and responding groan, comes from inside and my brows furrow.

What the hell was that?

I clear my throat, forcing confidence into my voice, and call out, "Mr. Ar—"

The door flies open before I can finish. A wall of heat and bare skin greets me, the rush of warm air laced with something faintly unidentifiable and far too masculine.

I blink. Then blink again.

Shit.

He really is hotter than a whore in church.

Chapter Three

Kade

Best Landlady Ever

The woman standing on my doorstep is either a dream or a gift from the best landlady in the world.

Either way, it doesn't matter.

All I know is that she's the prettiest thing I've ever seen in my life, and I'm probably too damn drunk to remember meeting her.

Fuck.

Chapter Four

Georgia

Who died? Oh.

The man before me grips the frame with one hand, the other braced against the door as if he might slam it in my face at any second. His barrel chest rises and falls rapidly, like he ran here.

Or maybe he's just exhausted from carrying around so many muscles.

Messy brown hair falls to his broad shoulders, and a beard any lumberjack would envy covers what I'm certain is a jawline sharp enough to cut glass. He's built like a linebacker, with a trail of dark hair leading from his pecs to a place I absolutely refuse to let my eyes linger. Black tattoos snake over his chest and shoulder, their details impossible to make out without risking my employment—*or my dignity*.

As if he knows exactly where my mind is, his full lips flicker with the ghost of a smirk as he shifts his legs, widening his stance. And like the weak trollop I am, my eyes drop.

Shit. Fuck. Shit.

The gray sweatpants hanging dangerously low on his hips are a problem.

A *big* one.

Especially when they show off the kind of V-cut that deserves its own zip code.

My mouth is so dry, I feel like I'm choking on sand.

I'm supposed to be professional and composed. But all my training apparently flew out the window the second he opened the door, because the only coherent thought in my head is, *I'm God's favorite today.*

His gaze drags lazily from my face, down the length of my buttoned-up blazer, pausing briefly at the ridiculous heels I immediately regret wearing. Then, just as slowly, his stormy-gray eyes travel back up, a rough, deliberate inspection that leaves my skin tingling and my brain scrambling for words.

Speak, Georgia. Say something. Anything.

"Hi." My voice squeaks, and my thoughts flatline. I clear my throat, attempting to recover. "I mean, I'm Walker. Georgia Walker."

Holy shit. Was that a Bond reference?

My eyes widen as I rush out, "From the county. Not the state. Or the government, technically. Just..."

Just what, Georgia?

"Official business," I answer myself because I've truly lost the fucking plot now.

His thick brows lift, and I can tell he's trying to not laugh. Humiliation burns through me, hot and fast, making my hackles rise.

"Official, huh?"

I nod once, internally berating myself for suddenly becoming a pile of useless goo on this man's doorstep.

Okay, so, he's hot as hell in that way no one ever truly expects to see in real life. The kind of muscular and rugged that only exists in books. But I have a master's degree, for fuck's sake. I've been on my own my entire life.

I refuse to be bested by a silver-flecked beard and gray sweatpants.

Shoving my shoulders back, I smooth my blazer and pretend he's not exactly the type of man who I'd let ruin me in any other situation.

I'm angry that he has this effect on me just by simply existing, and I force myself to hold onto the irritation.

"Like I said," I state, keeping my tone flat, effectively blocking out the last two minutes. They never happened. "My name is—"

"Walker. Georgia Walker," he quips, and I briefly consider throwing myself over the balcony railing. His gaze flicks over my face before sliding back to my shoes. "Whatever she's paying you, it's not enough."

"I...*what?*" My brows furrow.

He scoffs, voice deep and rumbling. "Look, I know Agnes well enough to know she's cheap as hell. If she told you I'm footing the bill, she's out of her damn mind."

My mind races, trying to put together the puzzle I can't quite make out. "Sir, I have no idea what you're talking about. I'm from Summit County Social Services, not—" I wave a hand through the air, mentally cataloguing his words again, and gape when they finally register.

"Wait, do you think…" I swallow, dropping my voice to a whisper. "Do you think I'm some kind of *sex-gram*?"

His head tilts. "Sex-gram? Never heard it called that before, but sure. We'll go with that."

It's then that I notice the glazed look in his squinting eyes, the bags beneath them. He looks like he just woke up from a three-day bender. I inhale discreetly, and sure enough, beneath the woodsy, masculine scent I assume is his cologne or body wash, is the tang of liquor.

Maybe he's still on said bender.

I glance behind his hulking form, taking in the messy apartment. My eyes land on an empty whiskey bottle next to the couch, surrounded by beer cans, confirming my suspicions.

Sighing, I make a note in the file. I hate dealing with drunks.

But hot ones who immediately assume I'm a stripper are a whole new bag of fun.

"What are you writing?" he barks, making me jump. "I told you; I don't want whatever Agnes—"

"Agnes has nothing to do with this!" I hiss, irritated as hell. "I told you. I'm from Social Services. I'm here for a home inspection."

His whole face scrunches, body stilling, before he glances over my shoulder where he stares for so long, I worry he's fallen asleep standing up.

"Never seen a state worker drive a Beamer," he mutters, lip curling. "Try that lie again, darlin'."

I pat my chest, looking for my lanyard, and wince when I realize I forgot to put it on.

"Don't call me that, it's condescending." I slip my badge from my bag and hang it between us, brow cocked. "Here."

"What the hell is that?" he rumbles.

"I can read it to you if the liquor's blurring your vision."

His shoulders square. "Look, ma'am. I don't know what the hell your problem is, or why you're at my doorstep right now hissing at me like some kind of pissed-off, feral cat—"

My jaw drops.

"—but you can take your high horse and ride it straight into a tornado."

Don't say it, Georgia. Don't say it.

"Do you mean ride off into a *sunset*?" I blurt.

"I said what I said."

My mouth falls open. "That's insane."

"It's metaphorical."

"It's a cry for help, is what it is."

We stare at each other, both breathing hard, both radiating heat that has nothing to do with the argument.

"You done?" he asks after a beat, voice lower now.

"Not even close," I whisper-hiss, much like the feral cat he claimed me to be.

He exhales sharply. "And you're here because…?"

Well, I'm officially over this exhausting conversation. I drape my badge around my neck and tug my hair free.

"You are, in fact, Kade Archer, correct?" I can hear the pissed-off reply forming on his tongue, but I don't have the time—or the energy—to deal with it, so I cut him off like he did me. "All I need is a nod. Yes, or no?"

His jaw ticks, and a vein pops up, pulsing across the side of his annoyingly thick neck, but he jerks a nod.

Thank fuck.

"Great." I shoot him a beaming smile and gesture to the pigsty behind him. "Then, please, by all means. Invite me into your lovely home so we can get on with it."

He jerks away from the door, steps forward, and crosses his arms, as if to physically bar me entrance from his house. I glare up at him.

Even in my heels, the man's tall. Really tall.

And frustratingly *broad*.

"Not happening."

"Mr. Archer, this is a court-ordered assessment. I'm not playing games or simply standing here for you to glare at. If you're denying me entrance—"

He cuts me off with a scoff.

"Are you always this serious?" His stormy eyes sweep over me. "And why are you dressed like you run a funeral home? Who died?"

Icy disdain pulses through me at the flippant tone. I may not know much about the case yet, but it's a tragedy. A baby girl lost her parents, her *mother*. And now the child is in the hospital.

Alone.

"Marlee and Travis Vernal," I state flatly. "That's who died. So, show a little respect, please."

The smirk vanishes.

For a moment, he looks as if I've slapped him. His mouth opens, but no words come out. True pain washes across his features, so thick, so heavy and deep, it punches me right in the chest.

Why does he look like he has no idea what I'm talking about?

The urge to flip through my measly file is intense, but I've already studied it front to back. No one said a damn word about me being the one to tell the next of kin their loved one died. That's not supposed to be my job.

It only gets worse when he croaks, "Marlee Vernal?" He shakes his head, throat bobbing with an audible swallow. "I don't know who—"

Oh, shit. Maybe she's recently married. The child *is* young. I quickly check the file and thankfully, her maiden name is listed on the death record. "Marlee Parker and her husband—"

"*When?*"

His broken question makes my eyes burn and my chest constrict.

"Six days ago," I say, voice tight. "There was a car accident. Marlee and Travis succumbed to their injuries, but their daughter is still in the hospital."

I search his storm-cloud gaze, seeing nothing but pain and devastation there. The drunken asshat from moments ago is gone, and in his place, there's only heartbreak.

"You didn't know." It's not a question when I already know the answer.

"No. I haven't seen Marlee in ten years."

Ten years? Why would he be listed as the guardian in the will if he's clearly not a part of their lives? Though, I suppose he could be lying.

"I… I thought you'd been notified," I say quietly, my mind racing.

What the hell have I walked into here? I've never had to notify someone that their loved one passed before.

My next words are more to myself than Kade. "You *should* have been notified."

"No. Nobody told me." He drags a rough hand down his face.

My stomach sinks, and I suddenly feel like I'm going to puke.

God, and I'm not even done.

Swallowing hard, I say softly, "I'm so sorry, Mr. Acher, but there's more."

His bloodshot eyes lock onto mine, his chest rising and falling like he's bracing for impact. Like I haven't already wrecked his world.

"You were named in the will," I say carefully, my hands trembling. "As the guardian of her daughter."

He flinches. "What?"

"Aurora Grace Vernal. She's eight months old."

Kade stares at me with a blank expression for so long, I consider checking his pulse. I can't even imagine what's going through his head right now.

But when he simply utters an empty *no*, my sympathy wanes.

"No?" I blink up at him, flashbacks of my own twisted past, racing through me. "You can't just say no. You're her guardian. She has no one else." I take a deep breath. "If you choose not to go forward with the guardianship, you'll need to—"

"She's not mine," he interrupts, fists clenching at his sides. "Marlee moved on a long fucking time ago. She started another family. The child—" He shakes his head. "She's not my kid, if that's what you're thinking."

"I'm not here to speculate your relationship to *Aurora*," I say, purposefully reminding him of the baby's name. "I'm here to follow the court's orders. And the order is that I inspect your residence to see if it's fit to bring a newly orphaned child into it."

And apparently, to break the worst news a person can hear to a man who looks like he's already battling demons.

Suddenly, Kade spins and half-stumbles, half-collapses onto a worn leather couch. A puff of dust erupts, swirling through the golden sunlight streaming in from the only visible window. The contrast between the bright day outside and the heavy, suffocating darkness inside isn't lost on me.

Unsure what else to do, I follow him in, leaving the door open.

The professional side of me knows I need to be doing my inspection. It's the perfect time. He's distracted, likely has no idea I'm even here, but when I hear him choke out a barely audible, "Oh, *fuck*," I find myself moving closer.

Closer to him, to his pain.

His huge hands drag over his face, gripping his temples like he's trying to wake himself from a nightmare. I don't talk, or ask any questions, letting him process, while I do the same.

"Is she okay?" He looks up, his eyes dim but coherent. "The baby? You said there was an accident."

"I don't know much, but from what I've read, she's stable and in a temporary hospital placement until further decisions are made."

He nods absently, but the far-off look in his eyes sends a pang of something uncomfortable through me.

I want to sit, but the room is chaos—wires tangling under furniture, clothes in piles, dishes stacked in the sink. The desk chair is blocked by a mountain of God knows what. The couch is clear, but for some reason, the idea of sitting next to him makes my nerves riot.

Instead, I dust off the least offensive spot on the coffee table and sit cross-legged, perching my notebook on my knee. Kade watches my every move in a daze, his eyes landing on my heels, where they stay.

The desire to kick them off and burn them races through me. I uncross my legs, dropping both feet to the floor and lean forward.

"I know this is a lot, Mr. Archer, but things need to move quickly here," I explain, careful with each word. "There's a court mediation hearing scheduled in Wildwood one week from today. The judge will assess your suitability as a guardian. I've been asked to conduct the preliminary oversight until the social worker assigned to Aurora's case returns from medical leave. I—"

I break off, biting my lip hard enough to draw blood, but inevitably, the words lodged in my throat break free. "I apologize for the way I informed you. That wasn't my intention."

He doesn't respond. Just stares at the floor, his broad shoulders hunched forward like the weight of the world has settled there.

I make a mental note to get his phone number for future contact. I'll likely need to go over all this again when he's processed the shock.

"You'll need to be sober," I add gently. "Showered. Dressed nicely. Try to get some rest before. The judge will expect—"

"Fuck." His head snaps up. "Do you even hear yourself right now?"

My spine stiffens. "Excuse me?"

"You walk in here like you've got it all figured out. Drop this shit on me, actin' like I've already failed." His voice is low, but the barely contained rage behind it crackles through the room. "You don't know a damn thing about me."

The weight of his words slams into me, but I refuse to flinch. Not for him. Not for anyone.

My jaw tightens, and I fight to keep the tremble from my voice.

"I'm doing my job, Mr. Archer. This is a child's life, not a game." I shove to my feet, the old coffee table scraping against the linoleum tiles, and step toward the door. "Maybe if you weren't halfway through a bottle of whiskey on a Wednesday afternoon, you'd have the sensibility to take the advice I'm giving you."

His head cocks, his lips lifting in a cruel smirk as he gestures to the room at large and leans back on the couch, legs spread wide.

"Well, go on then, darlin'. Tell me all the ways I've fucked up for just existing. Tell me how I'm not good enough."

My throat tightens, but, fine.

Fine.

If he wants to hear my initial impressions, he can have them.

"Where should I start?" I jerk my chin to the overflowing trash can, the sour stench of beer and old food practically radiating from it. "The scent of last week's leftovers? Or maybe the piles of dirty laundry on every available surface."

I point toward the low-hanging light fixture that's missing half its bulbs, the remaining one buzzing like a mosquito. "Mood lighting, very chic. Perfect for creating that warm, inviting ambiance *every* baby dreams of."

I shift to the wall of glowing monitors, their wires snaking across the floor like some tech horror show.

What the hell is this shit?

"But hey, if Aurora needs a nightlight, at least she'll have the comforting glow of whatever post-apocalyptic first-person shooter you're starring in, while drunk, midday."

My eyes snap back to him, voice dripping with false cheer. "Shall I go on, or are we both clear on why I'm concerned?"

He barks out a bitter laugh, shoulders shaking with the force of it. "Oh, is that what this is? You meet me once and I'm drunk, so that somehow equals deadbeat?" His lip curls. "Bet you've got all kinds of assumptions about the asshole in the sweatpants, don't you?"

Do not look at the asshole's sweatpants, Georgia.

"I don't need assumptions," I snap, jabbing a finger toward the empty bottle graveyard. "You're making it real damn clear."

He pushes to his feet, towering over me.

The sudden movement makes my pulse spike, but I stand my ground, aware of all my exits and the pepper spray in my bag.

Kade's broad chest rises and falls with each furious breath, and for a second, we're locked in a silent battle—my frustration meeting his fury head-on.

"You don't know shit about why I'm like this," he growls. "But that won't stop you from writing me off, will it? Just check the box. Another fuck-up unfit to be a..."

He trails off and looks away, his chest heaving.

I grit my teeth, every muscle in my body screaming to turn and walk out. But I don't. Instead, I lean forward, matching the fire in his gaze with my own.

"I don't write people off, Mr. Archer," I bite out, remembering all the times people did exactly that to me. "But I sure as hell report what I see. And right now? All I see is a man who's perfectly content to drown himself in cheap whiskey while the rest of the world picks up the pieces."

He scoffs, the sound low and venomous. "Yeah? And what do you see when you look in the mirror, Ms. Walker?"

I don't answer, I can't.

Not when his words are so close to my reality, I barely keep from flinching. Instead, I simply glare at Kade until he breaks.

"Get out," he barks.

"Gladly."

I don't hesitate. Every nerve in my body screams for the exit, and I'm more than ready to oblige. Snatching my bag from the floor, I shove the file inside and sling it over my shoulder. My spine stays straight, shoulders squared, and despite the trembling in my hands, my steps remain steady.

"I'll see you at the mediation." My voice is clipped as I grip the door, glaring at the bare expanse of his chest. "Try to be sober. And wear a shirt next time."

I spin on my heel, making it two steps before his low voice rumbles behind me, the sound crawling over my skin like a challenge.

"If you'll be there, I make no promises."

I'm still wondering what he was referring to when I walk into my rental that night.

The liquor, or the shirt.

Chapter Five

She Has Very Specific Amnesia

The sign for Heart Springs flashes by, just a blip on the highway, swallowed by an endless stretch of land.

Insignificant. Forgettable. Small.

Exactly what I feel coming back here. Exactly why I never do.

Don't even know where I'm going, just that I couldn't stand to be in my piece-of-shit apartment for one more second. I'm exhausted, and reeling from what happened the other day. Barely slept, too caught up in an endless cycle of *what-ifs, what-the-fucks*, and denial.

After the social worker left, I spent an hour checking and rechecking my emails—making sure I didn't miss anything. Nothing from Summit County, DCFS, or any other official notification about the shitshow that was about to rain down on me.

Rest of the night, I mindlessly cleaned the hell out of my house, not stopping until I passed out on my couch.

Threw the fucking thing out back and lit it on fire after that, like I could burn away the judgement that'd filled my apartment hours before.

Didn't work. My demons remained, and my reality never shifted. Still hasn't.

Marlee is dead.

The thought is a slow burn, a dull ache that builds in the back of my throat.

I think back to the girl who used to curl into my side on late summer nights, the one who knew exactly how to sneak out without waking her grandma. The girl who made me believe forever was something we could actually have, before she decided my life was too small.

Marlee was sunshine and laughter. Vibrant, and reckless. She was the girl who sat on the hood of my truck, counting clouds and dreaming up impossible futures.

And for a while, she was my whole damn world, until she turned it upside down and destroyed it.

But that was a lifetime ago, and no matter how much I loved her back then, we were never meant to survive the kind of storms that tear through South Dakota.

I adjust my grip on the familiar steering wheel, stretching my right leg as much as I can in the cab that still somehow smells like my dad. The deep ache in my thigh doesn't lessen, but it pales in comparison to the incessant throbbing in my chest.

Truth is, I haven't thought about Marlee like this in years. Not since the worst of it. Not since I finally stopped waking up angry.

Her name became a ghost that only haunted me when the nights got too long, and the whiskey wasn't strong enough. But it didn't linger. And eventually, her memory faded. I moved on. She moved away like she said she would. Apparently got married and had a baby.

A baby.

Aurora. Not even a year old, and in the fucking hospital.

Why the hell would Marlee leave her kid to me of all people? We haven't talked in years—never even tried.

After her letter, I may have re-upped my contract, but my information never changed. She could have reached out. Could have gotten word to me if she'd changed her mind, or fuck, just wanted to talk. But she didn't, and neither did I. After a while, I stopped thinking about her, and assumed she did the same.

Doesn't make any fucking sense.

A baby. A guardian. A father.

Makes me think of my own dad.

How he'd roughhouse with Hazel, Gemma, and me while simultaneously cuddling baby Clem or Colby to his chest. How he effortlessly guided us, taught us, and loved us, while also taking care of our mom and an entire massive farm production.

My dad was a superhero.

And I… *am not.*

There's a deep, painful itch in my soul to pick up the phone and make a call that'll never get answered. To talk to him. To ask him what the hell I'm supposed to do. Almost did it that night after Georgia left. Had the phone in my hand, his number a memory under my fingertips. Dialed it out—got far enough to know his phone's still in service for some asinine reason. Maybe for business, or just my mom's way to keep him close.

Either way, the sound of his voice scared the shit out of me, and I disconnected.

My heavy eyes stray from the road ahead to the rolling greens of early spring. With a slow exhale, I crank the window down, letting the familiar scent of damp earth fill the cab and wash everything away.

The air is thick with the fresh bite of new grass, the faint sweetness of budding wildflowers, and the sharp, clean tug of rain that hasn't yet fallen. Somewhere in the distance, the scent of tilled soil lingers, earthy and deep, mixing with the subtle smokiness of burn piles fading into the land.

It's the kind of smell that imprints itself into your soul. The kind that never leaves you, no matter how far you go. Even miles from civilization, in a country covered in sand, I could close my eyes and still breathe it in, still smell Heart Springs.

I lose myself to the familiar turns and gravel trails, letting the hum of an old country song fill the silence. But before long, my thoughts inevitably wind up back in the last place they should.

Because apparently, I'm a masochist.

Georgia Walker.

The hot as hell redhead with sky-high heels, a fancy-as-fuck car that'll never make it on our back roads, and a stick so far up her perfect ass, I have no idea how she managed to sit down on my coffee table like it was her goddamned throne.

She came in swinging, all attitude and sharp edges.

Hate that I noticed. Hate that even now, she's on my mind, when a hundred other things should be there instead.

The stubborn tilt of her pointed chin. The way the afternoon sun caught the blaze of her wild, curly hair. And eyes so green, so vicious, they burned. Every glare she threw my way felt like she was digging for something, peeling back the layers, waiting for me to fuck up.

Georgia Walker with a temper like a wildfire. And me, caught in the pull of her tiny, but mighty gravity.

Georgia Walker with her fair skin, delicate features, and freckles like stars. Freckles that somehow managed to etch themselves into my fucking brain, despite the fog of Jack.

Like the night sky lit her up just to mess with me.

Or maybe it was the alcohol and life-changing news making me see shit.

I scrub a hand over my face, muttering a curse under my breath.

I'm losing it. That's the only explanation. Grief, guilt, and whatever that meeting from hell was—it's all fucked me up, twisting me into knots.

No sane man would be thinking about a woman like that after the bomb she dropped.

With an exhausted sigh, I hang a right without thought. Call it routine. Familiarity. Maybe even an accident.

But I know the truth.

Before the social worker showed up, I'd been hellbent on getting blackout drunk and calling the day a wash. Better to sleep through hell than live it. I'd stared at the ceiling for hours, face up in bed, whiskey in hand, Hazel's words about Honey Bea failing spinning through my brain like a tornado.

The idea that the place my roots grew from might not even be standing anymore, guts me. It's where I watched my sisters grow up, scrapping over everything and nothing. Where I had my first kiss and got grounded for it after Hazy caught me and Tabby Stewart behind the tack shed. Where my parents got married. Where my mom's dreams came true.

Where my dad—

A pressure builds in my chest, tight and suffocating.

It's where he's buried, for fuck's sake. It's home. And no matter how hard I try, I can't forget that.

The road curves, and suddenly, the edges of the property are right in front of me. My stomach turns. Sweat tracks down my spine, and not because of the late March sun blazing through my window.

My fingers flex on the wheel, but I don't slow down.

The place is still massive—barns, silos, open fields. The house stands tall in the distance. White. Wide. That wraparound porch my mom always dreamed of is still cluttered with potted plants. Even from here, I can make out the yellow cushions she's had since I was in high school. If I got closer, I bet I'd see a pitcher of sun tea heating on the steps.

My vision blurs. The truck slows, but I don't stop. Can't.

A few minutes later, the bunkhouse appears. The siding's beat to hell, but it's standing. Same for the smaller homes, five of them scattered across the land. One for each of us.

I haven't stepped foot in mine in years. Probably never will. More than once, I've thought about showing up in the dead of night and setting the damn thing on fire.

Burning down the dream I once built before life blew it all to hell.

My jaw ticks as the wrought-iron sign comes into view. The one I've driven under a thousand times but haven't laid eyes on in years.

Honey Bea Farm is bold and curved across the top. Our family name hangs from a wooden sign beneath written in soft, delicate script. Below that, the year it all began—the year my parents were married.

My foot slips off the gas.

The truck idles in the middle of the empty road, engine humming quiet beneath the weight pressing on my chest.

I can't move.

Can't tear my eyes away from that damn sign.

How easy it would be to take the turn, to drive down the long, gravel driveway and park in front of my family's house. How simple it would be to just *go home*. To see the farm, my sisters. To sit at the old dining table and talk to my mom. Tell her everything that's changed. Open my mouth, bear my soul, and beg her to tell me what the fuck I'm supposed to do now.

It would be so easy.

Except, it's not easy at all.

Not a single thing in my life is simple right now.

My fingers flex around the wheel and my foot presses down on the gas a little too hard, making the fields skip by in a blur.

A flash of movement, small and fast, darts into the road.

My foot slams down on the brakes and my knuckles pop from the force of my grip.

"*Shit!*"

Instinct has me jerking the wheel just enough to veer off onto the shoulder, gravel skidding under my tires. My heart slams into my ribs as the truck shudders to a stop, pulse hammering in my throat.

I sit there for a second, breath heavy, hands still locked around the wheel. Then I shove the door open and step out, scanning the dimming horizon.

A few feet ahead, a tiny, scruffy dog sits in the middle of the road, staring at me like I personally offended it. Its dark fur is matted, its beady brown eyes full of judgment, but I didn't hit it, thank fuck.

Exhaling sharply, I rub a hand down my face, calluses scraping along my overgrown beard. "You've gotta be kidding me."

Without warning, the dog rolls over, giving me a full view of its manhood.

My head falls back, and I stare up at a sky heavy with puffy white clouds. Haven't even wrapped my head around the shitshow that's become my life. Now I'm dealing with a stray dog that has the survival instincts of a rock.

"Alright, asshole," I mutter, slowly stepping closer, careful not to spook it. "Let's get you outta the danger zone."

My leg protests when I crouch down, but I ignore it, reaching out cautiously. He sniffs at my fingers then throws himself at me, licking at my hand as if to congratulate me on my new family member.

"Not happening."

Taking a chance I sift through his thick mop of hair. Beneath the dirt and matts, I'm pretty sure he's a light brown color, but the breed's impossible to make out. Some kind of mix, probably. I also can't tell his age, but it's spastic as hell, so I'm assuming young. No collar, either.

"Guess we're both lost, huh?"

My eyes scan the road. Archer land still stretches to my left, and unless new homes have popped up in the last few years, this dog's a long way from civilization.

I stare down at the floppy-eared pup, and my stomach sinks. "You're a goddamned Archer, aren't you?"

It latches onto my beard and tugs, growling demonically.

With a sigh, I carefully pry its jaw away, saving myself from an impromptu wax, and cradle him to my chest. Shoving to my feet, I head back to my truck. Whether the dog is an Archer farm animal or not, it can't stay out here. It has no survival skills and won't last long in the country, especially with a big storm headed our way in the coming week.

There's no way in hell I can take it back to my place.

I glance at the little demon that's now curled up on my warm bench seat like it's his goddamn birthright. He licks a paw, barks, then lets out a sigh so content, it actually makes me jealous.

Snagging my phone, I thumb through my contacts until I land on Hazel. If anyone around here would randomly adopt a stray with attitude, it's my equally sassy sister.

The line rings once before she picks up—already yelling.

"Oh, now you wanna talk? You ignored all my calls, texts, and apologies for days. Now, suddenly you need something?"

I bite back a sigh. "Jesus, Hazy, can we skip the dramatic intro for once?"

"You can skip my ass. What do you want?"

"Do you have a dog?"

There's a pause. "What?"

"A dog, Hazel. You know, four legs, tail, drools like a toddler with a sinus infection—"

"No! When would I have time for a fucking dog? I'm running a whole-ass farm, remember?"

"You make it impossible to forget," I mutter, rolling my neck along my shoulders. "Does Mom have a new dog? Think it's a puppy."

"Call Mom yourself, asshole!" she snaps, then hangs up on me.

I stare at the screen. Then the dog. Then back at the screen.

"You should be the one making the calls, bud. It's your life on the line, not mine."

He gives me his ass and plops back down, curling into a ball.

I flip him off.

And even though everything in me screams that I don't have time for this—that I barely have enough in me to keep my own life from falling apart—there's something about the stupid, cute mutt that gets under my skin.

Whatever it is, it pushes me to do the very last fucking thing I want to do.

Call my mother.

"Kade?"

I clear my throat. "Hey, Mom."

"Hi, baby. Something you need to talk about, or did you just call to tell your mama you miss her?"

"No." My jaw snaps shut at the automatic reply. "I mean, sorry, not exactly."

I really do miss you.

The words hang on my lips, but I can't force them free, because, again, I'm an asshole.

"Well, color me disappointed." The sad smile in her voice makes my gut twist. "What's going on?"

"Do you..." I trail off, tug on my hair, and clear my throat. "Do you happen to have a new dog?"

There's a long pause, then, "*Huh.*"

My brows pinch. "Huh?"

"I might," she murmurs. "I can't really remember."

My lip twitches. "Forgot, huh? Do you have very specific dog amnesia I'm unaware of?"

"Not that I remember."

"Mom." I groan, long and annoyed. "Come on. Help me out here. The thing is stinking up my truck."

"Why would you have a dog in your truck that you think belongs to me, Kade?"

My throat constricts and it takes everything in me to answer her.

"Drove by the farm. Dog ran out in front of my truck." *Deflect. Pivot. Distract.* "If the dog's yours, you seriously need to get the fucking thing a collar, or leash, or fuck, a prison cell. Thing's a menace."

"Kade William Archer! Watch your language!" she snaps, then sighs. "What's your dog look like?"

"It's not mine," I huff indignantly and gently shove the pup from my lap. "Small. Brown. Long tail. Dumbass ears. Looks like a cross between a dirty goat and a suicidal rabbit."

"Oh!" She gasps. "That one!"

My jaw drops. "It's seriously yours?"

"Could be," she says brightly. "Might not. You'll just have to bring it by so I can be sure."

"Or, and *hear me out*, I know it's a wild concept, but you could describe the actual dog you lost."

"Sweetheart, I keep a lot of animals, you know this. They're all free range. It's impossible to keep track of their comings and goings."

"Free range? Don't you just mean outdoor?" The camera flashes with a photo. "I'm texting you a picture."

"That could help, but sometimes these phones distort colors and what-not."

"Brown is brown," I mutter, sending the picture. A moment passes. "So, is it yours?"

"I didn't get it."

I stare at the read receipt. "Yes, you did."

"Well, I forgot my glasses."

"You don't wear glasses."

"I think I might need to, because all I see is a dark brown blob."

"Because that's what it is!" I choke on a curse, drop my phone to my lap, and rake both hands through my hair, pulling hard. "So help me God—"

"You'll just have to bring it to me," she says sweetly, like I don't know exactly what she's doing. Like she didn't raise me. "Please, Kade."

My chest convulses and I press a hand to it, my panicked gaze flicking to Archer property.

Fuck. I'm not prepared for this shit. Not today. Not ever.

"I'm downtown," she quickly adds, and I swear, it's like she felt my mounting anxiety through the damn phone. "I'm at Thread and Thimble."

Relief hits hard and fast, knocking the breath from my lungs. For a second, all I can do is sag against the seat, chest heaving like I just crossed a finish line.

"Got it," I murmur. "See you soon."

"Drive safe, son. Love you."

The call ends, and my shoulders finally drop. I glance at the mutt curled up like he owns the place and smirk. "Buckle up, asshole. You're going home."

He tilts his head like he's considering it.

Then, he leaps off the seat, lands with a grunt, and locks eyes with me—full, deliberate, soul-piercing eye contact.

And shits.

I blow out a breath and sit up, shifting the truck into drive.

"Perfect," I mutter as I pull onto the road. "Just fucking perfect.

CHAPTER SIX

Kade

KNIT HAPPENS

Mom: *Text me when you're here. I'll come out.*

Me: *Funny how you can suddenly see the screen. It's a miracle.*

Mom: *Selective vision, sweetheart. Same way you thought I never saw the crunchy socks under your bed growing up.*

Me: *I'm leaving.*

Kicking one ankle over the other, I cross my arms and lean against the warmth of my truck, taking in downtown Heart Springs to the soundtrack of snores.

The puppy's curled up on my bench seat like he belongs there, nose tucked under one paw, breathing slow and easy. I opened the windows to air out the stench, but he hasn't moved since we pulled in, sprawled out like a cowboy after one too many beers.

Downtown is quiet. Quieter than I remember.

I haven't really been here since before the army. Not more than I have to. Mom and I meet at The Buttered Biscuit sometimes. We say our goodbyes in the parking lot, and I head straight back to Wildwood.

But standing here now, it feels like I've been gone a hell of a lot longer than ten years.

Some of the buildings are still going strong and look just how I remember them from childhood—brick and old wood with fresh paint. Others are worn and tattered, like the town's run out of money or people who care.

Moms favorite place in the world, Thread & Thimble is still on the corner, next to Between the Pages, the old bookstore that used to host summer reading challenges when I was a kid. I won once. Got a free cone from The Frozen Spoon down the block, which is still here, barely bigger than a walk-in closet. Today the door's propped open, and I can smell freshly baked waffle cones from here.

Across the street, The Shed, Heart Spring's general store, looks like a barn someone forgot to paint. Only place you can find live bait in the back next to winter socks, and a weird as hell display of collectable rooster figurines up front.

The streets aren't busy like they used to be. Back when you couldn't come downtown without running into half your classmates or someone's grandma who knew you when you were in diapers.

Now it feels like the town's just trying to hang on.

I glance toward Pine Street. If I turned right, I'd hit The Twisted Saddle, the country bar where I used to waste time during leave. Cheap beer, loud music, and old friends who stayed put while I went and got my ass shot at in someone else's desert.

A newer coffee shop called Snug As a Mug snags my attention.

White shiplap front, gold lettering on the windows. Looks out of place next to all the brick and weathered wood, but not in a bad way. Just newer—and cleaner. The kind of place that probably does fancy drinks with names I don't recognize and charges an arm and leg because it's sugar, dairy, and flavor free.

I smirk. Bet the city-girl social worker would love a place like that. Probably drinks twelve-buck lattes in her Beamer while listening to a podcast about irrelevant celebrity drama.

A shrill bark jolts me from my thoughts. The feral dog's on his feet, front paws pressed against the dash, tail thumping the door wildly, his attention riveted to the storefront. Following his gaze, I spot my mom through the front window, grinning like I just got back from war as she hustles to the door.

Shoving off the hood, I head across the sidewalk and prepare to open it for her like the gentleman she dragged me up to be, but before I can, it flies open.

From one blink to the next, my mom's standing an inch before me and Thread and Thimble's front door is banging shut, the sound ricocheting though my ears.

Stumbling back a step, I gape down at her. "The hell, Mom?"

"What?" She presses her back to the aged wood and blinks innocently at me. "Can't a mother be happy to see her only son?"

I wait for her to reach out, to hug me, smack a wet kiss to my cheek, or push me aside so she can see the dog, but she doesn't move at all. In fact, she seems to melt further into the door, eyes shifting all over the place.

My brows furrow.

Is it just me, or does she look guilty as fuck right now?

"What are you doing?" I murmur, my gaze flicking to the window of the only craft shop in Heart Springs. The same place she's gone for her weekly knitting club since I was a teenager.

She ignores me. "How have you been? I haven't seen you in forever. Are you sleeping? Eating? Dating anyone?"

My jaw ticks.

Beatrice Archer is a strong, bold woman. She takes shit from no one, including her kids. My entire life, she's been the heartbeat of our family. Best friends with my dad since the moment they met, and stayed that way until the day he passed. She's a force to be reckoned with—all five and a half feet of her.

But she's also transparent as hell.

I see through her scheming, her intentional avoidance. I also know when she's lying, and right now, Beatrice Archer is hiding something.

"I'll answer your questions," I hedge, not missing the way her blue eyes light up. "After you get the demon dog smelling up my truck."

Her gaze lands somewhere over my shoulder, and she swallows hard, but forces a quick smile. "It's nice seeing his truck back on these old streets."

Guilt claws at my throat followed by a rush of panic.

I get through my days by avoiding the ugly truths. It's not healthy, or smart, but it works for me.

Every time I climb into my dad's old truck, though, it's like his ghost is sitting right next to me, making it damn near impossible to ignore the ugliest truth of them all.

He's gone.

"How are you doing, sweetheart?" she asks softly, blinking back tears as she pats my cheek. "Have you found a way to talk to him yet?"

The world sways, and I drop my eyes to my boots.

She's always asking me if I've talked to my dad. Gone out to his grave on the edge of our land. He's buried under his favorite oak tree by the pond where we all grew up fishing, right next to his parents and older brother. No gravestones, just flowers—the way every Archer before him wanted it.

I went once for the funeral on emergency leave. Haven't been back since. Haven't said a word to him since, either. But I want to.

Fuck, do I want to.

"You know I haven't," I say, my voice rough as gravel. "Feels like shouting into the void. Doesn't change a damn thing."

She makes a soft, sad sound and slips her hand into mine, squeezing once before letting go.

"I'm sorry you feel that way," she murmurs. "For me… it helps. I still talk to him. I lay down the heavy things, the good and the bad, and some-times… sometimes I swear I hear his answer in the breeze. Maybe it's not about where you go, or even what you say—just that you try to let him in, however you can."

She sighs, eyes distant, the hint of a wistful smile on her lips.

"We all find our own way to carry people we love, Kade. Doesn't matter if it's a grave, the wind or water, or on the back of a horse. One day, you'll figure out how to reach him. You just have to want to."

If only it were that damn easy.

Mom lets out a breath and straightens, smoothing away her sadness in a way I envy. "Anyway. How's your life, hmm? Anything new?"

I deflect her question, and change the subject. "Your dog shit on the floorboard."

I'd cleaned it up the second I parked, but the stench remained.

"Poor thing's probably just stressed. He did have to ride with *you*, after all."

"Wouldn't have had to ride with me if you'd caged him properly." I narrow my eyes and jerk my chin at the door she's become one with. "Seriously. What are you hiding in there?"

"I don't think it's my dog." Mom tosses her hair over her shoulder, the brown and gray strands sticking to her Carhartt vest. "And I'm not hiding anything. Why would you say that?"

"You haven't even met the damn thing yet," I hiss, jamming a finger at the door. "And you're blocking the entrance."

"No. I'm *resting* on it." She smirks and sinks her weight back with a casual shrug. "Big difference."

"*Mom.*"

"*Son.*"

My mind races, trying to figure out her game. Her hands are tucked behind her body now, right booted foot tapping a restless tune. She's shifting like she has to pee, reminding me of my three year old nephew.

It's suspicious and shady, and I don't like it one bit. The hell would my own mother have to hide from me?

A deep laugh bounces around from inside the shop, and she jolts like she's been struck.

Then it clicks.

"*Mother,*" I choke out. "Do you—do you—" I press a hand to my chest and drop my voice. "Do you have a *man* in there?"

Her eyes flash, a glint of wickedness I hate. "And what if I do?"

"I—*what*?" My soul leaves my body. "No. No, you do not."

"I might."

"You don't."

She huffs, the sound so indigent, it's like she's been studying with my teenage sisters. "Why the hell not? I'm a grown woman, Kade."

"Because—" I flail a hand at the door like that explains anything. "Because you're supposed to be in *knitting club*!"

"So?"

"So," I splutter. "You can't be dating! You're my mother."

"Oh, Kade. Handsome as can be, but dumb as a rock." She sighs, real tragic-like. "Who says I'm dating?" Her mouth tilts up in a slow, devious smirk as she leans in and drops her voice to a whisper. "Last I checked, you don't need to be on a date to *get some*."

"Get..." I jolt backward, my hands flying through the air in a *hell no* motion repeatedly, like I can erase the last five minutes of my life. This can't be happening. "Get some? Why—who—"

"Is that not the right terminology?" Little lines pop up around her eyes as she squints and snaps. "Ah! Netflix and chill!"

I gape at her, reeling, my childhood flashing before my eyes like a tornado of casseroles and PTA meetings and Mom swatting Dad with a dish towel when he tried to steal food off the stove.

"Jesus Christ." I gag, dragging a hand down my face. "Who the fuck corrupted you?"

"The internet."

"Someone needs to take your phone." I hold my palm out. "In fact, give it to me now. I'm deleting everything."

She just smiles wider, pleased as pie.

"No, you know what?" My hands land on my hips as indignation rolls through me. "I'm going in there. Whoever the dude is, he's done for, so say goodbye to your little boyfr—" Another gag. I choke on my next breath and she cackles—actually laughs so hard, she cries.

"You're so cute, son," she coos. "But you're not going inside. You're not going to do a damn thing, and we both know it."

"I'm putting you in a convent right after I kick his ass." I try to move her gently, but she plants the heels of her worn boots like she's bracing for battle. "Move it, Ma."

"You can't!" she whisper-hisses, shoving me away. "No one's allowed in the knitting club but knitting club members!"

Before I can do something insane, like physically remove my own mother by force, someone slams into my side hard enough to send me stumbling a few steps.

A moment later, icy-cold seeps through my white T-shirt.

"What the fuck?" I spin toward the offender just as a plastic cup bounces off my chest and rolls under my truck.

The woman's got one hand clutched around a phone, the other still hovering like she meant to stop the spill and failed. My mouth opens to snap at her, but then our gazes lock.

And my brain short circuits.

Of course.

Of fucking course.

Wide, green eyes flare—brighter in the daylight than I remember. She looks like she's about to apologize, but then… recognition, irritation. And a flash of something hotter, low and dangerous, before it cools to pure frost.

Her giant bag's sliding off her shoulder, dragging an oversized black sweater with it, exposing an expanse of creamy skin and freckles I shouldn't be drawn to, but am.

And that just pisses me the hell off.

I tilt my head back, glaring at the sky like it's the one to blame, and mutter, "Anything else you wanna throw at me today, dickwad?"

Georgia Walker scoffs loud and exaggerated, snagging my attention. She's clutching her phone tighter—like she might chuck it at me next—and the words *I fucking dare you*, almost slip free from my dry throat.

"*You* ran into *me*!" she chokes out, her vision raking down my drenched shirt. "And you spilled my coffee!"

"I was standing still," I growl, tugging the offending material away from my skin. "And now I'm soaked in whatever overpriced, too-sweet bullshit you're drinking."

"*Was* drinking. Now it's gone because you were rooted like an over-grown tree in the middle of the sidewalk," she snaps, her cheeks burning bright red. "All giant arms and cowboy boots and—*and*—" Her eyes flick to my hair, my boots, my general existence. "*Broody*!"

"I don't brood," I grumble.

She arches a perfect brow and points at me. "You're brooding right now."

I cross my arms, tension coiling tight through my shoulders as I take her in—messy bun, more freckles than I'd originally thought, that fierce little chin lifted like she's ready to fight me.

There's a splash of coffee on her jaw and a fallen curl bouncing loose around her face, softening all those sharp, sarcastic edges. The urge to reach in, to wipe the coffee off and do something idiotic like *taste* it, is intense, but I shove that shit down where I bury all the inconveniences in my life.

Woman's trouble dressed in tight jeans and curves.

Much as I hate to admit it, today's outfit looks damn good on her. Hell of a lot better than the stuffy suit, though the heels did snag my eyes more than once.

Still, she's rude, stuck-up, and out of place.

Georgia Walker belongs in a city. Big buildings, shiny cars, endless crowds—somewhere she can judge people from behind a desk instead of on my porch.

Everything about her screams polished, professional, *not from here*. Just another city girl playing country for the weekend, counting the min-utes until she can get back to her real life and the fuck out of mine.

We have a silent stare off that results in my jaw ticking and my palms sweating, so I tuck them into my pockets. She follows the movement.

Her eyes don't come back up.

Rolling back on my boots, my lips lift in a cocky-as-shit grin, because apparently, fucking with Georgia Walker and pissing her off is my new favorite pastime.

"Eyes up here, *darlin'*."

Don't know where the heavy accent comes from, maybe I'm emulating Griff's Tennessee drawl, but it makes her blush, and I love the look of it.

She jolts her gaze to mine, and every inch of her is all wildfire.

"Nice to see you're still as welcoming as a rattlesnake," she snaps, shouldering her bag higher. "And don't call me that. As I said before, it's condescending and unprofessional."

"Professional, huh?" I drag my tongue over my lip and scoff. "You're doin' a mighty fine job of being professional all by yourself—" I tack on, all slow and dramatic, *"Darlin'."*

"You're *so* right. I must have lost my manners somewhere back in the *beer can graveyard*." She presses a hand to her chest and rolls her lip in a poisonous pout. "So sorry about your shirt, Mr. Archer. Maybe try vinegar and a prayer."

My mouth opens to tell her *exactly* what she can do with her vinegar when a voice purrs from behind me, setting my flight-or-fight instincts on high alert.

"And who might this be?"

Oh, fucccck.

My palm slaps against my face, knocking the brim of my cap to the side and I groan, long and low.

I forgot about her.

I forgot about my own mother.

Oh, my God.

Am I seriously sporting a half-wood in front of my *mother*?!

Better yet, why the fuck am I even hard right now? I can't stand the red-headed woman. Yeah, she's hot as hell—and okay, I love the way she's not afraid to go toe-to-toe with me—but she's rude and stuck-up.

It's annoying, not attractive.

"Um," Georgia says, clearing her throat and bringing me back down to reality. "I'm—"

"She's no one," I blurt, way too fast, way too brash. Georgia blinks, cheeks flushed, and looks away.

I could feel bad, but I don't, because I'm not ready for my mom to know about—*everything, anything.*

"Don't be so rude. I raised you better than that, Kade Archer!" Mom smacks my soaked stomach like she's swatting a mosquito and turns to Georgia. "Are you a friend of my son's?"

Her delicate throat bobs as she glances at me with questions in her eyes. I shake my head once while silently screaming, *no.*

No, she doesn't know.

No, I'm not ready to tell her.

No, you may not ruin her day like you did mine, even though I know it's your favorite pastime.

Clearly, she can't read my mind, though, because she steps forward and thrusts her little hand out like she's running for fucking office. "My name is Georgia. It's so nice to meet you, Mrs. Archer."

My mom's face lights up, bright and beaming. "Well, aren't you just the cutest little thing?"

I swear to Jesus, if she boops her nose, I'm out of here.

"Thank you!" Georgia beams right back, and the sight of it's enough to knock me on my ass. She winks at my mom, and I gape in shock. "I certainly try, ma'am."

"Oh, and so well-spoken too, but call me Bea." Her smile drops, and she gives me an accusatory look. "Kade, you didn't say anything about having such a darling *friend.*"

"I didn't say anything because she's not a friend, she's—" I choke, scowl, and stop myself before I say *a liability to my life.*

"Do you work with Kade?" Mom leans forward and brushes that stray curl from Georgia's face like she's already planning the wedding menu and what our babies will look like.

"Something like that," Georgia says softly, her voice honeyed and suspiciously innocent. Her throat bobs again, and I'm stuck on the sight of it.

The sight of *her.*

Here, in the sunshine. Here, in my presence. Here, in my hometown… with my mother who's still touching her.

Why is she touching her?

I can't stop staring at Georgia. Her lashes are long. Her smile is lethal. And those dimples? I'm sure they've killed a man before.

But her freckles?

Her freckles are a goddamn trap.

"We don't work together," I clarify, my tone rough as hell. I clear my throat, and Georgia watches. It's annoying. I flash my mom a fake smirk. "Sorry to disappoint."

"Then why do you look so squirrely?" Mom gasps, gesturing between the two of us. "Do you two have a little office romance going on?"

"Mom," I strangle out. "Christ. I don't even *have* an office."

"Right," she huffs. "You work from that cesspit you call a home."

Georgia's eyes flick between us like she's cataloging everything. I see the gears turning. I also see the moment she realizes I haven't told Mom a damn thing.

Beatrice Archer turns back to her, completely charmed, forgetting me altogether.

"Are you new in town, sweetheart? I can't say I'd forget meeting you before."

But you'd wish like hell you could.

Georgia twitches like the attention physically hurts her. "Uh, yeah. I just moved here."

My mouth opens to end this conversation, the urge to get in my truck and haul ass back to my *cesspit* is nearly too much to resist, but something stops me. Slaps my jaw shut. My feet shift against my will, tugging me a step closer, and my ears tune in a bit harder, like I give a damn what Georgia's life story is or something.

"How lovely! What brought you to Heart Springs?" my mom asks.

Georgia glances at me and bites her thick bottom lip, hesitating a moment.

Does she not want me to know? She looks so uncomfortable I almost crow with glee and make a show of settling in for story time.

How's it feel to be the one on display, freckles?

"I just needed a change," she finally murmurs, staring at her feet.

My brows draw tight. Pretty sure she's lying.

"Well," Mom says warmly, reaching out to touch her arm. I narrow my eyes at the connection. "How do you like it so far?"

"I haven't really been downtown until today," she admits, gaze flicking around. I expect her to curl her lip, to scoff at the rundown town. Instead, she smiles warmly. "But it's beautiful, and the air is so fresh compared to New York."

"Is that where you're from?" I blurt out before I can stop myself.

A look of shock twists her expression.

Shock at what? That I'm talking to her?

I glance away, forcing my features into something bland and disinterested, because no one's more shocked than me.

The hell was that?

Georgia makes some kind of grumbling, irritated sound that I expertly ignore.

"I've lived all over, but spent the last ten or so years in New York." Another smile, but this one feels all wrong. "South Dakota is just another stop on the map."

"Won't be here long?" my mom cuts in, sounding genuinely sad.

Georgia shakes her head. "My contract's only for six months, unfortunately."

I scoff. She's probably just here on some city-girl vacation, chasing her Pinterest dream of touching real grass. We get tourists like that every summer—roll in for the season, then disappear before the first snow hits the ground.

"Well, you should come out to the farm sometime soon, then," Mom coos. "The wildflowers will be blooming soon. Not something you wanna miss."

My stomach drops. What the fuck is she doing?

"Farm?" Georgia repeats, tilting her head.

"Been in the Archer family over a hundred years," Mom says proudly. "Out past the ridge. We farm honey, wild flowers, and wheat in the summer. You can even feed the animals. Do you like animals, Georgia?"

"You'd hate them," I cut in, tugging my hat off. I grip my hair, yank on it, and shove my hat back on. "They're big, dirty and smelly."

"What, like you?" she fires right back, then pauses to pointedly sniff me. "At least you're sober today."

I step forward, my hackles higher than corn in the summer. "Look. If you—"

"Do you knit?" Mom interrupts, shoving me back.

Georgia laughs, the sound so soft, it curls around me. "No, but I've always wanted to learn."

"Well, that settles it." Mom grabs her hand like it's the most natural thing in the world. "You can come to our knitting club. Everyone's inside."

I gawk. "I thought only members were allowed!"

Mom waves me off. "I meant *you're* not allowed."

What. The. Fuck.

Georgia opens her mouth, likely to accept the invitation and destroy what's left of my sanity, but to my shock, she pulls her hand back gently.

"Unfortunately, I can't. I have to work."

"What did you say you do for work, dear?"

I freeze.

Georgia hesitates just long enough to make my pulse spike. "I'm a social worker."

"How did you two meet?" Mom frowns slightly, eyes flicking between us. "Kade barely leaves his crap-hole. Not many places to run into a sweet girl like you when he's dealing with the termites and all."

Panic flares, too hard and fast to even defend myself.

"If you have to work," I cut in, my tone bordering on feral, "maybe you should go do that." Jaw pulsing, I grit, "*Now.*"

Don't say it. My stare begs her. *Please, don't tell her.*

Her lips curve up in a grin so smug it should be illegal.

She opens her mouth again and turns her full body to face my meddling mother.

I lunge.

It's all instinct and my dwindling will to survive that propels me into action. I wrap a hand around Georgia Walker's annoying, big mouth, dragging her into my chest, and start to haul her away.

I'm gentle—aware enough to avoid getting arrested, but also crazed enough to toss her over my shoulder if she starts to struggle.

"What do you say, *darlin'*?" I drawl just to piss her off. "Let's go get you a new coffee since you *tripped* and spilled that first one all over me. We can talk about dry cleaning bills while we're at it."

"Kade?" my mom cries. "Kade! What on Earth are you doing to that poor girl?"

"She's fine!" Pausing, I toss her my keys with one hand and a smile that got me out of trouble too many times growing up. "Get your smelly nutjob of a dog out of my truck before he shits again, Ma."

"Say please, Kade Archer!" she yells at the same moment Georgia peels my hand away and hisses, "Don't swear at your mother, asshole!"

Christ, these women are killing me.

"Please," I growl over my shoulder, before lowering my voice in Georgia's ear. "If you open that pretty mouth and say one more word, sweetheart, I swear I'll find a way to shut you up."

I'm pleasantly surprised when she goes still in my arms. Even more shocked at the shiver that wracks her muscles. I do all I can to ignore the way she feels tucked into me, all soft and small, her head barely reaching my shoulder.

And she smells damn fine. Something sweet, floral and wild, all at once.

It's good—*too good.*

The second we're inside the coffee shop, she elbows me in the gut and stomps on my toe. Neither hurt, but it's effective, and I drop her like I wasn't just huffing her shiny curls.

"What the—" Tabby Whitt cries from behind the register. "Georgia, do you need help?"

"She's fine," I choke back a growl of irritation and toss her a smirk. "Can you get her another drink, please? There was an incident outside."

"No, thank you, Tabby," Georgia says kindly before she whirls on me, her eyes blazing. "What the fuck?" she hisses, straightening her clothes, yanking her sweater back into place. "Why would you—"

"She doesn't know," I snap, rubbing the edge of my jaw, trying to keep my voice down. "My mom. My family. I haven't told them yet."

She gives me a long, considering look. Bites her bottom lip and keeps my attention right there.

"Why not?" she finally asks. "If you're going to give up your…" Her eyes flick toward the counter, then back to me. Her voice lowers. "No decisions need to be made yet. But ultimately, they're yours to make, Mr. Archer."

Unable to respond to the loaded statement, I deflect with a scoff. "I just had you in my arms, darlin'. You can drop the mister shit."

"Against my will," she mutters, shaking her head. "And I'm not your darlin'." With a sigh, she reaches into her bag and pulls out a business card and pen. "I meant to give this to you the other day. Should you have any questions, you're welcome to contact me."

She bends over a small table, scribbles something on the back of the card. My eyes slide to the curve of her ass in those fitted jeans, and my cock pulses to attention once more. Of course, she'd be the one to wake my balls up.

I look away just before she straightens and holds the card out to me.

"The date and time for the… *meeting* are on the back," she says, her tone low. "Please don't be late. It's important." Her throat bobs as she swallows. "And even if you decide to… *pass* on the opportunity, you'll still need to attend. You'll need to tell the judge in person."

I nod slowly, eyes locked on the card. The mediation. The courthouse in Wildwood. A day and time where everything could change.

One way or another, it will.

"Do you need to know anything?" I murmur, slipping the card into my back pocket.

She lifts a brow.

"About me," I clarify. "You said you were inspecting my place." Her grimace makes my jaw tick. "Do you need to ask me shit? Make sure I'm fit? Whatever it is people like you do?"

Georgia studies me, her face unreadable. Her fingers tighten around the strap of the giant bag slung across her body. A beat passes. Then another. Green eyes search mine, and I'm sure she sees it all. The anger. The guilt. The storm of everything I can't name.

She finally shakes her head.

"No," she says quietly. "I've got everything I need for now."

Then she steps around me, careful not to brush my arm. Doesn't look back. Just heads for the door where she pauses and turns enough to catch my gaze.

"Just remember," she says, voice steady, "it's not only your life you're altering here. It's hers. And she's already been through something unimaginable. Please don't make it worse."

And then she's gone.

The bell chimes. The door swings shut behind her. And I'm left standing in the middle of a coffee shop I've never been inside, trying to breathe around the pressure in my chest.

She's right. I know she is.

And that's the worst part.

But for the life of me, I don't know which choice will hurt Aurora more—keeping her in the wreckage of my existence, or letting her go.

Letting her have a new life.

One without me in it.

Chapter Seven

But Does He Smell Like Cow Shit?

"HE DID WHAT?" ABBY screeches, her messy, dark bun bouncing as she leans closer to the screen. "Say that again. *Slowly*."

"No, thanks." I scoff, shooting her a glare. "I'd rather forget the entire situation instead."

"Ah." She nods. "So we're still firmly planted in the land of denial. Got it." She gives me a big thumbs-up. "Super healthy of you, babes."

"I know, right?" I agree, propping my phone up on a stack of books.

Abby sticks her tongue out at me. I flip her off. She cackles.

Shifting from the couch to the entryway of my temporary home, I grab the next cardboard box, one of far too many stacked against the wall. Unpacking feels like some kind of personal torture to me. I don't even own that much, but somehow, every box I open feels like it's multiplying behind my back.

"But seriously," Abby begs, lip jutting out in a dramatic pout. "Please, just at least describe the manhandling to me. In great detail, leave nothing out. I promise I won't ask you anything else. And if I go off camera and on mute, just ignore me, but don't stop talking about that sexy cowboy of yours."

"My life is not diddle-material, Abigail," I shoot back, tugging the tape off the next box. "And he is not *my* cowboy. He's a client."

Just thinking about Kade Archer and his stupid arms and giant man-paws sends a full-body shiver up my spine. The man is far too attractive for his own good, and way too cocky for everyone else's.

"Whatever." She huffs, flopping dramatically onto her bed. "Tell me and I'll be your best—"

"You already are," I interrupt.

Abby groans, long and loud. "Stop being such a prude."

"You can't goad me into talking."

"You're withholding vital information," she accuses, propping her chin on her fist. "And we promised never to keep secrets from each other." Her voice dips as she hits me with a wounded look that smacks me right in the chest. "Are you seriously going to go back on our unbreakable vow of friendship so soon after abandoning me?"

I gape at her, bubble-wrapped frying pan suspended mid-air. "Low blow, witchling."

"Sorry, ginger tits." She's not. "Did it work, though?"

Of course it did.

I blow out a breath and glare up at the popcorn ceiling, already resigned to telling her all the gory details. Truth be told, I'm dying to talk about it. But talking about it will make it feel like it's a *thing*, and I'm desperately trying to avoid that.

"Georgie?" Abby coos, clicking her tongue. "Come back to the land of the living. Mama's waiting."

"He slapped his hand over my mouth, Abby," I say—deadpan. "In front of his *mother*."

Her eyes go wide with gleeful horror. "Shit just got real. Continue."

"It was so unprofessional. And rude. Annoying. Chauvinistic. Assholery—"

"One, that's not a word." I glare at her, and she grins. "Besides, it sounds hot as hell."

"He dragged me down the street like a caveman and said—and I quote—'*If you open your pretty mouth and say one more word, I'll find a way to shut you up.*'"

"Correction. *Super* hot." She's practically panting. "What did you do?"

Grimacing, I shrug. "Called him an asshole, elbowed him in the stomach, and stomped on his foot."

"Georgia!"

Yeah, that wasn't my finest moment.

"What was I supposed to do, Abbs? I was working!"

Not really.

I'd just finished my research at the coffee shop, where I've been going daily to use their free Wi-Fi. The ambiance is quiet, but not too-quiet, and the coffee is safe for my stomach.

When I ran into Kade, I'd been on my way to check out the bookstore a few shops down, but after everything that happened, I rushed to my car and took off.

Wound up parked in front of Heart Springs Emergency Clinic, and spent an hour debating walking inside under the guise of my job, just so I could poke around and ask questions about past patients.

It was stupid—probably fifty shades of illegal—and only my growling stomach pulled me away before I made a choice I couldn't take back.

"This is perfect." Abby beams and claps her hands. "I love this for you so much."

I groan, tip the box upside down, and start pulling apart the mass of gluten-free baking products to the sound of Abby planning my non-existent wedding.

Despite the midnight, alcohol-soaked decision that led me to finally pursuing Heart Springs after years of waffling, I did do my research—something I've learned to rely on ever since I was diagnosed with celiac disease.

There's no cheat day. No "*just a bite.*" Just strict cross-contamination rules and a whole lot of label reading.

That's why I had to pack all my dedicated products and supplies—the ones I've spent years, and way too much money, accumulating. This shit's expensive.

"So, I'm thinking spring. Small, intimate. Say, a hundred people?"

"A hundred people isn't intimate." I cock a brow, watching her write something down. "Are you being serious?"

She cackles and lifts a notebook, showing me a full page of black-inked scribbles.

"Dude, we've only met twice! We don't know each other. He's rude, impatient, condescending, and he has no clue how to use his big boy words. I'm also ethically bound from being with him."

"You said you're only covering. You'll be off the case soon." She waggles her brows.

"Just because I'll be off the case doesn't make it okay," I mutter. "There is no future for us, so pick a new dream to hang your tits on."

"And yet," she says, voice all sing-songy, "you're still thinking about how it felt to have his hand over your mouth and his arm wrapped around your waist. Admit it."

I freeze, a package of King Arthur flour clutched in one hand like a weapon. My cheeks burn so hot, I know she can see my guilt from across the room.

"I hate you."

"You love me." She bats her lashes. "Tell me, does he smell good?"

I swallow. *Hard.*

Because he does smell good—when he's not soaked in alcohol.

"Oh my god! He smells like leather, doesn't he? Leather and sweat, with a slight hint of cow shit. It's masculine as fuck, huh?"

"Cow shit?"

"Of course. All cowboys smell like cow shit. They try to cover it up and shower it off, but it's in their pores and DNA. The combo—" She kisses her fingers. "Chef's kiss."

"He's not a cowboy," I say automatically. At least, I don't think he is. "And he smelled like my coffee."

Actually, Kade smelled fresh, like rain and sunshine, mixed with something spicy.

"Does he live in the country?" I nod as she lifts a finger, counting. "Drive a truck?" I groan, but nod again. Another finger. "Kind of covered in dirt, even though he's clean?"

I shrug, but she ignores me, flicking up a third digit.

"Here's the big one."

"Can't wait," I mutter.

"Does he, or does he not, unironically wear cowboy boots with faded jeans that hug his thick thighs and juicy ass?"

My mind zeroes in on the memory of Kade standing in the middle of the sidewalk, sunshine wrapped around his dark, shoulder-length hair—hair that curled in random places and flipped in others, tucked beneath a worn black baseball cap.

Without the shadows of his porch, his beard—full but neatly trimmed—caught the light just right, revealing silver threads woven through the dark. I never thought gray hair would do it for me. But damn if I didn't nearly drool right there on the spot.

His fitted white T-shirt was covered in a layer of seven-dollar coffee, but that didn't take away from the way it hugged his barrel chest and biceps.

And the jeans… *fuck, yes.*

Jeans like that tell a story. The kind that says he knows exactly how to be on his knees.

How to take his time.

How to look up at a woman with those storm-gray eyes and ruin her with nothing more than his mouth, fingers, and a low, gravel-rough *"tell me what you need, darlin'."*

And God help me, I'd let him.

"Is Georgia Walker present, or has she descended into cowboy-shaped-dick-land?"

"What?" I drop the flour I'd been hugging like a safety blanket, grab my phone, and head to the kitchen. "Did you say something?"

"His jeans…" she drawls, brows high.

"Oh, I, uh—" I clear my throat and barely resist squeezing my thighs together. *Am I seriously turned on right now?* "You know what? I don't remember."

Abby cackles. "You so do. You remember everything. You have a brain like a steel trap and a heart like a puddle. In fact, your heart lives in your heavily-ignored, needy vagina, and now you're going to pine after him while pretending you hate his guts."

"I'm not allowed to hate his guts, but I really do," I mutter, stacking mugs in the cabinet while actively forcing myself to hate Kade's guts.

I do. I do. I do.

I shift to the next box, this one marked *pantry*, and grimace. Unlike my previous apartment, this place lacks storage. The cabinets are small, and I've already filled most of them with dishes, cookware, and baking stuff.

"You're still unpacking food?" Abby asks, thankfully changing the subject.

I sigh and nod.

"Dude, did you even bring any clothes or toiletries?" She gasps, pressing a hand to her chest. "Oh, fucking hell, did you bring your sex toys? You're gonna need them based on your obsession with the cowboy, so I really hope you did."

"Abby!" I cry, hands flailing. "I am *not* masturbating to thoughts of him! Holy inappropriate!"

My eyes flick to my bedroom, where my vibrators are stashed.

I couldn't. Could I?

Just to take the edge off?

No. No.

Bad Georgia.

"You say that now. Wait till that man has you ruining your own panties." She bites her lip and sighs. "If you really aren't going to fuck the grumpy cowboy, maybe you should go meet a different one in a bar. Find a way to take the edge off."

I scoff, but my stomach flips at the idea. "You know I'm not a one-night stand kind of girl."

"I know, you're boring," she whispers petulantly, eying the rows of food I'm organizing. "Wow. You seriously brought everything in your kitchen, didn't you?"

"I had to." I wince, holding up a crushed container of pasta. The sight makes my eyes burn. "Aw, shit."

"What is that?"

"It *was* gluten-free mac and cheese made with chickpea pasta and unicorn tears. Now it's dust and broken dreams." Tossing it in the trash makes me sad, and I give up unpacking for now, turning to give Abby my full attention. "You know, I don't think I've ever thanked you."

"For?"

"Helping me get my diagnosis. Surviving college while sick and depressed." I shake my head. "I couldn't have done it without you."

She scoffs, but her eyes are glassy. "Please. You're a badass, Georgie. You never needed me, but you're stuck with me anyway."

Maybe it's being so far from Abby—and the only home I've ever built for myself—but I miss her. And right now, I'm feeling more alone than I have in a long time. In a new place, searching for answers I doubt I'll ever find, with an illness places like Heart Springs haven't caught up to yet.

Celiac isn't just a *food* thing. It's an *exhaustion* thing.

A *trust-your-gut-while-it's-destroying-itself* thing.

It was a mystery that stole years of my childhood—years I can't get back. I was always tired. Always in pain. Always dismissed. I didn't get real answers until I was in my twenties, and even then, it took everything in me to keep fighting for them.

Sometimes I wonder if it would've been different—if it would've hurt less—if I hadn't grown up in foster care. If I hadn't been shuffled through seven homes by the time I turned fifteen. Maybe if someone had stuck around long enough to notice I was always sick, always small, always struggling... maybe then, I wouldn't have felt like a ghost in my own body.

Maybe if someone had just *seen me*, I wouldn't have disappeared for so damn long.

Abby saw me, though. She still does. That's why she's my ride or die.

"God, I miss you," I murmur, blinking away the burn behind my eyes.

"I miss you more," she says. Then she squints at the screen. "Are you crying *again*?!"

"No!" I sniffle and wave a hand through the air. "It's super dusty."

"You're crying."

"So are you."

She blinks, wiping her eyes. "I love you, ginger tits."

"I love you too, witchling."

After we hang up, I plug my phone into the charger and clean up the mess of empty boxes. There's still so much to do, but the thought of organizing this place, of trying to make it feel homey, is exhausting. I'm already running on fumes, and there's a bit of work I need to wrap up before I can crash.

Rain drums against the roof in hard, rhythmic bursts. I glance out the tiny window over the sink just as lightning splits the sky.

I used to be scared of storms. They felt too big, too loud—like the sky itself was angry, and I had nowhere to hide. I watched a lot of them from the porches of seven different houses across West Virginia. None of them ever felt like mine.

One of my foster moms once told me, "If you can hang on through the storm, the world always looks a little better after." I didn't understand it then. But somehow, the words stuck, and over time, they started to feel true.

Now, I love storms. The crack of thunder, the snap of lightning—it's chaotic, but it's beautiful. My favorite part, though, is what comes after. When everything goes still. When the air smells new. And, if you're lucky, a rainbow arcs across the sky like a quiet little promise.

I make a quick cup of coffee and set up at the kitchen table, opening the guardianship file for Aurora Vernal. I met her this week—spent time with her in the hospital. At first, it was just to collect medical notes and check in with the doctors… but then I couldn't stop thinking about her sitting alone in that room.

She's so small. Babbling and curious, but she cries a lot. The nurses say it's just teething, but I know better. I know what it looks like when someone misses their parents.

My gut twists, and my fingers hesitate over the keyboard.

Mediation is tomorrow afternoon, and I want everything to be perfect. This is my first case here, and soon I'll be handing it back to the original caseworker. I want to leave it better than I found it.

Once she's back, I won't have to see Kade anymore. He'll be out of my world, and so will Aurora. This will all just be a brief blip in the middle of my life. And Aurora? That sweet little girl will be one step closer to the forever family she deserves. I can only hope that family is Kade—and that he gets his shit together in time.

After an hour, I close my laptop with a soft click. My eyes drift to the window again. The rain has stopped, and…

And there it is—stretching over the green pasture behind my little farmhouse—a perfect, glittering rainbow.

I stand and stretch, my sore knees cracking, hips protesting in quiet rebellion. The ache is familiar, rooted in years of undiagnosed damage, and I make a mental note to take something for the pain.

Leaning over the sink, I rest my elbows on the edge and stare at the rainbow. It's not the first one I've seen here. But something about this one feels different—brighter, maybe. Like a sign that no matter what happens tomorrow, it'll be okay. That I won't screw this up. That somehow, I won't hurt a child who's already lost too much.

My eyes flutter closed.

And like always, I make a wish.

Chapter Eight

One Month Notice

I shove my phone into my pocket and stare up at the old Wildwood courthouse, doing all I can not to pass out or run back to my truck.

For the last week, I've gone back and forth on whether or not to even show up. Thought about calling Georgia. Thought about calling the judge. Thought about saying to hell with the whole thing.

Once, yeah, I wanted all of it. A wife. A family. Bunch of kids running through the fields while my old man laughed from the porch.

But that dream died with him and got buried in the desert with me.

Still, I spent the last week reading everything I could find online, just in case.

What babies eat. How often they nap. Diapers and potty training. Milestones. Car Seats. Preschools, for fuck's sake.

Turns out, they need a hell of a lot more than love.

They need structure. Safety. Stability.

A bedroom with four walls, at the very least.

None of which I've got.

The receptionist eyes me wearily as I step inside the lobby. "Kade Archer?"

My swallow sticks in my throat. "Yes, ma'am."

"They're waiting for you down at the end of the hall on the left."

My feet feel like they weigh a thousand pounds, and my heart's threatening to break a fucking rib, but I follow her directions, refusing to linger. I know if I stop, I might not go in at all.

The door's cracked, and a soft conversation filters through it. Can't make out what they're saying, but I recognize both voices.

"This is it," I murmur, squeezing my eyes shut. My knuckles pop from how hard my fists are clenched. "You've been to war. You can do this."

Correction. I *have* to do this. For Marlee, and Aurora. For me.

A sweet laugh has my eyes snapping open.

Not the clipped, professional tone she's used every time we've spoken. This is softer. Warm and real.

I inhale sharply, caught off guard by how it sounds—how it rolls over me. How it settles something sharp and frantic in my chest. I'm nervous as hell, seconds from bolting or throwing up, or both, but that laugh? It cuts through the noise in my head like sunlight through fog.

For a second, I let myself believe it. Let myself soak it in, soothe my nerves like the finest whiskey in South Dakota. Then I square my shoulders and step inside.

My boots echo against the linoleum as I walk through the door and all but ignore Georgia Walker as if she didn't just heal me for a breath. I'm pretty sure if she caught my eye right now, she'd see everything I'm trying to hide.

So, I focus on the man I knew as a kid, but haven't seen since high school.

Judge Romero is heavier than I remember, all gray hair and kind eyes behind wire-rimmed glasses. He looks up from a stack of papers laid out on a small table, gives me a familiar smile, and pushes to stand.

Pulling my Stetson off, I hold it to my chest with one hand and extend the other like the polite man I need these people to think I am.

"Kade," he says, his deep voice booming through the tiny room. I swallow hard, thankful it's not a full court room. "It's been a long damn time, son."

"Good to see you, Frank."

I shake his hand, firm, quick, then shove mine back into my pocket, and hope like hell he can't tell how terrified I am right now. My hat stays off since I'm in proper company, but I clutch the damn thing like a lifeline.

"I'm sure sorry about these circumstances," he says, voice low, hand squeezing my shoulder. "But glad you could be here today."

I swallow hard. "Thank you, sir."

He turns his attention to Georgia, and gives her a soft, almost fatherly smile. "Ms. Walker, I've gotta make a call in my office. We'll get started soon."

"Of course, Judge Romero," she replies, all sugar and silk. "Take your time."

I watch him disappear through the door, the latch clicking softly behind him.

And then it's just me and her. I take a slow breath, wait a beat, *or five*, and turn toward her, bracing for the sight of freckles and fire.

But all I find is frost.

I force a smile. Georgia looks away, ignoring me completely, and rolls her prim little shoulders back like a posh city girl too good for this town.

The hell's that about?

When I walked in, she was laughing with Frank like they were old friends. Now, there's not an ounce of the wildfire that burned through my apartment last week, or in my arms a few days ago. Just icy professionalism that grates on my nerves.

I shouldn't care. Hell, I shouldn't even notice.

But I do.

Jaw ticking and temper flaring, I stalk over and drag out the chair right next to her—*loudly*—ignoring the perfectly good one across the table.

"Nice to see you, Ms. Walker." My voice is a low rumble that'd scare the hide off a horse. She jumps, and on the inside, I'm fucking cheering. "Hope you haven't ruined anyone's day lately."

Slow as fresh, sticky honey, she turns to face me, cocking her head to the side. "Excuse me?"

"You ruined my shirt," I remind her, ticking off my fingers. "My time with my mom. My mood. And before that, you ruined a drunk daze I was desperate for by dropping the bomb that my oldest friend was dead like you were dropping the weather."

She pales, and a swarm of warring emotions battle for dominance inside me.

"I didn't mean to," she murmurs, gaze flicking to the closed door. "I'm really sorry about that. I thought you knew."

My nod is slow, assessing. She genuinely looks sorry—and something in me relishes her misery. Maybe because it's the first speck of real emotion she's given me today. Maybe it's because I'm miserable too, and it's nice not to be alone in it.

Or, maybe I'm just an asshole.

"Well, *darlin'*." I let the nickname she hates roll off my tongue with a thick-as-shit accent I don't have. "As my mama's always said, 'Sorry's like a rainstorm after the fire. It don't undo the burn.'"

My mom's never said that a day in her life.

Georgia's mouth falls open, and what looks a hell of a lot like another *sorry*, sits on her tongue.

Before she can say anything, I tack on, "And don't worry about the shirt. I look better without one anyway."

Her cheeks flare red, one eye twitching like she's short-circuiting.

Golden-red brows pulled in tight? Check.

Angled jaw working back and forth? Hell yeah.

Good. There's that fire.

A lazy smirk curls across my mouth as I lean back, legs spreading in the too-small chair like I own the damn place. Her gaze slides over me, and hell if I don't let mine return the favor.

She's in that stiff, starched suit again and those too-high heels, every inch of her polished and pressed. Her curls are slicked back into some kind of weird bun I hate, and the freckles I'd been looking forward to are hidden under simple makeup.

But *fuck*, she's still gorgeous.

Georgia's eyes trail down my body, all slow and clinical, pausing on my Carhartt before working their way down to my nicest pair of jeans—unlike the worn pair she gawked at the other day. Her throat bobs, and she jerks her gaze away, pausing at my boots. Same kind I've had since I was young, but these are newer—not softened by the farm or scuffed from a hard day's work.

Personally, I prefer them worn and battered. Comfortable. But today, I tried. Today, I wanted to look good.

For the judge.

Georgia's lips twitch, skin wrinkling around the edges of those grass-green eyes.

She laughing at me?

"You know? I think you've got it all wrong," she murmurs, leaning in close, gaze locked on mine.

"What's that?" I find myself mirroring her, the chair creaking under my weight as I fall forward.

She drops her voice so low, I have to share breath with her to catch her words.

There's that damn smell again. Sweet, floral, a little wild, like something that grows where it shouldn't but thrives anyway. This close, I can finally see her freckles.

Tiny little starbursts of distraction.

"I can barely stand the sight of you *dressed*, Mr. Archer," she purrs, the sound so warm and intimate, my eyes fall closed. *Goddamn, freckles.* "Not sure anything else could possibly help. *Shirt* or *no shirt*."

It takes me a second to register the insult and my gaze snaps to hers. My jaw tightens. I almost clap back, a cutting barb trapped in my throat, but before I can, the door swings open.

Thank fuck, too. Left to my own devices, I might have done something insane, like strip off my shirt just to prove a point.

We jolt away from each other like we just got caught with our hands down each other's pants in church.

"Alright, folks." Frank claps with a wide grin as he settles in his chair. "Let's get down to it, shall we?"

Georgia straightens so fast it's like someone pulled a string. Her expression shutters, mouth flattening into a tight, professional line. And me? I'm still trying to remember how to breathe without her scent invading my sinuses.

She taps something on her laptop, posture perfect, tone crisp. "Of course, Your Honor. I have the documentation ready."

Frank waves her off.

"No need for formalities here. This isn't a hearing, or the big city. We do things differently in Summit. Just a chance to sit down, go over what's been filed, and make sure everyone's on the same page for the sake of the baby."

Everyone. Like we're a team. Like I didn't just meet her a week ago and spend most of that time wanting to slam the metaphorical door in her face.

Georgia clicks a pen. My eye twitches. "I've compiled my findings based on my initial intake, a home visit, and a conversation with the probate attorney's assistant."

Romero nods. "Go ahead, Ms. Walker."

"If we're being informal, you can call me Georgia."

She shoots him a kind smile. My eyes narrow, and I shift uncomfortably.

"Mr. Archer had no prior knowledge of the child, Aurora Vernal, until my visit. According to the will filed with the probate attorney, the Vernals named Mr. Archer as Aurora's legal guardian following her birth. While Marlee does have a living relative—her younger sister, Oakley June Parker—she is only eighteen years old. Per the attorney's notes, Mrs. Vernal explicitly stated that she did not want Aurora placed with her sister, leaving Mr. Archer as the sole designated guardian."

I swallow hard, my fists clenched under the table.

What the fuck, Marlee?

"She and Mr. Archer were previously involved, I believe," Georgia continues, her brows furrowed. "Though, I was unable to determine the extent of the relationship—"

She trails off and glances at me as if she's hoping I'll fill in the blank.

I don't. Won't.

I'm not going there.

We stare at each other, the silence thick as hell. I do all I can to let my unspoken words fill the space between us.

You're gonna have to try harder, sweetheart. I'm not breaking first.

Georgia looks damn pissed as she huffs, "Can you help me out here?"

"No," I mutter. "Should have done your research better, *Georgia*."

"*You* can call me Ms. Walker," she says sweetly, flashing a smile that's all teeth. "And I'd really appreciate you filling in the blanks, Mr. Archer. Though my search was extensive, there's only so much I can verify without turning to the rumor mill, and that's just not something I believe in doing."

Interesting—and appreciated. I can only imagine what the old biddies in Heart Springs have to say about me and Marlee May, or the way things ended. Ten plus years, and I'm positive no one's forgotten a damn second of it.

Maybe they should have hit the whiskey harder. Worked for me.

Looking her straight in the eyes, I say the honest truth, "I have no interest in walking down memory lane."

"But—" Her hands flap at her sides. "I can't do my job if I don't know all the facts, and unfortunately, a big part of this story sadly passed away, and you're all that's left."

"You want the story?" She nods. My brows hit my hairline as my gut twists. "Marlee and I fucked for years, but that was a long ass time ago. The baby isn't mine. Marlee isn't mine. And this?" I start to stand. "This is a mistake—"

"Kade!" Frank chides. I slowly turn to look at him, and his expression has me dropping back down. He reminds me of my dad. "This'll only work if you want it to, son. You gotta put the past hurt where it belongs and handle what's in front of you for the people who can't speak for themselves. Can you do that?"

I hear what he's not saying. This isn't just about me. It's about Aurora and her parents.

It's about Marlee.

Frank knew the Parkers. Hell, the whole damn town did. Their name carried weight, and not the good kind.

People wrote them off as trash long before Marlee was old enough to prove them wrong. Her mom OD'd when Marlee was a teenager. The boyfriend died, too—same needle, same night. That left Marlee and her baby sister, Oakley, in the care of their grandma, Kim.

She lived in a rusted-out trailer on the edge of town and had no business raising kids. Barely raised her own before tossing Marlee's mama out on her ass. Cold, cruel, and sharp-tongued, she was the kind of woman who didn't believe in softness. She'd raised her daughter with fear and fists, and she didn't change for the next generation.

Marlee protected Oakley the best she could, but she was still just a kid herself. I tried, too. Got my parents involved, but things were different back then. Small town, no protection, and a tiny police force.

Eventually, Marlee got free just by turning eighteen, and shortly after, Kim passed away. Best thing that could have happened for Oakley. She wound up in foster care by the time she was eight, and last I heard, she had a good life a few towns over.

The reminder is like a slap in the fucking face. My palm rakes through my hair, tugging hard enough to hurt. It doesn't help. I still feel sick. And confused. And *sad*.

Maybe things between us ended badly, but the thought of Marlee's little girl winding up in the same kind of hell she and Oakley survived?

Fuck no.

I swallow back the acid clawing up my throat and shove the painful memories where they won't ache. Leaning forward, elbows braced on my knees, I pick a spot on the worn walnut table to stare at and don't look away.

"Marlee and I met in kindergarten. She hated me right off the bat, and I—" I swallow hard. "I loved her. Loved her from the second I saw her. Followed her around for years, begging her to look at me. To see me." I scoff and a sad smile spreads across my face without warning. "Every boy was after her attention, though, and I was just a scrawny little farm kid with a gap between my teeth and cow shit on my boots."

She didn't want a damn thing to do with me. She always wanted bigger. I should have known, even back then.

Marlee treated that cow shit on my boots better than she treated the boy wearing them. She flirted with and dated everyone else, barely sparing me a glance unless it was to throw an insult my way.

"Freshman year, I'd finally shot up, went through a round of braces, started putting on muscle from working the farm and hauling hay, but I wasn't a jock. No time for football or baseball like everyone else. Still, that year—"

I huff out a breath, remembering it clearer than I'd like.

"Every jock in school was falling all over themselves, begging her to be their date for homecoming. And then, one afternoon, there she was. All pompoms, swishing hips, batting lashes—prancing straight up to me. Demanded I be her date like it was the most obvious thing in the world."

A humorless smile pulls at the corner of my mouth. "To this day, I don't know why she picked me. Thought maybe it was a joke at first. But I said yes—showed up in a too-tight tux, my voice cracking from puberty, and a red corsage that didn't match her dress."

She was so fucking mad, too. Didn't let me hear the end of it for months.

"Didn't matter. I was gone for her after that. We were gone for each other. Fast and hard. That's how first love works, right? All in, no seatbelt, no second thoughts."

I scrub a hand over my jaw. "We had a plan. She worked her ass off to get into college, and I joined the military. She'd do school. I'd do the Army. Four years in, then we'd be together forever. I had six months left on my contract. I was ready for—"

A pause. I can feel the rest pressing against my chest, too heavy to speak out loud.

I was ready for everything. Had the ring. The house. The goddamn plan.

Telling them that makes me feel desperate, and foolish, but I force it out. They need to understand how perplexing this whole damn situation is. How out of her mind Marlee must have been to appoint me as her kid's guardian.

If they understand the circumstances, maybe they'll find a better solution.

"I was ready for the future," I say, my eyes fixed on a knot in the wood grain of the table. "But she had other plans in mind. Broke it off in a letter. Said she couldn't grow old and die in a shitty town like Heart Springs. Said it was too small; she wanted the city. And since the country was all I wanted—she didn't want me."

My fingers twitch, curling into a loose fist.

"Never spoke to her again after that. I extended my contract and stayed in nearly ten more years before I was discharged with injuries. I always figured she left for good. Moved in with her sister in Rydell or maybe Sioux Falls since it's a bigger city." I shrug, sighing. "Just knew she wasn't in Heart Springs when I came back."

When I finally lift my gaze to Georgia, I brace for the blow. Judgment, maybe. Sympathy, if she's feeling generous.

But I'm not prepared for the anger.

Her eyes are bright, blazing with something fierce and unspoken. Jaw tight. Shoulders tense. She looks like she wants to hit something. Or someone.

Like she's angry for Marlee. Angry at me.

I'm raw after opening up. Irritated I had to do it in the first place. My jaw unhinges, muscles locking up as I get ready to shove to my feet.

Fuck this. I didn't do a damn thing wrong.

"Such a shame," Frank mutters, sending a chill through the ire in my bones. I pause, fingers tight around the arms of the chair, and find his sad gaze locked on me. "Marlee was a confused, scared, and broken girl, Kade. Went through a hell of a childhood, we all know that, and it doesn't excuse the hurt she caused, but you were both young."

"All due respect," I choke out. "If I was old enough to go to war, she sure as shit was old enough to not be an asshole."

A laugh explodes from my left, shocking me. My eyes snap to Georgia's just as she slaps a delicate hand to her mouth and winces.

I'm so surprised by her outburst, I smile, despite the heaviness in my gut.

"Sorry," she murmurs, straightening her already perfect files. "Please, continue."

Her lips are curled in a soft smile she tries to hide, chin tucked to her chest—but for some reason, I'm riveted to that tiny curve. It takes me a long moment to drag my gaze from her profile back to Frank.

Behind his glasses, his eyes are flicking between us, keen and assessing. After spending nearly thirty years as a judge, I assume he sees too damn much too easily, and the realization has the smirk dropping from my face.

"Be that as it may," he continues. "I'm sure it was hard as hell coming back here, especially after your dad passed. I know how close you two were."

I drop back fully into my chair, knees suddenly weak. All humor evaporates in a split second.

"We're not here to talk about my dad." My words are harsher than I intend, but I don't give a fuck.

Truth is, the thrumming, burning pain inside me has nothing to do with Marlee, and everything to do with my dad. He *was* my best friend, and he died because he was working too damn hard doing a job I should have been at home doing. Instead, I was thousands of miles away, fighting an uphill battle that'll never be won.

That's the guilt I carry every damn day. That's the reason I struggle to wake up and find something to live for.

But mostly, that's the reason I haven't been home—and it's killing me.

And it all started with a letter.

Frank's nod is slow. "Understood." He turns to Georgia. "I've already read through your extensive notes, but go ahead and continue with your assessment."

"Um, of course," she whispers, tucking a stray curl behind her ear.

No idea when it worked its way free from that slicked-back bun, but the softness suits her.

Not that I'm looking.

"As Mr. Archer stated, he and the deceased had no contact for the last decade. Despite that, the probate attorney has confirmed receipt of the letter of designation and his assistant faxed over a copy yesterday." She blinks at me. "Everything is legal and notarized. Kade is the designated guardian."

She swallows hard, but my throat closes all together.

"At the time of the home visit, I conducted an inspection and found the residence to be unsuitable for a child, particularly one Aurora's age. It was not only unclean but also unsafe—structurally and otherwise." I inhale a shaky breath. "Mr. Archer was also intoxicated at the time."

I already knew all this—hell, I live it—but hearing it laid out in that soft, detached tone… it lands like a series of slow, deliberate punches.

And every single one hits dead center.

"There's also uncertainty regarding employment. Based on my records search, no current job has been documented."

Frank scribbles something down. "Kade?"

I clear my throat. "I, uh… I work remotely for a private security company out of Texas. I take jobs all over the place providing protection for people who need it on a short-term basis. I take gigs when I want them. Just got back from one the day before—" I glance at Georgia and dip my chin. "Before you showed up."

Just like Frank, she's taking notes. Me? I'm trying not to sweat through my clothes and stink up the place.

"Do you have a number for me to call? I'll need to verify."

Leaning forward, I dig out my wallet, grab a card with Griff's number on it, and hand it to her. The thought makes me ill, but I'll have to call him after this and let him know what's going on.

Frank nods slowly. "You think that work'll continue should we proceed with guardianship?"

Proceed? Like it's a done deal? My heart skips a few beats.

Holy shit.

"Don't see how it can," I say, raking a hand through my hair, my thoughts racing. "I'd have to quit."

"And income?" she asks, tone cutting. "If you quit your job, how will you afford to care for a child—"

"I have money," I interrupt, hackles high, heart rate higher. "Despite my shitty house, I do know how to balance a checkbook, Ms. Walker. I spent over ten years in the Rangers. Saved every penny. Now I live in a studio apartment that costs less than most people's weekly groceries." Her eyes narrow and my temper flares. "I could quit today and be set for years, so don't worry your pretty little head about how I'll provide for her. You can be damn sure I take care of what's mine."

The silence hangs thickly in the air between us.

Frank clears his throat, and leans back, fingers steepled over his chest. "So, let me ask you, son—do you *want* this? To be Aurora's guardian?"

I open my mouth.

Then close it.

Because I have no fucking clue what I want.

Georgia shifts awkwardly, but gives me time to process. They both do.

"I didn't ask for this," I say slowly. "But I… I don't think I can walk away."

He arches a bushy brow, but he doesn't look all that shocked. Maybe satisfied, or mildly impressed. Minutes pass, but they stretch on, tense and thick, feeling like a hell of a lot longer.

When he finally speaks, even Georgia looks nervous.

"Kade, I knew your daddy most of my life," he says softly, gutting me. "Known you since you were a baby. You've been gone a long time, and you've seen horrors only few can even imagine, but if you want this, I have every faith that you can handle it." He releases a breath. "William is in you, Kade. You hear me? You are your father's boy, and son, William Archer was the greatest man I ever had the pleasure of knowing."

I swallow so hard, it hurts, but he continues, barely letting me process.

"I just need you to understand that this is a serious responsibility. A child's life will be in your hands. Can you rise to the challenge, or are you walking away?"

I don't know what it is—my father's spirit writhing in my soul, or the reminder that he still lives on in more people than just me—but it's the push I need to do what my heart's been begging me to do since this whole thing started.

"I'm in—" My voice cracks, my eyes burn, but I square my shoulders. "I want to do this."

The man doesn't even skip a beat, just nods and gives me a serious look.

"You have one month to secure suitable housing that is far away from Agnes Whittaker's property. No drinking. No drugs—"

My jaw snaps open. "What? I don't do drugs!"

Frank ignores me and turns to Georgia.

"Georgia, I understand you're only with us temporarily?"

She jerks a nod, and my brows furrow. "I've been filling Ethel Sorrenson in on the progress. She's on medical leave, but should be back any day now." Her eyes flick to me, throat bobbing, before she glances away. "After that, I'll likely be moved to Serenity Falls and Ms. Sorrenson will take over where I've left off."

"Makes sense. I've known Director Finch a long time. Know he likes to keep one or two good people per town—less red tape, more trust. It's how we've always done things here in Summit. We look after our own." He sighs, smiling softly. "Serenity's got its own courthouse, so I won't see you much, but I'll be sure to let Finch know you've done a fine job here."

Her cheeks turn bright red, and she ducks her head. "Thank you, sir—I mean, Frank."

Chuckling, he gives her another soft look, then turns to me. The smile drops, and I nearly scoff.

The fuckin' man is taken with her, isn't he? Christ, it's my mom all over again.

"When we reconvene, I'll make a formal ruling on guardianship. If it all works out, you'll be able to file for adoption after that."

"Adoption?" The room sways, and I run my fingers through my beard, reality setting in. "I can adopt her—*permanently*?"

"If you don't fuck this up," he murmurs, brows high, smirk on his lips. "You have one month, Kade. Can you change everything you are for her?"

One month.

Thirty days.

Jesus, that's no time at all.

I have to move. Start over. Clean up my act, my life. But, I have no choice. This is happening. No one—and nothing—matters more than the innocent little girl lying alone in a hospital right now.

Fuck, she's probably terrified.

Inhaling deep, I let it out and meet his eyes.

"I'll be ready."

Frank stares at me for a beat, then smiles, big and wide. "Alright, son. Any questions?"

My gaze slides to Georgia, and I'm shocked to see her pretty green eyes filled with a sheen I sure as hell don't expect. She clears her throat and gives me a soft nod that hits me right in the solar plexus.

Just like her laugh. Just like her wildfire and starburst freckles, it settles something inside me.

I push to my feet and turn to Frank.

"When can I—" I swallow past the lump growing in my throat. "My—Marlee's daughter. I'd like to meet her."

CHAPTER NINE

IT'S A REFLEX?

THE HOSPITAL DOESN'T SMELL like bleach.

That's the first thing I notice.

It smells like plastic. Like rubber gloves and old vending machine coffee and trauma.

It feels even worse. Or maybe it's just me.

Georgia's already waiting for me, leaning against the wall outside a room with fish stickers all over the door. Her arms are crossed, giant purse pressed to her chest.

Unlike the other day, her curls are free—a reckless mess of oranges, reds, and every color in between.

I swallow hard, unprepared for what the sight does to my senses.

My eyes slide down her body, taking her in.

She's a hell of a lot more casual today, dressed in a long, flowy floral skirt that brushes the tops of her boots and sways when she crosses her ankles. A chunky cream sweater hangs loose over her frame, tucked slightly at the waist with a wide belt that draws my eyes straight to her curvy hips.

"Did you make the drive okay?" she asks, dragging my attention away from her body with a knowing look. "Rydell is farther than I realized. Took me forever to find the place the first time I came."

I blink a few times, jaw ticking—pissed off I've been caught checking her out when it's the last fuckin' place my mind should be.

"Obviously. I'm here, aren't I?" I shoot her a harsh look as I step into her space and cross my arms. Not close enough to smell her or go hunting for those damn freckles again, but close enough to catch the little crinkles next to her eyes when she glares at me.

"You don't have to be such an ass," she whisper-hisses, eyes darting toward the nurses' station behind me like someone might overhear and write her up. "I was just asking a question."

"A stupid one." My brow lifts, daring her to argue.

Georgia scoffs and pushes away from the wall. "Maybe I was trying to make polite conversation, then."

"Well, don't," I snap, dragging a hand through my hair. The moment my fingers hit my scalp, I wince.

Left my hat in the fuckin' truck.

My dad always said it was bad luck for a gentleman to leave the house without his cowboy hat. Worse luck to forget it somewhere.

Not that I'm a gentleman, and I'm already swimming in bad luck, so I guess I'm just keeping the streak alive.

"Insufferable," she mutters as she starts to pace. "Argumentative. Pig-headed. Emotionally constipated. Giant man-baby with stupid cow-shit cowboy boots and a stupid hat."

My brows climb higher with each insult, and I don't even try to hide the smirk forming. She's not looking at me, just muttering toward the floor like she's trying to curse me without getting fired.

She scoffs to herself and adds under her breath, "He probably snores like a freight train and chews with his mouth open, too."

I step into her path, interrupting the one-woman diatribe, and lean in close, voice low and drawling. "You got somethin' to say, darlin'? Feel free to say it to my face."

She snaps her gaze up, cheeks flushed, caught off guard by how close I am. Her mouth opens—probably to deny it—but nothing comes out.

"Didn't peg you for the type to fantasize about my sleeping habits…" My eyes drop to her lips. "Or what my mouth does."

Her face goes *full sunset-pink.*

Bingo.

Pink is step one in unraveling Georgia.

"You're impossible and so unbelievably unprofessional, Mr. Archer."

"And you're more fun when you're flustered, Ms. Walker," I murmur, winking as I step back, slow and satisfied. "Besides, you started it."

She bites her lip, turning it bright red. I have the strange urge to tug it free.

"I didn't know I said that out loud."

My brows go high. "You didn't know you were whispering non-sense about me?"

"I knew I was doing it in my head." She looks away. "I ramble when I'm nervous."

"I've noticed."

We stare at each other for a long moment that only breaks when a nurse pushes past and steps through the door with the fish. My eyes snap up, following her as if I'll catch a glimpse of what's waiting for me on the other side as if it'll somehow magically prepare me.

I hold my breath.

It opens and closes with a tiny *click*, and all I get is a peek of more bare walls and low lighting.

"She's in there?" I ask, my voice coming out rougher than intended.

"Don't ask stupid questions," Georgia says. Her eyes go wide, and she slaps a hand to her face so loud, I wince. "Shit, I mean, crap. I mean, I'm sorry." She sighs. "Would you believe me if I said it's a reflex?"

"To insult me?"

She lifts a shoulder and gives me an embarrassed smile. "Yes?"

I chuckle and shake my head. For some reason, her verbal diarrhea has me relaxing a bit.

"I am sorry, though," she murmurs. "Yes, Aurora is in there. I spoke to the nurse on call while I was waiting. She said she's been asleep for the last hour—and likely still is."

"Is she—" I feel like I'm being choked to death. "Did they say what happened to her in the—" *Fuck, just get it out.* "The acc—"

"The accident?" she finishes gently.

I give a sharp nod.

She looks at me for a long second, like she's trying to decide how much I can take. "Are you asking about the details of the accident? Or just Aurora's status?"

Do I really want to know what killed Marlee? How it happened?

I know if I hear it, if I can picture it, it might wreck me. Not because I still love Marlee. But because I *did*. And because I'm standing here for her kid… *and she's not.*

And never will be again.

But it's Aurora's story, and if this goes as planned, one day, I'll have to tell her what happened to her parents. How her mama died.

That thought makes me nauseous.

"All of it," I manage, voice shredded. "Like you're ripping a Band-Aid off."

Georgia's lips press together, her eyes searching mine, but she gives one, sharp nod and sucks in a slow breath.

"From what the EMT report said, the car left the road just outside Langley. Hit a tree. Hard. The driver and passenger were both pronounced dead at the scene. We're still waiting on the toxicology report."

My chest caves inward.

"Aurora was in the backseat. Properly buckled into a rear-facing seat. That seat, and the angle of impact, is what saved her."

The room sways, but I commit every word to memory.

"She has a concussion. Some bruising from the harness, and a few cuts from the glass. Worst was on her cheek. It'll scar, but nothing serious." She takes a breath. "There was a small brain bleed—"

Pretty sure my soul leaves my body. She must see the panic all over my face because she reaches out, grips my forearm, and squeezes hard as she rushes to finish.

"She didn't need surgery, but they kept her in the pediatric ICU for observation." Georgia's little fingers dig in, and she gives me a shake, drawing my gaze to hers. "She hasn't had any seizures, no vomiting since the second night. Pain management's the focus now. She'll be okay, Kade. She's healing."

Healing.

Jesus.

I nod, slow and unsteady. She stares at me for a few more seconds then releases my arm. I feel the loss of it like air in a confined space. Like I'm drifting at sea alone.

"You okay?" she whispers.

I almost laugh but it comes out like a garbled cry. "No."

"Want to talk about it?"

"No."

My hands are clammy, fists clenched at my sides as I stare at the door like it might unhinge itself and swallow me whole. A long moment passes before she finally speaks, voice soft and sweet.

"You don't have to be her everything all at once," she murmurs. "You just have to go in and say hi."

"Hi?" I shoot her a side glance. "I'm not ready for that."

"No one's ever ready." She gives me a sad smile. "Even the parents who had nine months to plan. No one is ever ready to be a parent, even when they think they are."

A parent? Fucking hell.

"Take your time," she says, stepping away. "I've got a call to make anyway. I'll be down the hall. When you're ready… just go in and say hi, Kade. That's all you have to do."

She walks away, and I'm left with nothing but a pulsing heartbeat in my ears and a trembling breath in my lungs.

The door's cracked open just enough that I can see the faint glow of machines inside. The fish stickers stare at me like they know I don't fit in, and I barely resist the urge to flip them off.

But I step forward anyway.

Because Marlee died.

Because Georgia, Frank, and Aurora, are depending on me.

Because it's what my dad would do.

Just say hi.

Chapter Ten

Just Say Hi

I PUSH THE DOOR open, slow and quiet, then just stand there for a second completely frozen.

The room's dim, lit mostly by the soft blue-white light of a monitor in the corner and the late afternoon bleeding through the edges of closed blinds. There's a chair, a couch too short to sleep on, and in the middle of it all, a small crib on wheels.

Another step. A slow breath. A shaky exhale.

The crib is small because Aurora…

Aurora is so fucking small.

It's the only thought I have, and it circles through my fogged-up brain on a loop. Not the machines. Not the quiet beep of her pulse on the monitor. Not even the butterfly bandage on her cheek, where a faded bruise still lingers.

Just how small she is.

Barely takes up half the crib.

She's curled up on stark white sheets, one chubby arm flung out to the side like she owns the place. Her cheeks are round and flushed, lips parted slightly in sleep—the top one fuller than the bottom.

Unlike Marlee's golden tan, Aurora's skin is pale—fair enough that the fading bruise stands out. Maybe it's just the hospital lights. Or maybe it's from everything she's been through.

And her hair's a wild, messy halo of soft brown curls that stick up like she's fresh out of a wind tunnel. There's a dried curl stuck to her forehead, and another twirling in the shell of her ear.

She looks like chaos. Like sweetness and strength, all knotted together in this tiny, impossible package.

Just say hi.

I take the last few steps till my thighs are bumping the crib. And then I stop, because my knees threaten to buckle.

"Fuck," I choke out. My throat constricts. "*Holy shit.*"

I'm not ready. I don't know what to do with this—this precious baby. This human that has no idea who I am. No idea why I'm here. No idea that someone she's never met just made a promise he's scared to death he can't keep when her world's already been turned upside down.

My fingers twitch at my sides. I want to touch her, but I don't. What if I wake her? What if she cries? I try to breathe deep, but it's like my lungs are full of rocks.

God, I don't know what I'm doing.

Suddenly, she stirs. Just a little. A shift of a tiny foot, covered by a tiny white onesie. A scrunch of her button nose. I hold my breath, my entire body tense as hell, waiting to see if she'll fully wake up.

She settles for a second—no more than a single breath. Then her eyes flutter open.

Big, deep brown eyes rimmed with thick lashes, blink up at the ceiling like she sees something I don't. I follow her gaze, stomach flipping.

Please don't be a ghost of your mama.

Nothing. Of course, there's nothing. My heart skips, stumbles, then slams. I look back down at the baby occupying the crib—flipping my world on its axis.

Aurora turns her head slowly—so slowly it feels like it takes a lifetime—and locks eyes with me.

And everything… *just stops.*

No sound. No panic. No spiraling. Just a weightless, breathless pause as this tiny girl stares up at me like I might *matter*. Like I'm not a stranger, or a mistake, or a man who's already wrecked too much to be trusted with anything soft.

My knees give out.

I drop into the chair beside her crib as if I've been hit. Elbows on my thighs. Hands shaking like I'm back in the desert, waiting for something to blow.

Out of nowhere, a tear slips free. Then another.

I wipe my face with the back of my hand, jaw clenched tight—hard enough to crack bone. But the tears keep coming. Thick and fast and stupid. *So fucking stupid.*

Don't even know why I'm crying.

I've seen worse. Lived through worse. Buried friends, dodged bullets, held men in my arms while they bled out and begged for their mamas.

But this?

This *wrecks* me.

She's so damn small. So new.

Unbroken.

She doesn't know what's out there waiting. Doesn't know about heartbreak or betrayal. Doesn't know the way the world kicks you when you're already down. Doesn't know that sometimes, one bad second is all it takes to fuck everything to hell.

Aurora has no idea that someday, when she's old enough, she'll learn she lost everything before she even knew she had it.

Her eyes are wide, dark, and innocent. She trusts me. Without hesitation. Without question. She doesn't know she's been alone. Has no idea she's not anymore.

I swallow hard, chest threatening to cave in under the weight of something I can't name. She's perfect. And I'm not. Not even close.

But in this moment—this one, impossible, breaking-open-my-ribs moment—I'd do anything to protect her from the kind of pain I've spent my whole life choking on.

The door opens softly behind me, and I sit up straight, trying to hide the worst of it, quickly wiping my face on my sleeve. Fuck, I haven't had to hide tears since I was a boy.

An older nurse walks in, short and round and kind-eyed. Her scrubs are covered in sunflowers, and her face softens when she sees me. "You must be Mr. Archer."

I nod, not trusting my voice, and shove to my feet.

She moves to the crib and checks the monitor, then the chart clipped to the side. "She's doing well. The concussion's resolved. The bruising's fading. The cut on her cheek will scar, but it's clean. No lasting damage."

My throat tightens again, and my voice is rough as I speak. "How long's she been here?"

I feel like Georgia's told me, but everything's been a whirlwind.

"Two weeks," she says gently. "She's a fighter."

I look at Aurora. "Yeah. I can see that."

"She's awake now," the nurse says, glancing at me. "Would you like to hold her?"

"I—uh—no." I wipe my sweaty palms on my jeans. "I mean—I don't know if I should."

"That's alright. I'll show you how." She leans into the crib and scoops Aurora up with practiced ease, cradling her against her chest like it's second nature as she quickly unhooks a tiny monitor from her foot.

"No, I know how, I've got nephews and little sisters. I've birthed calves and goats and puppies." *Shut up, Kade.* I sound like Georgia, rambling like a fool. "That's not the problem, I just—"

The nurse ignores me and circles the crib, stopping at my side.

"Here we go, sweetheart," she coos. "Let's get you settled." Then she turns and looks up at me. "You ready?"

"Not even a little."

I wipe my hands again, eyes flicking to Aurora where they stay.

"I feel like I should bathe in hand sanitizer or something," I mutter, swallowing hard. "I mean, I showered—I'm clean, I just—"

She chuckles and steps forward, placing the squirming baby into my arms. My hands instinctively adjust, supporting her head, her back.

"Just sway with her a bit," the nurse says, backing toward the door. "Walking helps. Talk to her, even if it feels silly. Your voice will comfort her."

Eyes locked on Aurora's face, I nod. The door clicks shut behind the nurse, and then, it's just us.

I pace slowly, bouncing her a little, careful not to scare or hurt her. I'm not exactly sure where her injuries are or if she's sore, and I sure as hell don't want to make her cry.

It's been a long damn time since I've held a baby this small. Was in high school when Colby and Clem were born, and overseas when both my nephews arrived. I'm out of practice. It feels clumsy and awkward at first, but she settles into me like she belongs there. Her head tucks under my chin, and I exhale for the first time in what feels like hours.

Just say hi.

"Hey," I whisper. "So uh… I'm Kade. You probably don't care about that yet, but you're gonna hear it a lot, so you might as well get used to it."

Aurora blinks up at me, eyes wide, curious, and unbothered.

"I don't know what the hell I'm doing," I admit, voice hushed. "Shit—I mean, crap. Crap. Gotta start working on that. You're a sponge, right?

That's what they say. Kids hear everything. My sister Gemma has these little ass—" I shake my head and groan. "Buttholes that repeat everything."

I shift her in my arms, trying to get more comfortable.

"Anyway, I read some stuff online. About sippy cups and baby-proofing and formula. But I also read that babies your age eat like, little fruit puffs? Is that right? I don't know. There was something about soft junk like mashed potatoes and stuff that's chopped real small."

My mind flies back to my shitty studio and the contents of my kitchen. Have absolutely none of those things.

"You're probably too young for jerky and beer, huh?"

A little gurgle slips from her mouth, and I freeze.

Suddenly, she's smiling, two little Tic Tacs halfway out of her gums on full display.

"You think I'm funny?" I whisper around a grin. "Shit, kid. You're in for a real rude awakening. I'm blander than Mrs. Whittaker's sweet tea."

I run a finger gently over the soft curve of her cheek. It's warm, chubby, and so pink, it reminds me of the hollyhock field at home in July. She's got a dimple starting to form when she smiles—just one. I shift her a bit and smooth down her dark curls. I'm surprised her hair is closer to my shade. Not Marlee's.

That thought does something weird to my chest.

I circle the room again, pacing, bouncing, talking. Tell her all about the dog I found, and then show her the pictures Mom sent me a few days ago.

"She said the little bast—" Groaning, I shake my head. "I mean *cute* little beast—wasn't hers, but look at him all clean and curled up in her lap like he belongs there."

Aurora's chubby fingers bat at my phone as she makes this bubbly, gurgling squeal that's too fucking cute to be human.

"That's what I said," I murmur, pocketing my phone with a smile. "You know what I think, sweetheart? I think my mama is a D-A-M-N liar."

She turns her wide eyes on me, her hands stilling like she knows how to spell, before giggling so loud, my ears pop. I take it as a sign she wants me to keep going, so I do. I don't stop walking, or talking. Telling stories about her mama, about Heart Springs, and about Honey Bea Farm.

I'm deep into a ramble about how I once stepped on one of my sister's Barbie shoes barefoot and swore like a sailor in front of Clementine when I hear a soft laugh echo in the small space.

I turn toward the door and find Georgia leaning against it, arms crossed, a grin lighting up her face.

She's smiling—*really smiling*—and it hits me square in the chest.

"You been standing there long?" I ask, bouncing Aurora a little more as she babbles into my chest and yanks on my beard.

My eyes stray to that little part in Georgia's skirt that splits when she steps closer, showing off an inch of her thigh. That inch shouldn't be so damn interesting, but for a second, it captures every ounce of my attention.

"Long enough," she says, voice warm. "I caught the full length of the Barbie story and the tail end of something about stealing a pickup when you were fifteen." She arches a brow. "It was riveting."

"Yeah, well." I shift awkwardly, my face on fire. "Thought I'd ease her into disappointment early."

Her eyes drop to the baby, and I swear I catch the faintest flicker of sadness cross her face. It's gone so fast, I might've imagined it.

"She looks better today," Georgia murmurs, surprising me. "Yesterday, her bruise was a bit darker. I'm glad it's fading."

"You were here yesterday?" I ask, throat dry, stomach twisting.

She nods, giving me a soft smile and a shrug like it's not a big deal. "Didn't want her to be alone."

Something in her tone catches me off guard.

It's not just admiration—it's longing. Like there's a whole story hiding behind the curve of those two words. But she doesn't offer more, and I don't ask. Not sure I'm mentally equipped to handle much more today.

"She's beautiful," Georgia murmurs, finger ghosting across Aurora's cheek.

My eyes don't leave her freckled profile as I choke out, "*Yeah.*"

We stand there a beat longer, the quiet stretching between us in a way that doesn't feel heavy anymore. It's nice, almost peaceful.

Until Aurora shifts in my arms and lets out a sound that's anything but.

Loud. Wet. Impossible to misinterpret.

I gape. Full stop. Staring down at her like she just detonated a grenade.

Aurora giggles—an adorable sound completely at odds with the unholy noises that just left her small body at an insane octave—and claps her chubby hands.

Georgia snorts, inhales sharply, then bends at the waist with a laugh so pure and wild, I swear it shakes my bones. She clutches her stomach, wiping tears from her eyes as she gasps for air.

"Oh my God," she wheezes. "The face you made—"

"She exploded on me!" I hiss, looking down in horror at Aurora, who's now smiling like she might actually like me. "What the hell was that?"

"She's a baby!" Georgia gasps, still cackling. "And she just introduced herself to you."

"I think she introduced me to her entire digestive system."

Georgia wipes a tear from the corner of her eye, her grin softening as she straightens. "Well, Dad, it's time you learn how to change a diaper."

The word hits me like a punch to the gut.

Dad.

It echoes in my chest. My arms instinctively tighten around Aurora.

I glance down at her—chubby cheeks, cooing mouth, eyes sparkling like she knows something I don't. She wiggles happily, kicking one foot against my side, hard enough to break a rib, and fists my beard like it's her new favorite toy.

For some reason, it makes me proud.

Dad.

No, it doesn't feel right yet. Not after everything. Not with how this came to be. But somehow… it doesn't feel wrong either. Not when she looks at me like this. Not when she settles so easily into my arms.

And fuck, I can see it. Not just surviving this, but being good at it.

Happy, even.

I clear my throat. "I don't need help," I murmur, voice thick with emotion. "I know how to change diapers. I've got a lot of family younger than me. Not my first rodeo."

Georgia tilts her head, amused. "You sure? She's… *potent.*"

"I'm not afraid of a little shi—" I pause, my eyes going wide. "Crap. I meant crap."

"Nice save." She snorts and points between Aurora and me. "You know, she doesn't understand the curse words yet. You're probably okay to speak freely until she starts talking."

"She could start talking any day," I murmur, frowning. "Actually, she could be talking already. Might just not be comfortable enough to do it around me yet."

"Did you learn that from your sister, too?" Georgia asks, questions in her pretty green gaze.

I nod solemnly. "Gonna need to work on my replacements. Gemma's kids repeat everything. I said 'hell' once and got slapped upside the head by a four-year-old."

She laughs again, quieter this time. "She really is beautiful. And you're good with her."

Her voice dips, like it carries more weight than it should. There's something in her eyes too—something deep and quiet and maybe a little broken.

But before I can say anything, before I can figure out what I'm supposed to do with that look, Aurora makes a face.

A very clear, very pissed face.

Then she opens her tiny mouth and wails.

I jolt like I've been shot. "Shit—uh, fuck—*No*! Crap—what did I do?!"

Georgia steps forward just as the door swings open again and the nurse bustles in, smiling.

"She's mad because she's stewing in her own shit!" I shout over the crying, voice panicked. "I don't know where the diapers are!"

"Kade!" Georgia chastises, like it's the most natural thing in the world to admonish me. "Don't cuss in front of the baby!"

"She's literally marinating in it!" I hiss back. "I think it's the perfect time to cuss! And you said she doesn't even know what I'm saying!"

"Sorry to interrupt, but that little one needs a change," the nurse says, eyes twinkling behind her glasses. "And if you don't mind an old woman's opinion, you two are such a cute couple."

Georgia and I snap in unison. "*We're not a couple.*"

I swear her voice goes up a full octave while mine drops to a growl.

She coughs, actually chokes, and presses a hand to her chest, backing away like the thought alone makes her sick.

"I'm sorry," she rushes out. "I'm one of the social workers assigned to Aurora's case."

The nurse raises both brows but chuckles and waves her off. "Well, it's good to meet you, then." She reaches for Aurora, gently lifting her from my arms. "I assume we'll be seeing you around a bit more while we've got this sweet girl here?"

I pale.

"Wait—sorry, does—do I have to go?" The words fall out before I can stop them.

The nurse's smile dips into something sad. "Unfortunately, it's not just the poo that's got your girl all riled up. She's due for pain meds. She'll be fussy till they kick in, but after that, she'll sleep for a good while. Probably out until morning."

I nod, throat thick, eyes fixed on Aurora's little face as the nurse soothes her. Her cheeks are still damp, her mouth puckering like she's about to cry again.

"When can I—" I start, but she cuts in before I can finish.

"Visiting hours start at eight tomorrow morning, end at five. But since you're the guardian—"

"Intended guardian," Georgia says crisply.

I shoot her a glare sharp enough to cut glass. She doesn't flinch, just lifts one of those sleek brows and shrugs.

"I have to say it, Mr. Archer," she murmurs, full of bureaucratic bite. "Until things are legal, they need to know the situation."

"But she needs visitors," the nurse says smoothly, saving me from snapping back. "All the love and cuddles she can get."

Stepping forward one last time, I brush my finger along Aurora's red, tear-streaked cheek. My heart's damn near lodged in my throat.

Why does this hurt?

I just met her.

I shouldn't feel anything yet. I shouldn't care.

But the idea of leaving makes the room spin.

"Feel better," I whisper, my voice too thick to clear. I meet her big, watery eyes and force a smile. "You sleep good, okay?"

She blinks once. Twice. A soft coo hums from her lips as she grabs for my beard like she's saying goodbye, and my ribs cave in on themselves.

"I'll be back tomorrow. I promise."

I don't even know where I get off making promises like that. But there it is.

The nurse untangles Aurora's fingers from my beard, so I step back and finally tear my gaze away before I do something stupid like steal a baby that's not mine.

When I look at Georgia, her expression's unreadable. She jerks her chin toward the door. We don't speak. Not until we're out in the parking lot where the sun's sinking low and painting the sky a lazy orange. The air's cooler now, wind curling around the edge of my collar.

I follow her blindly, my mind's still a thousand miles away, stuck in that hospital room. Thank God Georgia doesn't walk me into oncoming traffic, because I wouldn't have stopped her.

When she stops, I drag a hand through my hair. "What now?"

She flips through her file and I catch sight of the paperwork I filled out at the courthouse the other day.

"I have your number and email address. I'll send you the requirements the judge specified so you have a checklist to work through. I'm not sure how much longer I'll be your point of contact, but you're welcome to reach out if you need anything." The folder snaps shut. "You have less than a month, so please don't waste it."

"Christ," I mutter, irritation burning through me. "Despite the state I was in when you met me, I'm not completely fucking useless."

This whole thing's been one gut punch after another with no time to breathe. I feel raw. Exposed. Like my life's been ripped open and set under a microscope, and she's been the one reminding me it's not good enough.

"I never said you were," she whispers, throat bobbing.

My stomach twists as I glare down at her, holding onto the anger instead of the clawing ache in my gut to break down. "You didn't have to say it. You've made it damn clear from the beginning."

"I can tell you hate me, Mr. Archer," she says quietly, surprising me. "It's not uncommon. People in my position usually become enemy number one. Your whole life's changing at a hundred miles an hour, and I'm right in the middle of it. But I'm not trying to ruin anything. Believe it or not, I want a happy home for that little girl just as much as you do. Maybe more."

I catch her gaze just as a sad smile slips from her face.

"I know the numbers," she whispers, stepping back. "I know what happens to kids who fall through the cracks."

A shadow flickers across her expression, gone in a blink, but it slices straight through me.

"I don't want that for her," she says. "Because most of them don't come back from it."

She turns before I can say a word, but the echo of her voice and the sadness in her eyes stick with me.

And for some damn reason, I hate that she looked so heartbroken.

CHAPTER ELEVEN

ACCIDENTAL ALMOST ORGASMS WITH BRANNON

"That's it, you're doing perfect. Don't stop. Good girl."

Sweat trickles down my spine, and I bob my head rapidly in agreement as another heaving breath whooshes from my lungs.

"A little deeper. You can take it."

My eyes snap open, wide and slightly clouded from the strain. *Deeper? Are you fucking kidding me?* I glare through watery eyes at the person before me, internally cursing every decision that led me to this moment—primarily, taking my feral best friend's advice to find a way to blow off steam.

I shift my body, trying to find comfort in an impossible situation. But my knees are killing me, my finger bones ache, and my throat is nearly raw.

Can't do it. God, I might actually need my inhaler.

A tongue clicks in disapproval. "I know what you're thinking right now. It's all over your face."

Lies. You don't know shit.

"But if you dig deeper within yourself, I promise you'll find that extra bit of energy to keep going."

"Don't want to." Still, I won't give up. What kind of person would I be if I didn't see this through?

A happy one, my inner voice coos. *Just give up, Georgia. Give up and let's go find a cinnamon roll. Cinnamon rolls make us happy.*

I nod again, gluten-free, sugary goodness filling my thoughts.

"Beautiful. Now, let's take this a bit further," the sultry voice purrs. "Find a little movement here. Pedal the feet for five, hands planted flat on your mat for balance. When you're ready, *dive* for the earth on an exhale."

"Dive?" I gasp. "Pedal *how*?"

My neck snaps upward, and my eyes narrow on the athletic bombshell filling up my TV screen. She effortlessly bends and twists her body like the human gumby she is. Her breaths are even, inhaling on exertion, exhaling through holds, before repeating the process. All the while, she never gives up on her borderline sexual commentary.

"Perfect. Now that we're all warmed up, let's get a bit more comfortable as our partners join us."

Partners? My brows furrow and I lean back on my thighs, my attention riveted to the screen. The studio lights blanketing the instructor dim a fraction as a tall, shirtless man with lithe muscles appears, his sultry smirk fixated on the woman.

From one blink to the next, she's ripped off her form-fitting tank and her perky breasts spill free, bouncing against her perfect abs.

My mouth drops open.

The music changes from a soft, relaxing melody to something far more... *provocative.* It's a slow, sensual beat, one that makes my stomach flip for entirely different reasons.

What the hell kind of yoga is this?

"As your partner joins you," the bombshell purrs, "focus on the connection between your bodies."

Connection? I choke on a gasp. My hands are clammy, and I rub them over my thighs, feeling the overwhelming urge to run out of the room. I'm glued to the floor, though—frozen as the woman and her now equally naked partner entwine themselves together like some kind of spicy, tantric pretzel.

The guy settles behind her, his hands sliding down her sides as they move into a pose that looks anything but appropriate for a yoga class. My mind scrambles, trying to piece together how I went from a peaceful morning stretch to *this*.

I'm vaguely aware of the fact that I don't turn off the tutorial. Instead, I lean a little *closer*, focus a little *harder*.

Suddenly, working out just got a whole hell of a lot more interesting.

"Allow your partner to guide you deeper," she murmurs breathily as his hands travel lower, lower, *lower,* and I swear to all that is holy, my brain short-circuits.

"Deeper where?" I cry, watching raptly as his hand glides between her spread thighs.

As if in answer, he slips his palm beneath the band of her buttery-looking shorts. Her head falls backward onto his shoulder with a deep moan and her face instantly fills with a kind of bliss I can only achieve when I'm asleep—*or spending the evening with my vibrator.*

"Holy shit," I mutter, swallowing thickly.

Without my permission, my body scoots a few inches closer to the screen as my eyes adjust to my new reality. The woman whimpers, rolls her hips, and my nipples pebble in response.

Well, that settles it. I'm officially watching porn.

They grind together—him behind her, her ass pressed against his cock, and all I can think is, *fuck, that looks hot as hell.*

I'm debating grabbing my rabbit, or plucking out my eyeballs, when the guy whispers something in the instructor's ear that catches on her mic and echoes around my living room.

"You're so wet, darling. Is this all for me?"

The name tugs on something inside me, except in my mind, it's not a hippy yoga instructor with thin muscles and Gumby-like limbs, and he doesn't say *darling* like some sort of posh, British book boyfriend.

In my head, he's thick, tattooed, and grumpy.

Instead of short spikes, he's got a mess of dark brown waves that fall to his shoulders and are perpetually tucked under some sort of hat.

He's broken in a way that calls to my own fractured pieces, and his voice is a deep, rumble that's slightly accented, except when he's adding a thick drawl and murmuring *darlin'* in my ear just to piss me off.

His smirk is cocky, his body is insane, and he exudes so much Daddy energy, my ovaries actually *ache.*

Suddenly, the sound of murmured moans and groans is a blur in the background, overshadowed by the desperate need thrumming through me. My nipples are hard, and my clit's pulsing in time with my erratic heartbeat.

At some point, I dropped to my ass, back against my coffee table, and spread my thighs, just like the bombshell. But instead of watching them, my head is tipped up and my fingers are sliding under my leggings.

A whimper slips free the second my finger touches my clit.

God, how long has it been since I've touched myself? Let myself just fall apart? Attempted to quench the ache that never seems to quite disappear after I've come?

How long's it been since I got laid? Over a year, and it was over well before I was even close.

My eyes flutter closed, and my throat tightens. I try to focus on the sounds coming from the TV, and not the memories of Kade *fucking* Archer that are looping through my brain on repeat—but it's impossible.

I swirl my finger around my clit again, ignoring how utterly soaked I am. It's ridiculous. He's hardly ever touched me, and it was platonic at best, caveman behavior at worst.

But, hell, I loved the caveman behavior. I'd never admit it out loud, but being manhandled by him turned me on more than any bland sex I've ever had, which is depressing and exciting all at once.

Adding a second finger, I glide down, coating myself in my wetness, and slip them inside my pussy, curving them in a desperate need to find that elusive spot.

"Oh, fuck," I whimper, pinching my nipple through my sports bra.

My hips roll, my thumb presses down on my clit. I'm so close, and I just started. My core is literally dripping.

What am I doing?

I shake my head rapidly, trying to dispel the anxiety, and frantic thoughts competing with made-up images of Kade wearing absolutely nothing but a fucking cowboy hat.

"If you open your pretty mouth one more time, darlin', I swear I'll find a way to shut you up."

Did he mean with his mouth on mine, kissing me roughly, his tongue thrust between my lips, or something else?

Would he shut me up with his cock down my throat, or with my face stuffed into pillows?

My pussy clenches around my fingers, and I tug my nipple harder, twisting it the way I like. Hips rolling, fingers fucking hard and fast, thumb circling, and two yoga instructors moaning, whimpering, and groaning in the background, I'm seconds away from coming faster than ever.

I can feel it, feel it, *feel*—

"That's it, Brannon!" the woman cries.

I nod, but it's not Brannon I'm mentally calling, it's Kade, and as horrible as it is, the man in my mind is about to drag me over the edge with his mouth glued to my pussy, his fingers buried so deep inside me, I'll never be able to get rid of the feeling.

"Yes," I beg, voice breathy. "*Please, please, pl*—"

"Spank my vulva, Brannon!"

I freeze, heart pounding, ears fuzzy.

"Activate my chakras! I'm going to transcend into the ninth dimension!"

My eyes snap open, brows furrowed, and I flick my blurry gaze to the TV.

Where the hell are her pants? Holy shit, my screen is filled with the bombshell's literal bush, and Brannon…

Brannon is growling like a honey badger, and, and—

"Oh my God, they're actually fucking!" I cry.

Glancing down, I find my own fingers buried deep inside me, my other hand aggressively palming my boob, and suddenly, I feel gross.

More than gross, I feel…

I feel post-nut clarity, and I didn't even get to come.

"Oh, fuck," I breathe, tugging my hands free. My fingers are soaked, and my pussy feels disturbingly empty—as if Kade were actually there—and another wave of shame washes over me.

The sensual beat pulses in the background, and a garbled moan penetrates the air. My core clenches in anticipation like some kind of fucked-up Pavlovian response. I suck in a sharp breath and slap my clean hand against the *off* button on the TV.

Nothing.

I slam it again and again, but the only thing I see is Brannon pulling his dick out of the bombshell like they're preparing for a position change.

My eyes go wide and I half-run, half-stumble to the outlet. I drop to my knees, searching for the right cord in a sea of black wires.

"Let your sacred sun-seed spill into my cosmic garden, Bran! I want to blossom with your aura."

I rip out every plug in sight.

The sudden silence is deafening. My pulse is racing, and my brain is trying to catch up with what I just witnessed.

What I just did.

Holy shit. Was she about to come?

Was I?

My gaze flits to the mess of plugs, and for a brief second, I contemplate turning the tutorial back on—for research purposes. Clearly, the guy knew what he was doing. The woman was closer to combusting in five seconds than I was with either of my ex's.

I exhale sharply, my breath coming out in a rush as I drop to the couch in a daze. All I wanted was to stretch out my tired muscles, not witness—*wait.*

Was that seriously porn?

Fuck, I'm not a prude by any means, but that was a jump scare wrapped in Lycra and disguised as inner peace.

Note to self: Never accept yoga recommendations from Abby ever again.

I snag my phone and pull up my texts.

Me: Brannon? Are you kidding me? I hate you.

The timer on my bread machine goes off, and I jump up, rushing to the kitchen. I drop my phone on the counter, wash my hands, and grab my oven mitts, pretending the last however many minutes didn't happen.

"Come on," I murmur, my brows furrowed as I gently flip the pan over. "Don't fail me."

It slips from the tin perfectly, landing on the cooling rack with a tiny *thud* that makes my heart swoon. My smile is hesitant but real as I quickly wash the pan and unplug the bread maker, leaving the loaf to cool while I make my coffee.

It's still early, but I have to head to Serenity Falls High to investigate a new chronic truancy report I was just assigned, and it's a good forty minute drive from here.

A few days ago, I had to go into the county office to meet with Finch. He said Ethel Sorrenson, Kade's original caseworker, is returning to light duty this week. She'll be resuming her Heart Springs caseload, including Aurora's, which means I'm officially being reassigned to cover Serenity Falls full time.

It's what was supposed to happen eventually. But hearing it now, after meeting him and Aurora—I'm not sure how I feel.

On one hand, it's a relief. I was starting to lose my ability to stay impartial. I hardly know the man. He's grumpy, rude, and condescending. Being around him makes my nerves go haywire and my brain spaz out. I lose all composure and restraint—which isn't like me at all.

I know being removed from the case is a good thing. I was well on my way to slipping up and risking my job, not to mention my professional reputation.

But more than that, crossing any boundaries with Kade Archer would hurt Aurora the most, and that sweet baby girl doesn't deserve adults she hardly knows getting in the way of a possibly wonderful future.

Professional conflicts aside...

I haven't seen or spoken to Kade in days, and I still can't get him off my mind. I tell myself it's just attraction. That I'm only interested because I secretly love sparring with him. That his smile, his voice, his overwhelming willingness to step up for Aurora—mean nothing to me.

And then I remind myself: I'm a big, fat liar.

My phone vibrates, and I quickly open my texts.

Witchling: But did you come?

Me: Did you when you watched it?

Witchling: Watch it? I was in it. Didn't you get to the second act?

I gape at my phone, unable to tell if she's serious or not.

My best friend is a free spirit, wild in every single way, down to her brilliant bones. She's a senior financial analyst by day, but only because her uptight, Wall Street parents made her follow in their footsteps. But at heart, she's a green witch chasing her forever dream of opening an apothecary.

Based on all the adventures we've had and stories she's told me, I don't doubt her involvement in the porno at all, but...

Me: I want to say you're lying, but I already threw away my TV, so there's no way to know.

Witchling: Threw it away? Guess you didn't get to work cowboy out of your system, then. Bet you're all sorts of horny now.

Me: Goodbye, Abigail.

Witchling: Love you, have a wet day!

Sighing, I lock my phone and toss it on the table. Unfortunately, she's not wrong. I'm still horny, and now I have blue ovaries, which is way worse.

Once the bread is cool enough, I grab my serrated knife and pause, holding my breath.

This is it—the moment of truth.

The knife glides through the loaf with zero resistance, revealing the perfect, airy center. My jaw drops.

"Holy gluten-free grail," I choke out, staring at the soft, pillowy crumb. It's perfect.

I shake my head and exhale through a proud smile as I slice another piece and pop it in the toaster.

When I got my diagnosis, everything changed. Suddenly, I was saying goodbye to croissants, bagels, and late-night pizza binges—all my favorite things—and hello to endless ingredient labels and an obsessive need to Google *"is this gluten-free?"*

It was exhausting. Not to mention beyond expensive.

The simple act of shopping or eating made me mad, and when I'm mad, I bake. But even that looked different.

I was at a crossroads in my life—give up everything I know, love, and find comfort in, or adapt, and I've been adapting my entire life. So I learned. Bread, snacks, desserts, you name it. If it's gluten-free and edible, I've probably made it. And now, I don't just survive; I thrive.

Who needs a bakery or expensive grocery store when you can make sourdough *this* perfect?

The toaster dings, and I pile the slice high with avocado, salt, chili flakes, and a drizzle of olive oil. Grabbing my breakfast and coffee, I set myself up at the tiny kitchen table, back to the TV.

I don't think I'll ever be able to look at it again without thinking of Kade.

And apparently Abby.

Sighing, I take a sip of steaming hot coffee, letting the oat milk and sugar coat my tongue, and pull out the mostly empty binder I brought with me from New York.

My breath catches, and the coffee twists in my stomach, but I open it, eyes zeroing in on the first page.

A photocopy of a birth certificate that doesn't belong to me.

Lorna Iris Walker was born in the Heart Springs Emergency Clinic just over forty-seven years ago to Joseph and Sarah Walker.

There are no photos, no addresses or any other identifying information, and given that it was nearly fifty years ago, in a rural community, finding more details has been extremely hard.

I stare at it for a long moment and munch on my toast. It's cooked perfectly, but I hardly taste it at all.

Swallowing thickly, I flip to the next page.

Georgia Rose Walker, born on August twentieth to Lorna Walker—and a blank space for a father—in Saffron, West Virginia, population four hundred thirty-two.

A town so small, so in the middle of absolutely nowhere, that the doctors at the tiny hospital were unable to save her mom, Lorna, when she hemorrhaged during childbirth.

Only eighteen years old, and Lorna passed before she ever got to hold her baby. And that baby? She became a ward of the state before she even opened her eyes.

Fifteen years. That's how long I bounced around foster homes. In and out. Never a fit. Never wanted long enough to stay.

Not until Robin Donnelly.

She was older—mid-seventies and cranky in the mornings, but she loved me like I'd always been hers. She was a widow who lived on a small farm she and her late husband had dreamed of. On that farm, she raised me through heartbreak, taught me how to fight for myself, and made sure I believed I was worth something, all while riding a horse with a shovel in my hand.

She's the reason I made it through undergrad. The reason I applied to grad school in New York and got my MSW.

She's the reason I believed I could help other kids like me.

Robin died before she could see me graduate. That part still hurts the most, but I pushed through anyway. For Robin. For the mother who never got to hold me. For the father I've never known. For the family I dreamt of.

And for me.

It took me years before I could work up the courage to look for information about my roots, but I had to do it. It's been a clawing ache in the pit of my soul for as long as I can remember.

For years, I used to stare at the front doors or foster homes and imagine someone busting them down to get to me. To save me. Bring me home, and love me.

The places I lived were never particularly bad, but they weren't good either.

I wanted more.

I wanted happy mornings, and cuddles on the couch. I wanted birthday presents, and Christmas trees like my friends. Family vacations, where I was actually in the pictures.

But most of all, I wanted the family in the photos. A mom and dad, brothers and sisters. Big and happy and forever. I still want it. It's my deepest, and hardest wish.

A place to fit in.

A place that feels like home.

A place that'll *keep me.*

And after a month in Heart Springs, searching for answers, but finding nothing, I'm not sure my wish will ever come true, no matter how many stars or rainbows I ask.

Chapter Twelve

Wildwood's Most Wanted

This place is useless.

I should have just eaten the questionable banana I found in my car, and slept the hunger pains away.

It's almost seven. I've missed lunch, worked through dinner, and my fridge is emptier than my social life. The Wildwood Market's the only place open nearby, and judging by the flickering sign and split-pea-colored walls, I might be safer with the banana.

All I can do is hope the food is fresher than the decor.

I tug my sweater tighter and push my cart down the aisle with one hand while flipping over a box of crackers with the other. My stomach growls loud enough to draw a shocked look from a man comparing canned beans.

I don't even care.

"Contains wheat," I mutter under my breath, slamming the box back on the shelf. "Why does the world hate me today?"

The sudden burn behind my eyes has nothing to do with the crackers, and everything to do with the horrible day I'm having. I was yelled at by a client, had to drive two hours, back and forth across the county from one case to the next, and couldn't find a single place to eat while I was out.

I'm so tired, I hurt down to my bones, but it's the heaviness in my heart that threatens to split me in two.

The girl from the truancy case the other day, Tessa, wasn't at school again.

When I followed up at the house, the power was off and a six-year-old answered the door in a T-shirt and no socks. She said her big sister was at work. *Work*. She's fifteen. And they're mom—recently widowed, was working a double at her second job, just to get the power back on.

I left them with two bags of groceries, but it's a Band-Aid on a bullet wound.

They're slipping, a family completely under water, and I'm worried I won't be able to catch them fast enough.

Body sagging, I lean against the cart and shuffle through the store, desperate to just find *anything*. The basket's already full of chicken, salad, and fresh produce for dinner and lunches, but if this week's taught me anything, it's that this new placement means I'll be spending most of my day in the car.

I need safe snacks, and I need them *now*.

After five aisles filled with nothing but broken dreams and stomach aches, I finally spot a tiny section of hope.

An exhausted cheer escapes as I crouch to grab a jar of almond butter, and flip it over, reading the ingredients. *Gluten-free*. Thank the snack Gods.

Sighing in relief, I tuck it in the crook of my arm and grab three more jars, just in case they're out the next time I shop, then push to stand. My shoulder bumps the cart handle, and I stumble, dropping the jars.

They roll in four opposite directions, and my body sort of just… gives up.

Or, maybe it's me.

I fall to my ass, the skirt of my dress puddling around me like a white waterfall of depression. My back hits the shelves a second before my head, and I close my eyes, breathing through the sudden need to sob between the tuna cans and tampons.

This store really is backward.

Suddenly, the weight of the last month crashes down on me, heavy and unbearable. Maybe this whole damn idea was a mistake. Why the hell did I think coming to South Dakota alone, to find my long lost family, was a good idea?

I'm floundering here.

All I wanted was to finally feel like I fit in somewhere, like I have roots and branches, a whole family tree. But all I've found is dead end after dead end. Even the Heart Springs cemetery was a bust.

"You know, the mop here's as ancient as the floors they clean," a deep voice rumbles, making me jump.

I smack my head against the shelf and wince as half the gluten-free section reacts like it's under attack.

Jars clatter to the floor around me. Boxes shift and tumble. Something plastic bounces off my boot and glides down the aisle, like it's trying to escape.

Blinking up through my straightened hair—now half-stuck to my face—I find the last person I want to see while emotionally compromised and surrounded by spilled snacks.

Kade Archer stands at the end of the aisle, arms crossed, one brow raised like my mental breakdown inconveniences him.

"Jesus, freckles." His mouth twitches. "I leave you alone for a few days and you bring down a whole aisle. You always cause this much damage, or is the food just scared of you?"

My cheeks flame red hot, and my brain chooses that exact moment to remind me of what I did the last time I let myself think of him. I like to pretend it was just the tutorial—the overtly sexual innuendos provided by the bombshell, and the moaning and groaning Brannon supplied, but...

I know the truth.

And the truth is standing five feet away, glowering down at me with a big, perfect beard, giant muscles, and—*oh look*, he's wearing his cowboy hat today.

Brilliant. More material for my rub hub. That's the last thing my demented ass needs.

"Let me guess," Kade says, stepping closer, boots crunching softly over something crushed and probably expensive. "They just jumped off the shelf the second they saw you." He smirks. "Happen often?"

"Wow," I hiss. "I didn't think it was possible, but you're even more annoying in fluorescents."

I grit my teeth and swipe a sleeve over my eyes like I'm just brushing back my hair. The last thing I need is for this man—a man I stupidly, accidentally almost came to thoughts of, to see me crying.

And because today is the worst day of all days, he zeroes in on those barely-there tears like it's a sixth sense.

His smirk fades and he drops to a crouch in front of me.

"You okay?" he murmurs, grimacing. "You look..."

"Lovely," I bite out, scrambling to stand. "The word you're looking for is love—" My boot catches the hem of my dress, and I slip.

A strong hand closes around my arm just before I fall again. I land against his chest with a muted thud, heart thundering, breath caught.

His fingers flex gently, steadying me.

"Georgia," he says again, quieter. "You okay?"

The warmth in his voice undoes me. My eyes sting, throat tight, and I yank my arm free like his touch burns.

"I'm fine," I lie, scooping up the mess I made, haphazardly shoving shit back on the shelves. "Just go back to whatever cowboy errand you were on and leave me to unravel in peace."

He doesn't move.

Just watches me—arms crossed, brows cocked, face tight.

"You're not gonna help, are you?" I mutter, tossing my hair back.

His lips lift slowly. "I'm having more fun watching."

I didn't think it was possible, but somehow, my cheeks burn even more. "You would say that, asshole."

"Thank fuck I'm not one of your clients anymore." He scoffs, rolling back on his boots. "Not very *professional* of you to call me names."

My eyes squeeze shut as I force myself to breathe through the raging emotions battering around inside me. I'm raw, exhausted, and one more mean comment or disaster away from losing my shit.

I want to ask about Aurora. About him. About everything. But the words wedge in my throat and won't come out.

Before I can try, he nudges one of the rogue jars with the toe of his boot and lifts it.

"This that overpriced nonsense you city folk are into?" He squints at the label. "Almond butter. Don't y'all have normal peanut butter in New York?"

I snatch it from him like he's just insulted my bloodline. "For your information, most regular peanut butters aren't gluten free."

"Gluten free?" He stares at me like I've grown a second head. "Why the hell would you eat that shit? It's disgusting."

I drop the jars into my cart, expression hardening. "Some of us don't have a choice."

His brow furrows. "Wait, you're—"

"Yup," I snap. "Celiac. Shocking, I know. Go ahead and get your jokes in while you can."

But he doesn't say anything. Just stares.

Silence stretches between us. The overhead lights hum. Somewhere above, a terrible, warbly cover of *Every Breath You Take* starts to play through the crackling speaker system.

Our eyes lock. His flick to my mouth, where they stay, and my body *absolutely* comes to life under that stare.

So I drop my gaze to the almond butter still clutched in my hands and pretend like Kade Archer has zero effect on my senses.

"Your hair's straight."

I blink. "What?"

He gestures to my hair, brows pulled tight. "Most of the time, you wear it down and curly. Just look different, that's all."

Swallowing, I barely resist the urge to hide behind said hair, or shave it all off. Instead, I huff, and roll my eyes.

"And your hair's frizzy." I snatch the anti-frizz curl shampoo from my cart and thrust it into his stupidly hard chest with a sarcastic smile. "Here. Maybe this'll help you stop looking like you just rolled out of a hay bale after disappointing a rancher's daughter."

Kade catches the bottle with one hand, brow arching slowly. "Darlin', if I'd just rolled out of a hay bale with a rancher's daughter, trust me, she wouldn't be disappointed."

"Doubtful." My throat bobs, and his eyes are riveted to the movement.

"Maybe," he rumbles, voice gravelly, "but I've got a feeling *you'd* be a lot louder."

My mouth falls open, but I quickly snap it shut, fists clenched, body vibrating.

I want to punch him. Or kiss him. Or maybe throw him into a freezer aisle and file a restraining order. It's unclear.

"You couldn't make a woman scream if she stubbed her toe during sex, Archer."

With that, I shoulder past him, cart wobbling, and storm into the next aisle—pretending I'm not vividly imagining him proving me wrong.

Repeatedly.

Against a wall.

The dirty floor.

Back of his truck.

Or literally *anywhere*.

And because he's clearly on a mission to end me, he follows.

"Are you stalking me now?" I snap, grabbing a bag of something I don't need just to avoid looking at him.

"Just making sure you don't hurt yourself," he says. "You're a danger-ously clumsy little thing."

I whirl around, heat in my cheeks, fire in my blood. "For a guy who couldn't even find clean socks two weeks ago, you sure like to run your mouth."

"And you're just dying to keep my name in yours."

My jaw drops all over again. If I had any self-control, I'd leave. But I'm finding my mind and body have a serious disconnect where this man is concerned.

Instead, I glare, standing nearly chest to chest with the man who drives me insane. "You are such an arrogant, insufferable—"

"Careful," he drawls, leaning in just enough that his hair brushes my shoulder. "You might say something nice by accident."

Before I can fire back, a loud, cackling voice slices through the aisle.

"Well, well, well! If it isn't my two favorite sexy sluts!"

"Oh God," I breathe, flicking horrified eyes toward Kade. "That's your insane landlady, isn't it?"

He grimaces, already bracing for impact. "Ex-landlady."

My breath hitches. "Wait—you found a place?"

"No," he mutters, eyes catching mine. "Haven't yet. Just didn't want Agnes caught off guard when it happens."

"That's really sweet," I whisper, tuning out Mrs. Whittaker's incessant chatter about how hot we'd look together and how badly she wants to watch.

I also ignore the fact that her voice is getting closer, but, damn, I've been wanting to hear the updates since I was moved out of Heart Springs and off his case.

"Met Ethel," he murmurs, lip twitching. "She's a lot nicer than you."

I scoff, grinning. "Liar."

Ethel is really nice, though. We've been chatting nearly every day, and she's slowly helping me acclimate to how things are done in Summit. It's a world away from the strict policy back in New York. Things are looser here. By the book, but the book's a lot different than any I've read before.

"She has me working through that checklist you emailed," he adds, giving me a strange look. "Doesn't give me space, though." I cock a brow and he rolls his eyes. "Likes to hover."

"Ethel's just doing her job."

A couple days ago, I called the hospital to check on Aurora, and they gushed about how sweet it's been seeing Kade bond with her over the last week. Apparently, he shows up every day and stays pretty much the entire visiting hours, getting to know her, making sure she feels safe with him.

The nurses are all utterly obsessed, and half in love with the guy, and I…

I'm impressed.

More than that, I'm proud of him for stepping up. He seems to be really trying, and bad attitude and overly sexual banter aside—I truly think he's going to make a great dad to her.

I also think that information is terrible for my hormones.

"Jesus," he murmurs suddenly, tapping the back of my hand. "Don't think you can ignore her anymore, darlin'. She's about to steal your nut butter."

Cheeks burning from the nickname, I whirl to find Mrs. Whittaker grinning like a feral cat. Her muumuu is pink leopard print today, and—*bless us all*—she's wearing a bra.

"And Kade," she sing-songs, waving around one of my jars, "if you're gonna pick fights with pretty women in the grocery store, 'least buy her dinner first."

"Mrs. Whittaker, please—"

"Don't '*Mrs. Whittaker*' me like I haven't seen you buck-ass naked before."

Kade chokes and I gasp.

"You what now?" he rasps, beating his chest.

"Gotta go," she chirps, spinning her cart toward the produce. "My show's on. I'm just here for cucumbers, eggplants, and olive oil."

Kade blinks. "What the hell are you making with—"

I elbow him hard in the gut. He doubles over with a groan. "What the fuck, Walker?"

"Don't you dare ask," I hiss. "If she tells us, I will dig out both my eardrums."

Then I spin my cart and storm off down the aisle, heart racing, pulse pounding, and cheeks on fire.

I need space, air, and sanity.

Because if I stay one more second, I'm going to do something insane—like kiss Kade Archer.

Or buy a cucumber I absolutely do not need but will find a use for while imagining just how *loud* the grumpy cowboy can make me scream.

CHAPTER THIRTEEN

COME ON, LASSIE. YOU CAN DO IT.

"RISE AND SHINE, DADDY!"

I squint through the split in my fingers, brain foggy and absolutely not ready for whatever fresh hell this is. But no matter how many times I blink, the hallucination doesn't go away.

Griffin Sterling and Wilder Reed.

Two men I've trusted through gunfire, blackout nights, and too many bad decisions to count. Brothers in everything but blood.

Also? Two men who live several states away and have *no fucking reason* to be standing on my doorstep right now.

"Why do you look like you just woke up? It's four pm," Griffin barks as he shoves me aside and storms into my living room like he owns the place.

"Because I did," I mutter.

Wilder's right behind him, arms full of bags and a manic glint in his eyes like he's been snorting energy drinks. He spins in a slow circle, brows high, mouth open.

"This is…"

"Quaint?" Griff chokes out, Tennessee accent thick as he drops one singular duffle bag onto my kitchen table. "Small but—"

"It's a piece of shit," Wilder interrupts, throwing his haul next to Griffs. "You need to move out. *Immediately.*"

He has no idea how accurate that statement is.

The door clicks shut behind me. I lean against it, arms crossed over my bare chest, deadpan and disoriented.

A weird wave of déjà vu rolls over me—Georgia, showing up on this exact doorstep weeks ago. Me, shirtless and wearing the same sweats, half-awake and half-functioning.

Only difference is, I'm sober as hell today.

And despite her dropping a twisted bomb directly into my lap, her visit was a fuck of a lot more interesting for my dick.

Until it wasn't.

"So, where is it?" Wilder yells from my bathroom.

My brows snap together, stomach twisting.

"Where's what?" I rasp, voice shredded from a week of barely sleeping. I shove off the door and head for the fridge, frowning at the lack of beer. I grab a few waters and toss them on the tiny bar with a thud. "Who the fuck are you talking about, and why are you here?"

Griffin turns, a smug grin already living rent-free beneath his overgrown beard. I briefly consider waxing it like I did once in the military.

"What's got you all puffed up, princess? Parenthood got you in a mood?"

My hand stalls, bottle halfway to my mouth. My heart skips too many beats to be considered safe, and my stomach does a slow, ominous roll. Their words finally start connecting, and dread hits me like a tank.

Wilder stumbles out of the bathroom, still zipping up his fly. The toilet flushes behind him, but I barely hear it. He shoots me a dopey smile, all charm and zero awareness, and punches me in the good shoulder.

Small mercies.

"Where the hell's your kid?" He toes open my closet like I might've stashed a whole ass toddler behind my boots.

"I—" *What the actual fuck?*

I rake a hand through my hair, scrambling for anything to say.

To lie? To stall? To figure out how the hell they even know?

I never called them like I said I would. Meant to, but everything's been happening so damn fast, and my mind's been a mess since the mediation.

A week's flown by since then—a chaotic blur of long drives to Rydell to visit Aurora, house hunting, and running into ex-social workers and ex-landladies at my local grocery store.

Haven't been able to get that damn run-in off my mind, either.

Seeing her on the floor like that—eyes glassy, shoulders shaking—it scared the shit out of me. Took everything I had not to drop to my knees and lift her up, demand to know what the hell happened.

But then she looked up at me with that spark, that flash of wildfire that always burns just beneath her skin, and I knew she didn't need saving.

Not by me, anyway.

She looked… *beautiful*.

Too beautiful for a small town like this.

Long, flowy white dress, chunky cream sweater practically swallowing her whole—but somehow it made her look even smaller, softer. Her hair was straight, and it fell in this thick red sheet down her back, nearly touching the curve of her ass.

And I couldn't stop looking at the way it swayed.

Maybe because I'm a man with a pulse, and she looked like a goddamn fever dream standing there in the middle of a run-down store that still smells like old floor wax and expired cheese.

Or maybe because she's her, and I'm quickly becoming addicted to all things Georgia Walker.

She's chaos. Sharp tongue, quick temper, a walking contradiction of compassion and bite. And I fucking love sparring with her. Love the way she challenges me—pushes back, never flinches.

But this… *thing*… in my chest. This… *burn*… It wasn't just heat. It was something else. Something I don't know how to name.

Which means it's for the best Georgia's out of my life and moving on, just like she said she would.

Temporary.

Because in a few weeks, my life'll be anything but temporary. If things keep going as they are, soon enough, I'll have a kid.

A kid who I've spent every day getting to know.

The nurses told me everything they could—how to bathe a baby that's not quite yours without making it weird, how, what and when to feed her, milestones she'll have coming up, what kind of bed and shit I need for a nursery I have nowhere to put, and even how to encourage her to finally talk, despite what she's been through.

Despite it—like her entire world wasn't wrecked in a breath.

I've fallen for the tiny, little thing. She's sweet. A giggling bundle wrapped in barely-there curls that match mine. She loves blocks, especially when I trip over them and cry in pain. Makes her lose her mind with laughter.

She gets grumpy when she doesn't have her feet covered—which I learned isn't normal for babies. Apparently, hating socks and shoes is a world-wide baby phenomenon. But Aurora loves those tiny socks, and I find it so fucking cute, it makes me want to cry all over again.

I'm a sap where she's concerned, and she's not even mine yet.

"Jesus Christ. He's falling apart, isn't he?" Griff mutters. "Look at 'em. He's miles away."

"I think he's just sleeping standing up," Wilder whisper-hisses, snapping in my face. "Wake up, big boy!"

I slap his hand and blink back to the present.

Griff's leaning against the chipped Formica bar, back to the living room, rolling a water between his bear paws as he stares me down. It's the same look he used to give me in the army right before I got assigned some bullshit task.

Wilder elbows in beside him, bumping the six-foot-five bastard off balance.

"Fuck off," Griff grumbles, downing his water in one long drink.

Wilder cackles like the feral psycho he is and props his chin on his fist. "Nah, I'm comfy right here, big man."

As one, they turn to me, eyes sharp, seeing too fucking much.

There's a breeze drifting in through the open window behind them, but sweat still breaks out along my spine. My skin itches and my thigh throbs, like just looking at my best friends reminds my body what we all went through together.

For one wild second, I consider throwing myself off the roof just to get away.

Might even get some sleep in the hospital.

But of course, a peaceful coma is way too much to hope for when these assholes are involved. Wilder would probably curl up on my gurney with me, and Griff would sing until I woke up.

"So," Wilder drawls, tapping his fingers against his annoyingly clean-shaven jaw. He tilts his head, messy blond hair flopping into his eyes. "What's new with you?"

I swallow hard and nearly choke, because apparently my mouth is the Sahara. "Georgia called you, didn't she? She told you?"

It's the only thing that makes sense.

She took Griff's card. Said she needed to verify my job. That was over a week ago. Of course, she called. She's professional, punctual, and perfect. I, on the other hand, am struggling to stay awake, keep my shit together, and haven't told a single soul what's been happening.

"I don't know," Griff says slowly, green eyes narrowed. "Tell us *what*, Archer?"

"And who's Georgia?" Wilder pipes in, all curiosity and faux-innocence. "That's a pretty name. Not sure I would have forgotten it if I'd heard it before." He blinks up at our forever Sargent. "What about you, Griff?"

He shakes his head, man-bun whipping side to side. "No, Reed. Don't think I would have. Bet she's got a pretty-as-hell voice, too. All sweet and sunshine." His brows hit his hairline. "*Memorable.*"

"Jesus." I groan, dragging my hands down my face. "You guys are fucking assholes."

"Assholes who flew halfway across the country to meet our—"

"Okay," I snap, cutting Wilder off with a sharp look. "I get it. You want to meet your—" There goes my dry mouth again. "Your—"

They lean in, eyes wide, faces reassuring.

"Come on, Lassie," Griff coaxes, slapping my cheek.

"You can say it, boy," Wilder coos, ruffling my hair like I'm a fucking golden retriever.

I swat them both away and take a step back, needing air and space, and a temporary best friend transplant. My fists land on my hips, and I start pacing. Tiny, anxious stomps across my two-by-two kitchen.

Back and forth.

Back and forth.

Ten laps in, my pulse finally slows. Fifteen, and I can swallow again without gagging. Somewhere around lap twenty, I finally start to talk—still pacing, still avoiding their eyes, because if I stop, I won't get a damn word out.

I tell them everything.

Georgia showing up on my doorstep out of nowhere. The mediation. The probationary thirty-day period I've got to prove I can be a dad. The part where I need a new job. A safer house. A whole fucking lifestyle reset. And how it all ended with me at the hospital, holding a baby that isn't mine by blood—but is somehow already mine in every way that matters because she *needs me.*

I don't get into how it felt. I leave out the part about the way she looked up at me. The weight of her. The way everything in me cracked wide open the second she smiled.

I'm not there yet.

For some reason, I also leave out every fucking detail about Georgia and her addicting freckles and wildfire attitude. The idea of telling them any singular snippet about her twists my gut and makes me irrationally angry.

"Holy shit," Wilder breathes, throat bobbing. "That's... not what I thought you were gonna say. I figured a condom broke at some point, and a chick accused you of being Daddy. But your bitch ex writing you into her will?" He whistles low and tips his head back. "A baby instead of money is a wild thing to inherit. You win, man. That's a whole new tier of fuckery."

Swallowing hard, I shoot him a look. "You can't call her that anymore."

"Why?" he whines. "It's true."

"Because we don't speak ill of the dead. It's disrespectful." Griff smacks him on the back of the head and turns to stare at me for a long, tense moment. Finally, he exhales and runs a hand down his beard. "So what's the plan?"

"Plan?"

"Whatever it is, we've got you," Wilder adds, winking at me. "Don't think we can stay here though, bud. You don't even have a couch."

"I burned it."

He bobs his head. "Nice. Well, your bed's too small, so—"

"We'll find a hotel." Griffin sighs. "Doesn't matter. Point is, we're here, and you're stuck with us. So, tell us what you need, and it'll get done." His expression is somber, steady, and so damn honest it almost hurts. "You're not alone, Archer."

My eyes blur, and I have to look away before I embarrass myself by sobbing in front of my friends. I drop my face into my hands, breathing through the sudden rush of relief. I feel a hand squeeze my good shoulder, and know it's Griff. He offers me silent support to work through my shit, like always.

Even thousands of miles away, my team's never stopped being there for me.

Makes me realize how shitty of a friend I've been, and I make a silent vow to do better.

"Not to interrupt what I'm sure is a much deserved menty-B," Wilder says, "but when's the last time you slept?"

I look up just as Griff sniffs the air, nose wrinkling. "Or showered?"

"Fuck off." I glare at both of them, happy for a mood shift. "I've been busy." I inhale deeply and grimace. "And I showered this morning before the hospital."

After that, I passed the hell out.

I'd be lying if I said the drives back and forth to Rydell every day weren't getting to me. But every time I feel sorry for myself, I think of how much Aurora has lost, and the fact that she spends most of her days alone in a hospital room. Sobers me every time.

"Busy spiraling," Wilder says, deadpan.

I flip him off and take another long sip of water, which does absolutely nothing for my sanity.

"How many more weeks do you have to pull this off?" Griffin asks, flicking through his phone. "Three?"

I jerk a nod and run my fingers through my beard. "Bit less than now."

"And you have to move, right? You said the judge ordered it?"

"Yeah, I need a new place. I've been looking and can't find a damn thing." I must have contacted fifty prospects—apartments, rentals, fuck, I even called a realtor about buying, but it would take a hell of a longer than three weeks. "It doesn't help that part of the judge's orders were that I have to stay in Summit County."

Summit County's big, but a lot of it's rural. It only covers Wildwood, Heart Springs, Langley—a bigger town about fifteen miles south—and Serenity Falls, way out past the lake. The rest is all unincorporated land.

Anxiety creeps in as my mind spirals.

"I'm also ready to put in my notice with Iron Shield. I've got plenty to live off, but I'm not sure a new landlord would take me, freshly unemployed and all."

"Do it," Griff says, surprising me.

"The fuck?" Wilder runs a hand through his hair and tugs. "Look, I know we hate working for King Asshole, but we already live in three different states." He pouts. "If we don't work together, we'll never talk."

"That's sweet and all…" I start, lip twitching. "But I don't think I have a choice, man. And I can't exactly move anywhere else."

"I know," he grumbles. "But—"

"But we can," Griff cuts in.

Wilder's head snaps toward him, and my eyes go wide.

Griff just shrugs one thick, tattooed shoulder. "What? Neither of us are exactly tied down," he says, gesturing between himself and Wilder.

I tilt my head, taking his measure. Griffin—thirty-eight, freshly single—is Tennessee through and through. He loves being close to his siblings, but they're all married now, busy raising kids of their own. And from what he shared on the drive over, his mama met some guy last year and spends most of her time traveling.

Other than Iron Shield, he doesn't have much holding him there.

The idea of my two best friends living near me, especially with the big-ass life changes I'm facing, is…

My breath rushes out, and this time when I smile, I mean it. "Think you'd both like it here. Boring as hell, not much for jobs with the economy the way it is, but... it's nice."

Griff bobs his head, eyes distant like he's really thinking it through.

"Anything's better than where I'm at now," he says, flicking a look at Wilder. "And I'd bet the same goes for you too, Reed."

Wilder's jaw ticks, and he looks away, staring off into nothing.

He's the youngest of the three of us—only twenty-five. Grew up in Southern California, in a rough neighborhood. The second he turned eighteen, he bolted, getting out from under an alcoholic dad. He ran as far and fast as he could and wound up in a desert halfway across the world, stationed on base with us.

A year later, we were in a Ranger squad with Griff as our sergeant.

The accident that sent the three of us home also killed the fourth member of our squad, Rubin Drake. He was a damn good Ranger, an even better man. But out of all of us, he was the closest to Wilder.

The fifth member, Billy West, was the new guy—he'd only been with us a month before the IED hit. Rubin didn't make it, and the rest of us were done for, medically or otherwise. Billy was the only one who walked away unscathed. Last I heard, he made sergeant himself.

It was one of the hardest days of my life. Terrifying, unexpected, and world-shifting. I'll never be the man I was before that day. None of us will. We all grieve the losses we've suffered in the military, but some scars never heal. Rubin's death is one of them, especially for Wild.

He went straight back to California, partly because he needed somewhere for the hospital to release him, but mostly, I think, to punish himself for not doing more.

It's something we all feel.

But he hates it there. Hates being near his old man. Hates the city and the memories that come with it. Honestly, I think the only thing keeping him sane is Iron Shield. He takes more jobs away than Griff and I combined, spends all his time traveling, chasing danger, trying to save as many people as he can.

My eyes flick between the two of them, and I catch Griff's gaze. He's thinking the same things as me, it's written all over his face. His jaw twitches, fists clenched, as he watches Wilder disappear before us.

"It's not a bad idea," I murmur, surprising myself. "Don't know where you'll live—" I break off, a chuckle slipping out as I circle my finger around, gesturing to my apartment. "Actually, rumor has it, a studio's about to open up."

Griff barks a laugh, and just like I hoped, it pulls Wilder back in. He grins, tilting his head side to side. "Nah. I'll shack up with Mrs. W. Griff can take this shithole. He needs the space for all his beard products."

"Fuck this cockroach motel." Sarge scoffs, but he's smiling. "I'll move in with Kade."

"Who's homeless," I deadpan. "And also, the one who actually needs a new place."

"But are you?" Griff says. "Way I remember it, you've got a house waiting for you, Archer. Paid for, on land in your name."

My heart stutters, skips, then tries to beat right out of my chest. "No."

Undeterred, he cocks a brow. "No?"

"I can't." I swallow hard and shake my head.

"Why the hell not?" Wilder snaps, sharper than I've heard in a long time. Our eyes meet, and I'm honestly shocked at the anger there. "You have a home, Kade. A damn good one. A family who loves you—even when you're a pain in the ass. They never stopped, no matter how much you try to push them away. And that house? You built it yourself, with your best friend at your side."

"Wild—" I breathe, pulse racing.

He just shakes his head. "Nah, man. Enough's enough. We all have demons." He points right at me, voice dropping. "But you've got a little girl waiting on you. She has no one else. Get over the ugly in your soul and move forward. Stop punishing yourself for sins you didn't commit."

"You're one to talk," slips out before I can stop it.

He snorts. "I know. I'm just as fucked up as both of you, and I don't have room to say shit. But the difference is, I've got no one waiting for me to heal. You do." He looks at Griff. "Both of you do."

"Not anymore," Griffin grumbles, rolling his eyes. "That story's dead and gone. Ain't coming back."

"It could," Wild says softly. "If you wanted it to."

"I don't." Griff's cheeks flush, eyes a little bleary, but he blinks it away and deflates. "We're getting off track—and we're all way too sober for this shit. Fact is, Wild's right. You've got a house ready and waiting, Kade. Stop pussy-footing around, and take it."

"A *dream* house," Wilder emphasizes. "What is it? Four bedrooms?"

"Six."

His eyes go wide. "*Big* dreams then?"

"You know I've always wanted a big family."

"Daddy Kade's got a breeding kink," he sing-songs. "Gonna knock some sweet cowgirl up, keep her barefoot and pregnant while he starts his own—" His brows pucker. "What's the farmer version of a basketball team or band?"

Griff snorts. "A 4-H club."

Reed nods, clearly cheered up at my expense. "Maybe that's what you do for work."

"4-H?" I cock a brow. "Pretty sure that's volunteer."

"Nope." He cackles. "Start a daycare."

Griffin snaps his fingers, head bobbing. "Stud service."

"You two are idiots."

"We're just giving you shit," Wilder says, his voice softening. "We know you always wanted a big family like the one you grew up with."

"Somewhere along the way, those dreams just got lost," Griffin adds.

My cheeks burn at the honesty, the rawness of it all. "I don't even know where to start to get them back."

He knocks his knuckles against mine. "One step at a time, brother. Just like in the Rangers—you face the tough shit one step at a time, and never alone."

I rake a hand through my hair, my mind spinning.

Could I really do it?

They're right—the house my dad and I built on Archer land was more than halfway done when I joined the military. I haven't seen it in years, but with a lot of help, maybe I could pull it off. And if worst comes to worst, there are other houses on the farm.

I just have to get over my demons long enough to face the memories living in them.

Before I can say anything else, a text vibrates my phone across the table. The new social worker's name flashes, and my throat constricts.

Every thought, every emotion, narrows to a single pinpoint of dread.

> **Ethel Sorrenson: Hey. Sorry I'm not calling, but I'm in a meeting and wanted to update you. I just got word that Aurora's being released into the custody of the temporary foster family within the hour.**

My vision blurs, and it takes everything I have to breathe through the panic clawing at my chest. I knew this was coming—the nurses have been warning me all week.

Aurora's better now, which is good. But it also means she'll be with a new family, in a house with a fancy crib and a beautiful room just for her.

Not with me.

My fingers mash at the screen, and I'm surprised by the slight tremble.

> **Me: Can I still see her?**

> **Ethel Sorrenson: I'm sorry, Mr. Archer, but no. It's part of the Summit County DCFS rules. Once she's placed, you won't be able to see her again until the hearing, assuming it goes in your favor.**

I see what she's not saying. I need to get my shit together and fast.

And just like that, everything crashes in. The walls I've built between myself and Honey Bea Farm. The pain I've drowned in whiskey and tried to choke down. The ghosts I've ignored for too damn long.

None of it matters anymore.

Something bigger than me is at stake. Something more precious and innocent.

Peace, or maybe clarity, settles over me, edged with a new kind of resolve.

The guys are right. I have a place waiting for me. All I have to do is go home and claim it.

CHAPTER FOURTEEN

Georgia

THE CULT OF ARCHER

THE HEART SPRINGS FARMERS market isn't big, but it's got a kind of small-town charm I've never experienced before. Each stall's tucked between old brick shops and flower beds bursting with color. It's nothing like the sterile city blocks I spent years walking, and a world away from the wild, weedy patch around my rental.

I pass a table of homemade soaps shaped like celebrities. Chuckling, I pull out my cell phone and snap a picture, then flip to my texts and send it to Abby.

Witchling: If that's Daddy Pratt, I'll take five.

Chuckling, I buy her one—and Rip from *Yellowstone* for me. Something about a grumpy cowboy just does it for me.

Me: Done. But you'll have to come visit to get it.

Witchling: Also done. How are you feeling, ginger tits? Thriving or just surviving?

I grin and tap out a response as I weave through booths, careful not to run into anyone.

> **ME: Alive-ish. A little wobbly. Sun and shopping help. Joints still hate me, though.**

The truth is, I'm still lagging from yesterday's flare-up.

But with celiac, sometimes it's not about what you ate, but the damage that's already been done. I have bad joints, get chronic migraines, and if I overdo it, I wind up exhausted, in pain, and stuck in bed.

The day after the infamous grocery incident, I powered through two home visits and a stack of case notes at the coffee shop. I knew better, but I did it anyway. Adjusting from Heart Springs to Serenity Falls hasn't been hard, but the workload's heavier since it's a bigger town, and I don't want to fall behind.

By Friday, the damage caught up. My body crashed. Full-blown flare—fatigue, stomach misery, the works. So I stayed in. No makeup, no effort, no pretending. Just me, water, meds, broth, and my favorite cozy blanket.

But what I really wanted was a bathtub, my old bed in New York, and someone who would take care of me for once, without asking any questions or judging my bad days.

None of that happened, but today, I made it here, so I'm calling it a win.

> **Witchling: Don't over do whatever you're doing. Which is...?**

> **ME: The farmers market. Fridge was giving dust bowl.**

Because despite having just gone to the grocery store, I ended up walking out with only enough food to last a few days, and four jars of almond butter I'll never be able to look at without thinking of Kade. I shoved them in the back of my cabinet, but that didn't stop the cravings.

Not sure much will at this point.

> **Witchling: Are you secretly hoping to stumble across Walker family breadcrumbs?**

I'd be lying if I said I'm not hoping for more than vegetables today. Maybe a clue about my family. A glimpse of the town through my mother's eyes. Something that says I belong here too, or maybe this is the wrong place altogether.

Though, the longer I spend in Heart Springs, the more I fall in love with it.

Not just because of my familial history, but because I feel more myself here than I have in a long damn time. Truth is, I've only been here a month, but the idea of leaving when my lease is up like I'd planned, makes me nauseous. Almost as nauseous as the idea of not returning to Abby in New York at all.

Maybe that's why I tell a white lie instead of the whole truth.

> **ME: I'm just exploring today.**

> **Witchling**: *Right. And totally not hoping to run into a certain broody cowboy with biceps, a beard, and unresolved trauma.*

I scoff out loud, cheeks burning, and type quickly.

> **ME: Hell no. He annoys me.**

> **ABBY: Annoys your kitty. Nobody likes being wet and unfulfilled, babes. It's maddening.**

As if in answer, I lock eyes with a vendor.

"Cucumbers!" She grins at me as she holds one up. "We also have eggplants if you're interested."

I choke on my next breath and blush furiously, picking up my pace. "No, thank you! I'm all set!"

> **Witchling: You found him, didn't you? You're dry humping between the carrots and handmade jewelry!**

> **ME: Gotta go. Eggplants are calling. And no, not his.**

Chuckling to myself, I stop and buy a bunch of beautiful vegetables that smell incredible, then some fresh fruit for breakfasts. There's an adorable stand selling macramé butterflies, and I pick one Abby will love, then browse for a bit, munching on grapes.

I'm contemplating walking to the library to peek at their yearbooks for some information about my mom when I run right into the last booth I'd expect.

I stop dead in my tracks.

Of course they'd be here.

It's a farmers market. Farm is in their *literal* business name.

My swallow is all gravel as my eyes fly around, searching for a certain Archer in a cowboy hat who haunts my dreams—and a pair of too-tight jeans I've thought about way more than I should.

I hover a few feet away, watching who I can only assume are his twin sisters as they pass out golden plastic sticks to a line of little kids, all squealing and bouncing chaotically.

Someone bumps into me from behind, and I stumble forward, catching myself against one of the crates stacked beside their booth.

"Oh, honey, are you okay?" The voice is soft and warm—motherly in the kind of way that makes my throat tighten before I even see her.

A familiar face pops up from behind the crate, blue eyes kind and wide.

"Umm," I breathe, startled. "Hi, Bea. Sorry. I wasn't… uh… I didn't mean to…"

Get it together, Georgia! You have to stop stammering in front of this family!

"Hush," she chides, waving off my apology. "You're allowed to look before you leap, though I don't recommend leaping directly into the honey display. That stuff's not as forgiving as it looks."

I huff a small laugh, though my cheeks burn. "I was just… admiring from afar."

"Why?" she asks, tilting her head with a knowing grin. "We're perfectly friendly up close."

Before I can come up with a graceful excuse, Bea slips her arm through mine like we're old friends and drags me toward the booth. I tense for a split-second, then force myself to relax.

Apparently, not all Archer's are born with sticks directly up their asses.

"Girls!" she calls. "Look who I found sneaking around!"

The twins turn at the same time. One's got a golden stick in her mouth, the other a pair of shears in her hand.

"Georgia." Bea beams, giving my arm a little squeeze before shuffling around the other side of the table. "These two cuties are my youngest daughters, Colby and Clementine."

I smile, offering a small wave. "I love your names."

They scoff in unison.

"You can say that"—the one with the curls sasses, shooting Bea a pointed glare—"because your mom didn't name you after cheese."

"Cheese?" I echo, grinning as I glance between the three of them. That must make her Colby.

"At least you weren't named after a piece of fruit," Clementine mutters dryly, adjusting a flower arrangement on the table.

Bea cackles, not the least bit sorry. "What can I say? I was pregnant, emotional, and extremely snack-driven. Couldn't get enough cheese and oranges."

She throws an arm around each daughter, hugging them tight against her sides as they squirm and roll their eyes.

"Honestly, I almost named them Brie and Tangerine. Their father had to stage an intervention in the dairy aisle." Bea presses a wistful hand to her chest. "To this day, cheese is still my favorite food."

"Plot twist," Colby mutters. "We're both lactose intolerant now."

"We blame it on our mom," Clem adds with a nod.

They dissolve into playful bickering again, fast and familiar, overlapping stories and mock-horror recounts about Bea's pregnancy cravings and the time Colby tried to dye Clementine's hair orange to match her name.

And I just… *watch*.

Listen.

Smile when I should and try not to let it show that something in me aches.

Not because they're perfect, but because they belong to each other, loudly and unconditionally.

And I've never had that.

Not even once.

"So," Bea says, brushing a bit of windblown hair from her eyes as the girls begin restocking a crate of mini honey jars. "How are you settling in?"

I tuck my hands into the sleeves of my cardigan and hope she doesn't ask about where I live—or worse, my job. Does she know how I really met her son? Why he has contact with a social worker when he's all but a self-proclaimed hermit?

What if I accidentally put my foot in my mouth and drop a bomb I have no right dropping?

Have you ruined anything else lately?

Maybe it's the motherly tone in her voice or the panic swirling through me, but a little of the truth slips free without my permission.

"Oh. Um… slowly, I guess." I shrug. "It's been a bit of a whirlwind. Today's actually my first full day off where I've felt well enough to explore."

"Well enough?" The concern on her face is surprising.

"Nothing serious," I say quickly. "I have celiac, and the last few days were just… a little rough."

Her eyes soften. "You poor thing."

"It's okay," I murmur. "I'm used to it. But I am really loving it here so far. Heart Springs is—" I break off, shrugging with an honest smile. "It's special."

More questions are written all over Bea's face, so I quickly change the subject and gesture toward the golden sticks in the twins' hands. "What are those?"

More questions are written all over Bea's face, so I quickly change the subject and gesture toward the golden sticks in the twins' hands. "What are those?"

"Honey," they say in unison, holding them between us.

A giggle slips free at their uncanny response. It's a little *Shining*, but also adorable. When they don't back down from their offerings, I reach out and snag the sticks. The sunlight hits just right, and the amber liquid glows in my palm like warm glass. I turn one over, mesmerized.

"It's beautiful," I say, voice quiet.

"I agree," Bea says with a knowing little smile that makes me feel warm and squirmy all at once.

All three stare at me expectantly for long enough, my skin itches.

"What?" I ask, blinking.

"Well, aren't you going to try it?"

"Wait—try it now?"

They all nod, grinning identical Archer grins like this is a cult and I'm being drafted.

"Oh. Uh. Of course," I murmur, carefully tearing off the tip of one of the sticks and squeezing it until a bead of golden syrup hits my tongue.

The taste is like summer and warmth and something else I can't quite name. Something nostalgic.

My lips part around a surprised little hum. "Oh, wow! That's really good!"

"Hella good, huh?" Colby chirps. "The strawberry ones are my favorite, though."

She shoves another in my face, making me cackle.

"Colby Mildred Archer!" Bea hisses. "Watch your language!"

She ignores her mom and leans in closer to me as I suck on the second stick.

In a stage-whisper, she says, "Did you hear that? Not only did I get named after fruit, but I got the shitty middle name, too."

My brows go high.

"It's like she was trying to make sure I'd be a virgin forever."

Before Bea can give her daughter what I'm sure is a well-versed lecture, someone calls out the girls' names from across the market. We all turn to find a robust woman with platinum-blonde hair waving wildly.

They groan.

"Ugh," Colby mutters. "Mom, please tell me you didn't sign us up for more face painting duty."

"You said you wanted to make some money today," Bea sing-songs, already nudging them off with a playful swat.

"Not with Lizzy Simmons!" Clementine throws her a look of pure betrayal. "You tricked us."

"It's called parenting," Bea replies. "Now go make some little toddlers into tigers or butterflies or whatever their hearts are begging to be. Just don't make them cry."

The twins vanish in a flurry of eye-rolls and dramatic teen energy, leaving me alone with Bea Archer... who's now giving me a look far too knowing for comfort.

My mind scrambles for an exit—some excuse to bolt before she can unravel me with one of those warm, well-meaning smiles that remind me all too much of what I desperately want.

But before I can say a word, she reaches up and gently twirls the end of one of my French braids.

"Your hair is stunning," she says softly. "Especially in the sun. It's full of so many colors. And these curls?" She lets out a small, affectionate sigh. "I'm jealous. You don't see hair like yours very often."

Her fingers fall away, replaced by a motherly smile that curls like the honey she's selling—warm and sweet in the sun.

"Is it a familial trait?"

The world around me disappears at her otherwise innocent question.

My heart skips a beat—then another. Bea's voice fades, echoing through the hollow chamber of my chest.

Familial trait.

What if Bea knew my mom? What if she knows who my dad is? What if she knows why my mom was in West Virginia instead of here, with a family like hers?

I blink a few times, finding Bea giving me an almost knowing look that scares the hell out of me and makes me giddy all at once.

I'm still debating what to do when a new voice penetrates the long silence, distracting both of us.

"Hey, Mom. Ridge said one of the perimeter fences near the south pasture was down again this morning. Third time this month. He's not sure if it's the weather, the cows, or something else, but he's got a bad feeling and asked me to ride out with him."

I glance up just as a woman about my age steps forward. She's got the same dark Archer hair as the rest of them, a striped button-down tucked into worn jeans, boots that have clearly seen some shit, and a wide-brimmed hat that reminds me way too damn much of Kade's.

The image of Kade Archer clutching his Stetson to his broad chest like a true Southern gentleman flickers through my mind—his deep voice all rumble and charm as he addressed the judge.

Of course, that charm never extends to me.

No, when Kade looks at me, all that polite, fake Southern-boy energy flies straight out the damn window, and for some ridiculous reason, I like it that way.

What's that saying?

Cowboy in the streets, domineering, alpha daddy in the sheets?

No? Maybe I made it up. Actually, Abby probably said it.

I bite my lip, eyes flicking between the two women as they engage in a quiet, tense conversation. My fingers trail over the golden jars of honey in an attempt to give them privacy, but I catch the words *Cooper Ridge is here*, and *stay away*, before they drop their voices.

The honey really is beautiful, especially in the light. The label is modern, but rustic, just like their stand. I can tell every single aspect of Honey Bea farm was created with love and care. Did Kade help with any of this? The harvesting of honey or growing the dried herbs?

Bea said they have animals out on the farm. Does he know how to ride a horse, or are the cowboy boots just for show?

And with every single question, the reality that my interest in Kade Archer runs far too deep to simply be platonic. Every little detail I've found out about his life, whether from research, his family, or the man himself, has drawn me in a little bit deeper.

I'm attracted to him—that's obvious, but damn, why the hell did I have to go and start *caring* about the moments that make up his days? Pretty sure the man can't stand me, and I...

I don't know what I feel.

"Hazel Ruth, meet Georgia," Bea says, dragging me back to the present. "She's new in town. Isn't she just cute as a button?"

Hazel cocks a brow at her mom before slowly turning to face me. Her smile is friendly, but her body language is antsy, like she's ready to run and hates chit-chat.

Same.

"Cute as a button, huh?" she says, eyeing me from my worn Chucks to my braids, then doubling back to my shirt. Her brows go high. "Stevie fan?" She clicks her tongue. "You must love tequila."

A laugh slips free before I can stop it.

"I fail to see the correlation, but…" I shrug. "You're not wrong."

"Trust me, they're related." Hazel waves me off. "Stevie fans either cry to tequila or end up dancing on bars because of it. Sometimes both."

"Hazel Ruth," Bea chides. "Don't scare the poor girl off."

"She looks like she can handle it." Hazel narrows her eyes at me. "Right, *button*?"

I ignore the nickname and cock a brow. "Haven't had a tequila cry in at least a month, so…"

"Good. Then you're overdue." She grins. "And lucky for you, we've got the perfect watering hole to remedy the issue."

My head bobs, stomach flipping with excitement, nerves, and confusion.

I don't know what's happening right now—it feels a little bit like all the Archers are individually recruiting me, finding my weaknesses, and exploiting them in the kindest way possible.

They're like magnets, drawing me into their happy family circle as if I'm one of them, and that… *that feeling*… it's something I've wanted for way too damn long.

I could easily let myself get sucked into everything that is the Archers, and for that exact reason, I can't let myself get any closer—to any of them. Not when everyone I get close to eventually leaves, shattering my fragile heart in the process.

"I'm sure you do, but, uh," I say, thumbing over my shoulder, "I've got errands and, um, life stuff. You know how it is."

"Liar," she murmurs, challenge in her eyes.

My mouth falls open and she scoffs.

"Georgia, there are exactly three things to do in this town for fun: ride a horse, get laid, or get drunk. Lot of us do all three at once."

Next to her, Bea chokes on her water, but Hazel doesn't skip a beat.

"So, unless you're doing one of the above, you're likely just going home to rot on your couch and wish for a tornado to pick you up and take you anywhere else." She levels me with a serious look. "So, are you one of us, or are you just another sad city girl waiting for your Amazon packages and praying your Wi-Fi holds?"

I blink. Once. Twice. Then burst out laughing. "Wow. That was… aggressive."

"Motivational, actually." Hazel shrugs, smug as hell, and points across the street to a big, barn-shaped building with string lights wrapped around the porch beams and a swinging saloon-style door painted red. A large wooden sign above reads *The Twisted Saddle.*

"Every Saturday night, I'm at the *Saddle* with my best friend and a few of the local cowgirls. You don't have to drink. You don't have to dance. But it's an open invite. I'll save you a seat and defend your city girl ways with violence if necessary." She tips her hat. "You're welcome."

I stare after her long after she's gone, Bea grinning wildly at my side, my heart in my throat, excitement thrumming through my veins.

Could I do it? Go and make some finds? Plant some roots of my own in Heart Springs?

"You know, she's not wrong," Bea murmurs, bumping my hip with hers. I swing my head, and she gives me a slow smirk. "Doing all three at once? One of the best nights I've ever had." She waggles her brows. "That's how the twins were made."

A laugh bursts from me, and Bea turns to face me, grinning, but her head is cocked, eyes narrowed in that knowing way of hers.

My laugh dies, smile slipping.

"Are you usually free on weekends?" she asks, catching me off guard. "I assume you work a regular work week."

I nod, brows furrowed. "I don't really know many people here yet, so I've just been filling my time with exploring."

"Are you crafty, Georgia?"

"Crafty, ma'am?"

She tuts at me, rolling her eyes as she idly organizes her display, like it's all second nature at this point. "It's Bea, dear. 'Ma'am' makes me feel old."

"Sorry," I giggle. "And, yeah, I guess. I know my way around a hot glue gun, and I'm pretty great with paint. Just don't let me near the glitter."

"You sound like Colby." She laughs. "We've got this community event coming up at the farm. The girls are all busy with their own stuff, and I can't pull any of the ranch hands from their duties to help me get ready. Besides, I'd love to spend time with you, dear. Show you around the farm. It really is lovely."

"I'm sure it is." I swallow, biting my lip. "And that's so kind of you."

Just like with Hazel, I'm overcome with the kindness these people are offering me. Their sincerity, and inclusion. I can't remember a single time in my life when anyone's ever gone out of their way to bring me into their fold—especially not strangers.

And the fact that Bea wants to spend time with me...

Maybe I could use it as a way to get to know her, and if I do that, maybe eventually I'll be brave enough to voice the questions I fear she might be able to answer.

"So, you want me to come to the farm," I say slowly, heart racing. "To help you set up for…?"

"The Honey Bea Bash," she fills in, nodding and smiling adorably. "It's one of my favorite events. It kicks off the summer in Heart Springs. All the kids and families come. I've done it for years, but now that we don't have as much staff, because—"

Her smile fades, and the look that replaces it is so sad I want to hug her. Bea blinks a few times, then waves a hand through the air.

"The why's not important, but I can't quite do as much as I used to, especially not alone." Reaching over the table, she grabs my hand. "You'd *really* be doing me a favor."

Spending time with the Archers is dangerous—not professionally, not really. I'm not in Heart Springs anymore. Technically, I'm not breaking any rules, and the gray area is exactly that.

But that's not why this family scares me.

It's because every single one of them has found a way to rope me in, and my heart—my aching, yearning soul, has never wanted anything more than this.

Community, friends, people who see me as I am—and accept me anyway.

"When did you need me?" I croak.

Bea grins, tugging me into a warm hug that steals my breath and heals a tiny part of me all at once.

Fuck.

First Kade, now his entire family's roped me in.

The Archers truly are a cult.

CHAPTER FIFTEEN

THE WEIGHT OF WALLS

THE HOUSE BEFORE ME is the same one I left behind a decade ago, but it's painted in different emotions.

Once, it stood proud—clean lines of white shiplap against the green of the pasture, like a daydream for the hopeful.

My dad used to run his hand along the siding and say it was built to last. That no matter what storms came through, we'd made something strong enough to hold steady—

something to keep the love inside safe.

Now? The boards are faded, worn down by weather and time, and I missed every fucking minute.

The porch that wraps and curves around all the edges of my single-story home was designed so I could watch my family grow at every angle. Back then, I imagined sitting out here with a cold beer and a kid on each knee, watching the sun go down to the soundtrack of my wife's laughter.

Instead, the boards creak under my weight, and parts of the steps are split—not from the pounding of little feet, but from storms and neglect.

Life didn't grow here.

It stalled.

Got stuck in the same place I did the day I shipped out.

And then it got burned to hell when I chose not to come back.

I swallow hard, my throat tight, because it's not just wood and siding. It's him. Every nail, every plank… my dad's hands were *right here*. His voice still echoes in the way the gutters bend, the way the porch slants, just slightly wrong on the northeast corner, because I messed up the measurements and he let me fix it all by myself when I was sixteen.

Part of me feels like he built this for someone else. For a country boy who thought love could fix everything. The one who believed promises made in the sunlight would last forever.

But that boy died a long time ago, somewhere between the sandstorms and sirens, the blood and bone.

Still… some stubborn part of me moves forward anyway. Like maybe, if I just reach for it, there's still something in me left worth saving.

The key turns easier than I expect.

For a second, I wonder if maybe it won't work. But the door swings open without a sound. My eyes burn, and my whole goddamn body starts trembling as I cross the threshold. I force one foot forward, then the next.

And stop cold.

"What the fuck…" I breathe, stumbling over my boots, reaching blindly behind me to shut the door. It closes with a *click*, and then it's just me and this house.

A house that's not supposed to look like this.

When I left, the house was maybe halfway done. We'd framed the exterior, gotten it sealed up tight so the weather wouldn't ruin what we'd started. But the inside was just beginnings. All exposed beams and covered in dust. Plans scribbled on the back of anything I could get my hands on.

Now… now it's so much further along.

I walk forward slowly, like I'm stepping through someone else's memory. Because that's what it feels like—familiar and foreign at the same time. Every wall is up, covered in white paint. The kitchen's a blank slate, wires hanging out of the walls, waiting for life. No appliances, but the cabinets and sink are in.

I never picked them, never cared to.

Always thought I'd get to the guts when I had a partner by my side. Figured it wasn't my home alone, it was always meant for a family.

I shake my head, and yank my cap off, tossing it on the marble island that has my mom's hands all over it. The kitchen looks like something she'd dream up, replacing my shattered plans with her own spark of hope.

White shaker cabinets, gray-veined countertops, and a giant wrought-iron chandelier to warm the place up. I couldn't have chosen better myself.

The living room's wide open, sunlight spilling across the floor through clean, glass windows that line the entire back wall. Across from it, the fireplace I built brick by brick stretches all the way to the vaulted ceilings of the A-frame. The dark red color matches the knotty pine floors just like I imagined.

I drag a hand down my face, breath catching somewhere between my throat and my chest. My fingers shake when they fall away.

Every corner I turn, every detail I see—it's him.

Pieces I never planned now mirror some of my favorite parts of my childhood home—the first place he ever built.

From the doorways framed in raw, honey-toned wood—no stain or polish, just the kind of finish that lets the grain speak for itself, to the window seat in the kitchen. It looks just like the little breakfast nook we used to prefer over the giant dining table.

This wasn't a quick contractor job, it was my dad.

He fuckin' finished it.

While I was halfway across the world, chasing my pride in a war he didn't believe in, he was here, finishing my house. A house I didn't even know I wanted anymore. A future I'd shoved so far down, I forgot *how* to want it.

And he kept building anyway.

My boots echo in the hallway as I move to the back, toward what was supposed to be the primary suite. I remember standing in this space with him, arms crossed, arguing over whether the windows should face west or south. He said the morning light would be softer if the bed faced the trees, but I wanted to look out onto the wildflower fields from the bed and the tub.

The bathroom's half-shell, half-dreams—no tub, just copper lines and a stack of open tile boxes shoved in a corner like someone meant to get to it. A familiar mallet and tile cuter are next to a half-open can of dried-out grout.

Stepping back, I see the scene for what it is. A project barely started, but the tools are nearby—like it was next on a never-ending list and he just couldn't get to it in time.

And somehow, that's the part that wrecks me most.

Not the silence.

Not the emptiness.

But the proof that he was mid-motion—hands dirty, sleeves rolled, probably humming under his breath—just trying to make something better.

This space feels haunted, not by ghosts, but by intention. By fingerprints left on plans never finished. By the echo of a life paused mid-breath.

There's grief in the grout lines, loss in every tile not yet laid.

Like he stepped out for a break and never came back. Like love lived here once, and then ran out of time.

The thought steals the air right from my fucking lungs. I grip the doorframe to keep from crumbling. The weight on my chest is unbearable. Shame, grief, fury—aimed directly at myself. I want to punch something. To scream. Crawl out of my own skin.

I let him finish this alone, let him *die* alone.

Don't know how long I stand there. Long enough for the dust to settle around me. Long enough for the ache in my chest to bloom into something jagged and wild. Long enough for the memories I've tried like hell to outrun to start creeping back in. I shove away from the bathroom and head back to the front door, but the memories chase me, forcing me to remember every ugly second.

I was eighteen and barely fresh from graduation when I took off. Joined the Army despite my family begging me to stay. At the time, I couldn't see past Marlee's dreams of a future I didn't recognize, but I promised them I'd be back in four years. Promised I'd help. Promised I'd build a life here.

Dad was pissed. Thought I was throwing away a future rooted in this land for a war that wasn't mine, and a girl who was desperate for a bigger future than Heart Springs.

None of that matters when you're young and dumb, though—and hindsight doesn't save what you lost along the way to doing things right.

I trace my hand along the edge of the doorway, where the frame doesn't quite sit flush. I remember holding the level while Dad lined it up. The way he cursed at it under his breath when it didn't sit right. Said nothing was ever perfect, but that didn't mean you shouldn't try like hell to make it so.

My throat closes. Even after I re-enlisted—after Marlee's letter, after everything...

I can still hear his voice. *"Come home, son. Don't let her be the reason you throw your life away."*

And I didn't listen. I told him I was fine. That I was where I needed to be. That I didn't want to come back.

That was a lie, but I was young, stupid, and prideful.

God, we fought. Every fucking phone call turned into a standoff. Words that used to mean something came out ugly and bitter. Until eventually… there were no words at all.

By the time I came back that last Christmas, I'd convinced myself the bronze star in my pocket meant something. That saving those kids overseas made all the pain back home worth it. That maybe, just maybe, he'd finally see me as more than a disappointment.

But he just looked at me like I was a stranger. Said he didn't even recognize me.

He was right.

I was proud of what I'd done. Of surviving. Of saving lives. But he saw it for what it really was—just another way I kept running farther from home.

We fought in person that time. Voices raised, years of pain pouring out like gasoline. And I walked away. Stormed out like a coward. Didn't call. Didn't write.

The next time I heard his name… it was from my mom a month later. A heart attack. Out in the field, trying to move a busted trailer full of wildflower crates I was supposed to help with that Christmas. He died doing the work I left behind. Died thinking I hated him.

And still, he finished this fucking house. Still gave me this last piece of him.

I press my palm to the front door, breathing hard. My knees threaten to give out, but I hold on. I *have* to hold on.

Because this isn't just about me anymore. It's about a little girl who deserves roots, and safety, and love. And after all the time I spent with her this last week, I know one thing for damn sure. I can give her that. I don't have much, but I can love Aurora like she's my own kid.

Purpose pushes me forward. This part was hard as hell, damn near broke me, but I'm not done yet.

I quickly lock up the house and shoot a text to the new social worker to let her know I've found a place. She responds that she'll be out Tuesday for a preliminary inspection. The thought makes me wanna puke, but I confirm and pocket my phone, taking the stairs two at a time.

Thank fuck the guys are here. I'll need all the help I can get if I'm going to pull this off in two weeks.

The gravel crunches under my boots as I cut across the pasture toward the Big House, taking in Honey Bea and all the changes I've missed.

Last time I was really here was after I was discharged. Spent eight weeks holed up in my old room, recovering from multiple surgeries after the IED explosion. Shrapnel tore through my left shoulder, and the explosion broke my right femur. Left me with a chest full of scars and a limp I still feel more often than not.

Got out of here as quickly as I could. Moved to Wildwood and rarely looked back—except for on holidays. But those are in a dimly lit dining or living room, and I've always been buzzed enough to ignore the ache.

Now, I'm realizing how fucking selfish I've been.

The trek from my house to the one where I grew up is about half a mile, but it's a pretty walk. Five thousand acres, passed down from my grandfather. Five thousand more bought when my dad married my mom. Ten thousand acres of blood, sweat, and sunburns.

It's too much for one family and somehow still not enough for Archer dreams.

The wheat fields we use to supplement income when the flowers can't bloom, the acres that stretch long and golden in summer heat—those were Grandpa's idea. The working livestock, tractors, long days and weather-worn hands, that was my dad's dream. To work the land, build something solid, something that couldn't be taken away.

The wildflowers, though? The beehives? The bursts of color that flow like water across the hills in late spring?

Those were hers.

A honey bee farm. A wraparound porch. A house full of laughter and flowers. That was my mom's dream.

So they built it together.

When we were old enough, she taught us everything she knew. They grew when they could, scaled back when they had to. And somehow, it worked.

For a long time, they made it work.

Until it didn't.

Until we lost him.

Now, it's mostly my mom and the girls holding everything together. Colby and Clementine—seventeen, wild, and still figuring out their place in the world, but they love to help out at the farmers markets.

Hazel's got her own house on the far end of the property, tucked against the trees where nobody bothers her. She's always preferred the animals and crops to flowers and honey.

And Gemma... she hasn't lived here in years. Moved to North Dakota after her husband got a job up there. She visits, just not often.

Used to be more, but I'm the last person to be judging.

I pass the horse barn on my way up the hill. Two of the mares are out in the coral, flicking flies off their flanks with their tails. One of them tosses her head when she sees me, and I grin.

"Well, hey there, Dolly," I murmur, stepping up to the fence. She's a dapple-gray with big eyes and an attitude, but she's old enough to know me. "You givin' Clem hell again?"

She hooves at the dirt, tail swishing in fast snaps that make me laugh.

Next to her, a senior chestnut nudges closer, her muzzle more gray than brown.

"Hey, June Bug," I say, running my fingers down her velvet-soft nose, whiskers catching on my calluses. "Still the prettiest girl in the bunch, huh?"

She huffs like she knows it, pushing my hand away. Cocking her head to the side, she reaches through the bars and digs for my pockets like she remembers exactly what I used to keep in them.

Chuckling, I trail my finger down the white diamond between her eyes.

"Sorry, girl. I'll bring some sugar cubes before I leave."

I spend a bit more time with the horses, then goats, before moving on, passing the chicken coops and barns on my way.

Surprisingly, the familiar path helps soothe my nerves. This land is in my blood—every fence post, every worn trail. I could walk it blindfolded and still find my way home.

By the time I make it to the Big House, the sun is setting and a soft breeze carries the faint hum of music. I smile before I even round the corner. My mom always listens to classical music when she's with the bees. Swears it makes them smarter, sweeter. She says you can taste the difference in the honey. That the right song'll have them working twice as fast, building stronger combs, and filling the frames like they're drunk on the vibrations.

Sure enough, when I round the back of the house, I spot her in the distance by the apiary—white suit unzipped and hanging loose around her waist, veil pushed back off her short hair, bare hands moving calmly over the frames. Her mouth moves, talking to the bees in a low voice, like she's coaxing them to behave.

The apiary's gotten bigger since I last saw it.

Gotta be more than a thousand hives lined up in rows, each painted a different pastel color to help the bees find their way home. Wildflowers bloom in intentional chaos all around the area—purple coneflowers, black-eyed Susans, lemon mint, and bee balm.

Everything smells like sunlight and sugar. Like home. Feels better than I thought it would. Damn near cathartic.

She doesn't see me yet, and I don't call out. Because for the first time in a long time, I'm not in a rush to fill the space with guilt, grief, or explanations.

Right now, I just want to take it in.

The place that raised me.

The woman who never stopped loving me, even when I gave her every reason to.

After a while, she finally spots me and finishes what she's doing before stripping off her gear as she walks toward me. She doesn't call out until we're close, always thinking of her bees.

"Twice in one month? What do I owe the pleasure?"

My smile falters, and my heart flips in time with my gut. I swallow hard.

God, I'm a fuckin' dick.

"Ma…" I press my hat to my chest and rake a hand through my hair. "I gotta talk to you about something."

"Oh, my." She gives me a long look, then shakes her head like she's seen this coming. "This looks like a porch talk."

My throat burns, but when she wraps me up in a hug, some of the weight eases off my chest. She's a foot shorter than me, her brown and silver strands catching my beard as I bend down, but a hug from her has the power to soothe even the deepest cuts.

Don't know how I always forget that.

"Oh, baby," she whispers like I'm still five. "I'll get the sweet tea."

Few minutes later, we're sitting side by side on the old wicker bench with the faded yellow cushions—the ones covered in daisies and bees she refuses to throw out. She hands me a glass, doesn't say a word, just sips slow and gives me space.

It reminds me of Georgia, and for a second, I wonder if that's why I'm so drawn to the woman. It's familiar. *Calming.*

But I immediately know it's not just that. With her, it's something different entirely.

I stare at the fields stretching out in front of us, then finally say it.

Rip the fucking Band-Aid off, Archer.

"Marlee's dead."

Mom gasps, pressing a hand to her chest. Her iced tea glass nearly slips free, but she sets it down at the last second.

I wasn't sure if she'd heard through the gossip rings, or if the news had even reached Heart Springs, but judging by the tears in her eyes, it clearly hasn't.

"How?" she manages to ask.

And for the second time, I tell someone a tragedy. Only thing I hold off on is Aurora. I need another breath before I can slice into the wound again.

She listens, shoulders tight, hands bundled between her knees.

"I thought she moved away. Where did this happen?" Then she frowns—like the dots are trying to reach but can't quite connect. "Wait. How did you even find out?"

I chug half my tea like it'll make the words easier. It doesn't.

"A social worker told me."

Her eyes light up like a switch got flipped. "Georgia?"

I jerk a nod, biting the inside of my cheek as I watch her fight an incredibly inappropriate smile.

"Oh my Lord, I knew it. Saw her at the farmers market this morning, and I just felt it in my bones." She pats my leg. "Something's going on between you two, isn't it?"

"You saw her?" I ask, the words out before I can stop myself.

There's a look in her eyes that sends a tingle down my spine. Matches the look she had outside Thread & Thimble all those weeks ago. Like she's hiding something—plotting.

Before I can ask what the hell she's done, she continues, and her words have my jaw clenching.

"She met the twins—girls adore her. And Hazel invited her to girls' night at the Saddle."

My stomach twists knowing exactly what Hazel and her friends get up to on girls' nights in town. Hazel can drink more than most big men I know—and handles her liquor like any cowboy—but she's reckless and wild on a good day.

Drunk and surrounded by her feral girlfriends? I'll be surprised if someone doesn't wind up arrested, or in a random's bed.

Thought of Georgia in the middle of all that? Alone with my sister?

Hate it. Hate it hell of a lot more than I have any right to.

"Y'all shouldn't be inviting her to anything," I mutter, glancing away to hide my unwanted irritation. "'Specially not girls' night. Georgia's not from here, and she's not staying." I chug some tea. "Besides, she's not my social worker any more. We'll probably never see her again. Last thing we need is the girls getting attached."

"The girls, huh?" she murmurs, chuckling.

"You're already halfway obsessed with the woman, Ma. The twins spend any more time with her, they'll start calling her their new sister."

"Knew it," Mom mutters, voice laced with plotting and conspiracy. "You're unraveling at the seams, aren't you?"

I groan, scrubbing a hand down my face. "No, Ma. It's not like that."

Could be, my brain unhelpfully supplies, and I bite my cheek harder—until I taste blood. I *cannot* think about her like that anymore. I won't allow it.

Mom scoffs, almost as if in answer to my internal pep talk. "Please. I see the way you glare at each other. All fire and ice." She smiles, soft and wistful. "Just like your daddy and me."

I open my mouth to argue, but all that comes out is a sigh. I can't debate the right and wrongness of Georgia and me right now. Not with her. Especially not when I don't even know what the hell is going on…if anything.

Not when I still have more to tell my mom—the reason I'm here in the first palace.

"Forgot about Georgia for now, Ma. There's more."

She stills, waiting.

And then I tell her about Aurora.

How Marlee named me guardian.

How a little girl I've never met is now counting on me.

Mom's face crumples and then hardens again, confusion flashing across her features. "But… how? I thought you hadn't seen Marlee since that summer you went out to Ruthy Hatter's cabin on leave."

"Not in over a decade," I say roughly.

"Then why?"

I shrug. "Dunno. Your guess is as good as mine."

She stares at me for a long moment, then straightens her spine, nods like it's already decided.

"Okay. Well." She claps. "Where's my grandbaby?"

Just like that. No hesitation. No judgment. Just love.

I blink hard, the tightness in my chest twisting into something damn near unbearable.

"With a temporary foster placement," I choke out, hating the taste of the admission on my tongue. Her face falls. "That's one of the reasons I'm here. I need a new place to live, and…" I trail off, shrugging.

Because she's my mom, and knows my thoughts better than I do, she fills in, "You went home." I nod and she smiles, squeezing my hand. "He finished it for you, Kade. Wanted you to have something safe and familiar to come back to, no matter how many pieces your soul was in."

The weight of the truth sucker punches me, and a tear escapes before I can pretend it doesn't exist.

"From what I saw the last time I checked on it, there's a few leaks, and a couple rooms need finishing, but nothing your family and friends can't pull together in time." Mom smiles, tucks a strand of hair behind my ear, and says, "Since you're here... you wanna take a ride out to the lake with me? Might help you."

I shake my head, throat thick. Fuck. The hits just keep coming. "Not today."

She sighs, kisses my cheek, and pulls back just enough to study me, her blue eyes shining with pride and something even heavier.

"I can't believe you're a daddy," she says softly. "I always knew your dreams would come true."

"Oh my fucking God!" Hazel yells from somewhere behind the screen door seconds before is smashes open. "You've procreated?"

Before I can react, twin screams echo across the porch.

"You have a baby?!"

At the same time, a staticky voice crackles through the chaos. "Who has a baby? Kade?!"

All our heads whip around.

Colby's standing there, holding up her phone, and Gemma's face is frozen in mid-shriek on FaceTime.

"Tell me everything!" Gemma demands, clapping like a psycho.

I choke on a laugh, settle deeper into the old wicker bench, and let the chaos roll over me.

The sun dips lower behind the fields I grew up running through. The smell of honey and wildflowers thick in the air. The taste of sweet tea sharp on my tongue as my family gathers around me.

And for the first time in a long damn time, there's nowhere else I'd rather be.

Chapter Sixteen

Stuck Between a Goose and A Hard Place

"Follow the left curve?" I mutter, narrowed eyes flicking between the gravel drive and roughly sketched diagram clenched in my right hand. "What the hell are you talking about, Bea? There is no left curve!"

The note doesn't answer—because it's paper and useless—leading me in literal circles around a massive farm. I have half a mind to just park my car and search on foot, but I'm pretty sure I'd get lost almost immediately. Despite all the driving and circles, I've yet to see a single other living soul.

When I agreed to help with the Honey Bea Bash, I didn't realize Bea meant bright and early every Saturday… *for the next two months.*

Apparently, the summer kickoff festival hosted here is massive, and there's so much to do, it'll take nearly every weekend from now until June just to get it done on time.

But I'd already said yes. And really, what else am I doing with my free time? It's not like I have a social calendar to protect.

Sighing, I toss the map on the floor. It's getting me nowhere.

Rolling my window down, I turn up my favorite playlist and scan the sprawling property. It's huge—land stretching out as far as I can see, unraveling in every direction. In the distance, I can make out the outlines of quite a few buildings, and even a few silos, beneath a gray sky.

It's the kind of beautiful that steals the air right from your lungs.

I smile, heart skipping, and breathe deeply.

The scent hits first—wet alfalfa and freshly tilled soil, rain-soaked earth clinging to every inhale. There's a tang of coppery mud, sweet grass, and something floral, but not overpowering.

Beneath it all, there's the warm, unmistakable musk of animals, hay-damp fur, old wood, and manure baked into the bones of the place.

Robin's farm smelled like this—muddy and fresh and alive, a little wild around the edges. It wraps around me like a hug, and for just a second, I swear I can feel her with me.

My foot lifts off the gas when I pass three cats being chased by a—

"Is that a goose?" I breathe, eyes wide, smile wider.

A second later, a brown puppy with dopey ears flies after the goose, stumbling over its too-big feet.

Blindly, I reach for my phone and hit *record*, knowing Abby will lose her mind when she sees how cute the country can be. I may or may not be secretly trying to convince her to come out for a visit—via Heart Springs subliminal messaging.

The cats bounce over fence posts and around a tree, looping twice before crossing the road again. The goose never loses sight of the bunch—picking up pace, honking wildly, giant wings spread out at its sides—the yapping dog not far behind.

"God, Abby!" I laugh, wiping my eyes with my shoulder. "You'd seriously love this—*AH! Fuck! Shit! Oh my God!*"

My car thumps across rocks, bouncing and scraping at a slight downward angle. The steering wheel jerks, and my phone goes flying in my desperate panic to regain control of the vehicle—but apparently, *it's* driving *me* now…directly into a steep but shallow ditch.

I slam on the breaks, and my right leg locks up, sending a sharp pain up to my hip.

A second later, the car stops moving, so I throw it in reverse and slowly hit the gas. The engine revs. The wet sound of tires spinning through mud but not catching fills the air—nothing happens.

I try again and again, but eventually, give up and shift back into park.

With a defeated exhale, I drop my head onto the headrest and stare out the windshield.

What the hell just happened? One second I was documenting the adorable reality of farm life, and the next—

"Oh, fuck!" I cry, eyes wide, heart racing. "The animals!"

Did I hit one of them when I went off the road?!

My hand flies to the handle, and I try to shove the door open, but it barely budges an inch before getting stuck. Glancing down, I quickly discover why. I'm not just in a ditch, I'm in a ditch filled with nature—rocks, plants, and mud. *Lots* of mud.

I close the door carefully and reach over the center console, careful not to spill the coffee I stopped for on the way here—an iced latte for me and a black coffee for Bea, since I wasn't sure what she liked.

If she's anything like her *latte hating son*, I figured simple was best.

The second door is more stuck than the first, pressed up tightly against some giant, random bush scraping against the window.

Groaning, I flop back in my seat and stare out the windshield, unsure what the hell to do. My throat constricts, nerves completely shot, and the longer I stay here, trapped and tilted, the higher my anxiety soars.

Do I scream for help? That seems a bit dramatic.

I could climb out the window, but it's small, and I'm just clumsy enough that I'll probably get stuck halfway through and face-plant directly into a rock.

With no one around—possibly for miles—I'd just lie there, flopping in the wind, belly down, head bleeding profusely all over the rock that took me *and* my car out, until the cats—or maybe one of the cows I passed—found me and had my hair for lunch.

"Get it together, Georgia." I tug on my curls, groaning. "You're not lost in the wilderness. It's a farm. Someone will find you... *eventually*."

Except I have to pee—*desperately*.

I chugged two waters on my way, one with my pills, one with electrolytes since I'm still lagging and a little sore.

Shifting, I wince at the throb in my hip but shoot up a silent *thank-you* that it wasn't worse. At least I'm okay. My rental? I doubt I'll be getting my deposit back.

My eyes catch on my phone lying on the passenger-side floor, and I reach over, snatching it up.

Thumbing open my contacts, I pause.

Who the fuck am I supposed to call, the police? A tow-truck?

Where would I even say I am?

Hit the gravel road, follow the trees. I'm seven and a half curves past the third white barn, but not quite to the somewhat smaller blue shed? Oh, and while you're out there, please make sure there are no dead geese.

The only person who could even help me is the last one I should be calling, but I'm not sure I have any other options. I don't have a single other Archer's phone number, just Kade's from when I was on his case. It's been weeks since I've used it, and that was only to tell him Aurora's room number the day he met her.

My stomach twists, heart clenching as my mind fills with visions of her in his arms. He has about a week left to find a place and get it ready to move her in—if he has any hope of becoming her guardian.

Has he found one? Is she okay? *Is he?*

I'm as desperate for updates as my bladder is for peeing.

Fuck it.

Biting my lip, thumb hovering over his number, I suck in a breath, and press *Call.*

The phone rings. And rings.

And rings.

My eyes fall closed, palm clenching around the phone. I sigh, muttering a defeated, "Of course, the asshole's not going to ans—"

"I answered."

My mouth snaps shut so fast, I bite my tongue. Hard. "*Ouch!*"

"My voice that painful, darlin'?"

No. Not even a little bit.

In fact, the drawl sounds more genuine and less over-the-top on the phone. Just the sound of it has my stomach swooping low and pitching high, all at once.

"Uh…" I clear my throat, sitting up straighter. "It's fine. I guess." My tongue pokes the inside of my cheek, my lips tugging up. "A little nasally, though. Kind of high-pitched."

Kade grunts, but doesn't respond. The sound of hammering and drilling fills his end of the call, followed by men's voices in a low conversation I can't quite make out.

Is he working? Maybe he found a new job. Construction, or something else local.

I flick my gaze to the clock on the dash and grimace. I'm totally interrupting his morning. Of course, he's not going to stop whatever he's doing to talk to me, let alone come save me from a ditch.

"Sorry, you sound busy," I quickly say, shaking my head. God, I can't believe I called him. I'm so stupid! "I'll, uh, just call someone else." I suck in a breath. "By—"

"Wait," he barks, jolting me. A door closes, and the chaos quiets. "Sorry, couldn't really hear you."

I swallow hard, fingers tapping against the steering wheel. "You didn't have to stop whatever it is you're doing."

"It's fine, Georgia," he says, deep voice wrapping around the syllables of my name, distracting me. After a minute of silence, he drawls, "So, was there a reason you called, or did you just wanna ruin my workflow?"

This time, when my stomach flips, it's for a whole new reason. Part of me knows he's kidding when he says it—I can hear the laughter in his voice, but that doesn't stop it from twisting something deep inside me that's raw. An ache that never healed.

One that tells me I'm an inconvenience, a burden, *unwanted*.

And like always, when I'm hurt, my hackles rise.

"No, you know what," I say, voice sharper than intended. "I don't need anything. It's fine. I'll call someone else for help. Just go back to whatever it is you were doing before I *ruined* your precious—"

"Freckles!" he snaps, cutting me off mid-spiral. My teeth gnash together. "Stop rambling, take a damn breath, and tell me why you called, woman."

"Momentary lapse in judgement, clearly."

"Georgia."

"*Kade.*"

He huffs, long and dramatic. "What do you need help with?"

I tighten my grip on my phone and contemplate throwing myself from the window and finding that rock. But my bladder screams and then my hip throbs, and I toss my pride out instead of my body.

Sighing, I rub between my brows and close my eyes. "I was sort of in a little bit of a car accident," I whisper. "And—"

"You what?" he barks.

I wave a hand through the air. "An accident. It's not a big deal."

"It's a big fuckin' deal." He sounds breathless, like he's moving, and my brows crash together. "Where are you?"

My nose wrinkles as I glance out the window. This is humiliating. "About that."

Keys jingle in the background and another door slams closed.

"Spit it out!"

"Don't be so rude," I huff. "And I'm sort of on your family's farm." A swallow. "In a ditch."

Another door closes, and I think it might be his truck, but then he's pausing—silent and tense, before he rumbles out a slow, deep, "You're *where*?"

"Look, I know it's weird, and probably blowing your fucking mind right now, but I'm at Honey Bea because I ran into your mom last weekend, and she said she needed my help on a project. You've met her, she's incredibly convincing. I was supposed to find her at some supply shed, but I couldn't find it, and then there was this goose. The ditch came out of nowhere, and now I'm stuck."

"Stuck…" He draws the word out. "In a ditch on my farm."

"Yes!" I cry, hand flailing. "Stuck in a ditch. And I really have to pee! So can you please come get me, or find someone who will, because I might be in the country, Kade, but I'm not a guy. I can't exactly whip it out the window!"

He's silent for a beat, then, "Think I'd like to see you try, though."

"Oh my God!"

Kade chuckles, and an engine kicks on. "I'm on my way. Don't move."

He hangs up before I can remind him I'm literally stuck, and I drop my phone onto my lap, exhaling a shaky breath. I sink deeper into my seat and cross my bouncing legs. I wish he would have told me how far away he was. If he's home in Wildwood, I could be waiting for at least half an hour, and I'm not sure I'll last that long.

I turn up the music to distract myself from thinking about the discomfort, and sing along to one of my favorite songs, but it doesn't hit like it usually does.

Kelly would be so disappointed in me. I'm the furthest thing from "Miss Independent" right now.

I'm Sad, Trapped Barbie waiting for Cowboy Ken to rescue me.

For some reason, the idea of seeing Kade sends a wave of butterflies through my system, and my brain supplies a random image of him showing up shirtless like he was the day I met him.

Only in my fantasy, this time, he'd be in those tight jeans with the worn knees that hug his ass and thick thighs perfectly, a handyman belt strapped around his abs. Imaginary me is torn between him wearing his cowboy hat and the baseball cap he seems to love so much.

Both are hot as hell, especially when he turns the cap backward and calls me *darlin'* in that stupid, perfect, deep voice of his—that dramatic Southern drawl that never fails to make me wet and needy.

"Nope," I murmur, forcing the image from my mind. "No. No. No. I cannot fantasize about him."

I check my reflection in the mirror, and give myself the same pep talk I've been repeating since the day I met Kade Archer.

"You do not find him attractive. He's cocky, arrogant, and rude. His personality is equivalent to that of a rabid hyena. He's ugly and old. His face is annoying. Cowboy boots are not sexy. Hats are the Devil's wardrobe. He smells. And I *hate* his beard—"

"Arrogant, ugly, and old are one thing, but my beard?"

I scream and my eyes fly to the window—the *open* window, and the sadly, very fully clothed man outside of it. How the hell did he get here so fast?

"Now I know you're making shit up, freckles. Most people say my beard is my best asset."

Kade runs his fingers through his neatly trimmed, silver-flecked beard and shoots me a cocky, half smirk that sends butterflies through my veins. That smirk is quickly becoming my obsession—along with the man wearing it.

"Of course, some would argue it's my *rabid hyena personality*." He leans down and stares directly into my eyes as he murmurs, "Told you I could make you scream."

Annnd obsession tamed.

I stare at him for a long moment, brain fritzing, spiraling, and rewiring repeatedly.

"You didn't hear any of that," I state, chin high.

He cocks a brow. "You do know saying something doesn't make it true."

I toss my hair over my shoulder. "What'll it cost?"

"Cost?"

"For you to pretend you didn't hear anything."

Kade stares at me for a long moment, head slightly tilted, like he's actually considering it. His eyes slide across my face before gliding downward. They land somewhere around my chest, where they stay.

I follow his gaze and scoff.

"Either you love the Queen of Country," I murmur, referring to my Dolly Parton shirt. "Or my boobs. And if that's the case, they're not part of the deal."

"You have tattoos," he states, throat bobbing. "Multiple."

My mouth unhinges, then snaps shut. *That's* what he's looking at?

Self-consciousness swarms my senses, and I twist, letting the baggy sleeve of my vintage tee fall to cover the floral tattoo on my bicep. I feel exposed, the way he's staring at it—at *me*.

I lift my hand out the window and snap, getting his attention.

"If you're done gawking, can you please help me?" His eyes jolt to mine, jaw ticking. "I wasn't kidding when I said I was about to burst."

Kade rips off his hat—the baseball cap today—and runs his fingers through his hair. It's a bit longer than last time I saw him, but his beard is more trimmed and less wild than before. He looks rested and tan. Emotionally lighter than the first time I met him.

When I swallow, it sticks. He looks good. Really good.

No, Georgia. He's nothing. You've seen way hotter men back home. Kade is just a hillbilly with an attitude problem.

As if to prove me wrong, the man shoves his hat on his head—*backward*—and I'm pretty sure I start drooling.

He bends, and I hear him grunt, like he's in pain. "You alright? Did you get hurt?"

I lose myself in his stormy eyes for a breath—the dark ring of lashes that curl around them, the small scar that dissects his left brow, the little lines creasing around the edges, and the streaks of black and light blue that crash through his irises like lightning strikes.

Kade Archer is *beautiful.*

I'm still staring when his hand comes through the window and tucks a stray curl behind my ear. His fingers ghost my cheek, where they pause. My breath catches.

"Darlin'?" he murmurs, brows drawn tight with concern. He pads at my forehead. "Did you hit your head?"

In a daze, I nod, then shake my head, before settling with a shrug. I don't remember getting hurt, but I must have. Why else would I suddenly be losing myself in his eyes like they're the answers to every wish I never dared to say out loud?

"Do you need to go to the hospital?" he asks, voice threaded with concern that finally wakes me up.

"I'm fine," I breathe, blinking rapidly.

Hell, he's still touching me, but now, his thumb is softly stroking my jaw, palm cradling my face. His hands are calloused and rough, but they're also huge and so gentle that it makes my chest ache.

I pull away.

Clearing my throat, I force a smile.

He snaps his hand back and stands to his full, impressive height, tapping the hood twice. "Alright. Gimme a minute to get you hitched."

"Bit soon for that." I blame my flirty tone on the adrenaline crash. Kade flicks me a questioning look and I shrug, smirking. "Getting hitched. We only just met."

After a beat, his lip lifts in the ghost of a smile, and he shakes his head, stepping away. "Never been one for waiting around. See something I want, I go after it."

I say nothing, synapsis scrambling for purchase as I watch him walk away through the mirror.

Was he like this the last few times I saw him? Slightly inappropriate and flirty, masculine and broody, with a hint of over-the-top concern? Way too hot for his own damn good?

"And I'll take that extra coffee," he calls over his shoulder with a wink. "As payment for pretending you weren't just checking me out!"

And just like that, I'm annoyed all over again.

CHAPTER SEVENTEEN

Georgia

A HOUSE OF DIRTY DREAMS

THE GRAVEL PATH BEHIND me gave way to a muddy road with no driveway or yard—just wide-open space and raw potential. A single-story A-frame sits proudly in the middle of it all, big, charming, and utterly perfect.

From what I can see, the farmhouse itself looks finished. It's not landscaped or polished, but it's stunning. Clean white siding, tall windows wrapped in black frames, and a full-wraparound porch that practically begs for coffee, a warm blanket, and bare feet in the morning.

It's my dream home, on my dream farm—except it's not mine, and never will be. Closest I'll ever get to touching it is chaotic weekends helping Bea in a shed I still haven't located.

Out of the rear window, I catch sight of Kade climbing from his truck and stomping toward me, expression shadowed behind gold-rimmed sunglasses and his hat, now flipped right.

He towed me out of the ditch pretty easily, but apparently, the rocks gave me a flat. He wanted to replace it right there in front of God and seventy-five bushes, but then I reminded him of my desperation for a bathroom and lack of a whip-outable appendage.

After two minutes of tense contemplation—his jaw ticking, head swiveling from the direction of a giant white house off in the distance to a smaller one a bit closer and to the left—he climbed back in his truck and barked at me to follow him.

The drive was slow, bumpy, and beautiful. It was also a fuck of a lot easier with a tour guide. And thankfully, there was no sign of any casualties from the ditch disaster.

When he reaches my door, he doesn't open it or say anything.

Just *looms*.

Beefy arms braced over his equally beefy chest, annoying smirk plastered across his annoying face, he stares down at me from under that damned ball cap and cocks a bushy brown.

Okay, it's not bushy—it's kind of perfect.

I *hate* that eyebrow.

Swallowing thickly, hands shaking, I gather my stuff and jostle the two coffees between my hands while attempting to open the door.

And fail.

"Aren't you supposed to be a gentleman?" I hiss, struggling not to spill the drinks I suddenly regret buying.

Well, I don't regret mine.

My vanilla cinnamon almond milk macchiato is not only gluten-free—*tried and tested*—but also tastes like angels snowballed their golden seed directly into my cup.

Abby would call it a biblical experience.

I do, however, regret the drink he's claimed for himself, and the first chance I find a solid reason, I'm dumping it directly over his head this time.

"You're an independent woman," he drawls, stepping back to make room for the door. The second I swing it open, the music cuts off along with the car, and I nudge it shut with my hip. "Isn't that what you were screaming about a bit ago?" He winces, palms the back of his neck, and mutters, "*Talk about hyena.*"

And his coffee falls to the ground.

"Oops." I gasp, pressing my now free hand to my chest as we collectively stare down at the mess all over his boots. "Aw, crap. That one was yours." Stepping away, I give him a sympathetic smile. "Better hose that down. You don't wanna get ants."

I don't bother mentioning it was plain black coffee.

Without looking back, I make my way to the house, eyes scanning every inch. I pause at the front door to toe off my boots. They're basic—from a feed and hardware store I found in town, but they're already filthy and this house looks new.

Footsteps pound up the stairs behind me, and I hide my grin behind my hair.

"What the fuck was that for?" he barks, gesturing to his boots. They're the worn ones Abby suggested smell like poo, but all I smell is coffee. "Gonna take hours to get the stains out."

"Well, you're just a ray of sunshine today, aren't you?" I mutter, rolling my eyes. "And they're already stained. There's like five years of mud caked on them." Shooting him a fake grin, I bat my lashes. "If anything, I think I improved them."

He glares down at me, jaw ticking, shoulders heaving, and a shiver races across my spine at the sight.

Kade is taller than me, maybe by seven or eight inches. But with me in my socks and him in those slightly heeled boots and hat and anger—I feel downright tiny.

Hate how much I love it.

"Why are you here?"

I lick my lips, suddenly nervous, and glance away. "I told you. Your mom asked me to help her get ready for the Honey Bea Bash. I'm helping out here on the weekends."

He scoffs, crossing his arms.

"Look, I didn't know she'd have a booth at the farmers market," I hiss, narrowing my eyes. "What was I supposed to do? Tell your incredibly sweet mother *no* when she's telling me she's struggling to handle everything all by herself? That she's not as young and able-bodied as she used to be?"

Kade tenses. "She said that?"

I nod slowly and he rips off his hat to tug on his hair. A beat passes between us, and then he says, "Fine."

"Fine?"

"Fine," he echoes, petulant as hell. "Just stay out of my way."

"Oh, I plan on it." I huff, backing toward the front door. "I'll be out of your hair soon, and then you won't have to see me again."

Another step.

His brows lift. "Where the hell do you think you're goin', darlin'?"

Pretty sure he's just using the nickname because he knows it pisses me off. Unfortunately for the both of us, it's having the opposite effect on my system right now.

Brows tight, I gesture over my shoulder to the open front door. The sound of construction fills the air. I can hear men talking, but it sounds like they're outside. On the roof, maybe.

"I assume you brought me here because this place has a bathroom," I say, edging toward the door, bouncing on my toes a bit. "If not, the coffee on your boots will be the least of your worries."

There his jaw goes again—sliding back and forth like he's choking on an insult.

I give a fake pout.

He huffs, rolling his eyes skyward and bites out, "Fine."

"That your favorite word today, sunshine?" I murmur.

He snatches my coffee and storms past me, barking, "Let's go" over his shoulder.

"Hey!" I shout, tearing after him. "That's mine!"

"We made a deal, freckles. You owe me a coffee, and since you *tripped* and spilled mine, it's only fair, *again*," he says, moving across the plastic-covered foyer at a clipped pace—dirty boots and all.

Apparently, I don't need to be in just my socks, but I am, and unfortunately for everyone, they're unicorns flying on weed leaves from Abby.

They're also fuzzy.

I love them.

But the uncontrollable urge to rip them off and hide them in my bag gnaws at my brain while I follow him, eyes swinging in every direction.

"I never agreed to that deal," I murmur, taking in the open floor plan farmhouse with appreciation. "Both parties have to agree to something in order for it to be binding."

He scoffs and comes to a stop so abruptly, I slam into his back—face first. His addictingly masculine smell fills my senses just as I lose my footing, but I never hit the ground.

A big, calloused hand lands on my hip, wrapping around it like he has the right.

Stormy-gray eyes lock on mine, burning and unreadable, dragging me in and stalling time all at once. They flick to my lips, holding for a second too long. I stop breathing, heart hammering, and sway into him.

Is he going to kiss me? Do I want him to?

Yes? No? God, yes. I really do.

"Watch where you're going," he grits out, voice low and rough. "Christ, you're a walking hazard, aren't you?"

He drops his hands like I burned him, stepping back as if distance might undo the tension we just tied between us. The sudden shift has my mind spinning and irritation flaring.

"Have you ever stopped to consider that maybe I'm only a hazard when you're around?" I snap out. "Maybe if you'd stop freezing in the middle of walkways, I'd be able to avoid careening into your giant, stupid body!"

"Wasn't there when you drove into a fuckin' ditch," he mutters, bringing my coffee to his mouth so slowly, it borders on obscene. "That my fault, too?"

Before I can respond, his lips wrap around the lid—same place mine had not that long ago, and all I can think is, *I wonder if he can taste me.*

He tips his head back, throat working on a swallow, and then...

Gags, spraying the drink all over himself. I dodge out of the danger zone just in time, but it's too late for Kade—my coffee's already dripping through his beard and onto his gray shirt.

"What the fuck is that shit?" he snaps, wiping his face with the back of his hand. "That's fucking disgusting! How the hell can you even drink that?"

I laugh so hard, I snort and double over. The sound of him gagging and rinsing his mouth out in the kitchen has me wheezing for breath, but I freeze when I feel it.

"Oh, shit." Eyes wide, I meet his gaze across the open floor plan and drop my bag on the floor. "Seriously, Kade! Bathroom!?"

"First door on the left." His hand shoots out, pointing toward the opposite end of the room to a hallway. "Don't you dare piss on my new floors, woman! I don't have time to replace 'em."

I don't wait—half running, half peeling my hazardous socks off on the way. I can hear him muttering about me being a menace, and I toss my middle finger over my shoulder, making him mutter some more.

When I'm done, I wash my hands in the pretty bronze sink and force myself to breathe though the nerves buzzing through my system. Stepping back, I search for a towel, but there isn't one, so I dry my hands on my favorite jeans—a pair that make my ass look great but are broken in perfectly.

I check my reflection in the mirror, and quickly fix my hair. It's down today, my natural curls bright and bouncy under the pretty iron light fixture. My makeup is minimal since I'm supposed to be doing some form of labor or crafts today, and my shirt is a baggy green crop with a Dolly album cover in the middle.

My eyes flick to the closed bathroom door, and I hesitate, gnawing on my lip.

I'm not a model by any standard—my thighs and butt are thicker than my upper body, giving me a pear shape. My boobs are pretty small, and my hair is frizzy most of the time. But I love my freckles, and my eyes have always been my favorite feature, especially next to my red hair.

Yet I can't help wondering what Kade thinks.

Does he find me as attractive as I find him? Sometimes it feels like he's flirting with me. Other times, I'm pretty sure he hates my guts—or at the very least, finds me incredibly annoying. I swear I've caught him checking me out before—but maybe he looks at every woman that way.

Did he look at Marlee like that?

Groaning, I force the ugly thought away and open the door, leaving the beautiful, but simple guest bathroom behind me.

Kade's in the kitchen, back turned, phone pressed to his ear. I bite my lip and take in the house while he's distracted.

There aren't any furnishings yet, but the bones are incredible. It looks nearly done, like maybe he's just in the final stages of renovations or something. The kitchen's complete, and stocked with shiny stainless steel appliances that make my baker heart swoon. There's a giant range and two ovens that match a massive double door fridge I could fully stock with all my stuff and still never fill.

The walls may be white, but with the dark floors, dark bronze fixtures, and massive stone fireplace—it's warm and inviting, big enough to pack with all the friends and family a person could have.

I should leave. Grab my things and find Bea like I was supposed to half an hour ago. But if this is Kade's new place…

The house he moved into for Aurora…

I turn on my heel and quietly explore the other side of the house, peeking into rooms, closets, and cabinets like the nosey little mouse one of my old foster dads used to accuse me of being.

This wing has four bedrooms, but the one I'm standing in is clearly the largest. A wall of floor-to-ceiling windows wraps around the far side, with a sliding glass door at the center that opens to the back deck.

The view is stunning, just like the rest of them, but this room looks out onto the bigger house down the way that I assume belongs to Bea. It's lovely, weathered and worn in a way that screams of memories and *home*.

"That's the house I grew up in."

I jump, letting out an embarrassing squawk. My hip throbs in protest, and I wince.

Kade steps up to my side, brows drawn tight, eyes sliding over me in a way that makes me shiver. "You alright?"

Bobbing my head, I ignore his question and force my eyes away from the concern in his. Spinning around the room slowly, I murmur, "This is your house, isn't it?"

He doesn't respond for a long time, and when I finally look back at him, he's staring out the window, jaw tight, arms braced over his chest. I step up next to him and our arms brush, but neither of us backs away.

"I looked everywhere," he finally says, voice low and thick with something I can't place. "Wasn't a good house available in this whole fuckin' county?"

I scoff and nod. "Summit is seriously lacking in that area."

He glances down at me. "You lookin' for a place?"

"No," I say softly, then shrug. "I mean, I already have one. I sub-leased a little two-bedroom for the rest of the year; it's right off the highway. But I was still in New York when I signed the contract, sight unseen, and, well…" I trail off, huffing. "Let's just say I'll never make that mistake again."

"Off the highway?" His face scrunches. "There aren't any neighborhoods out there."

"I never said I was in one."

"Then where the fuck is your place?"

"Not that it's any of your concern, but my rental is in the country and overlooks a big field. The view's pretty, but the house leaves a lot to be desired." I smile a little and bump his arm. "Stop trying to change the subject."

Kade stares at me for a few more beats then looks away.

"This house has been on my family's property, sitting vacant and mostly built for years. I needed a place, and it was here, so…" He palms the back of his neck and points up to the roof where banging and shouts have become a constant echo in the background. "Couple of my buddies came into town, and we've been working on it nonstop to get it ready for the final inspection next week."

My heart soars at that. He really does want Aurora—he's working his ass off for her. Pride fills me so fast, the room practically spins.

"I know it's bare. It'll be tight, but I'll get it furnished in time. At least her room and mine. The living room, too." He glances at me, his expression so vulnerable, it hurts. "That's enough, right?"

My hand finds his, and I squeeze it, ignoring the sparks and tingles that fly through me at the tiny connection.

"Yeah," I breathe, chest hitching. "It's enough, Kade. Aurora will be very happy. You both will."

We stare at each other for a long, tense moment before I force myself to let go and look away.

"Well, it's really beautiful." My gaze moves to the hallway. "And big. How many bedrooms?"

"Six."

My brows jump. "Is this the primary?"

"Guest room," he murmurs, stepping toward the door where he pauses, watching me. "Four rooms on this side, mine and Aurora's are across from the family room."

My mind spins with the implications. Why would he need such a big place for just him and her? And she's so tiny. She doesn't need a house this big. Unless he's not single.

Oh my God.

Why didn't I ever ask if he was single?

He selected it on his intake paperwork, and said he'd be doing this alone, but that doesn't mean he's going to *stay* alone. And why would he? A guy like Kade Archer is destined for marriage and a happy future on this perfect farm next to an even more perfect wife.

"And the other three?" I ask, voice high-pitched. "You said there are six bedrooms. That's a lot." I bite my lip hard enough to draw blood. "Home gym?"

"Not really a treadmill kinda guy."

"Office, then?"

"I don't need an office anymore."

"Why not?" My nose wrinkles, mind flicking back to his tiny studio. "You have so many computers."

He lifts a thick shoulder. "I quit Iron Shield so I can be around for Aurora as much as possible. Gave my setup to a friend still in the field."

He. Quit. His. Job. For her.

Oh, shit. That news is excellent for him, for his case, and probably adoption—but so, *so* bad for my warring emotions.

"Do you have a girlfriend?" I blurt. My eyes go wide and I swallow hard. "I mean, or like a roommate or something."

"Girlfriend?" he drawls, brows climbing higher by the second. "Or a roommate..."

I jerk a nod and his lip curls in a smirk. "Why would you think I have either?"

"Your house," I say, voice bland, disinterested. "It's big."

"So I must have a woman who's gonna fill it with shit?"

I shrug, tracing a crease on the wall like I don't really care what his answer is. He pauses and I hold my breath.

Finally, he puts me out of my unexpected misery. "No, freckles. I don't have a woman, or a roommate, or anything of the sort. It'll just be me, that little girl, and my family when they inevitably show up."

"Then why did you pick a house with so many rooms?" I blurt again, then gnash my teeth together. What is wrong with me today?

His cheeks go a little pink, just enough to catch me off guard.

"You're blushing," I breathe, stepping closer. "Now you *have* to tell me."

He gives me a long look, something unreadable passing behind his eyes.

"Not sure you can handle the honest truth, darlin'."

The way he says it makes my blood heat in my veins—sticky and slow, like the very honey they farm here.

Unable to help myself, I murmur the first thing that comes to my mind, "You'd be surprised what I can handle, *sunshine*."

"That right?" He steps into me, leaving only a few inches of space between us.

I jerk a nod, doing my best not to combust on the spot.

"Oh, sweetheart," he murmurs, and leans in, close enough that the longer strands of his hair brush my cheek. I gasp. He makes this low, satisfied sound in the back of his throat, like he can feel what it does to me. "You really that desperate to know about what goes on in my bedrooms?"

"No," I rasp.

Yes, actually. Truly and honestly desperate.

"Liar," he mutters, gaze locked on mine. "If you're curious… all you gotta do is ask."

I scoff. "And you'd just tell me? Not that I want to know. Because I don't. *One*, that's gross—*ew*. And *two*, it's utterly unprofessional."

"You're not my social worker anymore." Kade tucks a strand of hair behind my ear and drops his voice to a low, seductive purr. "I can be as *unprofessional* with you as I want."

Oh my God.

What is happening right now?

I clench my thighs together, and my clit throbs in time with my heartbeat.

His tongue swipes over his thick lower lip, and my traitorous eyes zero in on the motion as my heart threatens to give out.

"I'll give you a little hint about the bedrooms."

"Okay," I choke out.

Kade dips closer, his cheek grazing mine. His beard scrapes my skin, and I swear to God my knees nearly buckle.

"But it's personal," he whispers. "Can you keep a secret, Georgia?"

Oh God. I can do anything you want. Just keep touching me.

"Yes," I breathe.

His breath fans down my throat, and I swear it leaves a trail of goosebumps in its wake.

"I have dreams," he murmurs, like it really is a secret, just for me. I soak up every word, an addict getting their fix. "Dreams I forgot for a long damn time. But lately, they've been coming back. Invading my head like a fucking plague I can't shake loose."

Oxygen ceases to exist.

"Dreams of having a big house filled with kids and laughter, messes and sticky fingers. Loud mornings with my family and quiet nights with my wife."

His voice cracks, and I feel that fracture in my soul.

"Quiet nights where I bury her face in the pillows and fuck her raw, long and hard, again and again, until she's sated, exhausted, and cum drunk, filled to the brim with me." His lip touches my ear, and I swear to fuck, the man might as well be fucking me just like his dream with how my body reacts. "And then do you know what I do?"

I shake my head, and swallow, but my mouth is dry, and I can barely breathe.

Kade tucks that strand back again, but leaves his hand braced on my jaw, tilting it up an inch. He inhales deeply and groans a quiet, desperate sound I feel all over.

"When I'm done, darlin', I start all over. Because in my dreams, my woman is just as fuckin' needy and desperate as I am."

My eyes snap open, and I whimper.

Holy shit, I fucking whimper, the sound desperate and raw.

He chuckles, leaning impossibly closer. We're touching nowhere else, just that tiny connection against the side of my face, his lips on my ear, hand on my jaw, beard burning through my brain cells, but it feels like he's *everywhere*.

"Because those rooms? They're meant for my kids. And I'll make damn sure every single one of them is filled someday."

And then... *he's gone.*

Chapter Eighteen

Grief Is a Hell of an Aphrodisiac

I SWAY FORWARD, GRABBING the doorframe at the last second to keep from stumbling.

While I'm still trying to steady my breath, Kade steps back and moves into the dim hallway. His body is rigid, cheeks flushed, and eyes suspiciously glossy.

If I didn't know any better, I'd say he's just as turned on as I am. But that can't be right. He just said all that to fuck with me. To make me feel stupid for prying.

He smiles and shoots me a wink, pointing to the hall behind him.

"You wanna see the whole house before my mom comes hunting for you, you better hurry up, Ms. Walker." His eyes slide down my body slowly before coming back up to my lips, where they stay. "Wouldn't want her to interrupt anything, would you?"

I'm so wet, I'm pretty sure there's a spot seeping through my jeans. And this man—this arrogant, asshole of a man—he's *unbothered*. Flirting and winking like this is normal, and not a complete mindfuck.

What is even happening right now?

Is this house some kind of aphrodisiac I'm unaware of?

I need to call Abby—*immediately*. Surely, there's something other-worldly going on. Maybe she did some sort of grumpy cowboy catnip spell or put pheromones in my luggage before I left.

"Holy shit," I choke out, shaking my head. "You… *that…*" My hands wave through the air, and I stomp past him, shoving him out of the way as I shout, "That was so, so completely inappropriate!"

And because I'm really fucking thrown, and confused, and *horny*, I shoot him a glare and add, "You're annoying, and I hate you."

He nods his head solemnly. "Right back at ya, darlin'."

I'm half-feral as I make my way through the last two rooms, the air thick and heavy with whatever the hell just happened back there.

One room is obviously the master—larger than the others, with perfectly placed beams in the arch overhead and uncovered floors beneath my bare feet. But it's the smaller room tucked just beside it with an adjoining door that makes me pause.

If even a single word of his unholy sex-monologue had a shred of truth to it, I assume it was built to be a nursery. And the fact that he said it's Aurora's room hits even harder, because out of all the rooms he could have picked, he put her right next to him, which is so perfectly sweet, my ovaries actually swoon.

Kade follows close behind, his presence brushing along my back like static. We reach the final room—an oversized bathroom attached to the master—and I stop dead in my tracks.

"This is beautiful," I choke out.

It looks nearly finished—a double vanity, beautiful mosaic tile floors in black, white and marble that match the rest of the room perfectly. There's a black arched window that's massive, overlooking the same field as the back of the house, but in here, it feels grander somehow, almost magical.

It's the kind of window you stare out of and *dream*.

I step forward, pointing at the wide, open space beneath it.

"You need to find the biggest soaker tub you can get your hands on," I demand as jealousy bubbles up my throat. "This window deserves to be stared out of."

He steps up beside me, close enough that the heat of him seeps into my skin, but he's careful not to touch me again.

I can't tell if I'm sad or happy about it.

"I know," he says quietly. "I designed the room around the view. It'll look out on the flower fields all summer and into fall."

I turn to him, eyes wide. "*You* designed this house?"

His expression tightens, mouth twitching like the question annoys him.

"Where'd you think it came from?"

"A designer?" I murmur. "A contractor your family hired. Isn't that what most people do?"

"Most people aren't Archers." He huffs, gaze flicking back to the window like it's safer than looking at me. "I assume you noticed the sign you drove under to get here."

"Of course I did," I hiss. "I'm not blind. I just figured this was an extra house on the property you claimed for the sake of the guardianship case."

Kade scoffs, tugging off his cap and running a hand through his messy hair. "You would think that, city girl."

"What the hell does that mean?"

He gives me a look like I've missed the punchline of a very obvious joke. I glare right back.

"There are no random buildings on an active ranch, darlin'. Every single one, every field, barn, and silo—they all serve a purpose. Those fences you drove by? They're not decoration. They keep cattle rotating through pasture so the land doesn't die. The trees along the ridge? They're a windbreak and shade for the livestock when we lease out the land. The flat patch near the creek is where we plant winter wheat. The low barn by the road is for sick animals, and the shed behind it stores our beekeeping gear. Without all that, this place wouldn't run half as well as it does."

I knew it, I think, almost dazed. *He's a cowboy. A real one.*

"But *you* built this *particular* house?"

"With my dad," he says, and his throat bobs with the words. "He helped all of us build our dream homes."

"That's incredibly sweet," I say, barely above a whisper, my eyes burning.

I glance out the window, my mind swimming with *what-ifs.*

What if my mom had stayed in her hometown and had me here, instead of alone in West Virginia? Would I have wound up with a kind, loving family like the Archers? Or with someone like that sweet man down at the farmers market?

Would my dad have shown up—swooped in to save me from a life of uncertainty, unanswered questions, and bone-deep loneliness?

And the hardest question, the impossible one that never ceases to plague me—*what if she never would have died at all?*

Would I have been happy here? Loved and adored. Would I have grown up surrounded by bees, and horses, and sun-drenched fields of wildflowers instead of packed bags, foster placements, and that cold, hollow ache I could never quite shake?

A long silence stretches between us, thick with things neither of us is brave enough to say, until he finally breaks it, taking my breath right along with him.

"I joined the Army before mine was done," he murmurs. "Always figured I'd finish it when I got out. But I was different. The war, shit that happened over there…"

He stiffens, and I get the sudden urge to hold his hand again, but I stop myself, not wanting to destroy this little corner of vulnerability we've carved out.

"It fucked me up," he continues. "Changed me. But the shit that happened back here while I was gone? It *destroyed* me. Didn't see much sense in building something meant for happiness and dreams when I was nothing but sand and ash by the time I came home."

He tugs on his hair again, jaw clenched as he finally looks at me. His eyes are hollowed, haunted, and the weight of that sadness nearly knocks me off my feet.

My mind flashes back to everything he told me in that courthouse. I'd been so irrationally angry at Marlee for what she did to him—for leaving him, for ending things while he was thousands of miles away, risking his life, planning their future, unsafe and alone.

She broke his heart, that was clear as day—written all over his face.

I'd be lying if I said a big part of me hasn't wondered if his commitment to all this—to Aurora and gaining custody, is because he still loves her.

The rational part of me says it doesn't matter what his motives or feelings for a dead woman are, but she was his first love, and judging by his story, Kade loved Marlee in a big, deep kind of way. A forever kind of way.

Does that feeling ever really leave you?

I know I still think about my first boyfriend, Stephen Tillby, every once and a while. I was nineteen, in my second year of college, and I think I loved him—as much as I've ever let myself love another person. Eventually, he ended things, said I never really opened myself up to him. Maybe he was right, or maybe we were just never meant to be.

Kade and Marlee, though…

That was a lifetime's worth of love cut too short in a letter while he was worlds away, and then again in a tragic accident.

He turns, facing me, and steps closer. "Tell me somethin'."

My throat tightens. "What?"

"Why's it easier to talk about this shit when you're around?" His eyes flit between mind, burning and glazed, like a storm raging and cresting, all at once. "It's been years, and I can't talk to anyone about… *before*."

"I don't know," I whisper, heart hammering wildly. My brain is begging me to run away while my body is screaming to close the distance between us.

"You know what I think?" he says, fingers brushing mine. "I think it's because you've seen wars, too. Might not have been as bloody as mine, but just as painful, just as destructive."

His eyes burn into mine, a storm of grief, heat, and history I'm desperate to know, but can't ask for, can't carry, when I'm not ready to give any of mine.

Too close. We're too close.

I suck in a breath and take a quick step back. My body immediately loathes the distance, and that right there, tells me all I need to know.

I'm not *just* proud of him for stepping up. I don't *just* find him attractive and annoying in the best way.

I like being around him.

I like sparring with him, flirting and arguing.

Worse—I like *him.*

He glares at me like he hates the distance just as much as I do. "What just happened?"

"What?" I clear my throat and force my face into the blank, expressionless mask I've worn for way longer than I've been a social worker. "Nothing."

It's easier this way.

I hike a thumb over my shoulder, letting cold condescension seep into my voice while actively ignoring the hurt, confused look on his too-handsome face.

"Anyway, you definitely need a good tub. Unless you *country boys* like to bathe in buckets."

With that, I brush past him, forcing my breaths into something easy and calm.

I need to get the hell out of here. I need to find Bea, tell her I'm sorry but I don't feel well, and I'll be back next weekend.

Better yet, maybe I'll tell her I can't do this at all. It's too much, too intense, and dangerous.

Heavy footsteps pound behind me, and I pick up my pace, searching for my bag as I tug my socks from my pocket.

"There you go again, freckles," he drawls, hot on my heels. "Asking about my habits. First it was me shirtless. Then my sleeping schedule. My mouth. The kinks I'm into. And now you wanna know how I bathe?"

He scoffs and I groan, rolling my eyes.

"If I didn't know any better," he adds, slow and smug, "I'd say you've got yourself a mighty fine list of all the things you're wonderin' about me."

A laugh bursts free, acidic and disbelieving, as I whirl on him, suddenly exhausted from all the whiplash.

He pushes, I pull. He goes too far, or sees too much, I shut down.

And then he's right back at it, and so am I.

Every single time.

"Don't flatter yourself," I snap. "You think just because you growl, smirk, and say *darlin'* in that fake-as-hell accent, every woman in town is wet for you?"

"I don't need to *think*," he fires back. "You admitted it yourself."

I press a hand to my chest and gasp, outraged. "I did not—"

"You did," he interrupts, stepping in.

"What are you talking about?" I whisper-hiss as his boots hit the tips of my toes. I glare up at him. "I didn't say a damn thing about that."

"No," he agrees. "But your body's screaming loud and clear. Has been since the second you got here today." His eyes trail down the length of me, stalling on Dolly—or what's beneath her. "It's still screamin', isn't it, darlin'?"

Between us, my nipples are sharp points, made more obvious by the heaving of my chest. As one, our gazes snag on them—and pause.

My throat bobs, and Kade groans, low in his throat.

"Say it," he demands roughly, and suddenly, I'm not so sure he's just goading me anymore. I think he really means to cross a line we can't come back from. "Say it and I'll show you just how fuckin' badly my body wants you right back—"

BANG.

"Georgia!" a sweet voice calls. "Are you here?"

We jolt apart.

"Fuck," Kade mutters, rolling his eyes Heavenward. "Seriously?"

I spin away from him and hustle down the hall, freezing when I spot Bea in the kitchen, hands full of reusable tote bags.

A massive body collides into my back with an irritated *oomph*. Hands land on my hips and squeeze. I wince, shifting my weight to accommodate my right hip. It's still sore as hell.

"Are you ok—"

"Kade?" Bea says sweetly, smile growing. "What are you doing here?"

"It's my house, Ma."

She laughs and goes back to unpacking her loot. "But what are you doing here with my Honey Bea Bash assistant? I need her, you know."

"Me too," he mutters, voice so low, I barely hear him.

I swallow hard, mind searching for an excuse but with his hands on my hips, body pressed into mine, the hard length of him digging into my back—my brain is suddenly mush.

"Everything alright?" Bea continues, clearly distracted. "I noticed the mud on your pretty car, sweetheart. A few scratches too. Something happen?"

"Bit of a mishap," I murmur. "But everything's fine."

"Got stuck in some mud. I towed her out," he adds, voice thick. "But she's got a flat. Told her to come here so I can fix it."

The fingers of his hand furthest from Bea's watchful gaze, rub in soothing, soft circles and I nearly groan, but then I blink, his words sinking in.

Shit. I forgot about my tire.

"Glad everything worked out." Her gaze collides with where we're hovering like freaks in the hall, and they slide down my body, landing on his hands on my hips. Her eyes flare, and I go to step away, but he holds me in place.

Before I can elbow him and run away, she smiles and glances up at him. "I brought you boys lunch for this afternoon. Wilder asked for my pot roast, but I added some pasta just in case you're still hungry."

Bea turns to the fridge and busies herself putting things away, but I'm rooted to the spot, heart in my throat, belly swooping and soaring.

Kade taps my hip and leans down to whisper, "I'm not done with you yet, freckles, so don't you dare go gettin' any wild ideas like running for the hills. Got it?"

I squeeze my eyes shut, barely resisting the urge to lean into his intoxicating touch.

"We can't do this," I say on a shaky breath.

"Says who?" he asks, just as quietly, burying the words in my hair. "I told you before, when I want something, I don't stop till it's mine."

My heart threatens to explode from my chest. Is it possible he actually *feels* what *I feel?*

Does Kade Archer like *me* the way I like *him*?

His free hand slides down my back, keeping his movements slow and hidden in the shadows of the hall. He squeezes my ass and my eyes snap open, staring at his *mother's* back as she hums a tune and straightens up, completely oblivious to her inappropriate son a few feet away.

I press back into him, drunk and delirious on his touch—at the forbiddenness of the moment, the risk of getting caught.

"And what is it you want?" I whisper, throat tight, smile lifting.

He brushes his lips over my ear and grips my ass tighter, fingertips ghosting the wetness between my thighs. "*This*."

With that, he lets go and steps around me, leaving my body hot and cold all over.

I watch in a daze as he kisses his moms cheek, murmuring a quiet *thank you* like he wasn't just two seconds from discovering how soaked he made me.

"*This*," he'd said. Not *you*.

He wants to fuck me. That's it. He's attracted to me, annoyed by me, hates me, and wants to *fuck me*.

Kade doesn't like me. He doesn't have *feelings* like I do.

He has a hard dick, and I'm...

Here.

Flirting with him, letting him touch me, tease me, turn me on. I'm just convenient, a distraction from the woman's ghost his life is now inundated with.

Suddenly, I feel dirty, just like after the *yoga tutorial that shall not be named*. I feel like I need a shower, a pint of ice cream I can't have, a good cry, and to puke, maybe all at the same time.

His hand wraps around my keys a second before the door slams open for the second time.

"What the fuck?" he barks, shooting daggers at the twins as they barrel toward us. "You're gonna dent the wall!"

"Georgia!" Colby says, grinning from ear to ear, clearly ignoring her brother. "Guess what!"

"We're going mudding!" Clem answers, clapping excitedly. She flicks her gaze to her mom. "Wanna come, Mom?"

She waves them away, smiling indulgently. "No, no, you go on ahead. Have a good time. Weather's perfect for it. Just make sure you wrap up the horses well and give them the full spa treatment afterward."

"Of course," Clem says, bouncing on her toes. She grabs my hand, dragging me toward the door. "You're going to have the best time!"

My mouth opens and closes, heart racing, stomach flipping. Mudding? Like with horses? I haven't done that in years. But while the idea sounds exciting, and appealing, that's not what I'm here for.

I'm not here for any of this.

Throat bobbing, I tug my hand free and force myself to look away from Kade's intense gaze, finding Bea across the room.

"I'm so sorry, girls, but I'm here to help your mom with the Honey Bea Bash. I can't—"

"Oh, don't worry about it, dear," Bea says, stashing her empty bags in a cupboard. "You go have fun. We'll worry about the event next weekend when you come over."

"See!" the girls cheer, snatching my hand back up. "Mom says you're off the hook. Let's go."

"Guys," Kade says slowly, and I look up just in time to see his jaw clench. "Don't know if that's the best idea."

They freeze and Colby slams her hands to her hips, glaring up at him. "Why the heck not?"

He stares at me for a long moment, but doesn't say anything.

And it's the silence that grates on my nerves the most. All afternoon, he hasn't shut up. Hasn't stopped making promises that sound like threats, opening up and battering against my walls like he has any right to.

And the touching… God, the *touching*.

With a few simple words, his eyes on my lips, hands on my body—he unraveled me in a way no one else has. Had my hopes high, and my lust higher.

Now that we're not alone, not that his family is here, he's quiet, refusing to speak, to lay his so-called *wants* out on the table between us.

Maybe that's why I smile at his sisters and nod, giving him my back entirely.

"Actually, mudding sounds perfect. Let's go."

Chapter Nineteen

Eat the Food

"This is a bad fucking idea," I mutter, tugging the cinch strap snug around Dusty's torso. The old boy flicks an ear back at me, more annoyed by my nerves than the pressure. "Really bad."

Griff chuckles behind me, his arms hooked over the stall door like he's got nowhere better to be. "Wilder'll be fine," he says, eyes tracking the scene across the barn. "And if he falls, he'll land in mud. How bad can it be?"

I scoff and toss him a glare while checking the girth again. "When's the last time you got trampled by a thousand-pound horse, Sarge? And for the record, it's not him I'm worried about."

My gaze finds Georgia immediately—jeans tucked into her boots, a Carhartt she borrowed from one of my sister's zipped to her chin, cheeks pink from the cold.

She's standing with Wiki—a new stable boy I just met—Wilder, and a ranch hand named Emmy—one of Hazel's old classmates, who can't stop staring at Wilder.

And Wilder? He's ready to mount Emmy, not his fuckin' horse.

At some point, Georgia tamed her wild curls into a messy braid that drapes down her back, swishing against the curve of her round ass with every laugh and nod.

My cock throbs at that curve, at the thought of wrapping that damn braid around my fist while I fuck her from behind.

I tip my hat up and run a hand down my face. I'm losing my mind.

Griff nudges a boot through a patch of straw. "You've been starin' at her for ten minutes, man."

"I'm not staring."

"Brooding, then."

"I don't brood. I'm supervising."

Wiki touches her arm, and my jaw pulses erratically. Kid may be young and dumb, but that doesn't mean I can't fire him.

"She's not learning a damn thing right now except how to get dead."

"Then why the hell aren't you the one over there showin' her?" he barks, brows furrowed. "You know a fuck of a lot more than that pimply-faced tween."

My throat constricts, keeping the words I want to say trapped.

Because if I go over there, I'm gonna put my hands on that woman. If I go over there, I'm gonna see her freckles and smile and sniff her perfume, and then I'm probably gonna kiss her, like I almost did back in my house.

What started off as an easy way to make her blush, to see that little line pulse between her eyes, and her tiny fists clench like she wants to choke me—became so much more, and way too much, all at once.

Worst of all is that what I said? It was the truth.

Wilder may have been fucking with me the other day saying I have a breeding kink, but fuck, maybe I do. The idea of a bunch of kids is one thing. Having them, loving them—I want that more than anything. Always have.

But the idea of making 'em?

What's worse is that Georgia didn't seem all that taken aback or opposed, and that thought is what's wrecking me the most.

I grab the bridle, and Dusty lowers his head so I can guide the bit past his teeth. I buckle the throat latch and rest a hand on his warm neck, letting my fingers press into the familiar muscle.

It's been over two years since I rode a horse—which is two years too damn long.

It feels good to be back in the barn my grandpa built. It's all rough wood and wide beams, but solid. Not quite as big as the newer barn a ways down the walk, but it's warm, clean, and smells like hay, cedar shavings, and petrichor.

The animals here are family. And Archers don't let family get hurt.

Satisfied with Dusty's tack, I snag my Stetson from the corner post and tug it down.

"You like her," Griff murmurs. I say nothing and he huffs. "Sure that's smart?"

"I can't stand her," I say roughly. "So smarts got nothing to do with it. I've got a week left to get shit sorted for Aurora." My throat constricts. "Sure as hell don't have time fuck around like this."

I'd been prepared to turn my sisters down. I have a list a mile long and enough stress to send me into a cardiac. But the second Georgia said she was down to go mudding with the crazy-ass ranch hands who have about as much self-preservation as my mom's suicidal puppy, I knew I couldn't stay back. Had to watch out for her.

"You can leave," he challenges, like he already knows what I'm thinking.

"Yeah," I grunt, shooting him a look. "Pretty sure I won't get custody if a social worker dies on my watch."

He chuckles, shaking his head and gestures to the pasture. "And I'm sure there are about fifteen cowboys out there that'll be more than happy to keep your pretty little Georgia safe."

"She ain't mine," I mutter, stomach souring. "And not a single one of those dicks will get near her."

Griff barks out a laugh. "Ain't yours, my ass."

Shoving down the strange twist in my chest his words cause is harder than it should be.

I glance up just as Wiki finishes inspecting the tack on Georgia's horse—a sweet mare named Pudding. He gestures to the stirrup, and I already know he's telling her to mount.

But even from ten feet away, I can see the cinch strap's hanging loose—low enough she'll slide sideways the second she tries to mount. And if that weren't enough, the fucking bit's not even buckled right.

My blood boils.

I charge across the barn, boots pounding the ground loud enough to make a few heads turn. "Don't you fucking dare, freckles!"

She freezes. Wiki freezes. All the horses in the stalls freeze. Wilder and Emmy? Oblivious. Probably about three giggles and an innuendo away from raw-dogging it in the tack room.

Georgia's mouth drops, arms snapping across her chest. "The hell is wrong with you?"

I don't answer. Just slow my pace as I near Pudding, keeping my voice low and hands steady so I don't spook her.

"Get out," I growl at Wiki, nudging him back.

"Wh-what?" he stammers, his straw hat flopping sideways as he stares at me, wide-eyed. "I—" His throat bobs, and he flicks his gaze to Georgia, giving her a look like she can save him.

Acid swims in my sternum, and my fists clench.

Eyes narrowed, I slide my attention down to his goddamn *tennis shoes* and jab a finger at them. "Get some real boots, kid. You're gonna lose a fuckin' toe. Don't come back till you have 'em."

"Kade!" Georgia gasps, stepping in like she's forgotten every single thing I've said today. All the ways we got too close. The feel of my hands on her hips.

She leans enough for her breath to graze my jaw. "Not everyone has money for fancy boots. And Wiki is nice. Don't yell at him."

Her shoulder brushes mine and my entire body lights up like a fucking livewire. And because I'm a masochistic fool, I inhale.

Jesus. Mary. And Joseph.

This woman's scent should be illegal.

My eyes cut to hers, and I'm seriously scrambling for composure here, so I say the first thing that comes to mind.

And because I'm slightly neurotic, and too-damn turned on, definitely losing blood flow to my head—I shout it in her gorgeous face. "Why are you telling me what to fuckin' do?"

Doesn't even bat an eye. She simply shrugs "Because someone needs to."

That mouth twitches. Then she bites her lip.

My cock punches my goddamn zipper.

"I'm sorry. I won't do it again."

There's not a lick of her that's sorry, but when she bites her lip and stares up at me with those big green eyes, I find I don't really give a fuck.

"I didn't say stop, darlin'," I murmur, voice low and rough. "But you should know—I'm piss poor at takin' orders."

"Ain't that the fuckin' truth," Griff hollers, stomping up with Dusty's reins in one hand and a grin on his face. "I'm takin' him out to warm him up."

"NO! You'll break the poor bastard's back!" Wilder cries, throwing himself onto his mare's back—a new one I haven't met yet.

Everyone gasps, and I prepare to grab Georgia and haul her to safety if Wilder sets off a chain reaction. The mare rears slightly, but he coos and pats her neck, and to everyone's shock, she settles.

"Oh wow," Emmy says, eyes wide and practically swooning. "You're a natural."

Griff scoffs. "Or he's just full of shit. Asshole spent three summers ridin' with me in Tennessee."

Emmy's head snaps to Wilder. "You said you'd never ridden before!"

His cheeks go pink, but the dick just winks.

"No, baby girl. I said I've never ridden *you*." He clicks his tongue and guides the mare down the barn aisle like he was born in a saddle. "But I've got a feeling that's about to change."

Emmy squeals and climbs on her own horse, galloping after him. Wiki chases her. And just like that, I'm left standing in the middle of the barn…

Alone with Georgia Walker.

Exactly where we shouldn't be.

"So," she drawls, rocking back on her boots, brows high. "Was there a reason you barreled over here like a—"

"Rabid hyena?" I mutter.

A beat, and then a giggle bursts from her ruby-stained lips. A smile sneaks up on me at the light sound, but I shake my head, sighing. My hands slip into the deep pockets of my jacket, and I pull out an apple, banana, and a bag of almonds.

My big hands hold the loot between us like an offering, and I look away, jaw ticking.

"What's this?" she asks. "For the horse? Wiki said she just had—"

"No," I grunt, digging a few pills from the pocket of my jeans. "You need to take somethin' for that hip before you ride. Looked up what's safe for your stomach. Internet said acetaminophen, but not to take it on an empty stomach."

I didn't miss the way she limped around my house, or every flinch and twinge from her hip. Must have hurt it slamming the breaks when she went in the ditch. I make a mental note to teach her how to safely coast when caught in the mud.

The I ask myself when the fuck I started caring enough to do something like that.

"Wh-what?" She looks shocked, a little confused, and maybe like she might cry. "Where did you…when…"

"It's not a big deal," I grumble, thrusting them at her. "I ran by the Big House on my way here."

"Kade…"

"It's a snack, not a million dollar condo!" I bark, cheeks burning red-hot. "Eat the fuckin' food, or I'll give it to the horse."

When she still doesn't take a single thing, I step into her, shoving each item into her pockets.

She sucks in a breath, staring up at me, all wide eyes and thrumming pulse. Her breaths puff against my jaw, and I can see a slight tremble in her frame. I'm half worried I might kiss her into submission, but a bigger part of me's worried she's going to pass out, or fuck, fall off the horse from the pain.

Gripping her chin, I drag our faces closer and pinch tight enough to make sure she's listening.

"You may hate my guts, Georgia Walker, but I'll be damned if I watch you slide off one of my fuckin' horses because you're too stubborn, or self-conscious to eat in front of me." I swallow hard, eyes flicking between hers. "Don't know when it happened, but I care about you and your wellbeing. Take care of yourself, I'll be forced to do it for you. Got me?"

"Okay," she finally breathes, nodding once. "I got you."

My fingers hover a beat longer than necessary and her eyes drop to my mouth where they linger.

Then her stomach growls like it's begging for what I'm offering, and like the caveman I am, I growl right back, releasing her.

"Eat," I snap, pointing at her pocket. "You don't like any of that, we'll leave and I'll take you to a diner. But you're eating."

She bobs her head and pulls the banana from her pocket in a daze.

I wait until she's eating to gesture to the cinch. "It's loose. You'd have slid right off the second your weight hit the stirrup."

Georgia hums around the fruit, watching me tighten it, and I do everything I can not to fixate on the sight of her lips and mouth stuffed full of a phallic-shaped item.

Clearing my throat, I check, and double-check, the saddle, blanket, and girth, giving each strap a firm tug before moving to the horse's legs. Just as I look away, I hear the plastic open and I know she's eating the almonds.

A smile tugs at my lips, but I hide it behind my lapel.

"She's wearing boots?"

"Wiki said she overreaches sometimes."

My eyes snap to hers, and she gives me a soft, knowing smile, meadow eyes bursting with hidden laughter. Squinting, I slowly push to my feet, knees cracking, thigh protesting like hell.

"What else did Wiki say?" I murmur, suspicion ghosting across my neck.

She taps a finger to her lips and makes this cute little sound I quickly memorize. Her free hand smooths down Pudding's dappled coat with so much love and appreciation, the horse's eyes fall closed.

"Well," she breathes, moving in a circle. I notice how she's careful not to get too close to Pudding's hind legs, like she already knows she could get killed by a back hoof alone. "He said she seems a little cooped up. Restless, like she hasn't been properly exercised in a few days."

"No way Wiki knew a fucking thing about that." I shake my head slowly, confused as fuck, but intrigued, too. *So damn intrigued.*

She smirks, lifting a delicate shoulder as she pockets the bag. "Maybe you're underestimating him. He's smart."

"He's young and dumb." I scowl.

"He's eighteen," she says softly, stopping at Pudding's head. Her fingers move, slow and deliberate, tracing beneath the mare's eyes. "And he may not be the best, but he's learning. He needs this job. Be kind to him."

I wanna tell her to stop bossing me around, but I like it too much to open my mouth. Not only that, but I'm transfixed by the way Georgia keeps her gaze locked on Pudding's, the horse staring right back, like they're exchanging silent words—some kind of instant connection between them.

And suddenly, I'm jealous of a fuckin' horse.

"You talked to Wiki for less than an hour. How'd you find out enough to vouch for him?"

"Wiki talked, and I listened." Georgia shifts slightly, adjusting Pudding's bridle like it's second nature, then runs her thumb along the bit. Her brows dip. "This wasn't seated properly. Was probably pinching."

She fixes it in a single, smooth motion and Pudding immediately huffs out a long breath, eyes going half-lidded.

And just like that, *I know.*

She's done this before. Not once. Not in some rich girl, summer camp way. This is instinct. Muscle memory.

"Where'd you learn that?" I ask, but it's not casual. It's gravel and curiosity and way too fucking intense.

"Must've picked it up from Wiki."

She smirks, mounting Pudding in one perfect, quick motion, and my heart leaps just as my dick rises.

The horse toes at the straw, prancing sideways for a beat, but Georgia doesn't even blink, just soothes her, cooing quietly. And then she's at my side, bending down and brushing something from my shoulder.

"Bit a hay," she murmurs, shooting me a wink. "Try to keep up, sunshine."

A blink later, my hat is on her head and she's racing off into the goddamn metaphorical sunshine, leaving me in the dust.

Fucking hell.

She's not just beautiful, she's dangerous.
And I'm so screwed.

Chapter Twenty

Mudding Ain't For the Weak and Willful

Mudding sounds reckless, but it's not.

It's an easy ride through the back pasture after a good rain. No race. No rules. Just a bunch of horses kicking up mud like overgrown dogs. We only take the ones who love it. The ones that damn near vibrate when the gates swing open.

We don't push them. They move if they want. Stop when they're done. Then it's baths, brushed coats, clean hooves, and peppermints for good measure. Out here, horses carry our weight, our gear, and sometimes our goddamn grief.

There's nothing like being back in Dusty's saddle, the scent of Honey Bea and worn leather burning through my senses, my family and friend's laughing and playing in the distance.

But watching Georgia Walker out here on the back of an Archer horse, braid flying, cheeks flushed, laughing and riding through the mud like an honest to God cowgirl with *my* Stetson on her head…

Now that's a fucking religious experience.

"I'm so confused," Hazy says, shooting me a look as she circles her Appaloosa, Orion, around me. "Thought you said your social worker was from New York."

"*I* didn't say shit. Mom did," I mutter, guiding Dusty toward the group. "And she's not my social worker anymore."

Pudding is prancing through the puddles with Colby and Clem's horses at her side. The three girls are laughing, shrieking when the mud splashes too high, daring each other to race through the deepest ruts.

Georgia leans forward in the saddle, easy and loose, guiding Pudding like she was born to do it. Her braid snaps behind her in the wind, cheeks flushed, mouth open in a wild, unfiltered laugh that hits me straight in the fucking chest.

Colby lets out a whoop and kicks her horse into a canter, slicing through the mud, sending a wave of it toward Clem, who shrieks and tries to block it with her arm.

Georgia spins Pudding to the side just in time to avoid the splash, then looks over her shoulder and tips my hat at them like she's a proper cowboy.

Dusty shifts under me, picking up on the energy, ears flicking as the other horses play.

He wants to join, and surprisingly, so do I.

Three young women I don't recognize run through the muddy grass, laughing and covered in filth—shorts too short, shirts too see-through. Nevan and Vander—brothers, and ranch hands—are off their horses in a flash, chasing after them, hats high, laughter higher.

Vander's horse doesn't miss a beat of freedom. He drops to his knees and rolls right in a shallow mud puddle, legs flailing in the air, saddle and gear be damned.

"You're cleaning that mess up, Van!" Hazel shouts, huffing like mud is beneath her. "And make sure you check his shoes!"

Vander tips his hat at her. "Of course, ma'am!"

"Ma'am." Hazy shudders. "Gross."

Georgia's eyes find mine across the short distance, and I'm shocked when she smiles at me and gives me this small, awkward but adorable wave before quickly turning back to the twins.

"She fits in well here," Hazel says quietly, pulling Orion up to my side. Her head turns, gaze off in the distance, where a few of the older ranchers are watching from a small hill, hats pulled low, mustaches even lower. "She looks happy."

There's a pained, longing note to her voice that pulls words from my chest I'm not quite ready for, but force out anyway. "I'm sorry, Hazy."

Her throat bobs and she glances at me. "For what?"

"Leaving. Staying gone," I say roughly with an awkward shrug, my eyes going straight back to Georgia.

For some reason, it's easier to say the hard parts when she's near, even if she's not the one I'm telling.

"Yeah, well, you're back now." She gives me a look that's all acid and threats. "Right?"

I jerk a nod. "Aurora's gonna need a community, and I'll need help."

What I don't tell her is that I've missed home—missed her, Mom, and the twins. The flowers, animals, and bees. I don't tell her my feet have missed standing on Archer soil, or that my hands are desperate for a hard day's worth of labor.

And I don't tell her that, whether I get Aurora or not, there's no place I'd rather restart my life than here.

She scoffs. "Nice."

My fingers tighten on the reins, smooth leather brushing my callouses. "What?"

"Nothing."

"Tell me."

"You don't wanna know what's on my mind right now, big brother, because it sure as fuck ain't sweet."

"Come on, Hazel," I say with a grunt, shoving her a bit. "You've never held back the truth from me before. Don't start walking on eggshells now."

She stares at me for a long moment, her body swaying with the heavy steps of Orion walking through thick mud.

I try to smile, try to reassure her I can take it, but honestly, I'm not sure. Hazel Archer has a sharp tongue and a deadly honest streak. She tells it how she sees it and never pulls punches. And I've got a decade worth of anger coming for me.

"Fine," she snaps. "You talk about family, but your family has needed you for years. I've called you, practically begged you to come help ever since Dad passed. You lost him, but so did we." Her chin drops to her chest, shoulders lifting on a deep breath. "I think what you're doing for that little girl is amazing, but I hate that Marlee dying is what's finally dragging you back here."

"It's not about Marlee—" I start, but she cuts me off.

"No, maybe not *her*, but in a way she's responsible, and I hate that. She pushed you to join the fucking Army in the first place. Wanted you to make money to build her dream life, and then when you were almost done, after you'd mailed her all your checks, she dropped your ass and moved on."

Heart racing, gut protesting, I choke on her words and try to breathe through the burn, but she doesn't stop—pushing on, determined to knock me off my own horse with the truth.

"She was a user, Kade. She used you and our family all throughout high school so she could get a sense of normalcy, and I felt bad for the girl, I really fucking did, but God, Kade, she hated the farm. Hated the country and all things Heart Springs, and you have country in your veins. That was never going to be fair to you."

She swallows hard, and so do I.

"She broke up with you in the worst way possible, while you were in a dangerous place, and without your family. And because of that, we lost you for a long damn time." Hazel sucks in a sharp breath. "I'm sorry Marlee died. But I'm not sorry that you're back. I just don't understand how, even from the grave, she's still found a way to leave you worse off than when she found you."

My mouth is dry, heart lodged in my fucking lungs, and while her words are built on truth and painful reality, there's something she said that rubs against my soul.

"You ain't wrong about Marlee," I admit, running my fingers through my hair. "It took a few years in the desert to work it out, but eventually, I saw it for what it was."

I think Marlee May loved me the best she could, and for a while, we *were* best friends dreaming up a future. But she always wanted out, she never kept that a secret.

Guess I always just hoped I could change her mind.

Maybe if the house was nice, the land was pretty, and the dreams were big, she'd find a way to share them with me—*for me*.

"Her decision to leave her child to me is mind-boggling, I know that. I still haven't wrapped my brain around it." I think back to the first day I met Aurora, the feeling of her in my arms while she babbled up at me—it was unlike anything else. "But having Aurora in my life, as my…"

I exhale and look her in the eyes.

"Hazy, having that sweet girl as my daughter, blood or not—it's not a fuckin' mistake and there's no way in hell it's leaving me worse off. That baby's not even mine yet, and she's already saving me."

Hazel hums, but doesn't say anything, just falls into step next to me. She's not one for extra words, or some grand declaration. I can count the times she's apologized to anyone on both hands, and the times she's cried on one.

Maybe that's why we've always gotten along so well. We both love the quiet—and hate talking shit out even more.

Allergic to emotions, she used to call it.

I guess things haven't changed all that much.

"What's been going on here?" I ask, eyes sliding across the ranch. "You said Honey Bea is failing."

It doesn't look all that different, and in the month or so since I've been home, it doesn't seem to be falling apart. I have noticed that they're a bit late with planting the late spring flowers, but that's not abnormal.

Walked the property a few times took my truck out even more. Equipment's in good shape, buildings are a bit worse for wear, but they're old.

Haven't talked to my mom about it yet, but we've all had shit going on, and for some reason, it hasn't felt like my place to pry. Like I lost that right when I walked away.

Hazel sighs, jaw ticking as she stares off into the distance. "Cooper Ridge happened."

My brows furrow. "Who?"

She scoffs, the sound so acidic, it hits me in the gut. "God, you really are disconnected from home."

"That's why I'm asking!" I snap, fingers tightening on the reins. "I'm trying, Hazel. I know I fucked up. Know I left you all in the lurch, but I'm here now. You gotta let me in if you want my help."

My sister's silent for a long time, and when she finally speaks, it's like the words are being dragged right from her soul. They're thick and heavy with a weight she never should have had to carry on her own.

"Cooper Ridge is a massive ranching operation," she says bitterly. "Moved into Summit County a year ago—big money, corporate backing, shiny equipment, paid help, and zero connection to this land."

She shakes her head, jaw clenched tight.

"They've been slowly edging in on everything we do—wheat, honey, flowers, grazing land, even the fucking farmers market. Offering bulk for cheaper, paying off distributors, undercutting everyone around them until we're the ones left scrambling to stay afloat."

My gut tightens. "They're trying to run us out."

"They're trying to *buy* us out," she mutters. "They already took three properties on the east side. And if Mom hadn't refused to sell last year, they'd probably be building a fence through our fields right now."

I glance toward the outer edges of the property, toward the place where the wheat should already be sprouting and the wildflowers should be blooming.

Cooper Ridge isn't just competition.

They're a slow-moving storm—and they're coming for everything.

"Damn, Kade, your girl's reckless!" Wilder shouts, jolting me, as he races past, heading into the fray.

"Let's go, Archer," Emmy calls, jerking her chin—and a smile—at Hazel as she hurries her horse after him. "Your clothes are way too clean!"

Hazy laughs, rolling her eyes, but I can tell it's forced. "You say that like you know a damn thing about coyboyin', Emmaline!"

She turns and gives me a long look, reaching over to squeeze my hand around the reins.

"I'm proud of you, Kade, and I'm really happy you're back." She jerks her chin at Georgia, who's off on her own now, watching me with a worried look on her pretty face. "You deserve some happy, too."

I swallow thickly, gripping her hand right back. "And when are you gonna get happy, Hazy Ruth?"

Something passes behind her eyes, gaze going back to that ridge of cowboys, except now it's empty.

"I'll find it someday." She flashes me a fake smirk and releases me, backing Orion toward the group. "Maybe when you're covered in mud and horse shit."

Scoffing, I cluck my tongue and tap my heel into Dusty's side. "Let's go, man. We've got mud to sling."

Dusty takes off like a shot, passing Orion and Hazy in a blink, like he's been waiting for the chance to show off. Neck back, teeth out, he hits the puddles, body skidding sideways a few feet. My heart thuds, a grin splitting my face as adrenaline courses through me.

I let him prance and kick the mess, coating his lower half in cold, refreshing mud and water, but the second his zoomies slow down a bit, I'm guiding him toward Georgia, unable to stay away a second longer.

Her eyes hold mine, and I dig in my heel, hands loose on the reins. She shoots me a little smirk and runs her finger over the brim of my hat—her *middle* finger.

My head falls back with a laugh that feels too damn good to stop.

The conversation with Hazel is still heavy in my gut, but the words I spoke are just as fresh. I meant what I said. Might not know Aurora very well yet, but in ways I can't quite figure out, she's mine.

"Took you long enough," Georgia says quietly, shifting on her saddle.

I slide my gaze over her legs, noting her form and posture, making sure she's not stretching too far to reach the stirrups.

She looks good.

Perfect, actually.

"How the hell can a city girl like you ride a horse this damn good, darlin'?"

She smirks, eyes gleaming. "I have secrets, and you haven't earned them yet, clearly."

"Why don't you tell me how to earn 'em, and I'll start right now."

"Oh, I've got a few ideas," she purrs, shoulder tipping, taking my stomach right along with it. "But unfortunately, they're also secrets."

"Seriously, freckles?" My mouth falls open, hand pressed to my chest in mock-horror. "You wound me."

"I think you're too full of yourself to possibly get wounded by words."

I waggle my brows. "You could be full of me too if you play your cards right."

Her head falls back with a sweet giggle that shakes her whole body.

That laugh—God, that laugh.

It's sunshine and honey, wild and unfiltered.

"You're a shameless flirt, Mr. Archer." She clicks her tongue, and shakes her head. "It's annoying."

Flirt? Is that what I'm doing? Fuck. Can't remember the last time I flirted with a woman—put in any real energy at all to get their attention. But it comes easy with Georgia.

And it's fun.

Being around her is *fun*.

When's the last time I had any fun?

"I think it's time you stop pretending to find me annoying," I drawl, pulling Dusty up to Pudding's side so we're next to each other.

"Between your over the top sexual innuendos and inappropriate touching, I assure you, I'm not pretending."

"Please," I mutter, rolling my eyes skyward, a smile tugging at my lips. "You loved the touching."

"Did not."

"And you *really* love my innuendos."

"I had no idea you had such good humor hiding under your rabid hyena tendencies."

"I'm charming as fuck, and you can't prove otherwise."

"Says the man who fired a young kid for wearing the wrong shoes."

My right eye twitches as I choke back the honest reason I sent Wiki packing. Somehow I feel, *because he touched you,* won't win me any points.

Instead I go with, "Or it's because he almost got you fuckin' killed."

"Except, I know more about horses than him, and I was never getting in that saddle!" she hisses.

"How was I supposed to know that?" I bark. "I hardly know you!"

"Exactly!" She stares at me, eyes sharp and dancing with waves of angry greens before her shoulders fall with a sigh and she drops her voice. "We hardly know each other, Kade. I started as your social worker, then I was nothing, and now, I'm caught somewhere in the middle, stuck between enemy and stranger."

I cock a brow. "Pretty sure most people call that a friend."

Her throat bobs, eyes flicking between mine. "That what I am to you, *sunshine*? A friend?"

Hell no, is the immediate response I want to shout, but I choke it back. Pretty sure she'd take it the wrong way. And I like the sound of that annoying nickname too much to piss her off right now.

Exhaling, I shake my head, and tug on my hair. "My point is, darlin', you wanna be somethin' other than whatever we are, you're gonna need to know me."

I gesture at the chaos around us.

"You wanna know what I'm all about? It's this. The land, the work, these people." My hand grazes Dusty's side, my throat catching at the truth of it. "These animals. The crops and very foundation Honey Bea was built on. That's me."

"Really? I thought you were a ten-by-ten box filled with dirty laundry, beer cans, and a bad personality," she says, deadpan.

"Maybe I was all that. Maybe I'm still dragging myself out of the pit you found me in." Jaw ticking, I glance away, unable to hold her gaze. "But I am tryin'."

Time stretches in tense, raw silence that grates on my nerves, but when her hand lands on my arm, squeezing softly, it stalls altogether.

"I know you are," she says softly. "I haven't known you long, but I see it. You *are* trying for Aurora, and…" Georgia breaks off, and I finally drag my eyes back to hers. "It might not mean much, but I'm proud of the changes you're making. Aurora will be lucky to have you as her dad."

My hand grips hers, mouth falling open, brain stuck on the word *will*.

That mean she thinks this'll all work out?

"Freckles—"

A loud curse cuts through the air. Our heads jolt to the sound just as Wilder sails off his horse, landing ass-first in a deep patch of mud.

Everyone gasps.

The laughter stops.

"Shit," I snap, already vaulting off Dusty. "I knew you'd be the one to get fuckin' hurt!"

He groans, head tipped high to the sky. Behind me, I can hear horses racing toward us, probably Hazy, or one of the hands, off to get Frank, the vet who volunteers here.

I skid to a stop, mud coating my calves and boots, and drop to a knee at his side. My thigh protests, but I barely feel it, heart ricocheting chaotically against my sternum.

"Wilder?" I call, scanning his body for obvious injuries. "Man, talk to me."

Nothing.

"Oh my God," a woman cries, probably Emmy or one of the randoms. "Is he dead?"

"No!" Hazel shouts, pausing before muttering, "Fuck, is he dead? God, this is going to be all over town."

"Swear to fuck," I choke out. "If you survived the goddamned war and got yourself killed by wet dirt, I'm going to light your ashes on fire."

My hand drops to his throat, and I swallow hard, digging my fingers in to check his pulse. Motherfucker better not be de—

Cold, wet mud flies through the air and collides against the side of my face with a loud splat.

Georgia lets out a horrified "*Oh, fuck!*"

The whole field goes silent.

I freeze. Wipe a slow hand down my face. Feel the tension stretch, like the entire world's holding its breath.

Then I bend down, grab a fistful of mud, and nail Wilder square in his too-pretty face.

"Always told you bare jaws are for the weak," I mutter.

He falls back, hitting the ground with a splash. His eyes are wide, but his grin is wider. "And I told you, it would be a crime to cover this mug with an overgrown gerbil hide like you."

I catch his fingers digging into the mud at his sides a split second before I hurl myself up and away.

A second later, he lets out a fucking battle cry that pierces my ears. "*Mud fight!*"

"Oh, motherfucker," I say, grinning from ear to ear. "*It's on.*"

CHAPTER TWENTY ONE

BUT MUDDING IS FOR MAKING OUT

SCREAMS ERUPT.

Wiki whoops and tackles Clem into a puddle. Hazy's swearing up a storm, boots stomping through the grass as she tries to dodge flying dirt. Colby is belly-laughing from the safety of her saddle.

And Georgia?

She's trying to sneak off. Turning Pudding in a wide arc, aiming for the outer pasture like we won't notice.

"Not so fast, freckles!" I shout, mounting in record time and slapping the reins.

She lets out a loud giggle that carries on a breeze and finds its way into my veins.

Dusty bolts after her, hooves pounding through the slop, kicking up water and debris as I gain ground. She glances over her shoulder, eyes wide with mock horror, then lets out a delighted screech as she kicks Pudding into a gallop. The sound of everyone drifts into the distance as we race deeper into the grass-filled pasture and away from the mud.

I catch up just as she veers right to avoid a massive puddle, and I cut her off, swinging Dusty tight and splashing her entire left side with a wave of cold, fresh rainwater.

She gasps. "You're dead!"

"And you look good wet."

"Do not tempt me to show you what wet is, Archer!"

God help me—I wish you would, baby.

My jaw clenches from the force of choking back my words.

"I thought you were supposed to be a cowboy," she taunts, letting Pudding prance back and forth in place. "Isn't that why you wear those boots?"

"No, darlin'," I drawl, edging closer, and backing her against a fence. "The boots are for work. My hat?" My chin dips toward the hat on her head. "That's for cowboyin'."

Georgia giggles, biting her lip. "Don't you mean *my* hat?"

I huff, slowly inching Dusty forward. Pudding mirrors my lead, tail swishing back and forth. She's open on either side if she wants to run, but Georgia's oblivious to what's happening.

"You do know what they say about cowboy hats, right?"

Her brows draw tight and she shakes her head once.

Smirking, I reach forward and grab Pudding's reins from her hands, using them to guide her closer.

"Kade!" she cries, gripping the pommel. "What the hell!?"

Dusty huffs and hooves at the ground, but they're both patient as hell, used to kids and crazy cowboys, and I easily get them side to side, where I keep Georgia.

My eyes glide all across her face—from her freckles to her eyes, down to her lips, where they stay.

"Rule is: Wear the hat, ride the cowboy," I rumble, voice full of gravel and lust I can't hide. She sucks in a sharp breath that goes straight to my cock and I meet her gaze. "So either give me my hat, or ride me, darlin'. Choice is yours."

And. Just. Like. *That.*

My wildfire is back.

Cheeks so red, even her faintest freckles pop. Eyes glassy and narrowed. Jaw ticking wildly. Brows tight, nose wrinkled.

She's pissed, and I find it so fucking hot, it makes me forget what I'm doing.

"How about neither, you pig!" she whisper-hisses, peeling my fingers off the reins. "I'd rather ride a murderous bull than your....your..."

"Come on," I prompt, tongue clicking. "You can say it."

"Again with the innuendos," she mutters, shooting me a glare. "This is why people find you annoying."

"Say it, Georgia. Say *'I want to ride your cock, Kade. Wanna swing your hat over my head while I bounce on your big, long, perfect, cowboy co—'*"

She slaps a hand over my mouth, blush full and pretty. "I. Do. *Not!*"

Eyes locked right on hers, my lips press against her palm in a soft kiss. She sucks in a sharp breath and shivers, so I do it again, flicking my tongue.

Georgia yanks her hand away like I've burned her and clutches it to her chest.

"*Liar.*"

A breath, an eye twitch, another shiver.

And then...

"I am not lying! Oh my God! You're a filthy, dirty, sex-crazed, brute!"

She's screeching now. This is a new level of Georgia's rage, and it's adorable.

I drag my tongue across my lip and her eyes fly to it like a magnet. She shudders, hips shifting against the rough leather of her saddle. Leaning forward, I drop my voice, breath fanning over her face, and murmur, "*Liar.*"

And then I wrap my arm around her waist, and *yank*.

She's pliant, body soft and distracted, and she comes easy. For a split second, before she realizes what's happening.

"Holy shit!" she shouts, arms flailing for purchase. "Kade! Oh, fuck, Kade! What—"

"You know," I grit out, tightening my hold as I heave her over Pudding and drop her ass in front of me sidesaddle. "I've pictured you saying that exact thing a time or two, but it was a hell of a lot less *dying cat* and more husky, bit of a moan."

She freezes, muscles going limp, and I chuckle, shooting her a smirk.

"Did I shock you into silence, freckles?" Georgia blinks once, twice, before batting at my hands. I tighten my grip and shake my head. "Don't do that, or I'll drop you."

I watch her look down and note the exact second she realizes she's dangling off a horse, held on by only my wavering grip. She's not far from the ground, but for some reason, she reacts like I'm dangling her from a fucking roof.

She screams, long, loud, and terrifying to everyone involved.

Pudding takes off like she's in the Derby, and all I can do is thank God that she'd already released the reins and was free from the horse.

"Now you've done it," I snap, huffing. My arms are burning, but my left peck is on fire. "You better hold on."

It takes a second, but I maneuver her so she's fully side-saddle in front of me. Once she's steady, I grip her left leg and she whimpers, nails digging into my forearm.

"Oh my God, what are you doing? You're going to get me killed!"

"I'm trying to keep you very much alive," I grunt out. "You wanna help me out with that?"

She inhales sharply and nods, wild-eyed. "Yes. Very much, yes."

Chuckling, I squeeze her thigh and tap it twice. "Swing your leg over."

"I—I can't," she stammers, shaking against me. "I'll just stay right here."

"Come on, now." I soften, but my grip tightens, worried she'll let herself fall. "You can, baby. Just breathe. Relax for me."

She shivers—*hard*—but lets out a slow exhale, her body starting to ease in my hands like she really trusts me. Like the idea too damn much.

"Good girl, darlin'."

"Don't say that to me," she chokes out.

Brows pinched, I murmur, "Darlin'?"

"No—I mean, yeah, that too, but…" She sucks in a breath and whispers, her voice all distant and entranced, "*Good girl.*"

"Why can't I call you a good girl when you're bein' good for me?" I ask, guiding her leg over as I scoot back, settling her right up behind the pommel. She gasps, going rigid again, and I tap her thigh. "Tell me, baby."

"Don't call me that either!" she snaps, but helps me settle her safely where I want her. "And it's like catnip. I'll go all feral and start licking you like you're my own personal cowboy-toy."

"Think I might like that," I whisper across her neck, wrapping her hands around the horn. "Hold on tight, yeah?"

"Yes," she huffs, adjusting her seat. Her ass brushes my cock and I swallow a groan. "I'm not an idiot."

I glance to the ominous, dark sky like it might spare me. "Never said you were."

"It was your tone!"

"Christ, woman," I mutter, adjusting us both so I'm not worried she's gonna yeet us into a ditch. "Can't you just say thank you and be quiet for once?"

"Thank you?!" she screeches, whipping around to glare at me. Dusty jolts, snorting, and hops into an irritated side-trot. "Shouldn't you be apologizing! This is your fault!"

"Easy, boy," I murmur, tightening the reins as I narrow my eyes at her. "Lower your voice. You're pissing Dusty off—and that's damn hard to do."

The brim of my hat collides with my chest, and I quickly reach up, snatching it from her head and shoving it onto mine.

"Hey," she murmurs, nose twitching, "I liked wearing that."

I give her a cocky, lazy grin and waggle my brows. "You know the rule now. Care to earn it back?"

Her eyes slice to my lips and for a second, I think she might say fuck it and kiss me, but a crackle of thunder far off in the distance has her whipping around.

I tighten my hand around the reins in case Dusty spooks, but he doesn't seem to notice, content to munch on grass while slowly moving forward.

"Another storm?"

"We've got time," I say softly, eyeing the sky. We're about a half a mile out, but the storm is farther. "Probably an hour before it's over us. That's how it is here. We get storms often in Spring. Big ones, small showers, flash storms that'll pop up out of nowhere and flood us in the blink of an eye."

"I've noticed," she murmurs, leaning into my chest. Her head hits my right shoulder, but for once, I don't feel the deep ache. "It's not too different from West Virginia, but after living in New York for so long, I guess I forgot how bipolar the weather can be."

I want to ask her to keep going, but I'm afraid opening my mouth will make her close hers, so I tighten my arm low on her waist, and when she immediately sighs into me, I decide no question is better than this feeling.

She feels so perfect against me. Too perfect.

But then she has to go and snuggle her ass against my dick, and like the traitor it is, it perks right up.

I haven't stopped thinking about how her body felt back at the house—soft and warm, those perfect tits smashing against my chest, nipples tight and begging to be sucked.

I shift in the saddle, torn between hiding my erection and grinding against her ass like an animal.

God, I want her.

I don't know if it's that damn body, curvy and strong, all that creamy skin dusted with freckles, or that face I can't stop thinking about. Her smart mouth and smoldering eyes. That hair I want fisted in my hand while I fuck her so deep she forgets her own name.

Don't know if it's the image of her cheeks flushed and lips wrapped around my cock while I watch tears build in her pretty eyes, or the way she laughs like she's never been allowed to be this happy before—but it's all stuck in my head.

She's in my fucking head.

"I love the rain."

The words hit me like a brick to the skull. I blink, dragging myself back to the moment—just in time to stop myself from rutting against her on the back of a goddamn horse.

I clear my throat, voice like sandpaper. "What's that?"

"I said I love the rain."

"Why?" I ask, eyes locked on the way tiny stray curls spring from her destroyed braid.

"I love the way it makes me feel."

"Wet?" I ask, low and teasing.

She laughs, soft and throaty, and mutters, "Not as wet as I am right now."

My arm tightens on instinct. "You can't say shit like that. I'm barely hanging on by a thread."

"I didn't say anything."

"We talked about this. Saying it didn't happen doesn't make it true."

"Yes it does," she huffs.

I roll my eyes, palm stroking her heavy jacket, every ounce of me mad it's in the way. "Fine. You didn't say anything."

"I know."

"I'm still thinking about the words you *didn't say*, though," I whisper against the crook of her neck. "You can pretend all you want, but it's burned into my fuckin' brain now."

She exhales sharply. A little whimper escapes—and it nearly ends me.

Then she moves. Subtle at first. A shift of her hips. Maybe keeping time with the horse. Maybe not.

Silence falls between us, but soon enough, she does it again, bumping the hard ridge of my cock digging into her back.

There's no way she can't feel it, right?

"Tell me about the rain, freckles," I rough out, teeth gritted.

She swallows hard, breath hitching as she leans deeper into me until not an ounce of space is between our bodies—her back to my chest, head tipped on my shoulder, ass digging directly in my groin.

God, I might actually come in my fucking jeans.

"I..." She wets her lips. "I used to live in the country for a few years when I was a teenager."

Her voice is barely there—breathy and soft, almost like she's trying to distract herself from how close my hand is to the button of her jeans, or the way opening up to me makes her feel raw, something I understand way too much.

"The country, huh?" I smile into her hair, inhaling her wild scent. "Knew you were hiding a cowgirl in there."

"No you didn't." She scoffs. "You called me a city girl. *Repeatedly.*"

I swallow hard, thumb pushing up under her jacket. When she doesn't stop me, I drag that finger up and down, up and down, then add the rest of my hand. My palm slides against her soft bare skin, and based on the reaction my body has, you'd think I'm palming her dripping pussy instead.

"And you thought I was a deadbeat alcoholic," I murmur, swallowing hard. "Guess we were both wrong."

She giggles, and her hips move again, only instead of rolling, they curve up, closer to my hand. The tip of my fingers dip beneath the edge of her jeans and we both suck in a breath.

"Tell me about the rain, Georgia."

"I loved the quiet of the country," she says softly, breath hitching when I slip in an inch. "The space. But the storms were so big, and they scared me."

"Keep going."

I sink in another inch and pause, thumb stroking, dick rocking against the saddle—rocking against *her*, because I'm losing my mind here.

She hesitates, so I do too.

"Because they'd come out of nowhere. And when you're small… and everything in your life keeps changing… you start to think storms mean something bad's coming."

Fuck.

My chest tightens, but I stay quiet. Let her keep going. My hand stops moving, but my thumb doesn't, passing back and forth in soothing strokes.

"But after, there was always something beautiful. A rainbow. The air felt clean. New." She smiles. "I love rainbows the most."

The horse has slowed to a crawl. The wind picks up just enough to mist our faces, and there's a drop clinging to her lashes.

She's stunning. Glowing. The most beautiful thing I've ever fucking seen—and I've been all over the damn world.

"Rainbows are pretty," I agree, eyes locked on her profile, throat tight. "But there are things in the world way more breathtaking than a stroke of colors."

"It's not that," she says breathily, swiveling her hips in an impossible circle, like she's begging me to keep going. "You can hang your wishes on a rainbow."

"And dandelions. Do you love those too?"

She smacks my thigh, and her hand stays there, gripping tight enough to bruise. I choke out a groan, and she shudders against me.

"I make wishes on everything." She says the words like they're a dirty secret. "Stars and pennies, birthday candles and rainbows. I never miss one."

"That's adorable," I admit, slipping my hand further until my fingers are dancing across the seam of her panties.

Christ, I can feel how hot she is, and I haven't even reached her pussy yet.

"Kade," she breathes, rolling her hips, whimpering up a storm. "*Kade.*"

"Your wet little pussy feel good against that saddle?" I tease. "I bet this whole ride had you seconds from coming all over yourself, didn't it?"

"You—" She breaks off, biting her lip hard. "You have an incredibly filthy mouth."

"Tell me to stop then, baby," I whisper, lips brushing her neck, inhaling hard, imprinting her and this moment into my senses. "Swear to God, I didn't drag you to my horse for this, Georgia, but Christ." I groan. "You in my arms, *fucking hell,* you fit perfect against me."

"I…know…it's so annoying." A throaty, quiet moan has her head shaking back and forth. "I…*oh fuck.* What is happening right now?"

"Does it matter?"

"Yes…no…I don't know."

"You don't have to know a damn thing right now. Just have to let go."

Her head bobs as she chokes, "Just let go. I can do that."

"Yeah, baby," I murmur, wondering when that name started feeling so easy for a woman I claim to hate. "You can."

I rock against her ass, and her nails dig into me as she moves with me, creating a steady rhythm that quickly has me losing all sense of right and wrong. My lips ghost the side of her throat, pressing soft, teasing kisses. I scrape my teeth down her pulse, feeling the way it bounces under my lips, and she shivers.

"Shaking already? We haven't even gotten to the good part yet."

My fingers dip another millimeter, meeting bare, warm flesh and promises of ecstasy. Her head shakes back and forth with a restless, needy exhale.

"Kade…"

"Getting mighty damn addicted to you saying my name like that," I say against her skin. She's so soft. So sweet.

"Kade, I can't.."

Another inch, and holy hell, she's *right* there, and my mind is a thousand miles away, and yet rooted deep in all that is *her*.

"We have to stop."

"I know…" I freeze. "Wait, what?"

Her hand falls away as she exhales hard, turning slowly to face me, eyes glassy, cheeks flushed, hair a wild mess of drenched, muddy curls slipping from her braid—she's never looked prettier.

But the seriousness and disappointment in her eyes, has me slipping my hand from her jeans and my throat constricting.

"Sorry," she breathes. "For the whiplash. I got carried away."

"*We* got carried away." Brushing a stray curl from her jaw, I nod, smiling softly. "This ain't our moment, freckles. If it's meant to be, we'll know it when it comes."

She bites her lip hard, face tight. "It would be so easy to fall for you, Kade Archer, but I'm not the kind of girl who hooks up on the back of a horse with guys who aren't…"

When she doesn't finish, I tilt my head and squeeze her hand. "Aren't what, darlin'?"

A breathe, and then… "*Mine*."

The word is so simple, and yet I've never hated four letters so much.

And I hate them, because she's right.

I don't know what the hell we're doing, or what I want, what she wants, but my hand down her pants before I've even tasted her sweet mouth ain't it. Georgia Walker isn't an easy lay, or a quick fuck from a few towns over. She's not a dirty secret to hide for a few stolen moments in a mud-filled pasture.

She's more. So damn much more.

A single lash slips down her cheek when she blinks, catching in the curve just above her smile. Without thinking, I reach up and catch it before the wind can steal it away.

She jerks, breath catching as her cheeks flush pink. "Mud?"

I hold the lash between my fingers. Her words about wishes are still fresh in my mind, sticky like honey I can't shake loose. And maybe I'm desperate to bring back her smile from a few minutes ago.

Maybe I'm just desperate for that smile to be because of *me*.

"Make a wish, darlin'."

Georgia's eyes go wide, then glassy. A myriad of emotions flash across her face, ones I'm not prepared for. Shock, sadness, something that looks a lot like hope.

Her gaze drifts to the lash and her lids flutter closed. One heartbeat is all it takes before she's leaning forward, lips pursed, and gently blowing the lash away, the ghost of a smile gracing her pretty face.

When her eyes slowly flutter open and lock on mine, a single tear is ghosting down her pale cheek, blending into the pre-storm dew.

"Fuck it," she chokes out.

And then, God help me, Georgia Walker's mouth crashes into mine.

It's soft, sweet—like something holy.

For a heartbeat, I freeze. My body's locked with the shock of it, adrenaline pounding so hard I see stars. But that single breath, that first inhale of her, snaps the world into motion.

My hand flies to her jaw, gripping gently but firm, holding her exactly where I want her. Where I've wanted her since the second she stormed into my life, full of fire and fury and the kind of hurt I know too damn well. My other arm cinches tight around her waist, anchoring her to me in the saddle, chest to chest, heart to goddamn heart.

She tastes like rain and wind and whatever the hell joy must feel like in your mouth.

Her hands are everywhere she can reach at the awkward angle—fisting in my jacket, tugging my hair, digging into my thighs like she's trying to climb inside my skin.

It's wild and messy and a little unhinged—and Christ, it's perfect.

The horse shifts beneath us, but neither of us flinch. We're locked in, consumed and completely lost.

I lick into her mouth, claiming her the way I've dreamed about for weeks, and she whimpers, soft and needy, and fuck if that sound doesn't short-circuit my brain. I kiss her like she's oxygen. Like this is the only chance I'll ever get, because maybe it is.

Because in a few months, she still might walk away.

Because I sure as hell don't deserve her—but God, I want her anyway.

She kisses like it means something. Like it's not just heat, but hope. Like every flick of her tongue is a secret, and every brush of her lips is a confession she'll never say out loud.

My hand slides from her jaw to the back of her neck, fingers threading through her damp curls. My forehead drops to hers, both of us breathing like we've just survived a war.

"Baby," I rasp, voice torn to shreds. I bite her bottom lip, pull it between my teeth, suck hard because I can't not. "Christ, darlin'. I'm not gonna survive you, am I?"

She goes still.

Then she jolts back—taking her warmth, her sweetness, and the entire damn world with her.

My eyes snap open. Hers follow a second later.

And just like that… she's gone.

Not physically. She's still on this damn horse, still close enough to touch. But the girl I kissed, the one I'm stupidly falling for, has vanished. And in her place is that icy mask I fuckin' hate.

"This…" She shakes her head, pale and shaken, refusing to meet my eyes. "This can't happen."

"Hate to break it to you," I say, jaw ticking, heart pounding, "but it already did."

"Well, it was a mistake."

"The hell it was."

Her gaze finally locks with mine—and it's the pain in it, the sheer terror, that shuts me the fuck up.

"Take me back," she whispers. "I need to go back. Right now."

She turns before I can answer, inching away like every molecule between us burns. But I see the tight swallow. The tension in her shoulders.

And when I guide Dusty back toward the house, I don't miss the tears slipping down her flushed cheeks.

What the fuck just happened? And why does it feel like I ruined the one good thing I never really had?

CHAPTER TWENTY TWO

ONE STEP FROM FOREVER

"YOU SHOULD COME OUT with us," Griff says, smiling as he leans against the hardware store counter, all giant, tattooed arms, and enthusiasm.

He's been spending too much time with Wilder.

"Out?" Holt asks, body stalling mid-action for a beat. He blinks, brain coming back online, and drops the screws in the bag. "To where?"

"We're going to the Twisted Saddle tomorrow night to celebrate."

"Celebrate…" Holt murmurs, brows tight. He drags his beanie lower and flicks his gaze to the old school register. "That'll be seven flat."

I pull a ten from my wallet, pass it over and give him an apologetic look. "Ignore him."

"Oh," he says, eyes flicking between us. "Alright."

"No," Griff drawls. "Don't ignore him, Holt. We're celebrating Kade finally getting his kid."

"Griff." I sigh, yanking my hat off. I tuck the bill into my back pocket and tug on my hair, anxiety practically strangling me. "Don't jinx it."

In the last few weeks, everyone in town has found out about what happened with Marlee and Aurora. It's been impossible to keep it under wraps with all the construction going on, and the trips I've had to make into town for supplies.

Not to mention, Griffin and Wilder tell everyone they see they can't wait to meet their niece.

"What?" he says, blinking innocently at me. "You finished that entire fuckin' checklist in record time. Your house is perfect. Aurora's room is done, and that stuffy social worker will be there at five to sign off on everything." He grins, squeezing my shoulder with a shake. "Stop stressing. Few days from now, that baby girl will be yours. Mark my fuckin' words."

I swallow hard, but don't respond. Can't.

"Congratulations, Kade." Holt passes me my change and bag, flashing me a quick smile. He clears his throat, looking away again. "I'm sure it'll all work out."

"Thanks, man." I tip my chin and heft the heavy mantle I custom ordered from him a few weeks ago. "And thank you again for doing this. It's beautiful. You do damn fine work."

"Might have to order one for myself," Griff calls, holding the door for me. "See you at nine tomorrow, Holt."

"Yeah, sure," he mutters, bearded jaw ticking. "Maybe."

The glass door sways shut gently behind Griffin and he stares down the three inches that separate us, giving me a disapproving look.

"That man has busted his ass to help you get the shit you need from other towns to finish your place. Least you can do is be polite and invite him for a fucking drink, you selfish prick."

"I've invited Holt Montgomery to get a drink at least once a month since I got home. He always says *maybe*, and never shows."

I carefully set the mantle on a blanket in the cab of my truck, right next to the cloud-shaped bookshelves I picked up for Aurora's room. They're bright white and soft-edged—*adorable,* apparently—which is why I had to drive two towns over to find them today. The Archer women are relentless when it comes to a vision.

"Let's grab Wild and get back," I mutter, jerking my chin toward the coffeeshop we left him at twenty minutes ago.

He nods, falling into step beside me.

Griffin's not wrong, the house is done. But I haven't laid eyes on Aurora's room since my mom claimed it as her personal grandbaby project the day Georgia showed up at Honey Bea.

Haven't laid eyes on Georgia, either.

Her showing up threw me for a fuckin' loop. I hadn't seen her since that day at the store. I figured I wouldn't see her again at all—especially with me moving to Heart Springs and leaving Wildwood behind. It was easier that way. Cleaner. But then she called me, said she'd been in an accident and needed my help.

I damn near lost my fuckin' mind.

Hearing her sweet voice again cracked something open. And seeing her? Walking around my house, all sunshine and fire, red curls lit up in the morning light, freckles on display, and that damn mouth running?

It was too much. Too easy. Too *comfortable*.

And because it felt so fucking good, I let myself relax. Dropped my guard. Talked more than I meant to, shared things I shouldn't have. All I could see was her in my space—smiling in my kitchen, toes curling in the hallway, laughter bouncing off the walls like she belonged there.

Wanted to kiss her, touch her, wrap her up and breathe her in. And yeah, maybe I crossed some lines. Maybe I scared her. But fuck, I couldn't help myself. Something about Georgia Walker makes me feel alive. Hopeful for shit I gave up on a long time ago. When she's near, I lose my mind a little bit, and fuck me, I love the way that feels.

I fixed her tire after she disappeared toward the supply shed with my mom. Then I waited around longer than I needed to—pretending I had things to do. Truth is, I was hoping to catch sight of her again. Say something that didn't come out wrapped in sex or sarcasm. Ask her what the real reason she agreed to help with my mom's project is.

She really just being a good, kind hearted woman, picking up the slack people like me are leaving behind, or was she secretly hoping to run into me?

Wanted to ask her more than anything else, but Georgia's smart. And if I had to guess, she was watching too. Waiting for me to leave.

The second I got called into the bathroom reno, she slipped in, got her keys, and slipped back out without a word.

Haven't seen her since.

But I haven't stopped thinking about her either.

"Really is nice down here," Griffin says, breaking the silence. "Hell of a lot nicer than back home."

"Yeah," I mutter, taking it in. "I've missed it."

He gives me a sidelong glance. "You happy to be back?"

We cross the street, passing *Slab Happy*, and a laugh slips free. "Where else can you find a butcher and party supply store in one?"

"Small towns are weird as fuck."

I arch a brow at him. "You're the one who wants to move here."

After three weeks, his comment to uproot his life—*and Wilder's*—hasn't gone by the wayside like I thought it would. If anything, Griff is more convinced than ever.

He's already talking about looking for a place to live, how long it'll take him to sell off his small plot in the country back home and get his horses here.

"Time for a change," he says simply with a shrug. "Nothing keeping me back there anymore."

I hear the words he's not saying, but I don't push for more. He's not like Wilder—when Griffin Sterling doesn't want to talk about something, there's no amount of prying, alcohol or otherwise, that'll get him to open up.

Wilder, on the other hand, needs a half a beer, a pat on the back, and a little bit of willing silence, and the floodgates inevitably spill open.

"What about work?" I ask, changing the subject. "JP was pissed when I quit. If you seriously move here, you gonna stay at Iron Shield?"

Griffin grins, green eyes twinkling. "I quit the same day as you."

I stop cold in the middle of the sidewalk and gape at him.

"So did Wild," he tacks on, rolling back on his boots.

I stare at the man I've looked up to since I was eighteen—my mentor, my brother in every way that matters, the guy who stepped in when my dad couldn't, and for the first time in the decade I've known him, he's actually managed to shock me speechless.

Griff slaps my back and chuckles. "Knew that one would short-circuit your system."

"The fuck?" I run my fingers through my beard, brain spinning. "What the hell are you gonna do for work? You love private security."

Like me, Griffin saved up a hell of a lot of his money over the years. But a nasty divorce left him with the farm he fought tooth and nail to keep and not much else. She got the vehicles, half the savings, and a monthly check big enough to make him cry. He needs the job.

He studies me with that long, assessing look of his—the one that always makes me feel like I'm under a microscope. "Do you love it?"

"Yeah," I answer automatically, but the word feels wrong in my mouth. "Truth is, JP's company is a mess of politics and power trips. I wanted to quit long before all this."

"So why didn't you?"

"You and Wilder," I admit. "Didn't wanna leave you behind." Then I frown. "Why are we talking about me? I already quit."

Griff shrugs. "I needed to know if you still cared about the work. Protecting people. Makin' a difference. Just without all the red tape and ego bullshit. If the scale was smaller, would you still want it?"

"I can't leave town, Griff." My voice drops, rough with the weight of truth. "Not now. Not when I'm this close to bringing Aurora home."

"You're gonna make one hell of a dad, man," he murmurs, grinning. "Damn proud of you."

My throat tightens.

He lets me sit with it for a beat, then gestures down Oak Street toward the block where a couple of the bigger buildings sit empty, "What if you didn't have to leave?"

I glance where he's looking, then shove my hands in my pockets.

Haven't thought much about what comes next—haven't had time to. These last few weeks without Aurora wrecked me. After spending every day with her, not seeing her feels like losing her before she's even mine.

I'd do just about anything to bring that little girl home, but that doesn't mean I'm not terrified about what's to come.

Most nights, I don't sleep.

When I do, the nightmares come—some from my time overseas, but most about her.

My brain fills in the blanks I'll never know—how the accident happened, what it looked like, what she remembers. Sometimes, it's me behind the wheel. Sometimes, she gets hurt because I don't know what the fuck I'm doing with a car seat. I wake up drenched in sweat, heart pounding, terrified I'll fail her.

Then I remember why I'm doing this.

The way she curled into me. How her little hand fit in mine like it was always meant to be there. The trust in her eyes, and the bond we built, in just a handful of days.

I'm one of the last people who can tell her who her mama was. Who can keep her tethered to where she came from—even if all I've got are the rose-tinted memories of a kid in love.

"I don't want to miss anything," I admit, voice low. "Not her first steps. Not the dumb little things like tantrums or bedtime books, or brushing her teeth. Wanna be there for all of it. Wanna be the one who makes sure she doesn't feel even a second of what she's lost when she's already lost everything."

I swallow hard, chest tight, and rub at the ache. "All I want is for her to know love. Not the ghost of her parents. Not the outline of the man who's supposed to be standing in their place. I want to be there. Really there. As much as I can be."

Just like my dad was for me, for my whole family.

Griffin nods slowly, a smile spreading across his face. "Good. Because I'm opening a private security firm right here in Heart Springs."

I blink. "You're what?"

"Want you and Wilder to do it with me."

Shock rolls through me again—but this time, excitement follows. I grin, shaking my head in disbelief. "Alright, man. I'm in."

Now he's the one to gape. "Just like that?"

"Not sure there's much need for security in Summit." I shrug and start walking again. "But if it gets you both here, and keeps us all sane, I'll do whatever you want."

Griffin barks a laugh and opens his mouth to reply, but I cut him off with a glare.

"I'm not giving you my truck. Don't even fuckin' ask again."

He starts to argue, but I grab his jacket and come to an abrupt halt.

"What?" he mutters, yanking free.

I jerk my chin toward the front window of Snug as a Mug, where Wilder is practically sprawled across the white waterfall counter, dimples blazing, hands braced like he's mid-sexual innuendo, as Tabby Whitt blinks her doe eyes up at him.

"Fucking hell," I mutter, charging forward. "Asshole's gonna get himself arrested."

The bell above the door jingles a second before it hits the wall with a thud. Griff's boots thunder in behind me.

"No!" I bark, grabbing Wilder by the collar. "Back away from her, man."

Tabby's eyes go wide, but Wilder just scoffs and swats my hand off him.

"What the fuck, Archer?" He groans, snatching his iced coffee off the counter. "We were just talking."

"No," I grumble, shoving him toward the exit. "You were just one dirty joke away from lock up."

He digs in, shooting me a confused look. "She's twenty, dude. I'm not some creep. Give me a little credit."

Griff chuckles, tossing a ten in the tip jar with a wink. He nods his chin like it's a cowboy hat and lays his Southern drawl on thick. "Have a nice day, miss."

I shove Wilder out the door, Griff right behind us, and steer him toward my truck.

"Her dad is the sheriff," I mutter. "And a raging bull where his baby girl's concerned. Doesn't matter if she's only five years younger than you, he'll kick your ass just for lookin' at her."

Wilder takes a long pull from his straw and glances over his shoulder like he might go back anyway. Griffin clocks him on the back of the head.

Wilder stumbles into my truck with a curse. "What the fuck, man? Jesus—you forget how massive you are?"

"Actually, I did." Griff opens the back door and gestures grandly. "Thanks for the reminder. I'm way too massive for the back. Climb in, princess."

"No." Wilder crosses his arms, glaring between us. "I'm not doing it again. My knees still hurt from the last time."

Scoffing, I yank open the driver's door and climb behind the wheel. "Get in the back or ride in the cab—I don't give a shit. But I'm leaving." I glance at my watch, and a full-body shudder rolls through me. "You assholes kept me out too long, and I still need to clean before Ethel shows up."

They stare each other down for a beat before Wilder finally huffs and folds his giant frame into the too-small back seat. Griffin cackles and slams the door before climbing in up front.

"Thank fuck," I mutter, pulling onto the road.

Downtown bleeds into country, and I lose myself in thoughts of my never ending to do list.

We're almost back to my place when my phone vibrates. I tug it from my pocket, and my heart skips a beat when I see the name on the screen.

"Turn it down, it's the social worker," I bark, heart hammering.

Fuck, what if she's canceling? What if something happened to Aurora? What if I already messed shit up before—

Wilder flicks my cheek. "Answer it!"

Swallowing hard, I swipe and bring the phone to my ear. "This is Kade."

"Mr. Archer, it's Ethel Sorrenson," she says, her voice kind but professional. "Just calling to let you know the final inspection went great. You did a wonderful job on the house—I'm thoroughly impressed with how quickly you pulled it together."

The truck swerves, my breath catching in my lungs. Griff's arm shoots out, correcting the wheel, eyes wide and panicked.

What the hell? She already did the inspection? How?

"Uh…" I clear my throat, brows drawn tight. "Thank you." I shoot the guys a confused look. "Sorry, ma'am, did I miss the meeting? I thought it was set for five?"

"Oh, no. I was free this morning, and figured I'd pop in. Your mom said you were out shopping for Aurora and let me in. No big deal—I got what I needed."

I exhale slowly, nodding even though she can't see me. "Okay. Well, thanks."

She chuckles. "I can tell I caught you off guard. Anyway, I've already shared my findings with Judge Romero, and he's signed off on everything."

Holy shit.

"Once you sign the paperwork I emailed over, we'll get it processed. Aurora will likely be with you by Monday or Tuesday."

"Monday…" I echo, dazed as I turn into Honey Bea. "That's fast."

Ethel laughs softly. "This town's small—things tend to move quickly. Especially when there's a valid will and everything's legally in order. At this point, it's just checking boxes."

My chest tightens. It's really happening.

"And after?" I ask, my voice thick. "How long do I need to wait to file for adoption?"

There's a pause, then a warm sigh.

"I'm really glad you're taking this seriously. If I've seen anything over the last few weeks, it's how committed you are. As far as adoption goes, I'll bring the paperwork when I drop Aurora off next week, and we'll go over it together. Sound good?"

"Yes, ma'am. Thank you for everything. I appreciate it."

"Of course, have a great weekend, Mr. Archer."

She hangs up just as I'm pulling into my new gravel driveway. I throw it in park and lower my phone, jaw unhinged, body thrumming with excitement, and shock.

"What did she say?" Wilder shouts, slapping my seat. "Dude! You can't leave us hanging like this."

"She's mine," I mutter, swallowing hard. "Aurora is mine."

And for some crazy, unknown reason, all I want is to tell Georgia.

CHAPTER TWENTY THREE

THE SPACE BETWEEN OUR SCARS

"WHAT THE FUCK?" I mutter, freezing mid-step.

My eyes are wide, heart hammering, and my family and friends? They're cheering, filling up every corner of my house, along with a hell of a lot of furniture that wasn't here when I left this morning.

The small brown leather loveseat I'd gotten just so the living room wasn't empty is tucked next to the fireplace to make space for a massive matching sectional. There are rustic barstools lining the island in the same shade of oak as the worn but solid dining table in front of the back windows. Fuckin' thing has enough chairs to seat my whole family—and then some.

A sideboard I recognize as my mom's is by the entry, lined with framed photos of my sisters, the farm, and my parents. My throat constricts when I see the two pictures of my dad and me, just off to the side, like whoever put them out knew they'd burn to see.

The walls are lined with more pictures, the floors are covered in massive soft looking rugs, blankets and pillows are on the couch, and somehow—somehow, my house feels like a real home.

"Welcome home, man," Griff murmurs, squeezing my shoulder. "Your little girl's gonna be damn happy here."

He brushes past me and heads to the kitchen where a bunch of ranch hands who've helped with renovations are drinking beers. They all slap hands and clap backs like old friends, passing him a beer as they turn back to the game playing on a massive TV I definitely didn't buy.

The group parts, groaning and shouting about a bad play, and I'm floored that the loudest voice comes from Agnes Whittaker. Gaping, I look away before she catches my stare and takes it as an invitation.

My eyes scan the crowd three times, and try as I might, it's damn near impossible to ignore the empty pit that settles in my gut when I don't catch sight of bright red curls.

The immediate disappointment should be a giant *what the fuck* to my system, should tell me I'm in way over my head where she's concerned, but I can't find it in me to care about the wrongness of it all.

I want Georgia here, and that want has nothing to do with her body or sharp tongue, and everything to do with the peace I feel with her by my side.

"Crazy, huh?" Wilder murmurs. "People in this town really care about your grumpy ass."

"What is this?"

"Your house warming party," he says quietly, shooting me a wink. "Surprise."

Grinning, I shake my head, still too shocked to move. Now I understand why they kept me out all damn day, refusing to let me come home.

"How the fuck did you pull this off?"

He barks out a laugh and smacks my stomach. "I love that you think I possess the ability to pull something like this off, but it was all your mom."

"And us," Colby says, skipping up to me, Clem right behind her. "We were sworn to secrecy."

"It was so fun," Clem agrees, smiling widely as she throws herself in my arms. "And you were so oblivious."

Chuckling, I catch her a second before Colby shoves her way into my other side.

God, they're so tall and grown up. When the fuck did that happen?

I squeeze my eyes shut and hold them hard, knowing damn well they won't wanna hug me like this for much longer. Soon enough, they'll be graduating high school, off to college or following their dreams.

And I've already missed most of their lives.

"We're so happy for you," Clementine whispers, sniffling.

Colby buries herself in my chest, curly hair tangling with my beard. "We can't wait to meet our niece."

The word punches me in the gut, but I barely have time to process it before another Archer voice cuts through the room.

"Move aside, baby sisters. The eldest and wisest has arrived!"

My eyes snap open and the girls giggle, slipping free from my arms as the oldest Archer child barrels her way into me. I suck in a sharp breath and hug the hell out Gemma, blinking back the burn in my eyes.

"What the fuck, Gem?" I breathe, tucking her short frame under my chin. "When… how…" Swallowing thickly, I push her back a bit and meet her glossy eyes. "You're here."

"So are you," she whispers, wiping away a tear. "You're in your house, Kade. On the farm, with your family…" Her throat bobs. "And a daughter? I'm so fucking happy for you."

Gemma hasn't been back to Heart Springs in over a year. Between Ryland's constant work relocations, and their oldest, Finn, recently being diagnosed with autism, she's had her hands full. And Grady—barely three—is already a whole damn whirlwind.

Jerking a nod, I glance away and rub the back of my neck. "I know," I say thickly. "I'm happy too."

At least, I think I am.

In reality, I'm still freaking the fuck out.

Barely got the call from Ethel twenty minutes ago. Haven't even had a second to process.

"Give the boy some space," my mom chides, tugging Gemma under her arm. She presses a kiss to her head and murmurs into her long, dark hair, "Missed you, sweetheart."

A quiet conversation filled with tears breaks out between them, and I step away, giving them a minute.

But as I pass my mom, I pause, kissing her cheek, heart heavy and soaring all at once. "Thanks, Ma. Love you."

She grabs my arm, yanking me into a quick, tight hug that nearly undoes me, then pulls back and gestures around us.

"Everyone in town came together," she murmurs, smiling softly. "Donated things from their homes, or bought things for what you're building here. Stocked the cabinets, and fridge. Filled your pantry with linens, and necessities. Susie Jacobs and Faith Clemmons both had daughters in the last couple years. They brought what their little ones outgrew. It's not everything, but it'll get you through for a while."

I have to blink a few times to clear my vision. Jaw ticking, body vibrating, I try to talk, but my voice breaks. Clearing my throat, I manage a tortured sounding *thanks*.

"Why don't you take a few minutes and go explore," she says softly, squeezing my hand. "Maybe spend some time in the nursery where it's quiet."

Unable to respond, I jerk a nod and move through the house with purpose. A few people try to pull me into conversations, but I quickly tell them all I've gotta make a call and step away, doing everything in my power not to fall apart in front of half the fuckin' town.

My boots are heavy on the shiny floors, freshly mopped and waxed by someone who wasn't me. I pause when I reach the hall that leads to my room, finding the walls lined with photos of the farm throughout the years. They're all blown up black and whites, framed in dark wood that warms the white walls.

Throat tight, heart hammering, I peek into the closets, master bath and my room, finding little things added to every single space, just like my mom said there would be.

But it's the closed door that connects my room to Aurora's that has my hand trembling. Haven't seen it in well over a week, and now that I know how over the top the rest of the house is, I can't even imagine what the Archer's pulled together for their newest member.

I swallow roughly, and exhale slowly, as I push through the door, body braced like I'm stepping into a battle zone instead of a damn nursery.

Light fills the dim opening, pouring in from the window, and my breath catches before stalling altogether.

But the lack of oxygen has nothing to do with the beautiful soft yellow walls, or the white furniture that matches the convertible crib I bought. It's not the bee theme dancing across every surface, or the massive bright rainbow mural that arches over the baby's bed.

No, it's the woman in the rocker—fiery red curls spilling down her back—folding baby clothes with tears in her eyes, and heartache written across her face.

My hand tightens around the doorknob. I freeze, caught off guard by the sight of her here. Georgia hasn't seen me. Hasn't heard me.

So like the fool I am when it comes to her, I stare.

A cloud shifts outside, sunlight breaking through the window and landing across her body. For a second, she glows. Not soft or angelic... no, that's not her.

She *burns*.

Golden strands of her hair catch the light like embers about to spark. Her freckles pop against skin paler than usual, flushed and wet with tears. And even with red-rimmed eyes and a crease between her brows that says she's hurting, she's still the most beautiful damn thing I've ever seen.

Throat bobbing, jaw pulsing wildly, I slide my gaze down her body, taking in a floral skirt that brushes the top of her cowboy boots pack a hell of a punch now that I know she can ride. She's got a thick sweater on, covering arms I now know are tattooed with thin-lined drawings that dot her skin like freckles—flowers falling from a tree dance across her bicep, a rainbow by her wrist. Words that were too tiny for me make out without looking like a creep.

They're simple and delicate. And maybe before, I would have said they suited a city girl like her.

But looking at her now, with tears trickling down her face, her small hands moving carefully over every piece of Aurora's clothes with love, and something like longing, I can't help but think how fuckin' wrong I've been.

Georgia Walker is far from simple. She's more than the wildfire I love igniting. She's not a storm I can ride out or ignore. She's layered and raw. Quietly wrecked in a way that makes my own broken pieces wanna lean closer.

I don't know what the hell's happening in my chest, but whatever storm was brewing there goes quiet just by looking at her.

And before I can stop myself—before I even think—I'm stepping into the room, breaking the silence with the only words that make sense.

"Who the hell made you cry?"

She bursts from the chair with a gasp, and the neat pile on her knee goes flying. Meadow eyes wide, Georgia whirls on me, hand pressed to her chest, hair sticking to her damp cheeks.

And because I've well and truly lost the fuckin' plot, I charge forward, stepping over clothes, boots sinking into a plush cream rug like a man possessed, halting less than an inch from her.

My hand comes up, and she jerks back, but I palm her hip, keeping her still.

"What… what are you…" she says, words thick and stuttering.

I slide my fingers through her hair, brushing it back as I murmur, "Why are you crying?"

"I'm fine." Her throat bobs and she glances away, dragging her face from my touch, but I don't let go, keeping her soft curls in my gentle grip.

My gaze collides with a bruise on her temple. Everything in me goes still, but the pounding of my heart threatens to bust through my ribcage.

"What the fuck?" The words are garbled, like they've been dragged over rocks. "Who the hell hit you?"

Anger like I've never known rages through my system until I'm practically fucking vibrating with it. I've never felt such a raw, feral need to defend someone, to lash out at whoever dared to *touch* her. It's irrational, but I'm quickly learning that sense is the last thing I possess where she's concerned.

Georgia's brows furrow, eyes meeting mine. "What are you talking about?"

"This." My thumb ghosts the mottled purple and red bruise. "Who did this? Is that why you're crying?"

She licks her lip, shifting in my arms, but she doesn't pull away. "No."

Teeth gritted, I tighten my hand on her waist, then force myself to soften, remembering she hurt herself in the accident last week. I flick my eyes back to the bruise. Did she hit her head when she went off road? But the coloring's all wrong. It's fresh, 'bout the size of a lemon, and looks painful as hell.

"Georgia. What the fuck happened?"

"I'm fine, Kade," she whispers, blinking back more tears that threaten to send me to my knees. "Don't worry—"

"Don't," I bark, making her jump. It takes work, but I lower my voice and smooth my hand through her hair. She melts into me, so I keep doing it. "Don't lie to me, and don't tell me not to worry. It's too damn late for that."

The surprise in her expression twists something inside me. "You're worried about me?"

Brows furrowed, I nod. "Of course, I am. You're cryin' in a nursery when a whole party's happening just outside, and you're hurt. Why the fuck wouldn't I be worried?"

"Because..." She trails off, red-tipped nose scrunching in confusion. "Because you don't like me."

Rearing back, I huff. "I don't?"

"It's obvious." She rolls her eyes, shuffling back a step, bumping into the dresser and trapping herself.

I follow her, not letting her get away that damn quickly, but I do drop my hand from her hair, much as it pains me. I can tell she's pulling away—not just physically.

Same way she has every time we've gotten too close, or things too heavy.

Georgia keeps shit close to the chest—something I understand far too well, but with her, it's different. Every time we're together, I find myself wanting to open up, find my walls crumbling whether I want them to or not.

But hers only seem to get taller, thicker—damn near impossible to climb.

Won't stop me from trying.

"Would I be touchin' you like this if I didn't like you?" I rasp, brushing my thumb across her hip. She drops her eyes, following my movements as I slip under her sweater, finding soft, warm skin that makes my cock throb between us. "Would I have kissed you like I did—stolen the breath right from your lungs, if I didn't like you?"

A shiver races through her. "That's called attraction. Doesn't mean you like me. You can hate a person and still want to fuck them."

I choke on my next breath. Christ, this woman doesn't pull punches, does she?

"You're right," I agree and she scoffs, expression pinched like I've hurt her feelings. That thought makes me unjustly ill. "You can hate a person and still wanna fuck them. Can hate fuck, 'em right through a mattress. Sometimes, hating someone can light a fire under your skin, burn you straight to your core, and fucking another person with passion like that burning through your veins? Can't be that damn bad."

I step forward another inch, towering over her. My palm travels higher, pausing on her ribs, and I slip my free hand under her top, surrounding her in every way. The heat from the swell of her breasts burns against my flesh, but I ignore it, not wanting to push, knowing she'll run.

She sucks in a breath and trembles beneath my touch, hands coming up to brace on my forearms, fingertips digging into my bare skin.

"So what you're saying is," she whispers, arching her neck to look up at me. "You want to fuck me because you have a thing for hate sex?"

Chuckling, I shake my head and lean in, drawn to her pain, her fight and fire.

"You're trying to distract me, freckles," I mutter, memorizing every single starburst etched into her skin. "Tell me what happened."

"I'll tell you the truth," she starts, eyes flicking to my lips for a beat before finding my eyes again, "if you do."

"Truth for a truth?"

A nod, a breath, another shiver.

"Deal."

Without pausing, I lift her onto the dresser, smiling at the adorable squeal that fills my ears. Her long skirt has a ruffled slit like the one she wore to the grocery store, and I use it to my advantage, stepping between her thighs.

"I can't think like this," she whispers. "When you're touching me. I…" Her tongue slides across that damn lip again, making my whole body thrum. "I can't think when you're this close. I lost my mind the last time you… we… I can't do that again."

"Don't think then, just tell me what happened."

Her eyes flick between mine, something vulnerable and unsure hidden behind thick lashes and irises a shade of green I'll never be able to name. I slip my hands from her ribs to her back, trailing my palms across her skin. She's covered in goosebumps, but she leans into the touch, just as starving for the contact as I am.

"I…" She swallows, but doesn't look away. "Your mom asked me to help her get all this ready. My job was this room."

"You did all this?" My gaze swivels around the beautiful room, taking it in with new eyes.

"Yeah," she breathes, smiling a little. "It was fun."

I stare at the massive rainbow mural painted over Aurora's new bed, and my mind goes back to our talk on Dusty.

She loves rainbows, and she painted one for my girl.

"Wait, you were the one sending me on wild errands for this room?" I ask, smirking. "Thought it was my mom."

Georgia's cheeks go bright red, freckles disappearing one by one. "The rainbow and bookshelves are for Aurora. The ridiculous errands were for me."

I blink, then bark out a laugh. "Secretly getting revenge on me, darlin'?"

Georgia shrugs, a hint of a smile. "I'm resourceful. People say it's one of my better qualities."

Cocking a brow, I murmur, "Thought it was your rabid hyena singing voice."

She pinches my forearms, face scrunched up in anger I find way too damn appealing. "You're rude."

"And you're changing the subject again."

After a long minute of glaring me down, she sighs, hands dropping with her gaze. They fall to her lap and bundle in the fabric of her skirt. The immediate reaction of needing to have her touch back should alarm me, but the sadness in her eyes reroutes my brain.

"Your family is wonderful," she finally whispers, the words so low I have to strain to hear them. "They've been nothing but nice to me from the very beginning. And they love you, Kade. God, your mom loves you so damn much."

My hands still on her back for a beat, but I shake it off. Moment's not about me.

"They wanted to do this big, wonderfully kind thing for you, for Aurora, and they haven't even met her yet. They're just so sure already that she's one of them, an Archer—no questions asked, past and the situation that led you here, be damned."

"And that makes you sad?" I murmur, heart twisting with every word. She shrugs and I let out a low breath, bending to catch her eyes. "Darlin', you gotta help me out here. I can't fix a problem I can't see, and Christ, much as I wish I could get rid of my family sometimes, I'm not sure during a surprise housewarming party they threw me is the right time."

Georgia giggles, this soft, sweet sound, but it quickly turns into a sob. I tug her into me, wrapping her in my arms. She buries herself in my chest, and I do all I can to ignore the way she fits so perfectly against me. I slip a hand free from her top and cup the back of her head, keeping her right where I want her while she cries.

Her fingers tangle in the front of my shirt, and soon enough, I can feel her tears seeping through the material. I don't know what the fuck she's working through, but the sound of it breaks my already confused heart.

"I'm so sorry," she chokes out, sinking impossibly closer until there's not an inch of space between us. "I'm sorry I'm a mess."

"Hey," I say, rocking her, fingers sifting through her curls. The smell of her shampoo invades my senses, all floral and sweet and addictive as hell. "Stop that. Not a damn thing you need to apologize for. I've got you. You can let go."

"I can't, though." Sitting up, she stares at me with so much pain, my breath catches. "Don't you see that? I can't let go. Not here, not with you, not in this town."

Shaking my head, I tighten my grip in her hair and draw our foreheads together, breathing her in. "You can."

"Kade…"

"Georgia," I say, voice thick and demanding. "Breathe, baby. Breathe through the hurt and everything that scares you. Breathe through all the shit in your brain telling you this is wrong or bad. Breathe through it with me, and lay your broken pieces on my shoulders. I swear to God, I can carry 'em."

She shudders against me, whole body trembling, and claws at my shirt like she's begging me to do just that.

"I've just… I've been alone for so long. I'm so tired." She inhales through another sob.

"And I thought if I finally just did it—jumped and came to Heart Springs—I could find answers. But all I've found are other people, other families, who are willing to do everything for each other, no matter the cost. And I… I shouldn't be jealous. It's so selfish. But fuck, Kade, I'm so jealous of you."

Of me? What's she talking about? A humorous laugh slips free.

"What the fuck for? Georgia, I'm a mess. Up until you dropped that bomb into my life, I was barely hanging on. I ignored my family for years—too fucked up, too broken and ashamed of…" God, now I'm the one tearing up, choking on my words. "Of what I did."

After a long moment, she pulls back and blinks tear-filled eyes up at me. "What are you talking about?"

My fingers tighten in her hair, and I let out a shaky breath. She's opening up, vulnerable as hell because I practically blackmailed her into it. Least I can do is reciprocate.

But I can't look her in the eyes when I do it, so I release her, stepping back. She lets out a pained whimper, like the distance hurts her, and I want to rush right back, but I don't.

Knocking off my hat, I toss it next to her on the dresser and tug on my hair. And with one last breath, I let out the hardest guilt, the deepest pain of all.

"I killed my dad."

Chapter Twenty Four

Georgia

The Cost of Wanting

MY FIRST THOUGHT SHOULD be *what the fuck is he talking about?* Quickly followed by a scream, a kick to his nuts, and me running for my life.

But, God… all I can think is: *He's broken. Just like me.*

Kade Archer is a good man.

An ass, sure—snarky, rude, brooding more times than not—but underneath all that rough-edged armor is something honest. Steady and solid. He's got a good heart.

How could he not, being raised by Beatrice Archer? She's the single most selfless person I've ever met. You don't grow up loved like that and not carry some of it with you. Even if it gets buried under guilt and grief. And it's clear he has enough of that to last a lifetime.

He's dark… broken in a way that calls to all the fractured, ugly parts of me I pretend don't exist. I've tried to stay away. Tried to ignore the tether between us that drags me back into his orbit every time we get too close. But it's getting harder and harder to pretend I don't feel it.

Especially when he holds me while I fall apart, rocks me and soothes me like I'm precious to him—*like I matter*. He was there for me, no questions asked. Worried on my behalf—angrily so, about what happened to me today to make me fall apart in Aurora's room like a crazy person.

He was here for me despite the shit I pulled on the back of that horse last week. I wanted to stay strong, but God, when he pulled that lash off my cheek and told me to make a wish like he *meant it*, I couldn't stop myself.

Kade didn't make fun of me or laugh, he just accepted my childish dreams as reality, and gave me the only kindness he could in the face of my meltdown.

And now he's the one unraveling.

I know how his dad died. William Archer passed from a sudden heart attack while Kade was halfway around the world. He had nothing to do with it.

No matter what logic says, grief makes liars out of us all, though.

I've been a liar for a long damn time, and it's a lonely way to live. Maybe that's why I move without letting myself overthink it.

Quietly, I slip off the dresser and smooth down my skirt. I step up behind him and press my chest to his back, wrap my arms around his waist, and just hold him the same way he held me.

He tenses at first, like he doesn't know what to do with comfort, but then his hands come up, fingers wrapping gently around my arms where the sleeves of my sweater have ridden up. His palms are warm and rough, calloused and big.

Perfect.

I inhale his warm, clean smell—the notes of cedar and leather tamer than usual, and I wonder if it has something to do with the cowboy hat or belt he usually wears.

"What happened?"

His fingertips dig into my arm, body shuddering with a deep breath, before he says, "He died because of me. Because I wasn't there. Because he needed me, and I left him alone."

It's on the tip of my tongue to argue, to tell him he's wrong, but I clench my jaw, knowing he doesn't need my opinion on his pain. He just needs to let it out, slowly and safely.

Kade told me to lay my broken pieces at his feet, promised me he could carry them. And maybe he's right, but I can be that for him, too. I *want* to be that for him.

I don't know what it means, but right now, I can't bring myself to care.

So I simply whisper, "Tell me your story, Kade Archer. I can carry your pieces, too."

The silence that follows isn't empty—it's heavy with the weight of every-thing he's never said out loud. Of guilt buried so deep it's woven into the way he *breathes*.

But slowly, his grip softens. His shoulders ease, just slightly, as if the act of being seen, *truly seen*, has loosened a thread inside him.

Outside, the sun sets, and warm, golden rays wrap around us like a blanket, broken only by the quiet ache between heartbeats.

And when he finally starts talking, finally lays down what he's kept in-side, I don't rush him. Don't fill the space with soft reassurances or hollow promises. I just listen and hold him, my grip never waning.

Because sometimes, healing doesn't begin with fixing.

Sometimes, it begins with someone staying long enough to witness the break.

Kade tells me all about the house he built with his dad. About enlisting in the army and how his family, especially William, hated his choice to go. He tells me about meeting Griffin and Wilder, the guys who came all the way to Heart Springs to help him get ready for Aurora, no questions asked.

The words slow, becoming more fractured the longer he talks, the closer he gets to the part where I know William dies.

And when he finally tells me about the biggest hurt of all—the ache he carries deep inside his soul, I pepper his back in kisses that I immediately pretend don't rewrite my DNA.

I told myself I could do this. That I could just be here for him. A friend, like he was for me. But the second his voice breaks and he softens in my arms like the weight of his pain finally found a place to land, *I know.*

Every wall I built to protect myself doesn't just crack—they crumble.

Because there's no coming back from this. No safe distance left to stand.

Not when he's giving me pieces of himself like they're sacred, and all I want to do is hold them like they're *mine*.

When he finally stops talking and darkness bleeds into the room, only lit up by the two nightlights I got for Aurora, I loosen my hold, but he clutches onto me like I'm the only thing keeping him standing.

"Don't," he rasps, voice thick. "Don't wanna see the look in your eyes yet."

"What look?" I breathe, blinking back more tears.

"Look that says you see me differently now."

I could lie, could promise nothing's changed, but that would be a dif-ferent kind of cruelty. Because something has changed. Not the way he thinks, though. Not in fear or pity. But in the quiet, terrifying way that feels a lot like *falling*.

I rest my forehead against his shoulder, heart thudding so loud I'm sure he can feel it.

"You're not the only one who's been carrying something," I whisper. "Not the only one who's been afraid of what the truth might sound like out loud."

He doesn't move. Doesn't press or prod. Just listens.

And maybe it's the way his body molds to mine so perfectly, or the way he lifts my hand to press a soft kiss to my palm, and then the other—but something inside me breaks open with it.

"I killed my mom."

Kade goes completely still. Doesn't turn around, but his grip on my arms tightens like he's trying to anchor me to him, or maybe the other way around.

"What?" he whispers, as if saying it too loud might break the bubble we've built around us. This moment, this pause, feels like a fragile truce. A sacred, shaky kind of peace I'm desperate for. "What are you talkin' about, darlin'?"

I squeeze my eyes shut and breathe slowly, just like he told me to when he was keeping me together, his body surrounding mine, holding me up and letting me fall apart, all at once.

"My mom," I repeat, voice cracking. "She died during childbirth. And I know I didn't actually kill her, I know it's not my fault, but…" I cling harder, and he clings right back. "But if she hadn't had me, or been pregnant or alone, she would still be here."

"Oh, Georgia." He sighs, trying to turn around.

I shake my head. "No, let me just… I need to get it out. I need to tell someone."

He stills for a long moment, then softens. "I wanna be that someone."

My breath hiccups, and I ignore the way those words make me feel.

"She was eighteen when she passed. Born and raised here, in Heart Springs, but she left at some point. I'm not sure if it was when she was already pregnant, or if that happened after she left, but she wound up in West Virginia. All I have is my birth certificate, hers, and her death certificate. No pictures, or records of anything else."

"How…" He trails off. "Never mind, you don't—"

"She hemorrhaged," I murmur and he flinches. "The hospital couldn't handle the extent of her blood loss. She passed quickly, I think, but she was alone, and she didn't list a father, so I…"

"You were in foster care, weren't you? Like Aurora?"

I nod against him, but don't I answer. For a long time, neither of us speaks, but when he finally breaks the silence, I'm surprised by how quickly he's put it all together.

"That's why you're here. In Heart Springs. You're lookin' for answers, then you'll go back." He releases a rough breath. "Said you only signed a six-month contract."

My eyes snap open, and I loosen my hold on him. "You remember I said that?"

He scoffs, chuckling quietly and glances at me over his shoulder. In the dark, I can barely make out his stormy eyes. "Spent nearly a decade in the Rangers fightin' for my life, baby. Really think I didn't pick up a skill or two?"

I blush, my body lighting up at the nickname—nearly fell out of the saddle the first time he said it. That paired with the smile on his face, laughter in his deep voice, and the feeling of his soft shirt against chiseled muscles brushing my skin—it's too much and not enough.

It's also a terrible time for my core to wake up, or my nipples to stand at attention.

Really terrible.

He's going to think tears and death make me horny.

"I guess," I murmur, stepping back. "But yeah, my contract is six months—so is my lease. I figured if I can't find anything in that amount of time, I never will."

Honestly, I'm not sure what my plan is. I love Heart Springs. Love the people I've met, the shops downtown, and the environment. I've missed the country. Missed the storms that rage, and the rainbows that follow. Breezes filled with petrichor and animals instead of smog.

There's not a whole lot tying me to my life in New York. I gave up my apartment to move here, sold half my belongings, and yeah, quitting Safe Haven was hard, but I've loved the work here just as much—maybe more.

Abby's in New York. But, she's about the only person I'd truly miss. My heart would ache for the other friends I've made, but nearly two months away and I haven't heard from a single one of them. Just her.

Could I leave Abby? Could I stay here? Do I even want to?

Kade crosses his arms and looks away, bearded jaw ticking. "And then it's back to New York."

The words sound like they were dragged over gravel.

"Are you..." My eyes narrow, my heart skipping a beat or five at his tone. "Are you mad at me?"

The thought makes my stomach hollow out and nausea crawl up my throat.

"No," he mutters, sounding very much mad.

I press a hand to his arm and his gaze snaps back to mine so fast, I drop it. He snatches it back up and uses the grip to tug me forward. I stumble into his body with a sharp inhale.

"You didn't keep up your end of the deal, darlin'," he rumbles, throwing me for a damn loop. I feel like I have whiplash. "You were cryin' because my family made you sad. Made you think of all the shit you've lost, right?" His Adam's apple bobs as he drops his voice and presses a hand to my chest, right over my heart. "You ran and hid away because *this* hurt too much to stay. Right?"

Why does it feel like he's not just talking about right now? Why does it feels like he sees me? Sees the parts I try to hide?

The ugly, painfully accurate, truth.

Nodding, I press my palm to his own heart. "And you came in here, eyes shadowed and haunted because *this* was too heavy. Because the way they love you is too much, and you…" My eyes search his, and, God, it feels like looking in a mirror. "And you don't think you deserve it."

Kade groans low in his throat, rough and pained and so fucking tortured; I feel it down to my marrow. His hand slides from my chest, up my throat, into my hair, and threads through the strands, thumb brushing my temple. "And this? What caused *this* hurt?"

My lip twitches, cheeks burning red hot.

I should have clarified earlier—when he was vibrating with anger and looked seconds from razing the world in my honor. But fuck, I just couldn't. It was too damn hot.

He's too damn hot.

"A baby," I murmur, full on smiling at the confused look on his face. "I was doing a home inspection today, and a baby chucked his full bottle directly at my head."

His hand stills on my face, eyes widening before settling on the bruise. It hurts, just not nearly as badly as it looks like it does.

"But it's so dark," he says. "Looks like someone clocked you."

"Oh, he sure did." I chuckle, biting the inside of my cheek. "And I bruise easily. It's part of my auto-immune disorder. My iron and vitamin K levels drop when I'm flaring. Comes with the territory."

Kade stares at the bruise for a long time before leaning forward and brushing his lips against it. His beard tickles my skin, but I love the feeling too much to move, or barely breathe.

The gesture is so soft, so sweet, I tear up all over again.

When he pulls back, we lock eyes and suddenly, everything around me disappears.

His gaze flicks to my lips, mine to his, and as one, we lean in—a magnet I can't seem to escape pulling us closer and closer—until his breath ghosts my skin.

Our confessions still sit heavy in my heart—the feel of his pain lingering like a physical touch, just like the memory of how it felt to kiss him.

Kissing Kade Archer was like coming up for air after drowning on my own for too damn long. There hasn't been a day—or even an hour—when I haven't thought about how it felt: the way he tastes, the delicious burn of his beard against my skin.

I want him—*desperately*.

Crave him with every cell in my body.

My brain riots and screams, telling me this is dangerous, that I'm getting too close, that I'm falling for someone I can't have, someone who's rooted in a place I won't stay.

A man whose life is changing, whose heart is…

Whose heart is *taken*.

A man who changed everything he is for the woman he loved enough to build a house for her. *This* house. And maybe the plans didn't turn out the way he thought—maybe the baby isn't his by blood, but Aurora *is* his now.

And Marlee, she's the ghost lining every wall, every shadow I'll never escape.

When he walks in this room, is it her he sees? When he falls asleep in bed, is it her he wishes were next to him?

And those dreams… those dirty, filthy, too-hot for my system to handle, dreams…

Those were about *her*.

It's too much, too scary, and I…

I'm not cut out for that. I've had enough of it. I can't do it again. I can't be someone's replacement while they wait for their forever. And I can't fill the impossible shoes of a dream he never got to finish.

"You," I choke out, pulling back, brain grasping for straws, for *anything* to save me from the storm of emotions battering inside me. "Your side of the deal. You never… you didn't…"

Kade's eyes narrow like he knows what I'm doing, but he doesn't call me out on it. Instead, he tucks my hair behind my ear and nods.

"You wanna know if I hate you. If the reason I want you so fuckin' bad is some misguided attempt at hate sex. You think this…"

He grabs my hand and drags it between us, pressing my palm against his very hard, very *large* erection. My breath catches, eyes widening, and because he's a cocky asshole—even now, he rolls his hips and pins me in place with his hard stare.

"You think I'm this goddamn hard because you're someone I'll be able to fuck out of my system."

He clicks his tongue and shakes his head, but doesn't release my hand, and thank fuck, because I don't want him to. He feels too good, too hot and hard and perfect, and suddenly, my confused system rages against the idea of putting a stop to whatever *this* is.

"That what you think, darlin'?"

"Honestly?" I breathe, dazed.

He jerks a nod. "All I ever want from you."

"Yes," I whisper, heart thudding. "Yes. I think you just want to fuck me. And…" I lick my dry lips, but it doesn't help. "I think once you fuck me, you'll forget about me, and Kade, as much as I wish I could, that's not me."

His brows pinch and he drops my hand, releasing me. "How the fuck could I forget you, freckles?"

I scoff, yanking on my hair, hands shaking.

"It's easy. Trust me. Give it some time, and it'll happen." *It always does.* "Either way, it doesn't matter. Whatever this is…" I gesture between us, stepping away, needing an escape, to run far and fast. "It can't happen. I already told you that."

"And I already told you it's too damn late. It's already happening."

Please don't push me.

"It can't!"

I'm already in too deep.

"Why the fuck not?"

Because I'll fall in love with you.

"Because I'm leaving, for starters," I snap, chest heaving. "In four months, I'll be gone."

"And? We have right now."

I gape up at him, my entire body trembling. What the hell is he talking about? His face is tense, *serious*. He's not fucking around. He really means to pursue… *something*, with me.

"And what about Aurora, Kade?" I ask, temper and anxiety rising by the second.

He shrugs. "I told you, I see somethin' I want, nothing stands in my way. Aurora is mine now. In a few days, she'll be with me and I'll take care of her. I'll be there for that little girl every damn day. Won't let her feel a second of the loss she's had. But that doesn't mean I'll stop living. Doesn't mean I have any intention of being alone."

My mouth opens and closes, once, twice. And, shit, the room actually spins.

Kade steps closer slowly, like he knows I'm easy to spook.

"You see, darlin', I've been alone. I've fought my demons in the dark for years. I buried my dreams with my dad, and for a while, I stopped living, content to punish myself. But I'm done with that. I can't do it anymore. Somewhere along the way since you walked through my door, I remembered what it was like to breathe, and I'll be fucked if I give it up now."

"You're insane," I mutter, shaking my head. "Whatever you're thinking… it's… insane and impossible."

"And you're making excuses."

"What the hell are you even suggesting? Friends with benefits? Fuck buddies?"

Surely it can't be anything more than that. We barely know each other.

He scoffs, ruffling his messy hair. "I'm thirty-one years old. The only friends I have are in the next fuckin' room, and I sure as hell don't think of them the way I think of you, freckles. And fuck buddies? Never been one for that kinda arrangement. Still ain't."

"Then…" My hands flail. "Then *what*?"

"I don't know!" he barks, chest heaving. "I don't know. All I know is that I *want* you."

I shake my head and step back, trembling hand wrapping around the door handle. My shoulders fall, breath heaving from my lungs. "And *that* answers all my questions. You don't care about me. You don't have feelings for me. You just *want*."

Tugging the door open, I turn, give him back and whisper the deepest truth of all.

"And wanting—" My voice cracks, but I force the words out anyway. "Wanting's never gotten me anything but heartache. So forgive me if I don't run toward it like it's something good."

CHAPTER TWENTY FIVE

WELCOME TO THE SADDLE, BITCH

THE RED SALOON DOORS swing in the evening breeze, all chipped and creaking, like they're daring me to walk into the most country-ass bar I've ever seen.

The Twisted Saddle's porch is wide and worn, the wood bleached gray from years of boots and spilled drinks. Music thumps from inside, muffled by laughter and the occasional holler.

It smells like beer and bad decisions. Like the kind of place where you lose your panties after a wild night on the dance floor.

Despite the butterflies battering against my insides, the thought makes me smile.

I adjust my faded cheetah print maxi skirt and cropped band tee, suddenly very aware that I'm about to stick out like a sore thumb.

Especially if Hazel and Gemma *aren't* here like they said they would be.

Yesterday, while we were putting the finishing touches on Kade's house for the big reveal, I spent time with all the Archer women.

I wasn't lying when I told Kade his family is incredible. They didn't just include me because they needed an extra set of hands—they went out of their way to make me feel welcome.

I see where Kade gets it from.

The Archer's have an uncanny ability to sneak past my walls, and God, I'm letting them.

Without anything else to distract me, I shove my shoulders back and push through the swinging doors.

It's instant sensory overload in the best way.

The music's live—a country-rock band on a low stage in the far corner, the lead singer in a battered ball cap and tight jeans. Somewhere, pool balls crack and people cheer. A hot guy is riding on the mechanical bull, his hat high in the air, his body rolling with the waves. The sight is so downright sexual, my mouth falls open.

Abby would eat this shit up.

I take a quick video before shooting her a text.

Me: You're missing out, witchling. You'd love this place.

I wait a beat for her to read the text, but she doesn't, and my stomach sinks, but I bury the sadness away. My eyes roam across a sea of cowboy hats, baseball caps, and everything in between as I hover just inside the door, clutching my bag like it might protect me.

What if Kade's sisters don't show? I probably should've gotten one of their numbers when they begged me to come to girls' night.

Maybe this was a mistake. I've barely recovered from what happened with Kade last night. Hanging out with more Archer's will only lead to trouble. But I'd already agreed, and for once, a little trouble doesn't sound so bad.

"You made it!" a familiar voice calls just as I'm debating turning around.

I scan the crowd and spot the girls at a high-top near the bar, both of them waving with wide smiles. Chuckling, I make my way over, sliding onto the empty stool next to Hazel with Gemma on her other side.

"Hi, Georgia," Gemma says, beaming. "We're so glad—"

"Yeah, yeah," Hazel cuts her off, shoving a shot glass into my hand. She leans in, dropping her voice. "We asked the bartender for gluten-free. It's 100% agave."

"Thank you," I say, voice a little rough.

"Don't hog her, Hazy!" Gemma cries, shoving her sister back. "And don't hog the tequila. I'm starving."

Hazel rolls her eyes, but she's smiling softly. "Then we should get food, not alcohol."

Gemma waves a hand through the air with a scoff and snatches a shot off the table. "Only thing I'm craving is the bliss of forgetting all my problems."

"Same," Hazel mutters.

Getting blissfully drunk and forgetting the chaotic emotions whirling through me non-stop sounds damn good right now, so I nod. "Agreed."

We clink our glasses together and tip our shots back. Before I've even swallowed, another one is thrust at me.

"Is this a hazing?" I choke out, eyes blurring from the burn.

Gemma cackles and passes me a bowl of sliced limes before coating her hand in salt. "Nope. It's just good form."

I suck on a lime to cleanse my palate, but skip the salt. We down the second shots. Mine hits like a punch to the esophagus. The Archer sisters don't even flinch.

A waiter passes, and I quickly order a water, already worried that tonight's going to wind up with me on my ass before I've even settled in.

"Make that a round of water, Jimmy," Hazel calls, swirling her finger in a circle that encompasses the table. "And another round of shots." She arches a brow at me. "Can you drink beer or just the hard shit?"

I wince. "Straight tequila is all I feel safe drinking in bars."

Though, I'm not sure I'm safe with Kade's sisters at my side. At least not my pride and morals.

"You heard her," she says to Jimmy. "Might as well bring the bottle."

He shoots her a wink. "You got it, Haze."

"Pretty sure if we split the bottle between us, you'll be carting me to the nearest hospital," I say with a nervous laugh.

Gemma smirks, tipping her chin. "Good thing we're not alone then."

I glance up just as three women saunter to the table and climb into the seats across from us.

"This is Loretta," Hazel says, pointing to an older woman in a leopard-print blouse holding a drink that's more garnish than liquor. "She keeps us in line, unless she's instigating."

"Which is most of the time," Loretta adds, her voice gravely and her smirk knowing. "And I don't apologize for it either."

Hazel gestures to a tall brunette with stunning eyes and a dark green hat that looks like Gemma's. "That's Shay. She's scary good at poker and will probably try to steal your boyfriend someday."

Shay jerks a nod in greeting and chuckles. "I get bored easily."

"And this—" Hazel waves to a blonde in a red dress and cowboy boots—"is Emmy. She's a menace."

"Only on Fridays." Emmy winks and twirls a straw between her lips.

"It's Saturday," Loretta chides, glaring at the row of empty shot glasses between us. "You drunk already, Emmaline?"

Emmy shoots her a harsh look but it softens when she stumbles. "Don't call me that unless you want me to find a biker chick to kick your ass again."

Shay and Hazel fall into a fit of laughter but Loretta scoffs, flicking Emmy between the eyes. "That bitch *tried* to kick my ass. *Try* being the key word."

Gemma sighs, propping her chin on her fist. She's smiling, but there's a sad look in her eyes. Like longing, but somehow deeper, more broken. "I've missed this place. I've missed all of you."

"Then move back home," Hazel says simply with a shrug. "Kade's back now, *finally*. It's your turn. Pack up my nephews, leave your prick of a husband, and come home."

"As easy as our brother made it look," Gemma murmurs, throat bobbing, "it's not. I can't just leave my life, or my husband, and come back to Heart Springs."

Shay scoffs and drops her elbows to the table, leaning forward. "Why the hell not? He's a dick. You deserve better."

It's on the tip of my tongue to snap at them. To tell them it wasn't easy for Kade to come home at all. I might not have been there for every step, but I was there at the beginning—when he was still drowning.

It took every ounce of courage and strength he had to come home, to move into the house he and his dad built together.

And in Aurora's room, when he opened up...

I swallow hard and down another shot while no one's looking.

"I came here to forget about Kade and all the words and emotions we let flow between us in the darkness of a quiet, sacred space last night—not to reminisce or contemplate all the ways I fucked up by walking out, when all I wanted to do was run into his arms, kiss his annoyingly handsome face again, and give in to whatever he was offering."

"Speaking of Kade," Emmy says. "How's he doing with everything?"

The whole table quiets and turns her way, so I do too—casual, like I'm not secretly starving for any scrap of information about the man.

Hazel shrugs, circling her finger around the top of her beer bottle. "You know our brother. He doesn't open up to anyone about anything. He could be ecstatic for all we know, but he keeps that shit locked down."

Eyes wide, I bite my lip hard enough to draw blood. I had no idea he kept things so close to the chest. My muscles lock up for a split second, worried everyone will turn to me for answers, but they don't.

And why would they?

For all these women know, I'm just the random social worker who dropped a bomb into Kade's life, then left it, only to be dragged back in by his mom.

Actually, they might not even know that much, and suddenly, I feel even more on the outside than before.

"When does the baby move in?" Loretta says, brows tight. "What's her name again?"

"Aurora," I blurt before I can stop myself. Everyone turns to me, and my cheeks burn from the attention. My mouth is dry when I shrug and murmur, "Her name is Aurora, and she should be with him in a few days."

And then, she'll be with him forever.

A smile tugs at my lips, and Hazel catches it, her sharp blue eyes narrowing in suspicion.

The smile vanishes, and I quickly look away, chugging my water like it might wash down whatever just gave me away.

"Her name doesn't matter," Shay says with a dismissive click of her tongue. "I don't know why the fuck he agreed to take that kid."

"Shay!" Hazel hisses, whipping her attention off me and straight onto her. "What the hell is wrong with you?"

The water slips from my hand but I catch it just in time. I can't stop the flip of my stomach or the way the bar spins around me, though.

"What?" Shay says, rolling her eyes. "It's Marlee Parker's kid."

"So?" Gemma demands, shoulders back, expression vicious. "Marlee died, bless her soul, and that baby girl has no one else. What would you expect him to do?"

She tips her shoulder. "Don't know. All I know is that if I were him, I couldn't stand to be stuck raising the love of my life's kid. Especially when I didn't have a hand in making it."

The alcohol turns in my gut, and acid claws its way up my throat, but I don't tune them out. If anything, I soak up every word like it's all the proof I need to steer clear of Kade.

"They broke up well before Aurora was born," Hazel says, fist tight around the glass bottle. "But..."

Her throat bobs and I gape at her. Surely, she's not going to agree with this woman. *Right*?

"Look, I'd be lying if I said I didn't have my concerns," she continues. "Kade just came back to us. I'm afraid being around a baby who represents everything he lost will send him back into that dark pit he hid away in for so long."

Shay nods and Emmy grimaces, but agrees quietly. Even Gemma looks torn.

My body shakes with the effort of staying in my seat. Of not running to some dark corner to cry. Of not jumping up and yelling at them—telling them to shut up and keep Kade and Aurora out of their mouths.

My brain reminds me it's not my place to speak for him—not my battle to fight. But my heart? The same heart Kade reached into last night with those gentle, calloused hands and held like it was something worth keeping? It's screaming that this is wrong.

That *they're* wrong.

But before I can act on the fire building in my chest, it's Loretta who speaks—and what she says stops me cold, confirming my biggest fear where Kade is concerned.

"I'm not so much worried about your brother. He's a damn good man. Stepping up is in his blood. Never would've taken him for the type to back down from a challenge." She takes a slow sip of her margarita, then sighs. "I'm just worried about the woman who comes *after* Marlee May. Far as I know, Kade hasn't been with anyone since her—and now that he's got her baby? Ain't a woman alive who could ever fill those shoes."

Everything around me blurs, and it takes a minute to realize I'm on the verge of crying.

Crying over a man I can't stand half the time, and feel way too damn much for the rest of it. A man I want, and like I told Kade…

Wanting gets me nowhere.

After a long, tense moment, I jump up, plaster a fake as fuck smile on my face and snag the bottle of tequila. "Enough with the sad shit! Who wants a shot?"

Because getting stupidly drunk is about the only thing in my life I can control right now.

After that, time passes in a blur of shots, chaos and random men. Men who come up to the table, asking for dances. Men who pout and flirt and buy drinks.

The first guy who asked me to join him on the dancefloor was yelled at by Hazel. Apparently STD-Stan is a *bad* man. The next guy got a thumbs-up from the Archer sisters but a no from me. Before he could feel sad about the rejection, Shay was crawling into his lap, and they've been making out ever since.

Clearly, he's not sad over me, and I'm… fine with being on my own. Been doing it my whole life.

The place is packed. I'm way past buzzed—probably drunk, laughing freely, and for once, not thinking about work or responsibilities, or what brought me to this town in the first place.

Definitely not thinking about Kade or how badly I wish *he* was here so I could crawl into his lap and kiss his stupidly perfect beard off his stupidly handsome face. It's probably for the best, though, because I don't trust myself right now.

The longer the night's stretched on, the more reckless my intentions have become. Pretty sure if I saw him right now, I'd do a hell of a lot more than kiss him, and I doubt I'd stop with sex.

No, knowing me, and the way my heart supposedly lives in my vagina, I'd probably go and admit all the crazy things I feel for the man.

Stupid, crazy, annoying feelings.

I hate them.

Still, every now and then, I catch myself glancing toward the door, stomach twisting, heart thudding.

Hazel catches me on the third sweep. "You looking for someone?"

"What? Me?" I press a hand to my chest and gasp. "No! I'm just taking it all in! It's *sooo* pretty here! So sparkly and dusty and—" I roll my empty shot glass between my fingers and grin. "*Drinky.*"

Her head falls back with a deep, smoky laugh that's all sex and fantasies for half the cowboys in the room. I glance around again and, *yep*—several men have stopped mid-sip or mid-step to watch her. One of them even has his mouth open.

"Close it, Wayne, or you'll catch flies!" Loretta hollers.

The man jerks and practically scrambles away.

A snort escapes me before I can stop it, and I slap a hand over my mouth. But it's too late. Everyone at the table turns to look at me for one beat, then two, before we all burst into laughter again.

I feel it before I see it.

The shift in the air. A ripple of attention. The subtle hush that happens when someone walks in who changes the temperature of a room just by existing.

Kade.

I spot him first, just inside the doors, flanked by two men I don't recognize but somehow know are Griffin and Wilder. I didn't get a chance to meet them last night before I took off, feigning a migraine.

The guy to his right is huge. Like, shoulders-for-days, probably-could-lift-a-bull huge. His beard is wild, streaked with silver, and his dirty blond hair is shoved into a man bun that somehow works. His shirt's tight. His jeans are tighter.

The other guy's a bit shorter, but still tall, pretty in a troublemaker way. Tousled blond hair, gray Henley, smirking like he's broken hearts in three time zones and isn't even sorry.

But then there's Kade.

And suddenly… they're both background noise.

It takes a second, liquid courage buzzing through me, to really look. But when I do, my stomach flips and something low and hot curls behind my ribs, traveling lower by the second.

Dark jeans. Thick thighs. Broad chest under a black tee that clings a little too well. Ink curls over one bicep, half-hidden under the sleeve. His beard isn't as wild as it was yesterday, like he took time to get ready tonight.

He's not doing anything special. Just walking, just existing. But my heart is beating like I ran here instead of drinking too much tequila, and my pussy is clenching around nothing but depression and need.

God help me, I want to climb him like a tree and never come down.

He's just so… so… *broad*, and sexy, and annoyingly perfect.

And then there's his favorite hat, smashing down a mess of thick, almost-curls. I've never found baseball caps sexy. In fact, I hate the sport. And judging by the size of Kade Archer's big, veiny muscles, I'd wager a guess that he's not exactly tossing balls anywhere.

Slapping them maybe.

Against a very lucky woman's ass as he pounds into—

My hand smacks against my face as if to shut my drunk brain up. Those are absolutely not thoughts we're allowed to have.

Hell to the *no*.

I glance up just in time to see Kade sit at a low table on the opposite side of the bar. He doesn't look around like he's trolling for women or familiar faces, just focuses on his blond friend and smiles at something he says. I find that smile to be arrogant and stupid and sexy.

I grip the edge of the table, nails biting into the wood, heart pounding in my ears.

Of course he looks good.

Of course he does.

Because why wouldn't the most infuriating man I've ever met walk into the bar on the one night I actually feel happy—and look like every bad decision I've never had the courage to make?

"Aww, fuck." Loretta groans, effectively dragging my attention from the last place it should be.

"What?" Emmy says, tipping back a beer.

"They're here," Hazel says, grimacing.

My heart skips a few beats, and the bar spins. Did she notice her brother? Is he coming over here?

Do I want him to?

Yes. So much yes.

"Who?" Gemma slurs, both arms wrapped around the tequila bottle like it's a teddy bear. "What's happening?"

"Them," Hazel mutters, tipping her chin at a group of broad-shouldered, denim-clad cowboys making their way through the crowd like they own the place. "Here come the boys from Cooper Ridge."

Shay whines, "Already?"

"Whatever," Emmy says, licking her straw. "They're hot."

"They're also responsible for this town taking a complete fucking nose-dive," Hazel mutters.

"That's the ranch trying to put Honey Bea out of business?" Gemma hisses, sitting up straight. "Oh, fuck no!"

My brows crash together. What the hell are they talking about? There's another big ranch here?

The group closes in fast—three guys, all tan, grinning white teeth, and obviously aware of how hot they are, heading straight for us. Everyone tenses.

"Well, well. Looks like the Saddle just got a whole lot prettier."

"If you're insinuating it's because you showed up, Clint," Hazel drawls, drumming her nails across the table. "I'd say it's quite the opposite."

Emmy flashes them a smirk and bats her lashes. "Sadly, I'd have to agree. All that money, and you still can't buy better personalities?"

"All beauty and no brains, ain't that right, Em?" The guy named Clint grins wider, his eyes rolling down her body. "Don't worry. A man don't care about smarts when you've got a tight little pussy, do they?"

Her cheeks turn pink and he chuckles like that wasn't rude as hell.

"Go find someone else to gawk at. No one here wants to look at ya," Loretta barks, waving them off.

"No." One of Clint's friends scoffs. "No one wants to look at *you,* Granny."

The two start to argue, but I tune them out, my gaze snagging on Hazel's hands. They're bunched up on the table, partially hidden behind her cur-tain of hair, fists so tight, her knuckles are bleached white.

And Gemma... Gemma looks like she's about two seconds from using the glass bottle as a bat.

Clint turns the full weight of his attention on me and saunters around the table, closing the distance between us and pinning me in place. His friends follow, and Hazel slides from her chair, jaw tight, Gemma right behind her. I spin my chair, not wanting the creep at my back, but I can't get up with him blocking me like this.

"Well, sugarpuss. Don't think we've met." He bites his lip, ugly sparse mustache twitching with the movement. "Get on your knees, and I'll introduce myself proper."

Ew. Absolutely not.

"You couldn't pay me to get on my knees for you, you tiny-dicked cretin."

Clint chuckles, dark eyes glazing over like he thinks this is some kind of fucked-up foreplay. "That right?"

I let my gaze drag from his overpriced boots to that smug, punchable smirk, and curl my lip in disgust. Hate men like him. He reminds me of Abby's ex.

"You clearly didn't hear my friends the first time, so let me break it down real slow in a way your tiny brain will understand: nobody at this table wants anything to do with you. Least of all me." I smile sweetly. "Now scurry along. Your fragile masculinity and tiny dick energy is dripping on my boots."

"Does *this* feel tiny to you, sugarpuss?" he mutters, licking his lower lip and grinding the hard ridge of himself against my thigh.

My temper flares red hot, as disgust and shock assault my senses.

"Don't touch me, asshole!" I snap, shoving Clint and his unwanted touch away from me.

He stumbles back and hits another table, sending drinks and a chair tumbling to the ground, but he quickly rights himself. His friends step back, eyes wide, and I sense the girls around me jumping to their feet, shouting words I can't hear.

Before I can blink, he's back in my face, his hand around my throat, and I just… *freeze.*

"I don't know who you think you are, you little cunt—"

"Get your fuckin' hands off my woman," a low, deadly voice rumbles. "*Now.*"

And then…

Clint is just *gone.*

CHAPTER TWENTY SIX

SEEING RED

RED.

It's all I see when I spot his fucking hand on her throat.

Not the lights. Not the crowd. Not even the cowboy hat tumbling off the smug asshole's head as I grab him by the collar and slam him into the nearest post hard enough to rattle the walls.

Georgia.

My Georgia.

He stumbles, gasping, hands digging at my fist like the little bitch he is. His face is red and mottled, but I can't see past the haze settling in around me, coating my world in a burning glow.

"What the fuck, man?"

"You ever touch her again, and I'll decorate this floor with your goddamn teeth," I snarl, body vibrating.

He shoves back, but I barely move. "She liked it rough—just playing hard—"

Crack.

My fist hits his face so hard it echoes. He drops like a sack of shit, catching himself against a barstool, blood blooming beneath his nose.

"You wanna finish that sentence?" I roar, stepping over him. "Go ahead. Try me, motherfucker."

I can sense Wild on my right, Griff on my left, and I vaguely realize the bar's gone silent, but all I see is *him.*

Him in her face.

Her pushing him away.

His hands on her throat.

Her. Throat.

His eyes are wild now, but he's stupid. Stupid enough to swing. I duck and slam my forearm into his gut, driving him back into the table. Bottles crash to the floor. Chairs scatter. Someone screams.

Doesn't matter.

He grabs my shirt, tries to yank me down—but I twist, lift him by the collar again, and slam him face-first into the bar, holding him there.

"You don't talk to her. You don't look at her. You don't even fucking breathe in her direction," I hiss, pressing him down, nose mashed against the wood, blood smearing across the grain. "You understand me?"

And because he's got a death wish, he keeps running his fuckin' mouth.

"She's just—"

I drag him back by the shirt and punch him again.

Harder.

This time, he slumps, dazed and sputtering on the floor.

"She's just *mine*," I snap.

"Kade!" someone yells behind me. "You're gonna kill him!"

Good.

I shove him off the bar, and he crumples, wheezing on the floor like the pathetic sack of shit he is. His friends are nowhere to be seen and the guys are flanking me, arms crossed, faces serious but confident.

Locking eyes with the piece of shit glaring up at me, I crouch—and for once, I don't even feel the burn in my thigh. All I feel is satisfaction and lingering rage.

"Get the fuck out," I growl, fists clenched. "If I ever see you again, I'll finish what I started. Got me?"

He scoffs, shoving himself off the floor. I cock a brow and step into his space and his face crumples a second before he tucks tail and scurries away.

Coward.

Only when the fuckface and his friends are gone, the door swinging behind them, do I finally turn to face her.

Georgia's frozen, her chest rising and falling fast, hands curled into trembling fists on her lap. Her eyes lock with mine—bright, wide and glassy.

The sight of her so scared sucks all the air from my lungs.

I take a step toward her and she flinches like she's scared of me. My knees damn near buckle.

"Darlin'?" I rasp, gaze trailing across her face, her body, before zeroing in on her throat. It's too fuckin' dark in here, and I'm too far to see any damage. "Georgia?"

She doesn't move, doesn't speak, doesn't look away, but I see the way her bottom lip quivers—and the instant it does, I'm moving again.

Don't stop till I'm right in front of her, surrounding her, not an inch of space between us, but I don't touch her, not yet. Her neck cranes back, eyes tracking my every move. Her throat bobs and she tucks that shaking lip between her teeth, biting down hard.

"You scared of me, freckles?" I murmur, muscles vibrating with the need to hold her.

Her mouth opens, and closes, brows tight, eyes blinking furiously, before she finally breathes, "Never."

Relief has my shoulders slumping, but I can't get a read on her. My hands reach out, hesitating, hovering between us. "What's going through that pretty head of yours?"

"You…" She swallows thickly, shaking her head. "You defended me."

"Of course I did," I say, scoffing. "Why the fuck wouldn't I?" My gaze snaps to the door, jaw ticking, pissed off all over again. "He touched you. Put his hand around your throat like he had any fuckin' right. I should kill—"

A soft, delicate hand grips my jaw, forcing my face back to hers. A shudder runs through me at the feeling.

"You called me yours," she breathes, fingers stroking through my beard absently. "You called me your woman, Kade. Called me yours. Defended me like you meant it, too."

"I did mean it…" I trail off, heart racing. Hadn't even realized what I'd been saying. Just knew that I could have easily killed him for what he did.

"Why?" she whispers, trailing her hand across my face, my cheek, smoothing her thumb beneath my eye with so much reverence, I damn near forget how to breathe. "Why would you do that for me?"

Goddamn, my sweet, soft girl. She has no idea how much she means to me, does she?

And why the fuck would she?

Last night, we opened up to each other, laid our demons down between us in the darkness, but when it came time for me to put my cards on the table, tell her the crazy shit that's been going through my head for weeks now, the damn near insatiable way I want her, *need her*... I froze up.

She was asking—begging me, to put a name on it, and I didn't, couldn't, too scared to fuck this up the way I fuck up everything else in my life.

All I knew in that moment was that I wanted Georgia Walker more than I wanted anything in my life other than Aurora, but that's a whole different kind of want.

I want Aurora to be safe and loved, protected and cherished. Want her to learn and grow with me.

With Georgia... I just want *her*.

In every way. In all ways.

Why the hell couldn't I have just told her *that?*

Exhaling roughly, I drop my forehead to hers and finally give into the need to wrap her in my arms. Her hands fall between us, tangling in the fabric of my shirt and she melts into me.

"Freckles," I murmur, kissing her forehead. "You wanna know why I defended you like that?"

"Yes." Her eyes flit between mine, fingers digging in deeper. "I don't understand it."

"How could I not?" I whisper. "You think I could stand there and watch someone put their hands on you? Talk to you like that? Not a fucking chance in hell."

A deep breath rattles out of me, shaking me down to my bones.

"You walked into my life like a goddamn whirlwind, Georgia. All fire and fight and freckles, and now I can't go a day without thinking about you. Wanting you. Craving you. Worrying about you." I swallow hard, tightening my grip on her. "You might not realize it yet, but you're mine, and I'm gonna prove it to you."

Her breath catches, and for a second, I think I've gone too far—but then she exhales in this quiet, relieved little laugh that's so soft, it brushes right against my ribs.

"That's really nice. Love the way it sounds."

"That right?" I murmur, confusion and shock bouncing through my system.

This is one-eighty from the way we left shit last night.

This is the Georgia who wrapped herself around my back and held on tight through my storm. The one who kissed me on the back of that horse, made out with me like we were lovesick teenagers, desperate to never let go.

"Yep." She wraps a finger around a chunk of my beard and tugs hard enough to make my eyes water, but I don't stop her, too caught up in the moment, too addicted to the feel of her.

"Your beard tickles." She giggles. "Feels like fuzzy sandpaper."

I blink, stunned—and then inhale, catching a wave of tequila so strong it singes my brain. "Drunk, baby?"

She lifts her head and gives me a squinty, slow-motion shrug. "No." She pauses. "Yes." A beat. "A little." Then she hiccups and boops my nose. "I like that name."

"Baby?"

An adorable nod. "Say it again. *Slower.*"

"I'll call you whatever you want me to," I say softly, grin tugging at my lips when she boops me again. "Think I'll start with *mine*, though."

Her pupils dilate and she sways. "Sounds dangerous, cowboy."

Christ, she's fuckin' cute.

"You like danger?"

"Yes." She nods, then shakes her head, shoulders slumping as she half-wails, half-sobs, "No! I'm too boring for danger! Abby always says I need to jump out of planes, but I don't want to! I hate heights."

"That's okay," I soothe, petting her hair. "We don't need to go skydivin', baby."

She pouts and hiccups again. "Can we have fries though?"

"Interesting," Griff mutters, eyes glued to Georgia who's back to playing with my beard and smiling. He shoots me a wink. "She's a fun drunk."

"And she really is hot as hell," Wilder adds.

My jaw ticks, and I bundle her deeper into my chest like I can keep him from flirting by osmosis or some shit. "Fuck off, asshole."

"We split this," Gemma announces, holding an empty tequila bottle like a trophy. "Damn good show, big bro." She cackles, stumbling. "Oh shit, that rhymed."

"Nice right hook," Hazel adds, flicking me right between the brows. "Could've stepped in earlier though. I almost had to kill a grown man." Her eyes narrow, sliding from me to Georgia—who's now fully snuggled against my chest, huffing me like I'm her emotional support hoodie.

"She drank a lot," Hazel murmurs, lip lifting in a soft smile. "But she's good people. Not many people can keep up with an Archer. I like her."

"So do I," I grunt, wrapping one arm around Georgia's waist, the other gliding through her curls, memorizing the way she feels wrapped up in my arms. "Who the fuck was that?"

"That would be Clint Cooper of Cooper Ridge," Hazel says, rolling her eyes so hard they might stick. Her gaze flicks to Griffin, then back to me. "Tiny-dicked ego maniac, according to your girl."

My brows lift, but I don't correct her. Because she's right.

Don't know how the hell I'm gonna pull it off, but she's mine.

I just have to prove it to her—*when she's sober.*

Georgia shifts again, murmuring something incoherent against my chest. I lean down, catching the words "*big pecs*" and "*leather*" and smother a laugh in her curls.

But then she sways hard, and my smile dies.

"I'm takin' her home," I say, chin jerking toward my sisters and their friends. "Can you handle the girls? Make sure they all get home safe?"

"Sure thing," Wilder says, not even looking up—too busy drooling over Emmy.

"He's talkin' to me, dickwad." Griff scoffs and turns to me. "No worries, man. I'll wrangle the herd. You just take care of…" His gaze drops to Georgia, who chooses that exact moment to lift her head.

"I'm tired," she says, blinking up at me. "And *starving.*"

"Okay, darlin'," I murmur, ducking down until my lips brush her hair. "Let's get you home."

"Don't remember where I live."

"That's alright." Wasn't taking her home anyway. "You drive here?"

Georgia nods, tugging her keys from her purse. She holds them up, blinking at me with the kind of soft, sleepy look that hits me dead center.

"Will you drive?" she whispers. It's the hope in her voice that damn near drops me to my knees. The vulnerability. The trust. Like she knows I'll keep her safe without her ever having to ask.

"'Course," I mutter, throat tight as I glance over my shoulder. "Griff—take my truck."

I toss him my keys and don't wait for a reply—just snag hers and guide her toward the door, one hand wrapped around her waist like she's already mine to protect.

Georgia stays close the whole way out, her thumb tucked into my belt beneath the back of my shirt, her warm palm ghosting my skin. She doesn't stumble, but I keep my arm locked around her anyway. Not because she needs it, but because I need her close after what happened tonight.

My eyes sweep the parking lot, scanning every shadow, every group of stragglers still loitering by the bar. Clint Cooper and his cronies are long gone, but tension still simmers in my spine.

"Where'd you park?" I ask, slowing to a stop. "Don't see the Beamer anywhere."

She giggles and points to an older black Jeep parked beside my truck. "Right there."

I blink. Hard. "Darlin', that's not your—"

"It is," she huffs, pulling away from me and beelining for it before I can snatch her back.

"I never wanted that stupid car," she says dreamily, brushing her palm across the paint.

"Tried to lease one of these, but they were all out. Only thing they had left was that fancy BMW." She turns, eyes heavy but shining, and grins up at me. "Had a hell of a sound system, though."

Chuckling, I thumb the fob. Sure enough, the Jeep chirps and unlocks. I open the passenger door, ready to help, but she beats me to it, reaching for the frame like she's gonna climb in herself.

Not on my damn watch.

Before she can even lift a leg, I catch her by the hips and lift her clean off the ground.

She lets out the cutest little squeal I've ever heard. "What the fuck, Kade!"

"Think you meant, *thank you, Kade*," I mutter, voice low as I lean over her and click the buckle into place.

Her chest brushes mine, little nipples so hard, my mouth waters. She gasps, just the faintest sound, but it shreds through me like shrapnel. Her hands land on my shoulders to steady herself, fingers flexing through the cotton of my shirt. My breath stalls as her wide, green eyes meet mine.

She doesn't pull away.

Neither do I.

"Beautiful," I breathe, tucking a strand of hair behind her ear. My knuckles graze her flushed cheek, and her lips part. "So goddamn beautiful, baby."

Her gaze dips to my mouth.

"Dangerous," she murmurs, throat bobbing. "You're so dangerous to my system, Kade Archer."

"Why's that?"

Her tongue glides across her lower lip, eyes still locked on my mouth, and whispers, "I could fall in love with you so easily if I let myself."

Air stalls in my fuckin' lungs. She's drunk, not in her right mind, and asking her questions feels like cheating, but fuck, how can I not?

"Why can't you let yourself?" I ask, throat dry and tight, fingers trailing across her jaw. She leans into that touch and words slip free before I can stop them. "Why can't you fall with me?"

"Because…" There's so much pain in her expression, it guts me. "Because you'll leave when I let you in. Everyone always does."

I want to tell her she's wrong. Wanna promise I'll be different, that I won't break her heart, or abandon her, but she's not in her right mind tonight and I don't think there's a damn thing I can say to prove that I'm, that *this*, is different.

Just have to show her.

Sighing, I lean in and press a lingering kiss to her forehead. "Let's get you home."

She smiles up at me, but her eyes are glassy, and I don't think it has a damn thing to do with the liquor. "Don't forget the fries."

CHAPTER TWENTY SEVEN

GLUTEN FOR PUNISHMENT

DID I EAT FRENCH fries?

My mouth tastes like them, and something else. Something sweet.

Rolling over, I blink my heavy eyes open slowly. The dark room spins. Not a slow, lazy kind of spin, either. More like someone tied me to the fan and put it on full blast. My heart kicks hard against my ribs, sending panic blooming through my chest. I stare up at the ceiling, breath held, trying to place anything familiar.

Nothing comes.

The ceiling's smooth and pale and *not mine.*

Where the hell—?

My fingers curl into the blanket, and I freeze. It's not the quilt from Robin I keep on my rental's lumpy bed. This one's soft, heavy, and clean. The sheets beneath me smell like fresh detergent and something warm and masculine… cedarwood, maybe?

Moonlight streams through a window somewhere to my left, slanting across the wall and catching on a polished wood nightstand. The silver drawer handle gleams like it's brand new.

Definitely not mine.

Oh, God. This isn't my room.

My stomach flips. Not emotionally. *Literally*. I jolt upright, and immediately regret it.

Pain claws up my sides, and my stomach lurches like it's being gripped in a vise. A low whimper escapes me as I slap a hand over my mouth.

No, no, no…

I scramble off the bed, limbs leaden and shaky, knees buckling the second my feet hit the hardwood. Pain shoots straight through the bone. My joints throb like someone's trying to screw them loose from the inside out, and my head—fuck, my head feels like it's wrapped in barbed wire.

I half-stumble, half-drag myself toward the bathroom across from me. The cold tile bites into my bare knees as I skid toward the toilet, fingers digging into the bowl just in time.

And I lose it.

Everything.

Definitely alcohol, definitely some kind of food.

And definitely bad.

I heave, dry and wet, as my throat burns and my ribs scream. My hands shake, my vision blurs. I can feel my lymph nodes swelling already—an ache blooming in my armpits, my neck. My hips throb like I ran ten miles. Everything hurts.

And I'm wearing—

I glance down and catch a flash of navy fabric and the worn white cotton letters across the chest that reads *Ranger*.

It's Kade's shirt.

I'm wearing Kade's shirt, and…

Using my free hand, I check what's underneath and my shoulders slump. Shirt *and* panties, but nothing else. I don't get a chance to think about what that means before the bedroom door slams open somewhere behind me.

"Georgia?" His voice is rough and groggy, but he sounds scared. "Darlin', you okay?"

Quickly flushing, I lean up and scramble for toilet paper, wiping my face even though I know this is only the beginning—the prequel to the horror show about to go down.

"I'm fine," I rasp, nausea already blooming again.

My head falls to the toilet seat, and I thank all the stars in the sky that the toilet is new.

The light coming in from his room is suddenly blocked out and without even looking, I know he's staring down at me with narrowed, stormy eyes and a ticking beard. His hand's probably gripping the handle like he's ready to yank the thing from its hinges.

"You're not fine," he murmurs, voice closer than I expect. So close, I shiver. Joints pop, and then he's there, brushing my hair from my cheek. "Drank too much, didn't you, baby?"

My heart skips a few beats at the name, and as if it's all I needed to unlock a hidden vault, everything comes racing back in.

The bar with his sisters, Loretta's words that pushed me to drink way too damn much, that asshole putting his hands on me and Kade fighting to defend my honor.

His admission, his feelings, his *wants*.

Sound of his voice when it wrapped around the words *baby* and *mine*.

I remember him bundling me into his truck and kissing my forehead—repeatedly. Remember the ghost of his beard over my flesh when he carried me inside and left me alone in his room to change while he made...

While he made me the French fries I wouldn't shut up about.

"No," I groan, rolling my head against my arm. "I mean, yeah. I drank too much but this isn't just that..."

God, he's going to think I'm a freak. Too much work. A nut job with a weird allergy and a body that's far too delicate for his rugged, country ways.

How could a guy like him, raised the way he was, understand a person with health issues like I have and not think I'm making it up? Other people have—*so* many people have discredited my illness. Told me I'm a hypochondriac. That it's in my head.

Happened my entire childhood. Every foster parent dismissed me, swept my pain under the rug. Both my exes rolled their eyes and scoffed at my flare-ups. The last one even nicknamed me *princess*, and it wasn't because I'm sweet and delicate. Whenever we'd go out, he said I was spoiled and difficult because I had to be careful with what I consumed.

Kade will be just the same, and maybe...

Maybe once I tell him, he'll realize everything he thought he wanted earlier was nothing but a pipe dream. That a future between us is exactly what I thought it would be...

Impossible.

He smooths my hair back from my face and presses his palm to my forehead.

"You're really hot," he grumbles, tone laced with an edge I can't discern. "Are you sick? Did you catch something?"

Water turns on, but I ignore the sound of it, focusing on the feeling of his hand pressed against my warm skin. He feels *so good.*

And of course, my stomach chooses that exact second to full Exorcist again. I sob into the toilet, and my cries only grow louder when he softly picks up my hair, bundling it at my nape and rubs my back.

"It's okay," he whispers, never letting up his kindness. "I've got you, darlin'. I'm not going anywhere, Georgia. I'm here, and I'm not letting you die."

And then I realize I'm begging him to leave me to die on my own between coughs and heaves.

When I'm finally done, he flushes the toilet for me and softly grips my chin, dragging my tear-stained face up to meet his gaze.

"What happened?"

"I ate French fries," I mutter, feeling miserable. "I'm just having a flare-up." Swallowing thickly, I drop my eyes, unable to see the rejection in his. "I can go home if—"

And then he's dragging my eyes right back up.

"Look at me." In the moonlight, I catch his face harden a split second before he grinds out, "You try to leave this house, and I'll throw you over my fuckin' shoulder and tie you to my bed."

I blink rapidly, mouth opening and closing at the vehemence in his tone. At the threat that should send me running for the hills but has a different part of me warming instead.

"Pretty sure tying me to your bed is the last thing you want right now," I say dumbly. "Really bad idea."

Kade's lip lifts in the hint of a smirk, but it drops just as fast. "Don't joke right now, baby. I'm seconds from losing my mind."

Squinting, I whisper, "Why?"

His shoulders fall an inch, and he tugs on his hair before pushing to his feet. I expect him to leave, but he doesn't, just busies himself at the sink. When the water cuts off, he pauses, head falling.

"Fuck," he breathes, hands braced on the vanity. "I did this? Made you sick?" He shakes his head and gives me a pained look. "I'm so sorry, Georgia. Recipe said homemade was safe. Took a while, and you fell asleep at the island before they were finished. Put you in my bed and you didn't even budge, but..."

My cheeks burn. "I got up and ate them."

He was asleep on the couch, and I leaned against the island, watching him sleep while I munched on delicious homemade fries he'd left to cool on the counter. I'd still been so drunk and craving something that sure as fuck wasn't carbs, but a hell of a lot more dangerous and I...

"I dipped them in your rocky road ice cream," I whisper, face red hot.

Before my diagnosis, it was my favorite. And going down, it still was. Coming back up, however... Not so much.

Reaching out, I squeeze his leg, the material of his sweats soft beneath my hand. "I did this, Kade. Not you. Sometimes, I forget. Shouldn't, but it happens, and I pay the price."

In all honesty, I don't think I truly forgot, but the alcohol was speaking for my stomach—and hormones—and I let myself be weak in one way so I wouldn't be weak in another.

He still looks tortured, so I add, "The fries were delicious and I really appreciate you going to so much trouble. But you didn't do this. I promise."

After a long moment, he sighs and drops to a crouch next to me. A warm wet cloth is pressed to my cheeks, my lips and jaw. It takes me a second to realize he's cleaning me up—caring for me, in the only way he can, and my eyes sting.

This man is *killing me.*

"What can I do?" he murmurs, breath ghosting across my damp cheeks. "Need to fix this."

This, not *me.*

Just like before, but I'm starting to see a totally different meaning where this man is concerned.

"Nothing," I whisper, leaning into his touch. "I'm okay."

"No you're not." His brows furrow and he grimaces, moving to clean my hair but he doesn't call attention to the mess I made. "Feel fuckin' terrible, baby. You're sick, miserable, and on the cold floor. Let me help you."

Kade pauses, eyes meeting mine, and the earnest look in his stormy iris' makes my heart swoon and soar all at once. I can feel my walls shaking, trembling with the need to let him in, but it's so damn hard.

I'm terrified of what'll happen when I finally do—and finally, because at this point, I know it's only a matter of time before he wins.

And as if he can see the battle happening inside me, can hear all my protests, he cups my jaw tenderly and says the one thing I'm helpless to resist.

"Please, darlin'. Just let me carry this. Can't take your pain, but I can take the weight of havin' to do it alone. You've done enough all by yourself. Time to let someone else stand beside you."

Beside me. Not in front of me. Not without me.

Beside me. Like a partner. A team. A family.

The words hit harder than I want to admit. Because he's not wrong. I've been doing this—all of this—alone for so long I forgot what it feels like to have help that doesn't come with strings, or pity, or the expectation that I'll owe them for it later.

Foster homes. College. Diagnosis. Grief. Work. Survival.

Every heartbreak, every hospital visit, every gut-wrenching flare, I've faced with no one but myself and a too-heavy bag of *just in case* supplies.

No one's ever said that to me before.

That it's okay to be tired. To not hold everything together. That maybe I deserve to rest too.

And God... how badly I want to believe him.

"I'd love that, but..." My throat tightens, and I feel the words before I can say them, "But you don't *have* to."

"I know," he murmurs, brushing his thumb across my cheek. "But I want to, because I want *you*."

Something cracks inside me—a slow, splintering release of years of being strong because I had no other choice.

And for the first time in maybe forever...

I don't feel so alone.

But...

Sighing, I can't help the small smile that curves my lips, or keep the embarrassment from my cheeks. With a slow, defeated but giddy nod, I press my palm against his hand on my cheek, thanking him the only way I can.

"What I really need," I murmur, brain swimming and spinning all at once. "Is the pill container in my purse. It's pink, you can't miss it."

He nods sharply, face serious, like he's making a mental list, and against my will, I smile.

"What else?"

"Water, please, and then, uh..." I thought I couldn't get any redder, but then I have to squeak out, "Some *privacy*."

"Privacy? What the hell for?"

God, he sounds and looks adorable when he's confused and possessive, but this is the last thing I ever wanted to have to say to a man, especially Kade Archer.

"Kade," I whisper-hiss, eyes wide, body vibrating with humiliation. "My stomach is rioting right now. What I need is privacy, extremely loud music—but not too loud because my head is killing me, some incredible-smelling room spray, and for this to not be happening, but we're here now. *Get it*?"

It takes a second, but then it clicks, and when it does, this foolishly wonderful, asshole of a man rolls his eyes and sighs, long and loud, like I'm the one being dramatic.

"Darlin', I've been cleaning up animal shi—"

I smack a hand to his mouth and lean in, hissing, "If you ever hope to see me naked someday, don't you dare finish that sentence."

His brows go high and he chuckles, pressing a kiss to my palm. That single kiss is equivalent to dynamite directly to my system.

"Naked's 'bout to come a hell of a lot sooner than someday," he mutters, pushing to stand.

I notice him wince and rub his thigh, but before I can ask him what's wrong, he steps behind me and the rush of loud water fills the bathroom. My head snaps to the side and I gape, fingers clenching the toilet lid.

I'd been in a desperate rush when I ran in here, and all the time I spent helping plan the housewarming party kept me in Aurora's room. Much as I wanted to snoop, I couldn't do it with his family around.

"You got it," I breathe, jealousy and excitement thrumming through my sluggish veins. "You got the dream tub for the dream window with the dream view."

He grabs a glass canister from the ledge beneath the giant arched window and pours something into the massive tub that's quickly filling with water. Steam clouds the window, but moonlight still pours in around us, along with the intoxicating scent of flowers.

Kade gives me a strange, but soft look and nods, palming the back of his neck.

"Yeah, well, a pretty girl once told me this window deserves the best tub a bucket-bathing hillbilly like me could get and…" He smiles, brushing my hair back. "I'm finding it's impossible to tell that girl no."

My heart races, brain rewriting itself before I can stop it.

"I'll drop towels, water, and your pills by the door. Tub's loud enough to block out any… *sounds* that may arise before I leave."

"Leave?"

My insides are confused.

I want him to stay as much as I want to have my vagina waxed—which is none and never—but the idea of him leaving… It makes me sicker than the ice cream.

He hikes a thumb over his shoulder. "Gonna run to my mom's real quick. I'll be back in…"

His cocked brow tells me to fill in the blanks, and I blush even harder. "Can I text you when I'm in the tub?'

Kade chuckles and nods. "Phone's on the charger. I'll leave it with everything else."

Before he can walk away, words escape me, loud and filled with way too damn much longing, and hope.

"I hate being alone, so…" I swallow thickly, and murmur, "thank you for staying even though you don't have to."

"Nowhere else I'd rather be, darlin'."

CHAPTER TWENTY EIGHT

POISON 101

"MA!" I WHISPER-HISS, HEART hammering, body begging me to go back home.

Home—where I left the girl I'm pretty sure I'm halfway in love with, violently heaving into my new toilet. Least that's what she was doing when I silently dropped off her supplies outside the bathroom door, pretending I couldn't hear a damn thing.

"Wake up!" My hand grips her slim shoulder a little tighter, and I shake her softly, but hard enough to get her attention. "Ma, I need you!"

"Kade?" she mumbles, rolling onto her back blinking slowly. "Son, that you?"

Crossing my arms, I scoff. "Who else would it be?"

"I have five children. Could have been any one of you—or maybe Wilder." She clicks her tongue. "That boy has nightmares."

My stomach flips, eyes flying to the spare bedrooms down the hall. Griff texted me hours ago that he got everyone back to my mom's safely. Emmy's sister picked her, Loretta, and Shay up, but Griff took care of Wild and my sisters.

"You've heard them?" I rough out, throat thick. "Wilder's nightmares."

"And Griff's," she says softly, eyes drifting closed again. "If you're just here to chat about your friends, can we do it in the morning, with coffee preferably."

"Not here for them. Need to talk to you." And because my emotions have well and truly taken a fucking nosedive, I add, "Really not safe to sleep with the door unlocked, Ma. Could have been a burglar."

She sits up and swings her legs over the bed, sighing in exasperation. "But if I lock the door, how the hell will my boyfriend sneak in when everyone is finally asleep?"

I gape, stumbling back a step. It's on the tip of my tongue to argue with her, to demand she explains herself, but another wave of urgency washes through me, and I shove the questions aside for later. *Much later.*

"Whatever." My fingers rake through my hair, heart physically aching to get back. "Need your help. I poisoned my—" I swallow hard.

Fuck.

Almost just called her my girlfriend, but the word feels all wrong. Not because she's not mine, she is, whether she knows it or not, but *girlfriend* doesn't even come close to what I feel for her.

Not serious or—Christ, it's not *permanent* enough for these *feelings* vibrating inside me.

Mom jolts to her feet, eyes wide, and smacks my gut. "Who the hell did you poison, Kade William Archer? Better not be my goats again. Swear to all that is holy, if you put cherries in—"

"Ma!" I bark, rubbing the sting away. Woman hits hard. "It's not the goats. I poisoned Georgia."

She stares at me for a long moment, mouth opening and closing.

I watch a myriad of facial expressions appear, disappear, and morph, before she finally settles on a knowing smile.

"You're together, aren't you?" I say nothing, and she practically screams. "I knew it! You two have been dancing around this since the first time I met her!"

Groaning, I turn around and stomp out of her damn bedroom.

Knew I shouldn't have come here.

She follows me, clapping and cheering like it's not nearly fuckin' dawn, but I ignore her, searching every cabinet and drawer in the upstairs bathroom for what I need. All the while, she never stops rambling about *kids with my eyes and her hair,* and *wedding next summer.*

I tune out the way her words make me feel, but they still trickle through my system like slow, sticky honey, invading my senses.

Would Georgia really want that? To be with me in a forever kinda way?

My gut twists.

First, I need to convince the woman to stay in Heart Springs before I go talking about marriage and having my babies. Need to get Aurora settled and comfortable, make sure that little girl is happy and healthy—with *both* of us, preferably.

"Ma," I drawl, shooting her a look. "Georgia's back at my place, sick as a dog because she ate something she can't have. She says she's set on meds, but I wanna make sure. Can you help me, or do I need to call the doctor?"

Before she can answer, Colby's door bangs open and she all but falls into the hallway, eyes heavy with sleep. "You poisoned Georgia? You know she has celiac! She can't have gluten, assface!"

"Can y'all keep it down? Don't want this to become a debate for the whole damn house. She's embarrassed enough as it is."

My mom's shoulders drop on a dreamy sigh. "Look, Colby. He's so protective of her already."

Colby grins, bouncing on her toes. "You two are so freaking cute. Can I be a bridesmaid?"

"I'm leaving," I say with a grunt, slamming a drawer shut. "You're both nuts."

"Okay, okay," my mom rushes out, hands up placatingly. "What are you looking for exactly?"

My throat constricts, and I quickly check my phone. She hasn't texted yet, but I don't wanna be gone much longer. I'll sit on the porch if I have to.

"She's really sick, and I drew her a bath and filled it with your salts, but I don't have any girly shit. So…" I spin, and snatch up the first pink bottle I find. "Can I borrow this?"

Colby scoffs and storms forward. "Have you seen Georgia's curls? Do you want to ruin her hair?"

She shoves bottle after bottle into my hands, talking a mile a minute about deep conditioners and body wash. Do I need a shaver or cream…or just soap? She spends a minute spinning in place, searching for a clean, soft towel that'll be gentle on Georgia's curls.

Mom runs in with a bag and fills it with the loot falling from my arms, murmuring, "I added in some gluten-free food for when she feels better, tea, and other things to settle her stomach. All safe for our girl."

Our girl.

Like she's family already.

Just like Aurora and my friends.

Just like every animal she's rescued and the bees she loves like they're her kids.

My mom's capacity for love is everything, and I missed out on it for too damn long.

Not anymore.

My eyes burn and I kiss her head. "Thank you for not giving up on me, Ma."

Her breath catches and she wraps me in her arms. "Never have, never will."

"Ah ha!" Colby spins, holding up a hair dryer and some weird, poky-looking thing with a manic sort of grin. "Do you use YouTube? You're gonna need this."

Everything in me deflates, and a laugh slips free.

These people are insane and over the top, but they're *my* people—and they're stepping up for Georgia like they're her people too.

Thank fuck, because my girl deserves all the community and family she's never had. She deserves to be loved like *this*.

And I'm going to show her exactly how that feels.

CHAPTER TWENTY NINE

Georgia

WANTING

I'M NEVER LEAVING THIS bathtub.

It's so big, and the water's so deep and hot, it covers all of me, soothing me down to the bones. Not to mention, the lavender and honey salts Kade poured in must have some kind of magical healing powers. After just thirty minutes, I'm half asleep and my stomach is settled way faster than it should be.

When I finally felt well enough to climb in, I opened the window, letting the cold early morning air counteract the steam coating the panes. The combination between that and the hot water is a kind of Heaven I've never felt before.

I flick my gaze to the slightly open bathroom door, and my stomach swoops for a whole new reason.

True to his word, Kade left me everything I needed and disappeared, including a new toothbrush I happily used. I took my pills, sipped on water, but after I climbed in, I hesitated to text him, needing a few minutes to wrap my brain around everything that's transpired.

It's a lot, and yet, something in me feels settled in a way that surprises me. While the desire to run that always thrums through my system is still very much here, gnawing at me, whispering that this is a mistake…

So is something else.

Something warm and addicting, exciting and… *new.*

And maybe it's time I grab onto it—consequences be damned.

That thought in mind, I send him a text, letting him know he can come back whenever he's ready.

I rush through washing my body with the cedar-scented soap I find on the ledge, a hum of pleasure slipping free. It smells so good—mostly because it's Kade in a bottle: addicting and comforting.

A grin splits my face when I find the frizz-free curl shampoo I shoved into his chest all those weeks ago at the store.

By the time I'm done with my hair, he still hasn't returned, so I reluctantly pull the plug and get out, wrapping my body in the towel. I freeze at the bathroom door, unsure what I'm supposed to do.

I slept in this man's bed. Got sick in his bathroom. Used his tub—probably all before he did.

And now, I'm pretty sure I'm alone in his perfect house, naked and without any of my things. The only clothes I have are what I wore to the bar, but… I don't want to wear them.

To be honest, I don't want to wear *anything.*

What I want is to lie naked in Kade's bed, and wait for him to find me. To show him how thankful I am for everything he's done for me. I want to thank him with my mouth and body, again and again, until he understands the feelings I'm too scared to say out loud.

But I'm not brave enough to lay myself out like an all you can eat buffet, especially after the whiplash I've put him through.

No matter how badly I want to.

Sighing, I search the room for my clothes, but come up empty. My eyes slide to the large oak dresser across from the massive bed, and I hesitate for less than a minute before saying *fuck it.*

I find a soft white T-shirt that smells like Kade and slip it on. It falls off my shoulder and lands mid-thigh. And as a small act of bravery, I forego panties.

After towel drying and finger-combing my hair, I quietly open the door and slip out into the hall. A bang followed by a quiet, masculine curse has my heart racing and stomach flipping.

Biting my lip, my feet pad across the cold, wooden floor toward the living room, eyes adjusting to the warm sunlight pouring in through the wall of windows across the back of the house. There are new, navy curtains pulled over the ones in the front, but it's still bright.

The scent of something light and earthy fills the air, layered with warmth from the fireplace and the sharp bite of a spring morning breeze drifting in through the cracked sliding glass door.

I freeze when Kade comes into view and just... watch him.

He's still in his gray sweats and a soft black t-shirt, dark, wavy hair falling into his face and catching in the scruff of his beard as he crouches in front of the coffee table, setting up what appears to be an entire salon in the middle of his living room.

A diffuser dangles from the end of a blow-dryer, clumsy in his hand as he scowls down at it like it just insulted his beard.

"What the fuck is this thing?" he mutters, face scrunched adorably.

A giggle slips free before I can stop it, and his head whips up, zeroing in on me with unnerving accuracy.

His eyes heat instantly, sliding down my body, lingering on my bare thighs and the long, white T-shirt barely grazing the tops of them. The same shirt I stole from his dresser, the same one I'm not wearing anything under.

The air thickens between us, charged and heavy, and my entire body goes up in flames under the weight of his stare. I shift on my feet, fingers tangling in the hem of the shirt, rolling it between my hands for something to do.

"How are you, darlin'? Feelin' better?" His voice is gruff and low as he crosses the room in three long strides. When he stops, there's barely an inch between us, and the warmth radiating off his body has me swaying, drawn into his gravitational pull.

"I feel a bit better," I manage, voice shaky. "The bath helped a lot. Those salts were amazing. Thank you."

"They're my mom's recipe."

I nod. "I figured. I bet people love them. They, uh…" My cheeks heat as I duck my head. "Normally it takes me longer to feel human."

"Don't think she sells them."

"Well," I whisper, feeling awkward and raw and so very alive, "she should."

His fingers find my chin, tilting it gently until I meet his eyes. His thumb brushes my cheek, and everything inside me lights up.

"Love your eyes," he says. "But goddamn, baby, these fuckin' freckles. Had me trapped from day one."

My throat tightens. "You hated me day one."

He huffs a quiet laugh, eyes dark with something deeper. "Never hated you. Hated how much I wanted you. Hated why you were there."

I reach up, wrapping my fingers around his wrist, holding him to me. "Because… I had to tell you Marlee died."

The thought makes me nauseous, as much as I try to ignore it.

His brows pull tight, his jaw flexing. "No. Yeah. I mean… I'd be lying if I said that didn't fuck me up. I'd known Marlee since I was five. But hadn't heard from her in over a decade."

But did you think of her?

He exhales slowly, eyes fluttering shut for a beat before meeting mine again. "What you brought to my doorstep was hell, but… that day was already hell. It was the anniversary of my dad's death."

Everything in me stills. My breath catches.

This man, this strong, silent, gruff man—he's been carrying grief in silence, walking through the dark with no one beside him for way too long.

"I'm so sorry," I whisper, fingers tightening on his wrist. "You've been doing all of this alone for so long, haven't you?"

His lips press into a tight line. "By my own design."

He built a life for himself filled with punishment—a desolate lifestyle, a tiny, crappy house secluded from everyone he knows and loves, a job where he saves people but forces him to move on before he can build any real connections.

"I'm sorry you felt you had to do that," I say, meaning it with everything in me. "I know how it feels to think you deserve loneliness."

"You don't deserve that," he murmurs, face tight.

I nod against his soft grip. "Maybe neither of us do."

Something flickers in his eyes. A crack. But it's gone just as fast.

He leans in, pressing a kiss to my forehead and threads his fingers through mine. "Come here."

Hand in hand, he leads me around the deep sectional and toward the coffee table.

I stop short, gaping at the sight of hair products, a handheld mirror, a diffuser-attached blow-dryer, and a lineup of carefully placed snacks. There's even a steaming cup of tea.

Between the table and the couch is a nest of pillows and the softest-looking blankets I've ever seen.

"What…" I bite my lip, eyes burning, heart hammering. "What is this, Kade?"

His cheeks pinken, color bleeding into his beard. He drops my hand and rubs the back of his neck. "Went home, asked my mom if she had any girly shit for your bath. Colby got involved. Apparently, *curly girls* take work."

A laugh bursts out, and I slap a hand over my mouth.

"She's not wrong." I giggle, noting all the costly products I've wanted to try but haven't had the funds for. Girl has expensive taste. I'm officially jealous of a teenager.

"The snacks and meds are from Mom," he says, dropping into the corner of the couch, spreading his thick thighs. "She said they're all safe, bland, easy on the stomach. Start with the tea."

My body trembles. My system is in overdrive—everything in me raw and aching and wanting. No one's ever done anything like this for me. No one's ever thought ahead or scrambled when I have a flare-up or get exposed. No one's even tried.

Abby does the best she can, but she has her own life, and to be honest, when I got sick and she was near, I usually kept it to myself, not wanting to be a bother. Maybe it's the way I was raised, or the treatment I've received from others in the past, but it taught me to rely on no one but myself.

Having someone—multiple someones—who not only believe me, but care enough to worry, to fuss…

It's everything.

"Thank you." It's all I can say. And it's nowhere near enough.

He raises his hand between us, palm outstretched and waggles his fingers in invitation. I practically dive into it, wanting physical contact with this man more than air.

He guides me between his thighs and nods to the pillows. Blushing, I give him my back and lower myself carefully.

The shirt rides up a little, and I tug it down fast, cheeks burning.

Should've worn panties. Definitely should've worn panties.

I curl my knees to my chest, sip the tea—chamomile with a touch of honey and lemon balm—and sigh.

"This is delicious," I hum. "Another of your mom's creations?"

"Yeah," he says softly. "Her and Gemma, my older sister. Gemma's always loved planting—herbs, mostly. She loves the flowers, it was her favorite part of Honey Bea, but she's got a hell of a green thumb. She created the recipe for the tea, and the salts."

"You guys have quite the operation here," I murmur around another sip. "What else do you make?"

Kade pauses for a beat, exhaling roughly, knees tightening around my shoulders. "I'm not really sure what they make or sell these days."

There's something thick, something painful, in his voice, and I turn, catching his eyes.

"Because you've been away?"

A sharp, tense nod. I kiss his knee—the only thing I can reach at this angle.

"You're back now," I whisper. "That's what counts." Grinning, I turn back around and shrug. "Besides, your mom has a new assistant who's eager to learn the ropes around here, so for all you know, you might get replaced as her favorite child soon."

His bark of laughter is magic to my ears, and the way he squeezes my shoulders, digging into my tense muscles, is magic to my system. I groan, body softening in his grip, and he takes it as his cue to work out the knots there.

"No doubt in my mind, darlin'. My mama loves you already."

Warmth spreads through me, and I hide my happy smile in my drink.

Once I'm nearly a pile of happy goo, he moves to my hair. I watch with rapt attention as he picks up a bottle of leave-in for curls and squirts some into his palms. A sweet, sugary scent fills the air a second before his big, calloused hands begin working it through my hair.

My breath catches and the teacup almost slips.

"You're… you're doing this?"

"Of course I am." He scoffs. "May not know what the fuck I'm doing, but Colby wrote a step-by-step list."

"A list," I repeat, dumbstruck.

I kind of just figured he was waiting on me to dive in and do it myself.

"If I can birth a calf in a thunderstorm and disarm a roadside IED, I can do your damn hair, baby."

And just like that, he slips into the role of caretaker.

And I…

God, I let him.

His hands are slow, tender, never rushing. Massaging, detangling, moving with care. The silence between us is warm, and natural.

The sun climbs higher, casting golden light over the fields outside. The fire crackles softly. A tutorial plays low in the background, but I tune it out, content to sip my tea, nibble a cracker Bea packed, and revel in this luxury.

When he's done prepping me, the blow-dryer hums. Warm air flutters over my curls, his fingers tugging gently, shaping. Quickly, the rhythm and sounds lull me into tranquility, but it's the love and care in his movements that comforts me and heals me all at once.

But it's the occasional rough glide of his calluses against my neck, my ear and throat, my scalp, that wake me up in a different way. I clench my thighs tighter, and my clit throbs in time with my heartbeat. Under my stolen shirt, my breasts are heavy and aching, my nipples begging for his touch.

I'm raw and wet and so very empty, but I loathe the idea of stopping him.

No one's ever done this for me.

I think back to that day in the grocery store when I ran into him. The way he looked at me. Hovered nearby. Followed me like a shadow.

At the time, I thought it was to irritate me. Now, I see it for what it really was. Kade loves to take care of people, and that day, I'd been on the floor, mid-breakdown, stomach growling, and frustrated with the lack of food choices. Maybe he thought I'd been about to pass out, or maybe he just sensed how close I was to losing it—but he stayed. Bugged me, followed me, but he stayed, just in case.

And he's been doing it ever since.

He's done it again and again—arguing with me, but still caring. Still seeing me. Still showing up.

And now… Aurora's coming in a day or two. He should be worried about that. Instead, he's here, taking care of me, protecting me, cherishing me.

My heart twists, body thrums, brain races…

But it's my soul that cracks.

The blow-dryer clicks off and the room falls quiet—nothing but the sound of birds and wind outside, and the quiet crackle of the dying fire fills the air.

In true gentleman fashion, Kade doesn't tell me to get up, or rush me out the door now that I'm feeling better. He doesn't tell me to get dressed, or go home.

He just waits, letting me decide the next move.

Part of me wishes he'd stop being such a gentleman, but then I remember that day on the back of the horse—his hand down my pants, fingertips an inch from finding out just how soaked my pussy gets every time he's near and I…

I stopped him.

Then I kissed him. Pulled away. Told him to take me back where I dutifully ignored him the whole time he repaired my tire like a spoiled maniac, and then…

Fucking hell, then I almost kissed him again, muttering nonsensical shit into his chest while I played with his beard.

I'm giving the man seven different versions of myself—of what I want. It's mixed signals on steroids.

And I know, I know, Kade won't be the one to make the next move. He won't be the one to ask me what I want or take things between us to the next level. He stepped back because I was scared and told him to, and now...

Now I need to fix it.

His fingers skim through my dry hair, tangling in my curls, tugging in a way that sends a pulse directly to my wet core.

A shiver races through me, vibrating all the way down.

"Cold?" he rasps, shifting like he's about to stand. "Lemme add another log—"

"No," I breathe, hands snapping out to clench his legs.

Inside my chest, my heart is slamming against my ribs, but for once, every part of me is in agreement about what I want.

He freezes. "What?"

I stand on legs that are weak and trembling—not from the flare-up, but from *him.*

Two steadying breaths is all I let myself have, and then I slowly turn to face him.

Kade's gray-and-blue-flecked eyes are dark with desire, lips parted, chest rising and falling like he's just as keyed up—just as strung out—as me.

"I'm not cold," I murmur, fingers twisting in the hem of his shirt. It lifts an inch, and those dark, stormy eyes snap to the newly exposed skin like he's committing them to memory.

"You shivered."

"I know." Another step.

His eyes flick to mine, searching. "Sick?"

"No." My knees hit the couch and this time, it's my gaze that falls, fixating on the way the hard length of his cock tents his sweats. The sight makes my mouth water.

He leans back into the couch and spreads his arms across the back, thighs falling open around me. Throat tight, body crying out for the feel of him, I climb onto his big lap, one knee at a time, bracing his thighs.

Like he can't stand to not touch me either, his hands snap to my bare legs, fingers digging into my flesh with desperation I feel down to my bones.

"What are you doing, darlin'?" he rasps, voice rough.

I cradle his jaw, fingers weaving through his addictive, sexy-as-sin beard, and draw our mouths close, leaving only a breath between us.

"Wanting."

And then my lips are on his

CHAPTER THIRTY

RIDE MY TONGUE, DARLIN'

HE DOESN'T HESITATE, WRAPPING his arms around my body and groaning into my mouth. "*Fuck*."

Our mouths battle like a storm, messy and raw and utterly *starving*.

It's the kind of kiss that steals your breath and refuses to give it back. The kind of kiss that alters your brain chemistry.

And I know, with just one touch, I'll never be the same after this.

His hands roam—wild and reverent—gripping my ass over the shirt, using his massive palms to direct me where he wants.

I gasp into him, fingers messily clawing at the soft fabric of his shirt, my mind spinning, heart racing. I've never wanted anyone like I want him. Never had this insatiable, unquenchable lust, no matter how reckless and stupid I know it is.

Maybe heartbreak is waiting for me on the other side of this. Maybe I'll wind up alone in New York, devastated and missing the glimpse of good I finally had. Maybe I'll regret every second I spent sinking deeper and deeper into Kade Acher.

But right now, I don't care.

Right now, all I want is to burn with him in my arms, his mouth on mine and our wild, broken souls between us.

"Need this off," I say, yanking at his shirt desperately. "Need to feel you."

He pulls back just enough for me to tug it up and over his head, tossing it behind me like it's on fire.

And God, he's even more beautiful than I remembered.

Thick chest dusted in dark curls. Carved abs. Deep grooves along his sides that beg to be licked. Bold black tattoos stretch across his right shoulder and down his arm, partially covering the raised scar that starts at his pec and slices across to his shoulder.

The tattoo is one I've wondered about, but never allowed myself to get close enough to really look at. But I'm looking now, and all I feel is *more.*

Black and grayscale, it's a ripped and worn American flag blended into three dog tags, and even though it's not obviously sad—I can feel the heartache, the loss, bleeding from it like the wound it now covers.

I trail my fingers across that scar, following it with gentle reverence. Kade swallows hard, his hands finding my hips, tightening with a groan as my touch glides over his skin.

Jaw ticking, throat bobbing, his mouth opens, breath caught on a word, but I press a finger to his lips, silencing him. Eyes locked on his, I lean down and kiss the jagged tissue. He exhales roughly against my fingertip, his grip flexing around me.

So I do it again, and again.

Silently, heart hammering, world spinning, I map the pain he's carried with my mouth—every single inch of it.

And when I reach the place where the scar vanishes into ink, I press my lips to each of the three dog tags tattooed on his skin.

One for every name. One for every soul—the last one belonging to his dad, the hardest hurt he carries.

Kade groans, low and broken.

"You gotta stop," he breathes, voice thick, head shaking. "You're wreckin' me, baby, and I haven't even gotten to taste you yet."

He doesn't give me a chance to respond, just grips me by the throat and tugs me forward. Not hard, not enough to hurt, but enough to bring us face to face. His thumb glides over my pulse, drawing sweet circles, Adam's apple bobbing.

"Could have fucking killed that asshole. Nearly did when I saw his hands on you."

"But you stopped him before he could hurt me," I whisper, brows tight at the honesty of it all. "You stopped him. Defended me. You were there."

His eyes flick to mine, holding for one painfully soft moment before he rasps, "Always wanna be there."

My breath catches when his lips replace his hand, mouth dragging along my jaw and throat, beard scratching deliciously as he licks and nips at my skin.

There's no bruise—I already checked—and Clint was barely standing long enough to leave an ache, but that's not why Kade's doing this. He's doing it for the same reason I kissed his scar, and God, that hits me deep in my chest.

He's healing a hurt he couldn't stop, even though he tried.

And I think...

I think he might be healing me, too.

His mouth and lips and teeth don't stop moving as his other hand slides across the top of my shirt, cupping my breast, fingers finding my nipple blindly, twisting and pinching in a way that makes me needy all over.

I whimper, head tipping back. My pussy grinds down on his cock, every thrust of my hips dragging the thick ridge of him against my pulsing clit.

"Kade," I gasp, nails digging into his shoulders. "*Please.*"

He chuckles darkly, biting down on my throat. I cry out, rocking harder and he hums. "My girl likes it a little rough."

His girl.

Fuck, I like the sound of that too damn much.

He drags his mouth across my chest, sucking one nipple through the shirt, then the other. Every flick of his tongue sends jolts of heat to my core.

I reach for the hem of my shirt, needing to feel him on my skin like I need my next breath, but he stops me, gripping my wrists and dragging them behind my back in a quick, single handed move that leaves me breathless.

"No," he growls, eyes burning as he leans back and takes me in. "Sight of you when you walked out here in my fuckin' shirt, perfect tits bouncing with every step..." Biting his lip, he groans low in his throat. "Almost came in my fuckin' pants."

He thrusts his hips up, and I moan, trembling all over.

"Can't wait to see what's underneath. Been dreaming about it since I met you. But I wanna see you come while wearin' my shirt first. Can you do that? Be my good girl and come all over my cock just like this—hands behind your back, ridin' me like I'm yours."

I whimper at his words and grind down harder, aching for friction, desperate for more.

I want him. All of him. And the thought of him being mine...

Really and truly *mine.*

It makes something in me crack and cave and burn, all at once.

"Kade," I breathe, body shaking in his hold. "I need—"

"You'll get it," he growls, mouth on my neck again, hands stilling my movements. "But you gotta tell me, baby. You gotta tell me you're mine."

I want to.

Fuck, I want to so badly, it hurts. But a few kisses don't rewrite years of trauma, pain, and fear. They don't change who I am at my core, as much as I wish they did.

And who I am at my core is someone who desperately wants a family, a forever kind of love, but is *petrified* to reach out and grab it.

"And if I don't?" I rasp, holding onto the chaotic swirl of emotions battering around inside me. The fear, the want, the desire, the *love*. "What if I don't say it?"

His eyes gleam, thick lips lifting in a cocky smirk. "I'll leave you aching and dripping and pissed off."

I scoff, dropping my weight directly on his cock. His smile slips a fraction, fingers digging into my hip so hard, I know I'll have bruises tomorrow.

But unlike Clint's depraved, disgusting touch—I want all Kade's marks.

"I could just go home and get myself off without you. Leave *you* hard and aching and alone." I drop my voice to a low, seductive purr, just to mess with him. "Or you can let me go, and I can ride your big cock just like this, until we both come and make messes of each other. What do you say, sunshine?"

Kade glares at me for a long, painful moment, then releases my hands with a defeated sigh and a shake of his head. "Knew it."

"Knew what?" I ask, hands snapping to his shoulders to anchor myself as my hips pick up pace, my orgasm so damn close, I can taste it.

His head tips back on the couch, hooded eyes meeting mine, an addictively genuine expression painted across his handsome face. "You're impossible for me to deny, Georgia Walker. Pretty sure I'd give you anything you want, and I'm in too fuckin' deep to care."

My heart skips a beat, then another.

I swallow hard and drop my mouth to hover over his, body shaking so hard, the room spins. "You know what I want?"

His big hands squeeze my thighs, calluses dragging across my skin. "Whatever it is, it's yours."

Fuck, a statement like that is dangerous. So dangerous.

"I want you to make me come," I whisper against his lips. "And then I want you to do it again and again, until I'm sated and exhausted." My teeth latch onto his lower lip, eyes meeting his as I murmur, "Isn't that what you *dream* about?"

Kade *snaps.*

He bucks up into me, dragging me down to meet his thrusts. His mouth devours mine, tongue claiming, lips bruising. We kiss and dry-fuck like we're starving, like this is the only way we'll survive. Like it's the last time we'll ever touch.

His hands grip my ass, guiding me as I grind harder, faster.

The pressure builds fast—*too fast.* My breath comes in pants and every muscle in my body locks up.

"Kade!" I cry out as my orgasm slams into me, stealing my breath. "*Oh, fuck!*"

"Another," he growls, dragging me, practically fucking me through his sweats, controlling my hazy, bliss-filled body like I weigh nothing.

My head shakes, heart hammering, bleary gaze meeting his intense expression. "I c-can't."

He sucks my nipple into his mouth and bites down gently as he slows the aching roll between us. I tremble in his grip, fingernails digging into his skin, pussy clenching around nothing like it's just as desperate for this man as I am.

"You can," he murmurs, switching to my other nipple as the cool breeze catches on the wet spot left from his mouth. I shiver again. "You can, baby. Another. Exhausted and cum drunk. That's what I want."

And like his words and body alone command mine, I come again, burying my moan and teeth into his throat. This time, it's a slow, delicious roll through my system, but just as intense, just as perfect.

When I finally come down, I sit back on my thighs and look between us. His cock is digging into his sweats, pointing toward the band at the waist where a big wet spot is seeping through the material.

My heart skips a beat, lips lifting in a smug, excited grin.

Men coming in their pants is the hottest thing I've ever read about but never been lucky enough to experience firsthand.

"You came?" I ask, breathless, ghosting my thumb across the wet patch.

He bucks under me, grunting like he's in pain and I drop my hand, eyes snapping up.

Kade chuckles, shaking his head. "Nah, baby. That's all you."

I swallow hard, shifting on his lap, suddenly becoming aware of how soaked I am. He drags a hand under the shirt, his fingers sliding between my legs, and he freezes, breath catching.

"No panties?" He groans, eyes boring into mine. "You tryin' to fuckin' kill me?"

A giggle slips free but it dies on my tongue when his fingers find my soaked clit, circling it with enough pressure to have me trembling all over again.

And when he sinks one inside me, thick and perfect, we both moan. I fall forward, catching myself on his shoulders and stare down at the space between my thighs where Kade is lazily finger-fucking me.

I clench, the ache inside me that never seems to disappear, no matter how many times I come by myself, already alive and throbbing again.

"Look how wet you are, Georgia," he says, voice guttural as he slips free and holds up his finger, slick and glistening. "You're dripping all over the place."

"I'm always this wet when you're around," I whisper, cheeks burning as we stare at the wetness and I silently wonder if he's going to taste it.

Taste *me*.

"That's a dangerous thing to tell a man," he rasps. "Very fuckin' dangerous."

And in true Kade fashion, he blows my mind by doing the exact opposite of what I expect him to do.

Some men would ignore that wet, sticky finger entirely. Some would bring it to their mouths and suck the flavor from their skin.

But this man, *my man*, does neither.

Instead, he brings that finger up and paints it across my lips slowly, pupils dilated, eyes heavy and chest vibrating with a groan.

"How do you taste, freckles?"

A whimper escapes me, skin prickling with awareness as I drag my tongue across my top and bottom lip and swallow.

"I don't know," I whisper, dragging my nails down his chest, reveling in the goosebumps that break out under my hands. "Why don't you try me for yourself?"

His fingers drop between my thighs again, and he doesn't hesitate to thrust two inside me, curving them to hit my G-spot. I arch against him with a cry.

"Take the fuckin' shirt off, darlin'. Wanna see your pretty tits bounce while you ride my face," he demands, slipping free from my core and pushing me to my feet.

My mouth falls open, knees damn near buckling beneath me at the whiplash. "What?"

But he's already shifting, sliding down the wide couch so he's flat on his back. He dips a hand into his pants, slowly stroking himself while he watches me.

I bite my lip, and glance at the back wall of windows. "What if somebody sees?"

"Who the fuck would be out back?" He grunts, brows furrowed.

"I don't know." My hands flap, heart racing. "Your friends? Your family?"

He scoffs, rolling his eyes. "Barely six in the morning, baby. Anyone's creepin' outside my windows this early, they're gonna get a fuck of a lot more than a show."

"Like?" I breathe, fingers dancing at the hem of the shirt.

"My fist in their fuckin' faces. Now lose the shirt."

Before I can let myself overthink anything, I whip my shirt over my head and drop it on the floor.

Kade goes utterly still.

His hand freezes inside his pants, the slow, rhythmic drag of his palm halting as his eyes eat up every inch of me like he's starving.

"Holy fuck," he mutters, voice wrecked. "*Georgia...*"

The way he says my name, hoarse and shocked, like it's the answer to every question he's never asked, makes my knees tremble and my throat tight.

I've never felt so exposed. Bare and vulnerable in every way. My arms twitch to cover myself—some instinct I learned from the men who came before him.

They looked at me like I was something to tolerate or tame.

But it's the slow bob of his throat, the way his breathing quickens, muscles bunching... that has me feeling *wanted.*

Kade looks at me like I hung the moon and it has me wishing with everything in me that I never have to know what it feels like *after* him.

"You're so goddamn beautiful, baby," he breathes, eyes locked on mine before they drift lower—slow and hungry. "Jesus Christ. *Look at you.*"

He strokes himself again, this time rougher, like he can't help it, like touching himself to the sight of me is involuntary.

"I knew you were sexy, but this..."

He shakes his head, eyes dragging down to my breasts, lingering on the way they move with each shuddered breath before falling to the space between my legs.

Kade groans, stroking harder, faster, before dragging his gaze back up to my face.

"Every curve and freckle and dip of you is perfect," he murmurs, eyes holding mine. "But if you took it all away and never let me see or touch you again, I'd still be wrecked and desperate."

"Kade…" I shake my head. That can't be true.

"You've got no clue what you do to me, do you?"

I swallow hard, heart pounding against my ribcage like it's trying to escape. Instead of answering, I gesture to his pants.

"Wanna see you," I whisper. "All of you."

His jaw tightens, teeth gritted, and slips his hand free, holding it up between us in a loose beckon.

"This isn't about me," he murmurs, voice raw. "Not today."

I take a trembling step forward. "Why?"

His hand wraps around mine and tugs me the rest of the way until I fall into the couch, knees braced on either side of him again. His hands come up to hold my hips, big and warm and strong, grounding me.

"Because, baby," he says softly, brushing his thumb over the back of my hand like it's the most important part of me. "You're sick, and I'm takin' care of you."

My throat goes tight. I flick my gaze to the coffee table—the cold tea, the carefully lined-up products, the snacks I still haven't touched. "You did take care of me."

Before I can blink, he grabs my hips and lifts me with ease, guiding me over his body. I gasp, hands scrambling for the armrest to catch my balance as I straddle him.

His palms slide up the outside of my thighs, callused and rough and so goddamn reverent it makes my eyes sting.

"That *was* me caring for you," he agrees, voice low and thick. "So is this. Every orgasm. Every scream of pleasure. Every drip of your cum sliding down my throat—that's all part of me making sure my girl is happy and cared for. And when you're exhausted and soft and sated, me wrappin' you up in my arms and holdin' you while you sleep… that's me takin' care of both of us."

My throat tightens with something terrifyingly close to tears.

No one has ever said something like that to me.

No one has ever made me feel like this—with their words, with their hands, with their *soul*.

"I want to take care of you too," I whisper, reaching up to brush his hair back from his face. "How can I do that when you won't let me?"

His smile is soft. Devastating. It punches me straight in the chest.

"You wanna take care of me, darlin'?"

"Yes." I nod, eyes glassy. "I really do."

He hums low, then smacks my ass, and the sound that rips from my throat is a broken moan.

"Then climb on top of my face and fuck my tongue, because I'm fuckin' dying for a taste of you."

Heat crashes through me, my whole body going tight and trembling.

I blink, lips parting in a stunned, breathless gasp. "Kade—"

He cuts me off with another slap, firmer this time. "Go on, baby. Get up there. Lemme take care of you."

And before I can second guess, before my trauma or fear or the voices in my head can talk me out of it—I move.

Knees braced on either side of his head, my hands grasp the back of the couch as I hover over his face, heart pounding so loud it drowns out everything else.

Kade looks up at me like I'm his last meal. Like I'm sacred.

His hands grip my thighs and he pulls me down, dragging my soaked core over his mouth. And then—

"Oh my God," I choke out, head falling back.

His tongue parts me with one long, rough lick and my knees nearly give out.

"Fuck," he grunts, sucking me between his teeth. "You taste like sin and sugar, and I'm starvin'."

And when he starts to devour me, slow and messy, like he's got nowhere else to be, I lose every coherent thought I've ever had.

Kade Archer eats me like he worships me.

Like he's not going to stop until I've screamed myself hoarse.

And when I do two minutes in… he keeps going, dragging another orgasm from me.

True to his word—to his *dreams*, the man doesn't stop bringing me over the edge, no matter how long it takes. He eats me like he's trying to prove a fucking point, I just don't know what it is, but I sure as hell won't stop him.

I'm sweating, shaking, on the edge of another, but it's too much. My fingers claw at everything—tug on his hair, drag across his shoulders, the couch, my own body.

He groans into me, mouth wet and hot and perfect, his beard scraping my thighs in the best way as he sucks my clit into his mouth and bites down, just enough to make me jolt.

Another finger fucks up into me, stretching me in the most deliciously, drugging way possible, making me slowly lose my mind to pleasure.

"Kade, please!" I cry out, slapping the arm of the couch, body twitching from the overstimulation. "Come with me!"

He shakes his head against me, and I feel the rumble of his voice all the way through my spine.

"Next time I come," he rasps, voice wrecked, "it'll be deep inside this perfect, needy cunt. Bare."

I whimper, my thighs shaking on either side of his head, my whole body teetering on the edge again as I clench around him.

"You want that, baby?" he growls, tongue dragging down to circle my fluttering entrance before licking me clean. "Wanna feel my cock fucking into you, raw and warm, filling you up with my cum?"

My eyes roll back. I nod frantically, lips parted, breathing shallowly. The image alone has me spiraling.

"Tell me," he demands, fingers thrusting up into me, hard and deep, fucking that spot inside me that makes me see stars.

"Yes," I cry out, shaking my head back and forth, hair sticking to my sweaty face. "It's too much, Kade. It's t-too mu-much. I—"

"It's not too much," he barks, teeth grazing my clit again. "Just relax, baby. Relax and let go. Squirt all over my face. Gimme this sweet cum."

I gape down at him, body shaking so hard I can barely make out his features in the bright light of day.

"I—" I choke, everything inside me winding tight.

"I said give it to me," he growls, voice unhinged, desperate, raw. "Gimme every fuckin' drop, Georgia. You're mine, this pussy's mine, and I wanna wear your cum like a fuckin' badge of goddamn honor."

That does it.

I explode.

Screaming his name so loud I'm sure the walls shake, my body convulses and I shatter, drenching his mouth, his beard, his throat. He moans into me like a man possessed, dragging out every ripple of pleasure, every throb, until I can't take it anymore.

I collapse onto him, my body limp, boneless, my cheek resting against his slick chest as he shifts us. One of his arms cradles my back, the other strokes my back as I lie on top of him, panting and twitching while my heart pounds wildly against his.

For a long time, I can't speak. Can't think. The only thing I can do is float in the afterglow, totally spent.

Eventually, my pulse slows and I shift slightly, just enough to realize the sticky warmth pressed between our stomachs.

I grin into his chest.

Lifting my head slowly, I blink up at him. His cheeks are flushed, his beard glistening, lips parted, pupils blown wide.

"Thought you were waiting till you could fill me," I rasp, brushing his hair back from his face.

Pink tinges his cheeks even deeper, and he scrubs a hand through his beard, huffing out a breath.

"Tried to hold out," he mutters, "but how could I when you were screamin' my name like that?"

"Like what?" I whisper, voice thick with emotion—with everything that just happened.

That was… a lot.

His smile softens, and he tucks a damp curl behind my ear, fingertips brushing my temple with maddening care.

"Like you're really mine."

I swallow hard, blinking fast, my heart folding in on itself.

Because I am.

I'm already his.

But I can't bring myself to say the words yet, so I just smile and lower my head back to his chest, breathing in the wild scent of sweat, sex, and *him*—and hope he knows I'm trying. That I'm getting closer.

That I'm already his in all the ways that count.

Chapter Thirty One

Kade

More Than a Weekend

The scent of coffee's what catches my senses first, followed by something sweet and warm. I reach out instinctively, patting the space around me like I'm still in a dream. But it's empty.

I force my eyes open, the morning light soft and golden through the windows.

Getting up is easier than it's been in years, maybe longer, and the reason why is notably missing from my side.

Didn't have a nightmare last night.

Don't know if it was having Georgia curled up in my arms, her soft breaths grounding me in a way no sedative ever could, or if it was the simple fact that I was bone-deep exhausted after spending the day wrapped around my girl. Either way, I slept like a damn baby.

I shift to a seated position, bare feet hitting the floor. The rug beneath me is warm and soft—so different from the old laminate I used to wake up to, it rattles something deep in my bones.

Christ, things have changed.

And they've changed fast.

My house. My job. My whole damn future.

Just a few months ago, I was living in a shell, detached and half dead on the inside.

Now, I'm waking up in a home I'm building from the ground up, waiting on the arrival of a little girl who's about to change my life. Aurora could be here as soon as today, depending on how fast the paperwork from Ethel's office is cleared. I emailed it back last week as soon as we hung up, and she promised once everything was processed, she'd pick Aurora up and bring her to me.

If Georgia hadn't been here this weekend, distracting me, making me laugh and groan and lose my fuckin' mind in all the best ways, I probably would've driven myself insane waiting.

And Georgia...

Tried to go slow. Tried to keep my thoughts to myself and my mouth shut, but then she was sick and in my house, wearin' nothing but my shirt, a weary expression and bare feet, and I was done for.

Couldn't stand to see her hurting, or upset. Couldn't stand the thought of her being unwell because of something I did, even if she swore up and down it wasn't my fault.

And once I started taking care of her—really taking care of her—there was no going back. It wasn't just about making her feel better. It was about making sure she never had to do it alone again.

Didn't plan it. Didn't even see it happening.

But somewhere between blow drying her hair and holding her while she slept... she became *everything*.

She doesn't even realize how fast she's become the brightest part of my day.

It's terrifying.

And it's the most alive I've felt in years.

Shaking my head, I drag my gaze across the living room. My brows crash together, pulse ticking up. Everything's as we left it last night—blanket tossed over the couch, pillows askew from where she passed out on top of me while we watched some old sitcom, but it's too quiet.

Standing up with a groan, I stretch out my chest and arms as I make my way around the house, calling out her name as I go.

I come up empty, but I find every room just as clean as the living room, and something about it sets my nerves haywire.

It's like every sign of her is gone... erased.

Fuckin' hate it.

Only proof I know it wasn't all a dream is the folded-up shirt she wore yesterday lying on my bed. Possessive bastard that I am, I grab the thing and bring it to my nose. All I smell is my body wash and the curl cream I used in her hair—but underneath that is her. That soft, wild scent I can't name. Something I've come to crave.

After the intense round of back-to-back orgasms, my fingers buried deep inside her, mouth wrapped around every inch of her sweet pussy, my girl passed out on my chest.

I let her rest as long as I could, but we were both a mess, and she still needed to be looked after. I'd carefully rolled her onto the couch and stepped away to shower quickly, not wanting to leave her alone for too long. But I needed a minute to myself. Needed a minute to wrap my mind…. *my fuckin' heart*, around what was happening between us.

She let me care for her.

Let me in.

Never thought I'd want this again. Not after Marlee. Not after what that kind of love cost me. I swore I'd never let anyone past the wall I built the day I re-upped my contract.

And I lasted for over a damn decade, but then Georgia burst into my life, vicious and burning and unafraid to meet me exactly as I am—broken and angry and bitter and a fuckin' mess.

She saw it all and took me on, pushed me, pulled me, and dragged me right over that fuckin' line I'd drawn in the sand back in the desert and fuck, I think I dragged her right over it with me.

After my shower, I lifted her soft, sleepy body up and bathed her, bringing her to two more half-awake, quiet orgasms in the tub.

All day, we lazed on the couch, watching TV, relaxing, talking about everything and nothing while I smothered her with questions. Asked her about her family, and how her search for answers has gone. What she's found, and about her life in foster care.

Asked her what she does for fun, why she became a social worker, and what her favorite food is. And when she was sleepy, and passing out on my chest, I kept going, desperate for everything I could find out about this damn woman. I'm fuckin' greed for it.

Even after all we talked about, I still want more.

It's a sickness and I… don't really give a fuck.

Sighing, I drop her shirt on my pillow and get dressed quickly. Her keys are gone from the entry table, so she probably left for work like she said she would. Thank fuck I brought her Jeep here after the bar.

Still stings that she didn't wake me.

The smell of coffee pulls me toward the kitchen, and I stop short when I spot a plate covered in foil next to the stove and a folded note tucked just beneath it.

My heart stutters, skips a beat, and picks back up at a dangerous pace. Don't know if it's the product of seeing a note written in feminine scrawl with my name etched across the top or the clear heart drawn at the bottom, but the room blurs out of focus for a beat.

Shaking my head with a huff, I snatch the note up and my lips lift in a grin that quickly falls.

Kade,

I didn't want to wake you. You looked too peaceful. And when you still didn't wake up, despite the banging around in your kitchen ten feet away, I figured you needed the rest. Thank you for taking care of me this weekend. It means more than you know. Also, your stomach was growling while you slept, so I made you breakfast. All I could find were supplies for pancakes, but I couldn't try them, so, sorry if they suck and super sorry if you get food poisoning.

Talk soon, Georgia

My stomach sours, heart clenching, as I slip the note into an empty kitchen drawer and unwrap the plate. A stack of thick, fluffy pancakes sits on a dish I didn't buy—one that showed up during that wild day the town came together for me.

Who shows up for Georgia like that?

They all donated, bought, and celebrated me doing the bare minimum for a little girl who deserves the world. And Georgia...

Does anyone see her? See how much she struggles just to find a fuckin' meal every day? Does anyone see how hard she works—at her job, at life—all by herself?

That same painful pit that opened up the other night at my mom's shows up again, sharp and nauseating.

She deserves a community to rally around her—everyone fuckin' does—but Georgia? I think she might need it more than most.

And I wanna be the one to give it to her.

That thought in mind, I roll up one of the pancakes and shove it in my mouth, food poisoning be damned. It's sweet, and perfectly cooked, making my decision all the more easier.

During our long talk, Georgia said she loves to bake. Said baking looked different after her diagnosis, but she never stopped trying. Fact that she can't even try a fuckin' pancake in my house means baking here will be hard for her... and it doesn't have to be.

Pouring a cup of coffee, I sip on it while scrolling my phone for gluten-free baking shopping lists. Once I find a comprehensive one with tips for keeping it safe and not cross-contaminating anything, I head off to Amazon. May be in the cuts out here, but we still get packages delivered to a stop in town.

I drop onto a barstool and spend hours researching, filling my cart, and eventually, checking out, all while eating the food she sweetly cooked for me, knowing damn well she couldn't have any.

While I was reading, I found articles about keeping items separate in the house, even down to pots, pans, seasonings, and sauces.

One of them suggested having an entirely separate drawer, color-coded if possible, for everything gluten-free. Another mentioned storing gluten-free baking ingredients above the standard ones to prevent dust contamination.

So I do it.

I clear out the bottom cupboards under the island and move all my baking and cooking shit there. I'd toss it, but it's new, donated from friends and family, and I'm sure with Aurora here, I'll need regular supplies, but I don't bake, so they get tucked away.

After moving everything for Aurora to the left, I designate the right side for Georgia, leaving Post-its marked with a *G* on every door. When that's done, I shoot a text to Clem to ask if she still has that dumb label maker she used to tag everything in her room.

By the time I'm done, there's space for whatever's on the way—new baking trays, measuring cups, mixers, gluten-free flours and sugars and syrups in sealed containers. I even cleaned the damn toaster and added a second one to my Amazon cart just to be safe. Separate tongs. Separate cutting boards.

Hell, I even spring for a new spatula set just so hers never touches something that could hurt her again.

She deserves that.

Deserves a space where she doesn't have to second-guess everything, where she can bake without fear, eat without thinking, and live without worrying she's about to get sick.

Once everything's organized, I open the back door for some air and sit at the table, coffee in hand, scrolling through articles on wheat sensitivity. One link leads to another, and pretty soon I'm reading about airborne gluten exposure during harvest. Some people get sick from walking through fields during peak bloom. Others react just from being downwind and some are just fine.

Shit.

My gut twists. Wheat won't be harvested for months—not till August, maybe late July if it's an early year, and I'll be out there helping when it's time. Hell, I'll be out there before that. When the heads start to ripen—when the pollen lifts off in the heat.

I glance toward the open window, the fields stretching green and endless in the distance.

Is that gonna be safe for her? Is this place gonna make her sick?

I don't know. Not yet. But I'll find out. And if it's not—I'll figure it out. Do whatever it takes to make her okay. Because stupid as it may be, as fast it feels, I want Georgia here. And I'll move fucking mountains to make sure she stays.

All that done, I stand, stretch out my legs, and make my way toward Aurora's room.

The door creaks a little as I open it—still new, freshly painted, and smelling faintly of lemon-scented cleaner and baby powder. Light spills in from the hallway, casting soft shadows over the pale yellow walls and the rainbow mural on the far one. My chest tightens instantly.

Still can't believe this was all Georgia.

Sure, I know my family had a hand in stocking the room with gear.

Gemma bragged about the play mat and fully stocked toy box she picked. Colby and Clementine were over Saturday morning, organizing baby books on the cloud shelves I hung.

And my mom… practically had to drag her out of her when I left for the bar with the guys.

But the soft things? The details? The night-lights in every outlet, the cozy curtains, the matching bee-patterned sheets and mobile, the way everything smells clean and warm—like lavender and love?

That's all her.

And she didn't do it for credit. She didn't even tell me until I walked in and saw it.

She did it for Aurora.

For *me*.

I move slowly, reverently, like I'm in a church. My fingers ghost over the bee-print crib sheets, then up to the soft hanging mobile. Bees with little smiling faces spin lazily in the breeze from the cracked window. My throat closes around the sudden pressure that builds behind my ribs.

This room is perfect.

It's ready for Aurora

And, God, I think I am, too.

I've missed Aurora for the last three weeks—a deep ache in my chest that shouldn't be possible, but it's there.

Thought about her every damn day, worried and stressed over how she's doing with the foster family. Blew up Ethel's phone more times than I can count, just to check on her. All she could say was that Aurora's teething up a storm, and to be prepared.

My eyes land on the car seat in the corner. Still in the box. The sight sobers me, reminds me that no matter how perfect this room is, the second I strap that seat into my truck… everything changes.

Her life's about to be in my calloused hands.

I pull out my phone.

First instinct is to Google a video tutorial, make sure I don't fuck it up, but instead, my thumb hovers over the number I know by heart. One I've called countless times over the last six weeks.

I don't even have to look.

Breath in my throat, eyes squeezed shut, I press call, bring the phone to my ear, and lay my soul on the line.

Chapter Thirty Two

History in Her Bones

She's here.

In my house, in my arms, staring up at me with a gummy smile, her chubby little fists tangled in my beard like she remembers me.

My breath is trapped in my lungs, muscles locked tight, but my heart? It's fuckin' *soaring*.

"And here's the adoption paperwork we talked about," Ethel says softly, passing me a folder. "The probate attorney is back in the state. I've received all the necessary documentation. I did a deep dive into the Vernals, and there is no other living family capable of taking her. So as long as this is still something you want, the paperwork just needs to be filed. After that, it typically takes a few weeks for final approval. Could be faster, depending on the judge's docket. But you know Romero. He'll push it through for you if he can."

"What about Oakley? Marlee's little sister." My gaze slides over Aurora's face—a face so much like Marlee's, like Oakley's. "She's eighteen now, I think. Is she still around?"

Ethel's brows furrow, but she nods. "Oakley's nineteen, living in Rydell. But she's not…"

She trails off, adjusting her large wire-rimmed glasses. Her curly, gray-streaked hair is pulled back into a thick braid, a few stray curls escaping around her temples.

"She's what?" I murmur, shifting Aurora against my chest so I can hold the cold teether up to her mouth, ignoring the drool pooling against my fingers.

Ethel smiles softly at us.

"Oakley's not in a position to care for a baby right now, and I didn't feel she was the best choice." Clicking her tongue, she shakes her head. "You're it for this little one, Kade. Still sure this is what you want?"

I meet Aurora's big brown eyes and my hands instinctively tighten around her.

"Yes." And I am. "She's mine."

Ethel lets out a slow breath and squeezes my shoulder, pushing to stand. "That's what I love to hear. I'll be in touch to check on you in a few days, and I'll continue to do that until the adoption is final."

Chuckling, she smooths a hand down Aurora's dark, messy curls. "Honestly, I'll probably still check on this little one well after that, if that's alright with you. She's special."

"She is," I rasp, forcing my gaze away from her tiny face scrunched up in concentration as she gnaws on the rubber. "Anything else I need to know?"

Ethel pauses, expression falling. "Actually, yes, but…"

Her gaze slides around the room, finding the playpen I put up after I installed the car seat this morning.

"Maybe we could speak in the kitchen. In private. She may be small, but we never know what they pick up on."

Nodding, I stand, hardly feeling the throb in my thigh from doing so much around the house today, and quickly move across the living room to the open space between the couch and kitchen. I laid a soft rug out and put the playpen around it, along with some soft, safe toys, but I still feel sick putting her down. Still feel worried she'll get hurt the second she's out of my arms, but I know this is just the beginning.

Bending, I gently set her down and pass her a bear I bought her a few weeks ago. She stares up at me and smacks the teether against my cheek, screaming happily. Smiling, I brush her hair back and stand to my full height, turning to Ethel at the island. My smile falls at the serious look on her face.

Clearing my throat, I join her and gesture to the coffee pot. "Coffee? Or water?"

"Coffee'll be great," she says, heaving herself up onto a barstool. "Black, please."

Nodding, I pour us both a cup, my hands shaking slightly. Inhaling deeply, I pass her the mug and flick my eyes back to check on Aurora, who's waving her bear around and gnawing like it's her damn job.

"What's going on?" I murmur, dragging my attention to Ethel. "Something wrong?"

She sips her coffee slowly and sighs. "I wanted to fill you in on some information I received this past week from the hospital."

My heart skips, hands clenching on the edge of the counter. "About Aurora? She okay?"

Christ, I feel like I'm going to pass out from all the whiplash.

"Is it the concussion? The accident?" I tug on my hair. "Is she—"

"Kade," Ethel interrupts, squeezing my hand, "She's okay. Aurora is fine. Teething like crazy and struggling to sleep through the night, but that's to be expected. She's going through a lot of changes. Missing her parents, I have no doubt. Her life's changing, and it's changing fast—something I'm sure you can understand. But she also spent some time in the hospital, had a lot of tests done, and they found some things that sparked..."

She trails off, setting her cup down with a ragged exhale.

"Things that prompted me to dig a bit deeper."

Nodding slowly, I brace myself, mind whirling, heart hammering, and fuck, I'm surprised my first thought is: *I want Georgia here.*

Want her at my side, to lean on, to ask for help and support. Just plain want her here.

But she's not. I'm on my own. Signed up to do this on my own, and as of now, that's where I'm at. Need to learn to be a dad by myself just in case...

Just in case she ends up leaving in a few months.

So I gesture to Ethel to continue and wait for the words I already know are gonna fuck me up.

"Aurora shows some history of abuse," she says quietly, and my body goes utterly still. "Some minor but telling fractures in her wrist and collarbone, consistent with rough handling. A few small scars. The kind that don't come from normal childhood bumps."

My heart skips a beat, room spinning, but I force my legs to hold me up.

"Because of that," she continues, her tone carefully measured, "I looked deeper into her parents. Marlee Parker-Vernal had a relatively clean record—just a few minor incidents, short-term arrests, but they were from years ago. As I'm sure you know, she had a rough upbringing. Both her parents died from drug overdoses."

She sighs, clicking her tongue softly. "I knew Kim Parker—Marlee's grandmother. That woman had no business raising anyone, let alone Marlee and Oakley after their own mom passed."

A beat of silence stretches between us.

"I thought Marlee had escaped the cycle," she murmurs, fingers tight around her mug. "But from what I found, it looks like she got pulled back in… and it seems to have started around the time she met Travis Vernal. His record paints a very different picture."

I grit my teeth, listening.

"Travis Vernal had two DUIs in the past five years, both quietly pled down. Several reports of domestic disturbances from neighbors, but none that resulted in charges. A few hospital visits for unexplained injuries to Marlee and Aurora, but nothing concrete. Still, it was enough to raise red flags."

My hands shake and I grip the counter to keep from punching something.

"That brings me to last week. I received the toxicology report for Aurora's parents the day they passed." A breath as she meets my gaze. "Travis Vernal was highly intoxicated. Nearly twice the legal limit. Marlee was also drinking, though her levels were lower."

"Why are you telling me all this?" I rasp, barely holding it together.

Her eyes cloud over and she looks down at her cup before steeling herself and looking back at me.

"There were no skid marks at the accident site, Kade."

I lose it the only way I can.

Spinning around, I yank at my hair and breathe through the rage clouding my mind. When that doesn't do a damn thing, I pace, quietly working through the chaos swirling inside me.

My eyes repeatedly slide to Aurora. The need to go to her, pick her up, hold her close and protect her is hard to ignore, but I don't want her in the middle of this. Never want a single ounce of this… *hate* to touch her.

"You're saying that piece of shit crashed on purpose?" I whisper-hiss, jerking a finger toward the playpen. "With his baby in the fucking car?"

She holds her hands up but doesn't seem put off by my reaction. "We don't know that for sure. Could have been too drunk to see the lines, or fallen asleep at the wheel. We don't know it was intentional—"

"Nah, fuck that," I bark, shaking my head. "He got behind the wheel drunk as hell, with his baby in the backseat. He did that shit on purpose. And Marlee…"

I grip the sink and lean over, dry heaving. "She knew. She was there. She was drinking. She *knew.*"

Silence hangs between us like smoke, and I hate how long it takes me to pull myself together. Hate that it's happening now, on a day that was supposed to be filled with love and happiness.

Swallowing hard, I shake the lingering anger from my system, put it away for later, and turn back to the social worker who's quietly wrecking everything I thought I knew about my ex.

Ethel sighs, her voice softer now. "I know this is a lot to process. But it also explains a lot about why Aurora struggles with certain things. Why she reacts the way she does to loud noises or sudden movements. Why she clings to you the way she does."

My knees nearly buckle. But I don't fall. Not with her watching. Not with Aurora watching.

"She won't have to be afraid anymore," I say, voice ragged. "Not for a single fucking second. Not with me."

Ethel nods slowly. "I believe you. And I think she does, too."

I drag a hand over my face and glance again toward my little girl. And she is *mine.* Knew it from the second I met her. Maybe it wasn't like this... this dire need inside me, something almost vicious, to protect and cherish her, but it was solid.

Now... now it's sure and final.

"I'll do whatever it takes," I whisper. "To keep her safe. To give her a new life."

Ethel stands and pulls me into a hug that smells like lavender and strong coffee. "You're not alone, Kade. Not in this. You have a community around you." She pulls back, giving me a meaningful look. "Don't be afraid to lean on those who want to stand by your side. No matter how they came to you."

My heart skips a beat and it's on the tip of my tongue to ask if she's talking about Georgia, but I leave it be for now, my brain already too messy to interpret a damn thing.

Ethel grabs her cane and walks slowly toward the door. I follow, heart aching, arms already itching to hold Aurora again. To pick up the phone and beg Georgia to leave work early and come be with us—to hold those pieces she promised she'd carry for me.

When the screen door creaks open, she looks back once more.

"You let me know when you're ready to file. And if you need any-thing—anything at all—reach out. If I don't hear from you in a week, expect my call."

"I will," I promise, voice gravelly.

She nods and slips out into the spring sunlight.

Ethel's SUV disappears down the long drive, kicking up dust in the distance. I shut the front door slowly, the latch clicking louder than it should in the quiet. My body feels too big in the silence she leaves behind, the weight of everything she just told me pressing hard on my chest.

After a few long, deep breaths, I turn around, and there she is.

Aurora.

Unable to help myself, I close the distance between us in a few short strides, but slow my pace when I near her, the shit Ethel told me battering against my senses. She blinks up at me with those puppy-dog eyes, and for the first time, I notice the way she holds her little body tight, like she doesn't know what to make of me.

And I can't help but wonder if she thinks I'll hurt her like her piece of shit dad did.

After stepping into the pen, I drop down to a crouch across from her, arms on my knees, making myself as small as fuckin' possible.

Part of me wants to make promises—to bear my soul and erase all the shit she's been through with my words alone, but I'm not stupid.

I know nothing will rewrite this little girl's history. All I can do is draw out a better future and hold her hand while she lives it.

"Uh… hey," I murmur, dropping to my ass slowly, leaving a few feet between us. "Remember me? I'm Kade."

She freezes mid-gnaw, tilting her head just slightly and stares at me.

"So, Ethel said you already ate. That's cool. Great. Less pressure right off the bat." My eyes flick to the island where I set out all the formula and baby snacks the foster's sent over. "They gave me a schedule for you, but all the shi—" Groaning, I bite the inside of my cheek and look back at her. "Crap I read online said you'll probably rebel the fu—"

I smack a hand to my mouth and mutter a nearly silent string of curses. This is ridiculous.

Aurora knocks the teether against the floor, then back to her mouth it goes. All the while, she stares at me like she's judging my entire existence.

"Not very helpful," I whisper, running a hand through my beard. "I don't know what I expected. Like you'd be able to tell me what's next? Nap? A diaper? Favorite activities?"

She shrieks and flings the rubber teether at my face.

Jolting, I gape down at her and rub the ache from my jaw.

"You've got a hell of a hand on ya, sweetheart." I chuckle, handing her back the projectile. "Aim's spot on, too."

Aurora giggles, kicks her feet, and shoves herself forward onto her hands and knees, and then this sweet girl... this brilliant, tiny little survivor, crawls to me.

My heart damn near stops, breath stalling in my lungs.

The nurses weren't sure if she was crawling or toddling yet. Whole time in the hospital, she never tried to talk or do any of the other things she could be doing at her age—or at least attempting. They did make a list of the few things they noted, a list I added to my phone so I could keep track eventually.

But they didn't know about the crawling... and I...

Christ, I wasn't ready for what the tiny little milestone would do to my heart.

Once she reaches me, she wastes no time climbing into my lap, and again, the organ in my chest finds a way to grow and shift, all from one beat to the next.

Aurora blinks up at me with sleepy eyes, and I waste no time cuddling her against my chest, abs already burning from the angle. When she settles into me, thumb between her lips and pinky wrapped around a chunk of my beard, I decide I don't care.

"I'm here," I coo, rubbing her back, eyes burning, mind a fuckin' disaster zone. "I'm not goin' anywhere, sweetheart. I've got you."

After a while, Aurora passes out, and I carefully climb from the pen, dropping onto the couch. If she wants to nap on my chest, I'll let her.

How could Marlee let this happen?

She'd been through so much. Her mom was an addict, in and out of jail her whole childhood. No father around. And when her mother died, she got dumped with a grandmother who barely tolerated her. Marlee grew up angry, desperate for attention, desperate for love. I knew that. I saw it. Hell, I lived pieces of it with her.

So how the hell did she end up with a man like Travis Vernal?

How could she let this baby—this perfect little girl—get hurt?

My gaze drops to Aurora's chubby arm, bare and soft. Her tiny overalls are light pink, the white onesie underneath already rumpled. And just above her elbow, on the inside, is a small, faint scar. I thought it was from the accident.

Now... I don't know.

My stomach turns.

Did Marlee do it? Did she watch it happen? Was she too scared to stop it? Or worse... did she just not care? Maybe she was too drunk or high to give a shit. Maybe she was just as much a victim as her daughter.

Either way, it doesn't stop the violent rage pelting my system.

I'm desperate for a bottle of whiskey right now, but the judge said I'm banned from a good buzz and now that I have Aurora, drinking feels wrong. Never been one for drugs or beating the shit out of random, swinging objects to get my head right.

For a while after the military, I spent my days drunk—and weekends drunker. I'd find some random woman in Wildwood or Langley to fuck the pain away with. It's been more than a year since I was that low, and I'm not proud of using it to cope, but it worked. The thought of doing it now has nausea clawing through me.

Only thing that feels like it would help at all right now isn't a shot of whiskey—but a shot of Georgia.

If I close my eyes, I can practically *feel* the way her laugh rolls over my too-tight skin. The way it burns and wakes me up like nothing else can. The husky sound of her voice—a mixture of faded and blended accents I can never make out but find endearing and adorable.

I've never found anything endearing in my life, but here I am, missing the cadence of her syllables the way addicts miss their favorite fix.

With the baby on my chest, I don't dare let myself think about all the other shit I miss—all the other ways I could lose my mind and fix my ragged emotions while lost in Georgia, but it's there—an ache in my soul.

Glancing at the island, I catch sight of my phone and contemplate grabbing it to call her. I haven't heard from her all day. Didn't want to bug her while she was at work, so I kept busy. Cleaned. Organized. Prepped everything I could for Aurora's arrival. I didn't even know she was coming today. Thought for sure it'd be tomorrow. But then the doorbell rang, and there she was.

Ethel holding the car seat, Aurora looking up at me with wide, glassy eyes and a tiny, perfect smile, like she really remembered me. Like she'd been waiting, too. The hours since passed in a whirlwind.

I want to tell Georgia what happened. Wanna talk about Marlee. About the crash. About everything that's ripping my goddamn heart open right now.

I want to lay every shattered piece of me down at her feet, just like she begged me to.

But what if it scares her off?

What if I'm too much?

I'm still spiraling when the front door bursts open, and my mom's voice floods the house.

"Was that Ethel's SUV I saw pulling away? Why was she—*Oh my God*! Is that my grandbaby!?"

"Ma!" I whisper-hiss, hiking Aurora higher on my shoulder while bouncing her softly. "She's asleep!"

A second later, two familiar voices echo through the room.

"Look, man, I know you told us to stay away so you could be alone with your sweet, freckled Georgia Peach, but I'm leaving in a few days, and I miss your stupid face," Wilder grumbles, followed by a thump as he comes to an abrupt halt.

Griffin crashes into his back, both of them staring down at me, eyes wide.

"Holy shit," Griff breathes. "Is that—"

"Mom? Are you here?" Clementine calls from the hallway. "Colby and I want to—"

"Holy shitballs!" Colby screams, cutting her off. "She's here!"

My mom whips around, hands on her hips and quietly snaps, "She's asleep!"

And then they're all silently barreling toward me, wordlessly crying, cooing, and prancing around like a herd of wild birds.

My too-quiet, too-heavy house is suddenly alive with joy, excitement, and so much fucking love I can barely breathe.

Aurora blinks her eyes open like she can sense all the eyes on her and wiggles around, fist tightening in my beard, and I hold her closer, kissing the top of her head.

I'm not alone.

Not anymore.

I've got a baby in my lap, a family at my back, and a future that terrifies the hell out of me—but I'll fight for it with everything I've got.

CHAPTER THIRTY THREE

Georgia

EVEN IF IT BREAKS ME

FOUR DAYS OF RADIO silence.

Four days where I stewed, panicked, and spiraled.

Four days where Kade William Archer didn't say a word to me after I left him sleeping on the couch, snoring quietly, and wrapped in a soft blanket that smelled like *us*.

I could have called him, or shown up, but honestly, in those four days, I lost my damn mind.

Because when you've spent your whole life learning that love is conditional, that people leave, and that no matter how careful you are, you're never quite enough.

You learn that silence doesn't feel like space—it feels like punishment.

And it didn't matter that he'd kissed me like I was air and he was drowning. Didn't matter that he'd touched me like I was sacred, murmured things that felt too sweet to be lies, or pulled me into his arms like he wasn't planning to let go.

The moment I walked out that door and didn't hear from him? My heart whispered the one thing it always does.

Of course he didn't call.

Why would he?

Why would anyone fight for the girl who was never chosen? Not as a baby in the hospital. Not in a string of foster homes. Not in relationships, or friendships, or families that always left just enough room for her to feel the edge.

People don't hold on to girls like me.

They forget us.

They let us go.

And if they do come back, it's only long enough to remind us why we never should've believed in the first place.

I tried to rationalize it. Tried to believe he was busy, or overwhelmed, or sorting things out in that quiet, broody way of his. But the longer I went without hearing from him, the easier it became to rewrite the weekend into something shameful.

Sure, he'd taken care of me. Fed me. Bathed me. Held my hair back when I puked and wrapped me in his arms like I was something fragile. He'd drawn a bath, blow-dried my hair, rubbed my back when my migraine hit like a freight train, and shut out the world with blackout curtains and whispered questions in the dark.

And when my alarm went off that Monday morning, tearing me from the warm cocoon of him? Climbing out of his bed felt like ripping off my own skin. Getting dressed in my clothes from the bar was its own special kind of torture. Walking out the door nearly broke me.

But I did it. I told myself he'd wake up and call. That we'd talk. That everything he said, everything he promised, wouldn't turn to ash the second I was gone.

Four days.

That's all it took for the self-sabotage to kick in—loud and cruel, whispering things I've spent my whole life trying not to believe.

You're too much.

You're not enough.

You made it up.

He used you.

He regrets it.

He. Regrets. You.

By the time my phone rang this afternoon, in between house visits, and his name lit up my screen, I was too far gone. And when my emotions get the best of me, I get angry. I get snappy and sassy and pissed off.

When I declined the first call, it wasn't a mistake. And when he called again, and again, until I finally answered—I was short and painfully cold, my voice held together by threads that were already unraveling.

But then he brokenly rasped the only three words that could've soothed the storm in my chest.

"I need you."

Just like that, every wall I'd spent four days rebuilding crumbled like dust. His voice was ragged, worn, full of defeat—and I didn't even hesitate.

How could I?

Because in the space that had grown between us, I'd started to forget the *truth*.

I'd started to forget the man I walked away from wasn't just the one who made me feel good. He was the man who held me like he was afraid to let go. The man who cried in a nursery over the story of his dad. The man who drank himself sick trying to outrun grief so deep it swallowed him whole. The man who held me while I broke, and promised he'd carry my pieces.

A promise I made right back.

I forgot.

But the second I heard his voice again, it all came rushing back. Every soft word, every shattered piece he let me hold.

I told him I'd be there soon, and I meant it.

Even as guilt clawed up my throat for being such a goddamn coward. For punishing him for disappearing, when maybe he was just barely holding it together.

Now, the sun is down. The breeze is cold. The scent of blooming flowers is thick in the air as I stand on his wraparound porch, heart pounding behind my ribs like a drum.

I stare at the door, debating whether to knock or just walk in.

Would he expect me to wait, like I'm some polite guest? As if I didn't ride his face and soak his beard just a few days ago? Or do I walk in like I already *belong to him*?

I shift my bag on my shoulder—this time packed with clothes, toiletries, and my backup meds. Because I'm starting to learn that when it comes to Kade Archer, I should always expect the unexpected. And right now? Standing on this porch, skin prickling with nerves and hope and something dangerously close to falling…

Nothing about this feels predictable.

My shaky hand lifts to the door but it flies open before I can knock.

Kade stands there—shirtless, barefoot, wearing a pair of ratty gym shorts and looking like he hasn't slept in days. His hair's a greasy mess, falling in strands around his face, and there are dark circles etched deep beneath his bloodshot eyes. He looks horrible.

And somehow, *he looks beautiful.*

My breath catches.

He stares back at me like he can't believe I'm real, then drags in a shaky breath, his hand tightening on the doorframe like it's the only thing keeping him upright.

"You're here," he says, voice hoarse and low. His shoulders drop, chin falling to his chest.

Before I can speak, before I can ask what the hell happened, a cry pierces the air—loud, devastating, and raw.

Kade's whole body tenses. His spine goes rigid. And when he lifts his face, the look in his eyes guts me.

A choked, broken sound slips from his throat.

"I can't do this."

The cry cuts off abruptly, leaving behind a quiet so heavy it nearly topples me. My heart slams against my ribs, eyes flying to Kade's. His breath is shaky, lips parted, shoulders drawn up like he's bracing for impact.

Awareness dawns on me like a gut punch.

Aurora's here.

A smile breaks across my face, wide and unfiltered, and before I can think better of it, I step forward, closing the space between us and wrapping my arms around his bare, exhausted frame.

"She's here," I breathe, the words catching in my throat as I squeeze my eyes shut.

He melts into me, his weight forcing my knees to bend as his arms lock around me. The relief of his touch nearly destroys me.

"Aurora is yours, Kade," I whisper, eyes blurring. "Fuck, I'm so happy for you."

He nods against my neck, fingers digging into the back of my sweater like he needs me just as much as I need him. Like he's terrified I'll slip away.

It's scary and exhilarating and desperate.

"And she fuckin' hates me," he chokes out, voice cracking as his body shudders.

My brows pinch together, and I try to lean back to look at him, but he won't let me go. One of my hands strokes gently down his back, my nose wrinkling as I breathe in fatigue, sweat, and something stale and sour.

"What are you talking about?" I murmur. "That little girl adores you."

"No," he mutters, burying his nose in my hair and inhaling like I'm the first full breath he's taken in days. A full-body shiver ripples through me at the feel of it, but I shut it down, overtly aware of his breakdown right now and how inappropriate getting turned on is.

But, God, it's like a knee-jerk reaction to being in this man's presence. Especially after the way he…

Nope.

No, Georgia. Not now.

"She won't stop cryin'. Won't sleep. Barely eats. Just spits up and drools and throws shit. And *shits*."

I bite down a laugh and press my face to his chest to smother it.

"Ethel says she's teething," he grumbles. "But Christ, I don't remember it being like this with the twins. Don't remember them hating the world this fuckin' much."

"Well," I say softly, my voice trying to sound steady even though my brain's still short-circuiting from everything that's happened in the past five minutes. "The twins were your sisters. You weren't their parent. And you were still a kid."

"I was thirteen when they were born," he defends, fingers weaving through my hair.

It's down and curled by a curling iron today because I was so over *overthinking* him, I spent hours blow-drying, straightening, and curling my hair in front of the same stupid TV show we binged when I was here, being a masochist to the extreme.

"This is pretty," he hums, low and warm. "Miss your curls, though, baby."

Baby.

The word settles something wild and frantic in my chest, anchoring it in place. I finally manage to pull back enough to meet his eyes, cupping his face as I search him.

"You haven't slept, have you?"

He shakes his head in my hands, eyes closing.

"She showed up Monday," he mutters. "Was gonna call you, but then my whole family showed, and the guys…"

He trails off, shrugging helplessly before pressing his face into my palm.

"Everyone hung out, getting to know her. Mom stayed two nights, but she had to take Gemma to the airport yesterday and got stuck in Rydell because of the storm. Hazel's out of town with Ridge at some equipment sale up north."

"Ridge?" I ask gently, sorting through all the pieces. "The ranch manager?"

He nods, something like guilt flickering across his face. "They handle most of the shit for the farm these days."

"And the twins?" I ask, eyes narrowing as protectiveness swarms my system. "They aren't at the big house alone with your *buddies*, are they?"

He snorts. "Fuck, no. Mom's got them staying with a friend till she's back tomorrow. Griff took Wilder to the airport this morning."

I nod, the tension in my shoulders finally starting to ease. "I'm sorry I didn't get to say goodbye to Wilder. Your friends seem like good guys."

His eyes snap open, arms tightening around me.

"They're not that damn good," he growls, and I catch the hint of possessiveness in his tone that sends shivers down my spine. "Don't get any fuckin' ideas, freckles."

I scoff, stepping away—only to be yanked right back into his arms. My nose wrinkles.

"I want to hug you again," I whisper, smiling faintly, "but you smell, Kade." I tap his abs, grinning when they twitch under my hand. "Really bad."

"I do not," he grumbles defensively.

Aurora immediately starts crying again.

He winces, shoulders tightening as he glances down the hallway, tugging at his hair. "Shit, I need to—"

"You need to shower," I interrupt firmly, planting my hands on my hips. "Maybe even bathe. With salts and lots of soap."

He blinks at me.

"When's the last time you ate? Or drank water?"

He glances out the window, eyes widening slightly. "The sun was coming up."

"Well, it's going down now." I huff, grabbing his shoulders and steering him down the hall. "I'm starting a bath. Go say goodnight to your little girl, but don't worry about settling her. I'll take care of it."

He resists, heels digging into the hardwood like a stubborn mule. "Georgia…"

"No," I say, firm and low. "I know you want to handle everything on your own. That's your thing. But you're not alone. And I don't just mean because you've got a family that loves you, or friends who'd drop everything to be here."

My voice quiets, throat thick with the weight of what I'm admitting.

"I don't know what this is yet, or where it's going, but I'm here." *For now.* "I *want* to be here." *Forever.* "If you want me to be." *Please say you do.*

"Want that too," he murmurs, eyes heated. "A lot."

Then you should have called me.

I swallow back the words, shrugging helplessly, feeling stupid, and vulnerable and too damn needy.

"Well," I say instead. "I'm here now. I'll take care of everything."

I'll take care of you.

Leaning in, he presses a lingering kiss to my cheek, his beard brushing my skin in a way that's anything but innocent.

"Wanna do a fuck-ton more than this, darlin'," he murmurs, voice thick with exhaustion. "But not only have I not showered in four days… I, uh… haven't brushed my teeth either."

I grimace. "That explains the crying baby," I say, deadpan. "Probably scared her half to death. You smell like a—"

"Rabid hyena?" he finishes, smirking as he shuffles toward Aurora's room. "Some say it's my best quality."

And no matter how hard I try, I can't stop the smile that splits my face.

The mans an exhausting, heart-wrecking, annoying asshole.

He's perfect.

Kade is asleep in his bed, the house is clean, and Aurora is finally… peaceful*ish*.

It took hours.

I walked her for miles in his living room—swaying, humming, bouncing gently on my toes until my calves burned. I gave her a lavender bath, massaged her legs with baby-safe balm, and rubbed frozen teething rings along her gums until her sobs turned into whimpers.

Thank fuck for whichever Archer or friend donated all the goodies, because they came in handy.

We rocked together until she stopped pulling away, and I fed her slowly, letting her take her time, letting her know she didn't have to cry for comfort.

The sink is empty. The dishes are washed and dried and stacked neatly on the counter because it didn't feel right to dig through his drawers or cabinets while he slept.

There were a ton of shipping boxes tucked in a corner, so I broke them down and quietly set them on the porch, not wanting Aurora to get into them when she feels better.

The floors have been swept, and mopped. I wiped down the sticky surfaces in the kitchen, scrubbed the counters, and ran a few loads of laundry.

And somewhere between folding onesies and disinfecting pacifiers, I opened all the windows to air out the house. Lit a candle. Put a soft blanket on the couch. Made the place feel like a home again.

Now, it's almost sunrise.

Kade slept through the night without moving, and I'm... *wrecked.*

But I can't bring myself to put her down.

She's curled against my chest, her soft yellow blanket wrapped around her like a cocoon. One tiny hand is tucked into the fleece, the other is curled tight around a strand of my hair. I tried to pry it free more than once, but every time I did, her face crumpled, and that little fist found it again.

So I let her keep it.

Who am I to take comfort away from something so small and sweet?

The low hum of "The Mother" by Brandi Carlile plays softly through the TV, the fire crackling quietly behind us, filling the room with a golden glow. The warmth on my skin makes me drowsy, but I don't dare move. Not yet.

And because I'm really weak where this man is concerned, I rescheduled my two appointments for tomorrow. My weekends are always free. So for the next few days... I'll be here—if Kade needs me.

Maybe it's fast and stupid and reckless. Maybe my heart will crack open and bleed all over this floor when all this ends.

But as I stare down at her, at this beautiful, brave little girl sleeping against my heart, I know I'd do it all again.

She stopped sucking on the bottle a while ago, her lips now puckered in soft little snores. I slip it gently from her mouth and rub slow circles on her back with one hand while my other fingers trail through her damp hair, still soft and sweet-smelling from the bath.

It shouldn't be this easy.

Not for someone like me.

I'm a social worker. I've been trained to create boundaries, to build walls between myself and the families I work with.

I know the dangers of attachment. I've lived the worst-case scenarios.

And yet... from the second I walked into that hospital room and saw her tiny face, red and scrunched and screaming for someone who'd never come, it was already too late.

Maybe it's because I see myself in her—a helpless little girl, alone in the world, born from tragedy and crying out for someone, *anyone*, to choose her.

That was me.

Only I didn't have a Kade.

Didn't have a Bea—or even an Ethel.

I have no doubt the social workers who tried to help me cared. You don't do this job if you don't care. But the times were different, the system was thinner, and the community I was born into makes Summit County look like LA.

I fell through every crack. Every gap and fracture. Again and again.

But Aurora didn't.

She won't.

Because Ethel won't let her.

Because Kade won't let her.

And neither will I.

A lump rises in my throat, thick and unrelenting. I shift her upright and gently burp her, holding my breath when she stirs, then settles again with a sigh that makes my heart ache.

When she's fully asleep, I stand, slow and careful, my legs screaming in protest from how long I've been sitting, and carry her into the nursery. I lower her into the crib, settling her into the firm mattress, making sure her blanket is tucked loosely around her hips, not near her face. Her pacifier rests nearby. The teether ring she finally accepted earlier is still clutched in her tiny hand.

I double-check the monitor, adjust the angle, and gently draw the blackout curtains shut. The soft glow of the nightlights spills across the room in warm patterns of dancing bees and rainbows. They flicker gently on the pale yellow walls, and my chest throbs with something I don't know how to name.

I brush a hand through her dark hair, lingering for just a second too long, and my vision blurs. I blink hard, swallowing down everything I feel but can't say.

How did I fall this hard? And what the hell am I supposed to do if it ends?

Because this—this baby, this man, this messy, beautiful life?

This feels dangerously close to home—the one thing I've wished for my whole life but never found.

Maybe that's finally changed. Maybe all my wishes have finally come true.

CHAPTER THIRTY FOUR

DOMESTIC, DERANGED, AND HOT AS HELL

"WAKE UP, DARLIN'," I rumble, voice thick with sleep as I brush Georgia's mess of hair from her face.

She blinks up at me, a soft smile ghosting her lips before jerking upright with a gasp, moving so quick, her head knocks into mine.

Grunting, I shake the throb away and glare down at her, jaw ticking as I prod at her forehead. "You hurt yourself—"

"Oh my God! Aurora!" she cries, jumping off the couch. The blanket wrapped around her drops, tangling with her feet and she stumbles forward, arms spiraling like a damn windmill.

I snatch her up, arm around her middle and haul her into my arms, her back to my chest.

"I didn't mean to fall asleep," she whimpers, nails biting into my arm. "Shit. Let me down—"

"Hey, hey, relax," I interrupt, moving her from the danger zone of the blanket and coffee table. "She's okay. She's playing with my sisters out back."

Georgia freezes, body tense for a split second before the fight drains right out of her. Confident she's not about to fall or run, I drop her feet to the ground and slowly release her.

She smooths her hands down her clothes—black fitted pants and a soft sweater. Same thing she was wearing when she showed up last night and rescued me from severe sleep deprivation brought on by a screaming, drooling, pooping toddler.

Only thing Georgia's missing is those damn sky-high heels that kill me every time she wears them, which isn't much. My girl prefers her cute little fake cowgirl boots. I make a mental note to get her some real ones.

With a slow exhale, she turns to face me, lip tucked between her teeth, hands clenched in front of her.

She looks nervous as hell—awkward even. And she's silent, which isn't like Georgia. Even when she's mad, she's rambling a mile a minute, or biting my head off at the very least.

Only time I've seen her so… *stand-offish*… is when she's pulling away, walls up and feet halfway out the damn door.

"You slept," she finally whispers, body language closed off.

I nod slowly, eyes narrowed.

"I'm glad. You needed it."

Gesturing to the couch, I grumble, "Why didn't you come to bed with me?"

"With you?" she asks, voice a little high-pitched, cheeks burning red. "Oh, I, uh—" She takes a step back… a step *away* from me. "Just fell asleep. I was going to make you breakfast, but I wasn't sure when you'd be up, or if you'd want me to hang around after you slept. I can…" Brows furrowed, she gives a sharp nod. "I'll go—"

Nah. We're not doing this shit.

Unable to take the distance—emotional and physical—I haul her over my shoulder and stomp toward the kitchen.

"AH! What the hell are you doing, Kade?" she snaps, little palms slapping against my back. "Put me down, you big brute!"

I grin. There's my wildfire.

My hand claps down on her perfect, round ass before I drop her on the island. Don't give her a second to overthink a damn thing before I'm on her, forcing my way between her thighs, hand gripped around her jaw, fingers threaded through her wavy hair.

"Talk to me," I demand, voice rough, muscles corded with tension as my eyes flick between hers. "What the hell happened between last weekend and now?"

Her throat bobs beneath my grip, fingertips digging into the counter like she wants to touch me but doesn't know if she can, or *should*.

I hate it.

She drops her gaze. "Nothing."

"Don't do that. Don't look away." I tighten my grip, still keeping it gentle, but enough to tip her head back, forcing her to look at me. "Gotta help me out here, freckles. Know it's been a few days, but—"

"Four days," she huffs, and I'm shocked to see her eyes gloss over. "But I didn't... you didn't..."

She trails off, swallowing hard.

My mind races through an invisible battlefield I can't quite see, trying to put the pieces together.

I know Georgia is quick to run when shit gets scary. Don't blame her for it after all she's been through, but I'd be lying if I said it didn't make it hard to navigate whatever... *this* is.

To me, what we have between us feels a hell of a lot like the start of something permanent. Something I've dreamt about my entire damn life.

Thought she wanted that, too. Thought she felt the same way.

Did I fuck it up already? Get it wrong? Push too hard?

But then her words come tumbling back, the vulnerability on her face, the *hurt* in her eyes.

Last time I saw her, she was wrapped in my arms, and holding me like she never wanted to let go. And then she left for work, and Aurora showed up, and everything after that was a whirlwind. I'd been so caught up, that I didn't think to call her...

Fuck.

"I didn't call you."

The way she flinches tells me all I need to know.

Cupping her face with both hands, I tilt her neck back and drop my forehead to hers, inhaling the sweet, wild scent that's all her, and let it calm the chaos still clawing under my skin.

"Saying I'm sorry won't fix it," I murmur, brushing her cheek with my thumb, "but I am. I'm sorry, Georgia. I shouldn't have let it drag on so long without reaching out. That's on me."

"No," she whispers, voice tight and raw as her hands finally leave the counter and grip my wrists hard enough to leave nail imprints. "*I'm* sorry. I let my brain fill up with all sorts of ugly thoughts about what happened between us." A shaky breath escapes her, but it sounds too close to a sob. "I'd like to say it was a one-off, but it happens a lot with me."

I press a kiss to her forehead, trying to pour comfort into the contact, trying to stitch together what I've unknowingly torn open. "I'm not afraid to fight your demons, Georgia Walker."

"I'm a lot of work," she says, like she's trying to scare me off.

"I'm not afraid of hard work," I murmur, my lips ghosting her skin. "And you're worth it."

Her breath catches, body shivering against me, but the tension in her shoulders doesn't fade, so I continue, rambling the truth like a madman.

"Wanted to call you the second I woke up to an empty house. Missed you more than I probably should, but I don't give a fuck."

"You did?"

I nod, keeping her close. "Wanted to beg your perfect ass to come back and never leave."

"Kade…"

"It's true," I murmur, thumbs tracing the soft skin of her jaw as I pull back far enough to see her eyes. "If I told you all the things I feel where you're concerned, darlin', you'd run for the hills and never look back."

Her tongue drags across her lower lip, slow and sexy, before she breathes out, "Try me."

And God, it yanks me right back to that day all those weeks ago when I showed her around this very house and she begged me to tell her why I wanted so many rooms.

Meadow eyes flare up at me and for a second, I wonder if she's thinking of it too. She brought it up while her bare, wet cunt was rubbing my cock the other night, so clearly, my dreams are on her mind as much as they're on mine.

"You really wanna know?" I ask, my voice rough.

She nods, gaze flicking to my lips and then back to my eyes. "Yes."

It hits me then, that maybe I've had it wrong.

Maybe Georgia's need to run when shit gets scary isn't because she's afraid of me going all in—it's because she's afraid she's falling alone.

Maybe she needs the reassurance that what's between us isn't one-sided.

Don't know if it's love yet. Don't know if I'd recognize love if it hit me in the chest. The only time I ever thought I had it was with a woman who turned out to be more manipulator than partner. A woman who lied to me, used me, and weaponized her pain in ways I'm still untangling.

Did Marlee ever love me? Did she even know how?

Doesn't matter. Not anymore.

All that matters is Georgia. This moment. This woman sitting in front of me, holding on with her fingernails and heart.

"I want you, Georgia Walker," I say, voice low and steady. "In a big, scary kind of way."

Her eyes widen, lips parting, but I'm not done.

"Called you mine the other night, and I meant it. Want your softness and sass. Your stubborn mouth and your tendency to overthink every-thing. Want the girl who's had to fight for herself every goddamn step of the way. Want the woman who never got chosen and still shows up for everyone else anyway. I want the parts of you that you think make you too much—your fear, your fire, all of it."

Her chest rises in a sharp breath, tears flooding her eyes so fast it nearly unravels me.

"I'm not sayin' I've got it all figured out," I admit, brushing a tear from her cheek with my knuckle. "And I'm not sayin' I know what comes next. But I know what I want. And it's you. Aurora. Us."

"But…" Her head shakes. "What happens when my contract ends?"

My stomach flips and turns, heart kicking at the thought.

Don't want her to leave. Not now, not never.

But that's not my choice.

If she doesn't find what she's looking for in Heart Springs, she might leave and never come back. Part of me wants to run out right now and dig hard for her roots just so I have something solid to give her.

Georgia has to want this, though.

Has to be in this with me.

I'll fight tooth and nail for this woman, but she's gotta fight at my side.

If I learned anything from my past, it's that a person who wants to go, will go. One way or another, they'll find an exit and bolt through it first chance they get—no matter what, or *who* they're leaving behind.

Tried to be everything I could be for Marlee. Tried to show her that I was worth choosing. But she chose herself, and from what Ethel said, she kept making the same choice 'till the day she died.

Didn't want to fall into someone who had a foot out the door… tried to avoid it. But Georgia isn't just someone, and ignoring what I feel for her is as useless as it is painful. All I can do is hope this shit doesn't blow up in my face eventually.

"Can't force you to stay," I rasp, pressing a kiss on the corner of her lips, body shuddering. "But I want you to. Want you to pick this place, this town, this house." *Me. Us.* "But I can't ask you to do that. You gotta want it, baby."

"I… I do." An audible swallow. "I still have a few months left before I have to make any decisions."

I nod. "Then we take it day by day."

"Day by day," she whispers, shoulders falling an inch. "I can do that."

There's a million things I wanna say. Questions I want answered, promises I want made. But if this little thing is all she can offer today, I'll fuckin' take it. Take it with both greedy hands and hold onto it like a man possessed.

Because where she's concerned, pretty sure I am.

"Okay," I murmur, leaning in, hands tight on her face. "One day at a time."

"Just us?" she asks, looking worried and a little green.

A possessive growl catches in my throat. "Just fuckin' us."

"Day by day." She inhales sharply, mirroring me, letting her lips hover a breath away. "You and me."

"Us."

With that, I finally claim her mouth the way I've wanted to since yesterday. She melts into me with a tiny, breathy moan that shoots straight through my bloodstream and lights up every raw, aching nerve in my body, ending in my cock that strains to get to her.

It's always like this when she's around. Even when she's not, and I'm thinking of her. Every inch of me is always desperate to get back to every inch of her.

Georgia's hands fly to my chest, fingers curling in the fabric of my shirt like she needs something to hang on to. I cup the back of her head, threading my fingers into her red strands and tugging just enough to tilt her jaw the way I want it so I can deepen the kiss.

She parts for me with no hesitation, and the second my tongue slides against hers, she whimpers into my mouth—and *fuck*, I nearly lose it. The sound is soft, desperate, real. She kisses like she feels too much and trusts too little, like she's trying to memorize me in case it all disappears.

But I kiss her like I'm trying to rewrite every lie she's ever believed about not being wanted.

Her thighs lock around my hips, and I step closer, grinding my throbbing dick against her warm pussy. A pussy that tasted like honey, and sin, sugar and *mine*. A pussy I can't wait to have my lips and tongue wrapped around again.

I slide my hands down her body, slipping them under her to cup her ass so I can drag her against me roughly.

"Kade," she whimpers, crossing her ankles for more leverage as she claws at me. "I need you."

"Not yet," I rasp, diving in for another wild, deep kiss that has her moaning into my mouth, hips grinding and thighs clenching.

Christ, this woman makes me lose my fuckin' mind.

"Please," she begs, hands gliding beneath my shirt, nails raking across my abs. "I'm so wet for you."

A groan rattles my throat, and I seriously rethink the plans I made for us today. Unfortunately, I can't reschedule nature, so after another minute, I reluctantly pull away.

With a huff, she tugs me right back by the band of my jeans.

Chuckling, I shake my head, heart hammering, blood burning through me. My lips work across her jaw, down her throat, and I sink my teeth in, mumbling against her,

"I'm not fuckin' you on the counter today."

"Why the hell not? It's as good of a place as any."

It's the petulance in her voice and the cute pout that damn near drags me back in, but I pull away, forcing a few feet between my dick and the place it desperately wants to live inside.

"I said not *today*," I whisper, swallowing hard. "Not never."

Panting hard, I stare down at her, thumb brushing her swollen bottom lip, eyes raking over the damage I did. Her hair's a mess, eyes are glazed, lips red and puffy, beard burn across her jaw, and there's a nice pink mark on her neck from my teeth.

Pride and possessiveness swell inside me.

"Still want to run?" I ask, voice hoarse, ignoring the way she's trying to draw me back in. If I allow it, I'll lose myself in her, and I can't. Not right now.

She shakes her head, breath shuddering. "I really don't."

"Good," I rasp, pressing another kiss to her mouth, slower this time. "Because we have plans I can't reschedule."

Her brows pinch, but her lips curve into an excited smile as she asks softly, "Really?"

It takes more effort than I care to admit to step away from her, but I do, grabbing my hat from where I left it on the island and tugging it over my hair.

"Yeah," I say, flashing a grin. "We've got somewhere to be in about an hour."

"It's early," she murmurs, sliding off the counter. "Where are we going?"

Chuckling, I move to the fridge and pull out a water for each of us, passing her one. "Check the clock, darlin'. You napped all day."

Georgia's eyes gape and she nearly spits her water out. "How the hell did I sleep so long?"

I lean against the counter and stare at her, gratitude and something deeper washing through me. "You took the night shift with Aurora, and that girl, sweet and perfect as she is, is a handful. Somehow, you still managed to clean every inch of the house. Did laundry, for fuck's sake."

Her cheeks turn bright red, and she shrugs like it's not a big deal. Like she didn't get my life back together in a single night. Like she didn't save me from a ledge it only took a few days to dangle me on.

No fuckin' idea how single parents do it. After all my friends and family disappeared—already adjusted to the excitement of having a cute new family member, I scrambled to pick up the pieces. Thank fuck I slept while my mom was here, but after…

I fell apart.

"Thank you," I murmur, shaking my head. "Appreciate the hell out of you for showing up."

She nods, bare foot scuffing the ground. "Thank you for calling."

I seriously fucked up.

Closing the distance between us, I brush her hair back. "Won't hesitate next time."

If I have it my way, there won't be a next time. She'll just be here. Always.

"So, where are we going?"

Smiling, stomach swooping with excitement, I tell her the truth. "It's a surprise."

One I'm hoping proves how much she means to me in a way her sweet, terrified mind can't argue with.

Chapter Thirty Five

Georgia

Where the Sky Falls

"Are you sure she's okay?" I murmur, narrowed eyes flicking over my shoulder in the direction of Honey Bea. "She's only been with you for a few days. Maybe we shouldn't leave her yet."

Kade reaches over the truck's shifter and grips my hand, squeezing it gently. "Mom has her."

I bite my lip to stifle a gasp.

Him referring to Bea as *Mom* instead of *my mom*, shouldn't have the effect on me it does. Shouldn't mean a damn thing, but, God, every time he says something like that, all easily and plainly like it's *normal*, I swear, it rewrites my DNA.

The fingers of my free hand tangle in the thick gray crewneck sweatshirt I borrowed from him. Paired with my leggings and some thick country-and-mud-approved boots, I feel overdressed for spring, but with the sun going down and the weather so unpredictable, especially not knowing what our plans are, I guess it's for the best.

After he told me tonight was a surprise, he sent me off to his room to change into warm clothes—and to borrow whatever I needed—while he disappeared to get Aurora settled for the evening with his mom, who's back from Rydell now.

I tried to argue that we really shouldn't be leaving her so soon, and though I could tell he was reluctant, especially as we were finally loaded up in his truck and driving away, but he said this can't wait—whatever that means.

Turning back to face the windshield, I take in the dark landscape stretching for miles on every side of us. "Are we still on the farm?"

He nods, flicking on his high beams. "Yeah, we're not leaving—just driving a couple miles west."

"How big is Honey Bea?"

"Bit over ten thousand acres."

I gape. "That's huge."

Kade chuckles, pressing a kiss to the back of my hand. "Prefer you said that while staring at my cock, but I'll take it."

Scoffing, cheeks red-hot, I tug my hand away and flick his cheek. "You would say that, pervert."

He barks a laugh that makes his giant shoulders shake, and I get caught up in how *big* he is. Wide and thick and muscular all over. His eyes flit to me, hands tightening on the wheel as he cocks a brow.

"Who's the pervert now, darlin'?" he drawls, wetting his lower lip. "Like what you see?"

"No," I say, deadpan, tossing my hair over my shoulder as I force my gaze to the window. "Just thought I saw a bug in your beard. Don't worry, it was only your gray's, old man."

"Well, geriatric must be your thing, because you were screaming my name a few nights ago and squirting all over this old man's beard, weren't you?"

My mouth falls open, a denial already forming on my tongue, but the sight of him smug, eyes glazed and heavy with lust, sends a sharp bolt of need down my spine. Clit pulsing, nipples standing at attention, he's impossible to deny.

It's always like this when he's around. Even when I was swearing up and down I hated him.

"Cat got your tongue?" he taunts, lighter and freer than he was yesterday, weeks ago, months ago. Slowly yet surely, Kade Archer is coming back to life before my eyes.

"Sorry to break it to you," I say around a laugh, "but age-gaps aren't really my thing." Clicking my tongue, I settle into the seat, letting the warmth from the heater coat my skin. "My best friend, Abby, however, loves older men."

"How old we talkin'?"

I think back to the guys she's had crushes on over the years. They were all at least ten years older. Even her ex-husband—and still-boss—Steven is twelve years older than she is. But the age difference didn't stop him from being a lying, cheating prick who stole her freedom, her money, and her condo in an ugly divorce.

"Never seen her date or like a man less than ten years older than her," I finally say with a shrug. "Not that she's out here actively hunting sugar daddies. It's just... she's got a thing for the emotionally unavailable with a hint of salt-and-pepper and trauma."

Kade laughs. "Sounds like she'd love Griff."

I snort. "Griffin's a six-and-a-half-foot-tall teddy bear. Abby would eat him alive."

"Maybe you're right," he mutters. "He hand-raises rescue ponies."

"She's more candlelight, tarot cards, and *'let's move to Bali to sell macramé'* than barn boots and farm chores."

"In his defense, the man makes the best damn bourbon-glazed ribs I've ever had."

"One, Abby's a vegan," I say, chuckling. "And two, it sounds like you want to date Griffin." My brows waggle. "Bit of a bromance thing going with your beloved Sarge?"

"He wishes." Kade smirks, eyes dragging over me like he's starving. "Fact that your best friend likes older men doesn't surprise me."

I arch a brow. "Why not?"

"Because if her type's anything like yours, she's probably got a thing for big, capable hands and the kind of experience that ruins a woman for anyone else."

My mouth drops open. "I didn't... I never..."

He chuckles low in his throat, all gravel and sin. "You didn't have to, darlin'. You've been starin' at my hands since we left the house."

"Only because they were on my thigh," I shoot back, voice breathy despite myself.

And because they're perfectly calloused and huge and felt so damn good inside me, I'm literally panting for a repeat.

"Exactly." He winks, then slows the truck to a quiet, rumbling stop. The headlights stretch out across an open stretch of dark green field, rimmed by trees and swallowed by night. "We're here."

My brows pull together in confusion as I glance around. "Already?"

"Yep." He kills the engine and opens his door with a creak. "Stay put."

Before I can argue, he's jogging around the truck. The tailgate squeaks open, followed by the soft bounce of him climbing into the bed. I shift in my seat, trying to get a peek at what he's doing, but it's too dark.

After a few minutes, I've determined he's setting something up, but I have no idea what it is. The sound of Fleetwood Mac's "Chains" fills the silence, and my brows furrow.

What the hell is he doing?

By the time he's climbing out and rounding to my side of the truck, every nerve ending in my body is buzzing with anticipation.

Because with Kade Archer, the unexpected always turns into unforgettable.

He opens my door with a flourish, tipping his baseball cap like it's a Stetson, and I blush all over again. "My lady."

Giggling, I lift my hand to his but squeal when he reaches for my hips instead and…

Throws me over his shoulder again.

"I'm not a ragdoll!" I hiss, fingers clenching his jacket. "Don't you dare drop me in the mud."

"Not a doll," he drawls, "but fun as hell to toss around."

My teeth clack from how hard I snap my mouth shut, and he laughs, free hand inching up my thigh. A moan slips free when his fingers graze my center and his laugh dies a quick death.

It takes everything in me not to beg for more. To spread my thighs wider and whimper like a wanton hussy.

I'm so damn keyed up after the other night, it's becoming a serious problem—for my panties.

He sets me gently on the tailgate, and I toss my head back, righting my messy hair. When I meet his gaze, red is spilling out above his beard, tinting his skin in an adorable, nervous flush.

"Are you…" My heart skips a beat, stomach flipping wildly. "Are you *blushing?*"

"No," he mutters, lip twitching. "Maybe."

"But why?"

Stepping forward, he grips my thighs roughly, hands rubbing up and down like he's trying to warm me up.

Little does he know, I'm already burning alive on the inside.

"I'm really fuckin' sorry for what happened the other night," he murmurs, surprising me. My smile falls, and he's quick to jump in, shaking his head. "No, not that. *Definitely* not *that*. But before…" He sighs. "I'm fuckin' this up."

"No," I breathe, tucking his wavy hair behind his ear, thumb ghosting his jaw. "You're really not."

He presses a kiss to my palm and sinks into the touch.

I'm quickly realizing, Kade is just as touch starved as I am, maybe more, and I make a mental note to be more physical. It doesn't come natural to me—or, it didn't. Not before him.

But now, I'm finding it difficult *not* to have my hands on this man at any given moment.

"Anyway," he continues, voice rough. "I'm really fuckin' sorry you got sick. Know you said it's not my fault, but fuck, Georgia, seeing you like that—sprawled out and sobbing on the floor, and after… the migraines and pain. Never knew food could do that to a person."

I tip my shoulders, stomach swooping. "It happens. I'm used to it."

Pain lances across his features at that. "Well, next time it does, you won't have to go through it alone."

And that promise is enough to make me fall infinitely deeper and further into the abyss of *him*.

"Brought you here to replace that shitty memory with a better one. Was our first night together, and yeah, ended good as hell, but started rough."

Unable to help myself, I lean forward and kiss him, driven my nothing but instinct and *want*. He doesn't miss a beat, kissing me hard and groaning into my mouth. His fingers weave into my hair, tipping me back as his tongue traces my lips. I open, greedy for more.

More.

Always *more* with him.

When he finally pulls back, we're both breathless and panting, and I'm seconds from stripping down and asking him to bend me over and fuck me on this tailgate.

Before I can, he's smiling and stepping back.

"Can't go losing my head before I tell you what our date is."

"This is a date?" I ask, butterflies breaking out in wild, chaotic wing beats. "A real one?"

He scoffs, climbing into the truck with ease. "Obviously. Dating is like the official first step in a relationship, is it not?"

"A…" My mouth opens and closes, the butterflies throwing a full blown rager in my gut. "A… *what?*"

Kade laughs and tips my jaw shut, kissing my lips once more. "We're a thing, baby. Get used to it."

Clearing my throat, I nod dumbly and turn to face him. "Okay, what's our—"

I freeze mid-sentence and gape at the setup before me.

The truck bed has been transformed.

A thick flannel blanket lines the bottom, layered with soft quilts and a tangle of pillows. A small camping lantern glows softly from the top of a cooler in the corner, lighting the setup softly. An oak tray is perched in the center, laid out with what I can only hope is a gluten-free charcuterie dream: crackers and cheese, sliced meats, fruit and veggies, a plate of chocolate-covered strawberries, a jar of honey, and a few glass bottles nestled in ice.

And him.

He's sprawled out on his side, propped up on one elbow, wearing dark jeans and a black shirt under his worn Carhartt jacket, cowboy boots crossed casually at the ankle. That damn baseball cap pulled low, and a smirk—the one that promises ruin and worship all at once—painted across his stupidly handsome face.

"Our date is a picnic?" I breathe, my voice cracking, eyes burning. "A nighttime picnic in the back of your truck."

His smirk falls, replaced by something serious and vulnerable.

"No, darlin'. The picnic is because you need to be fed and looked after. Blankets and pillows are to keep you warm and comfortable. Music's to make you smile. The dancin' we'll do is so you fall wildly in love with me. But the date?"

He points up.

"The sky is the date, baby. And it's fallin', just for you."

I look up slowly, almost afraid of what I'll find—because I already know whatever it is, it's going to change something fundamental in me.

And it does.

Above us, the sky is glittering and alive. Stars scatter like sugar across velvet, and right on cue, one streaks across the heavens, then another, and another—each one brighter than the last.

"The meteor shower's supposed to peak around two," he murmurs. "So I asked Mom to keep Aurora overnight. Just in case."

"You…" I choke out, body trembling, tears streaming down my cheeks. "You brought me to see shooting stars?"

"Millions of 'em." His voice is thick. "Figured you could make as many wishes as it takes to find whatever you're lookin' for."

My gaze reluctantly drags away from the prettiest sky I've ever seen and lands on him, the man who made it all possible. All because I told him I make wishes—one offhanded conversation weeks ago, and he did…

He did *this.*

And suddenly, I know.

I love him.

Don't know when it happened. Whether it was a slow burn built between anger, bad misconceptions, and heated arguments, or in the quiet, broken moments where we simply existed together.

Maybe it was watching Kade grow and heal for the sake of a little girl who desperately needed him.

In the promise to carry each other's pieces without judgment, or his willingness to show up and remind me that he wants me as I am. That he sees me and chooses me anyway.

Maybe it was this exact moment.

But it happened, and for once, I'm not afraid.

"Come here," he demands softly, hand held between us. "Let me show you what being mine feels like, Georgia Walker."

Wiping my tears on my shoulder with a sniffle, I take his hand and barely resist the urge to dive onto him and never let go.

Instead, I let him lead me to his side, careful not to knock anything over. Kade tugs a blanket over me and fluffs a pillow behind my back so I can lean against the cab.

"You did so much. I'm blown away," I say, voice raw and shaking. "No one's ever done anything like this for me."

"It was easy," he says simply, tipping his shoulder. "Know the things you love and made it happen."

And somehow, he finds a way to make me swoon harder.

He gives me a worried look. "You're not a vegan, right?"

Giggling, I shake my head. "No. Luckily it's only gluten I avoid. And seafood, but it's preference, not allergy."

He nods, dragging the board closer. "Everything here is gluten-free. I checked, and double-checked, but I also brought the packages just in case you wanted to—"

"I believe you," I interrupt, smiling softly at him. "I trust you, sunshine."

His cheeks turn pink again, and the sight makes me warm and fuzzy all over.

"Nickname used to piss me off," he mutters, cracking the cap off one of the bottles.

I scoff. "Like darlin'?"

"You never hated that name, *darlin'*." Kade laughs, passing me the drink, which I note is sparkling, gluten-free cider.

Everything in me melts all over.

Taking a sip, I watch him assemble some cheese and meat on a cracker then drizzle honey over the top like he's done this a thousand times. I expect him to shove it in his mouth like most men would, but Kade isn't like most men.

He's… he's *my man*.

And in my man's true fashion, he brings it to my mouth with an expectant look. "Eat."

Rolling my eyes, I open my mouth and accept the demanded snack. The flavors burst on my tongue, and I cover my lips, chewing and moaning in bliss.

His eyes heat, and he's quick to make me another. "Could listen to that sound all fuckin' night."

Swallowing with a grin, I shake my head. "You need to eat, too."

"But I don't moan when I eat," he says, practically pouting.

I bite my lip and my core tightens. "You sure about that? Pretty sure you moaned when you ate *me*."

Kade's head falls back with a breathy groan that goes right to my clit. "Christ, woman. I'm tryin' to be good here. Let me feed you before you go seducing me."

"Then feed me fast, because I'm starving," I whisper, voice shaking, body on fire. Our eyes meet and his throat bobs. "And it's not for food."

Tension, hot and aching and needy, burns between us. "Fever" by Peggy Lee—spills through his phone speaker, the crooning seduction of it wrapping the night around us.

Kade's jaw ticks. His knuckles flex as he sets down the honey jar, fingers shaking just slightly.

And I feel it—that razor-thin line between restraint and surrender snapping tighter with every breath.

"I'm not tryin' to rush this," he murmurs, voice hoarse, like he's warning both of us. "I wanted tonight to be slow. Romantic. Thought maybe we'd dance under the stars. Feed each other strawberries. Talk about shit that scares us, lights us up, and everything in between."

My breath hitches. "We still can."

"Yeah, but it's hard to think about talkin' when you're sittin' there lookin' like that," he rasps, eyes devouring me like he's starving. "Wearin' my clothes. Freckles bursting all over your skin. Moaning like you've already got my cock in your mouth."

"Then put it in my mouth," I demand, shoving the charcuterie board gently away and climbing to my knees.

I stop an inch before him and drop back, sitting on my ass.

The air between us shifts. Tightens.

My thighs clench together on instinct and his gaze drops, tracking the movement with heat so sharp it slices through the cool night.

"Freckles, I'm about five seconds from tearing those leggings off and making a whole new memory on this goddamn truck bed. You gotta tell me what you want here, baby."

I shiver and ache, and I can't pretend I don't know exactly what I want.

Leaning forward, I drop my shaking hands onto his chest, pushing him onto his back. He shifts, making room for me to straddle him. My fingertips dig into his shirt, and his find my hips, gripping tightly.

"Remember what you said when I was riding your face?" I whisper, feeling his cock pulse between my thighs. "Next time you came, it would deep in my pussy—raw, and bare, and filling me with your cum, *again* and *again* and *again*." I drop my lips to his ear, shuddering with need. "That's what I want."

He groans, the sound so desperate and primal, it makes my whole body shiver.

His fingers find my jaw, dragging my mouth to his as he chokes out, *"Fuck it,"* and smashes his lips to mine.

CHAPTER THIRTY SIX

Kade

DRIP BY DRIP

HER KISS IS SWEET and dangerous. Sparkling cider and wildflower honey with a bite of something that's all Georgia.

I'm already drowning in it, in *her*. In the way her hips rock against mine like she doesn't give a single damn about taking her time or the way she's quickly destroying my will to wait. My hands roam without restraint, gripping her ass, kneading the soft swell of it through those tight leggings I plan to ruin.

The music swirls around us—something slow, sultry, female. Don't know the artist. Only recognized like a third of the songs I stole from her phone while she was sleeping. Tossed them all into a folder and named it *Freckles*, like a lovesick dumbass, just for tonight.

Because I wanted to make her smile.

Wanted to make her mine.

She moans against my mouth, warm, wet center grinding down harder. "Fuck, Kade…"

That sound—my name said like *that*? Desperate and wrecked and right on the edge of breaking?

Christ, I could come just from hearing it.

But I won't. Not yet.

Not until she's come apart as many times as it takes for her needy cunt to feel satisfied. Not until my tongue has memorized the taste of her again, and my fingers have wrung every whimper and gasp from her pretty mouth.

I grab the back of her neck, twisting my fingers into her hair and tilting her head back, forcing her eyes to mine.

"You gonna let me have you tonight, freckles?" I rasp, breath sawing in and out of my lungs. "Let me touch every fuckin' inch of you? Worship that perfect body like it's the only thing that's ever mattered? Gonna let me make you come on my fingers and tongue?"

Her lips part and she nods.

But I don't want her nod, I want her voice.

"Say it."

"*Yesss,*" she hisses.

I groan, tugging harder on her hair, devouring the moan that slips free with another kiss.

"And what about my cock, baby?" I breathe against her lips. "Gonna let me make you come on that, too?"

"God, yes," she chokes out, voice shaking. "I want all of it. I want you."

I flip us before she can blink—one hard roll of my hips and I'm on top of her, thighs bracketing her sides, chest rising and falling like I've run miles.

Her breath whooshes out in a soft gasp, eyes wide, lips red and kiss-bruised. I trail my finger over the pink marks my beard left across her jaw and throat, shuddering in approval.

Goddamn, she's beautiful.

Still fully clothed in my old Ranger sweatshirt and leggings, hair messy and cheeks flushed, she's the sexiest thing I've ever laid eyes on.

But I want more.

My hands find the hem of the sweatshirt and I drag it slowly up her body, knuckles grazing her sides, watching goosebumps bloom in my wake. She shivers, and I know it has nothing to do with the cold, because I feel it too.

It's this.

It's us.

She lifts her arms and lets me peel it over her head, baring her completely. No bra or undershirt. Just soft, freckled skin and two palm sized breasts tipped in tight, flushed little nipples already begging for my attention.

My cock throbs to the point of pain.

"No bra?" I murmur, pinching a rose-tipped bud. She moans, but doesn't respond, so I twist it the way she likes. "Answer me or I'll stop, baby."

Her back arches, head whipping back and forth. "Hate bras."

Me. Fuckin'. Too.

Shifting, I quickly work her boots and socks off then grip the waist of her leggings and panties, sliding them both down her legs in a slow, maddening tug.

When she's fully naked, I sit back on my heels, boots digging into the blankets as I take her in.

She's spread out like a feast—wild red hair fanned across a pillow, breasts heaving with every rough breath. Her skin is covered in goosebumps, but her thighs are parted, showing me everything and hiding nothing.

But it's the way she stares up at me, body lax and trusting, that flays me wide open for.

I'm one lucky bastard.

"Christ, Georgia," I whisper, hands gripping her calves. "You're incredible."

She blushes hard, biting her lip. "You saw me naked five days ago."

"Doesn't mean I'm not still obsessed."

"I wanna see you too." She yanks at my shirt. "Please, Kade."

My swallow is rough. The sound of her begging already nearly snaps my patience, but I'll be damned if I rush this. I strip down without finesse yet the whimpers that slip free from her throat make it sound like I'm putting on a damn show, and fuck if that doesn't inflate my ego.

And then I'm back on my knees, hand wrapped around my leaking cock, letting her look her fill.

"You…" she breathes, brows furrowed. Her eyes trail over my body, pausing on the scars and tattoos, my chest and abs, before settling on my cock. "You're perfect." She flicks her gaze to mine, and fuck if she doesn't look seconds from pouncing. "So perfect."

Groaning, I drop my mouth to hers, kissing her with all I've got. She thrusts her hips up, kitten-like nails digging into my hips as she tries to pull me down, but I flex my muscles, resisting.

Every part of me knows that if I let her win, if I close the distance between my bare cock and her bare, wet pussy, I'll be sliding home from one breath to the next.

And I'm not ready for that.

It takes work, but I pull my mouth away, putting enough distance between us to trace my fingers down her sternum, over her belly, across the curve of her hips. She bows toward me, needy and impatient, jerking beneath my hands.

"You cold, baby?"

"No."

"Then what's got you shakin' so hard?"

"You," she breathes. "Why aren't you fucking me yet?"

A laugh breaks free, and I shake my head at her adorable impatience.

"Because, freckles. Wanna see if I can make you lose your mind for me. Can you handle that?"

Her little hand darts out and wraps around my cock, tugging hard and circling like she already knows exactly what I like.

"I don't know," she murmurs, licking her lips when I groan hard. "Can you?"

My eyes drop to where she's jacking me off and my hips thrust into her grip. Ecstasy shoots down my spine, and I almost say fuck it, but I can't. So much I wanna do with the woman. So much I wanna taste and touch and explore.

Precum leaks from my tip, and with great pain and effort, I drag her hand away. "Wait your turn, Georgia. I wanna play with you first."

Before she can complain, I grab the honey I set aside earlier. It's open, wooden dipper still coated and sticky.

"If by lose my mind, you meant pause for a snack, I'm gonna get myself off," she says with a huff, small hands gliding down her body in a way that's too fuckin' distracting.

"Not yet." I click my tongue, shoving her hands aside, then lift the honey stick above her chest. "You're the only thing I want more than sleep, whiskey, or breathing. And tonight, I'm gonna prove it." I tip the stick, letting the honey fall. "*Drip by fucking drip.*"

It's slow and sticky, trailing down the curve of her breast like sunlight made liquid. Her back arches as the liquid hits her nipple. She gasps, spine bowing, and the sight, the sound, goes straight to my throbbing cock.

I circle the honey dipper around the peak, watching her body react. Her skin tightens, nipples hardening further as the honey glistens in the low light.

"That's..." she chokes out, eyes wide. "That's so hot."

I laugh, low and dark, and lean in—licking the trail between her breasts, tasting her and honey and heaven all at once.

She moans.

God help me, that sound unravels something in me.

Still gripping the honey stick, I drag it across the other nipple, watching her twitch and squirm. Then down. Past her ribs. Along the dip of her belly. Across her hips.

She's panting now, breath shallow and fast.

Slowly, I reach the place I've been starving for since the second she showed up at my door. The place I spent hours buried in the other night, and still didn't get enough of.

Her thighs part automatically, cunt already glistening, neatly trimmed red curls damp where she's been aching for me. I reach for the honey again, dip and swirl, and let it fall between her legs in one slow, decadent ribbon.

She gasps.

I groan.

And then I bring that stick down and coat her pussy with it—trailing it across her folds, circling her clit, dragging it through the mess she's already made like I'm painting her in gold.

"That's so unsanitary," she murmurs, but it ends with a cry of pleasure as I tease her entrance with it. "Don't you d-dare b-bring that home with u-us."

"You think I'd let a single person touch or eat a damn thing that's been near this cunt?" I click my tongue, shaking my head as my free hand cups her jaw, holding her gaze. "All of you is mine, baby. And I'm a greedy, possessive bastard."

With her eyes locked on me, I bring the dowel up and suck it into my mouth like it's my favorite fuckin' lollipop, moaning around the sweet, heady taste. I drag my tongue over the rounded grooves, removing all the honey, and coating it in saliva.

"Wh–what are you d-doing?" she stumbles around the words, meadow eyes wide, body shaking hard. "Kade..."

And then I slip it inside her, curving it up like a sex-toy, a single word on my lips, "*Mine.*"

Georgia's back arches off the truck bed with a sharp cry, hands tangling in the thick blankets beneath her. "Oh... *oh shit!*"

I fuck her with the honey stick, using the small, rounded part to graze against her G-spot slowly as I tease her, licking the honey from her body. It's warmed against her skin and melted down her ribs, but I chase it, not leaving a single, sweet drop.

With every flick of my tongue and shift of my hand, her cries grow louder, her fingers more restless—clawing at my skin, my hair, my shoulders.

She's frantic and wild, and perfect.

"I love you like this," I murmur, sucking her nipple between my teeth and biting down. "Unrestrained. Uncaring and free."

She inhales sharply, stilling for a beat, but relaxes again when I move to her other breast, giving it the same treatment. By the time I've worked my way down her body, she's begging relentlessly, and practically fuckin' feral.

Her hips lift, needy and wild. "Kade—*please*—"

"I know, freckles. I know." I kiss the crease of her thigh, right where it meets her slick center. "You want me to eat this sweet little cunt? Clean you up so I can make a mess of you all over again?"

She makes a strangled sound and nods furiously, heels digging into the blanket.

"Thank fuck."

I flatten my tongue against her clit and lick—slow, deep, unrelenting. Her cry splits the quiet and I moan, the taste of honey and her, driving me fucking insane.

She bucks beneath me, thighs threatening to close, but I hold her open, mouth locked to her like I've got something to prove.

And I do.

I want her ruined.

Want her so sensitive she begs me to stop—and then begs for more.

She's so damn wet, she's dripping all over my beard, so I lose the dowl and swap to my fingers, slipping three in without hesitation.

Georgia screams and throws her legs over my shoulders, squeezing my head so damn hard, I chuckle against her.

"Hell yeah," I rasp, curving my fingers, hitting her in a place that makes her squirm. "Come, baby. Come all over my face."

I wrap my lips around her clit and suck hard, flicking the tip of my tongue fast and light, then slow and hard. She thrashes, fists in the blanket, breath catching on a sob of pleasure. "*Fuck… Kade… oh my god…*"

She's right there. I know her body now—know the way she tightens, the tremble in her thighs, the frantic drag of her fingers when she's about to lose it.

"That's it," I growl against her, fucking her rough and fast. "Let go for me."

Her body bows off the truck, a keening sound tearing from her throat as she shatters. I don't stop. Don't fucking slow down. I keep working her, licking and sucking through it, grinding my cock against the blankets like a goddamn animal.

Because nothing's ever felt this good.

Nothing's ever tasted this fucking perfect.

She sobs my name again, voice hoarse, her whole body shaking. I ease up—just enough to let her breathe—but I don't pull away. Not yet. Not when she's still soaked and dripping, slick and raw, and twitching with aftershocks.

I kiss my way up her body—over her belly, her ribs, between the curve of her perfect tits—and grab the honey again.

She whimpers, eyes wide as I swirl more onto the stick.

"You gonna let me make you come again?" I ask, voice low and dark, my beard soaked in her.

"I don't know if I can," she whispers, wrecked and breathless.

"Oh, baby." I grin, feral and possessive, dragging the honey down her sternum. "You don't have to know. You just have to lay there and take it."

I circle her nipple again and suck it into my mouth, tongue lapping up the sweetness, then switch to the other side. She writhes, breath stuttering.

"God—Kade, it's too much—"

"No," I growl against her skin. "It's not enough. Never gonna be enough."

I slide back down and bury my face in her pussy again.

This time she screams.

A real scream—shocked and raw and punched straight from her chest.

And I don't stop. Not for a second. I tongue-fuck her like a man deranged, honey and cum mixing on my lips, beard dragging against her swollen clit.

I don't stop until she's sobbing my name and falling apart all over again, thighs locking around my head, body twisting in ecstasy.

And when she comes again, harder this time, shaking like she's being exorcised, I finally, finally pull back, wiping my mouth on the back of my hand.

"Please," she chokes out, wiping actual tears away. "Please fuck me. I want you so bad."

I wrap my hand around my cock, and stroke once, twice, dragging the tip through the wet mess we made together, but I pause, breathing like I'm the one who just shattered.

Swallowing thickly, I drop to my elbows on either side of her head and drag her mouth to mine. She doesn't hesitate to kiss me, sucking my tongue between her lips with a moan so wild, it vibrates against me.

"Georgia," I breathe, drawing back to meet her eyes. "You with me, sweetheart?"

"Yes," she chokes out. "God, yes."

"Wish I could say I was fuckin' around when I said I wanted you bare," I whisper, brows furrowed. I brush her sweat-soaked hair back. "But I wasn't. I'm wild—half demented when it comes to you, baby. I'm obsessed. Wanna feel every inch of you, nothin' between us. But if you don't want that, I'll wrap it up. Don't want you to be uncomfortable or feel pressured."

She licks her lips, eyes flicking between mine, heart hammering between us. Then, she smiles, soft, slow, and sweet, and grips my jaw, pulling me in for another kiss.

"I'm on the pill," she murmurs against me. "And I've only ever…"

Her nose wrinkles and she glances away but I drag her face right back. "What, darlin'?"

"I've only ever been with two guys, and it was a long time ago."

My nod is slow, my hands reverent as I cup her jaw. "Been a long time for me too. Never gone in bare before." I swallow, but it sticks. "I'd never put you in danger like that. Never."

"I trust you," she murmurs. "And I… I wouldn't either. I'm clean."

That's all I need to know. My mouth collides with hers in a deep kiss that steals my breath as I press in, slow and careful, grinding against her clit as I fill her inch by aching inch.

A groan catches in my lungs, body shaking just as bad as hers. Georgia digs her nails into my shoulders and folds her body around mine like she needs the closeness, and fuck, so do I.

She shudders, whimpering into the kiss.

I sink in an inch, then pull back out, then in a bit more, and out. Again and again, until I'm buried to the hilt, my hips flush with her.

"You're…" She gasps, back aching, breath caught somewhere between a sob and moan. "You're huge. Fuck. I… *Fuck*. Hang on!"

"Christ, baby." I exhale roughly, brushing her hair back, soothing her the best I can. "Did I hurt you?"

She shakes her head, then nods, squeezing her eyes shut. I slip a hand between us and find her clit, circling gently until she relaxes against me. After a minute, her body sags into the blankets, and her eyes flutter open, meeting mine.

And something in them… something in her… makes time stand still.

Nothing about this feels casual. Nothing feels fleeting. It's raw and brutal and soul-deep. The way she inhales sharply, eyes glossing over, tells me she feels it too.

I vow then and there to do everything in my power to make this girl happy. To make her dreams come true. To make this work, no matter what it takes.

"Okay," she finally says, hips tipping up. "Okay, you can move."

I pull back, nearly slipping all the way out, and thrust back in. She cries out, nodding rapidly, so I do it again, harder.

And when her walls clamp down around me like she was made for this—made for me—I lose whatever thread of sanity I had left.

"Jesus fuck, Georgia," I growl, a chaotic ramble of praises slipping free with every thrust, every drag of my cock against her. "You feel like fuckin' heaven, darlin'. Warm, wet heaven. So damn tight. Never felt anything like it. You're killin' me."

She whimpers, hips rolling up to meet mine, greedy and perfect and already dripping down my cock. Her hands land on my chest, digging in like she's trying to yank my heart from my body, and fuck, I think she might have already stolen it.

I shake my head, arms trembling, a sense of helplessness swelling inside me along with a hell of a lot of emotions I wasn't prepared for.

"Tell me what you want, baby," I practically beg, heart hammering. "Whatever it is, you can fuckin' have it."

"I just want you to fuck me like I'm yours."

That's all the invitation I need.

I grip her thighs and spread her wide, bending them back until her knees are damn near brushing her ears, and drive into her.

Hard. Deep. Unforgiving.

"You like that?" I growl, pounding into her, sweat dripping from my temple, more words, more feral sounds, tumbling free. "Like havin' me fuck you so hard, you'll never not feel me? Fuckin' you so hard, you'll know exactly who you belong to when you wake up?"

"Yes—fuck, yes—"

"You'll take everything I give you, won't you? Take it because it's yours. This dick? These hands? This fuckin' mouth?" I lean down and bite her neck hard enough to leave a mark. "All yours, Georgia. You earned every broken, filthy fuckin' inch of me."

She's gasping now, wrecked and beautiful, legs shaking as I hammer into her, chest flushed and hair wild against the blankets.

"More," she begs, eyes rolling back. "Kade... don't stop...don't you fucking stop—"

"I'm not stoppin' till you come again," I grit out, one hand moving between us to rub her clit in tight circles. "Want your cunt to cry for my cock, baby. Wanna feel you milk it."

And she does.

Less than a minute later, she shatters around me—loud and sobbing, her pussy clenching like it never wants to let me go. The moment it hits,

I swear I black out. My whole body locks, every muscle seizing as I lose control.

I groan loud and low, hips slamming forward one last time as I spill inside her, cock pulsing with wave after wave of pure fuckin' bliss.

Hot, endless, mind-erasing pleasure like I've never felt before.

For a long, breathless second, neither of us moves. I'm still buried in her, panting against her neck, her fingers twitching in my hair like she's forgotten how to let go.

When we're both relaxed and my cock is softening, I slowly pull out.

My cum leaks from her swollen pussy, wet and slick, and I watch it like a man possessed—because where Georgia's concerned, I am.

Without thinking, I scoop it up with two fingers, slick and glistening, and slide them right back inside her.

She gasps, full-body shivering. "Kade—what are you—"

"Shh," I rasp, curling my fingers, watching her twitch as I smirk. "Told you, darlin'. I've got lots of bedrooms to fill."

Georgia moans, back arching, thighs trembling around my wrist.

"I told you, I'm on birth control," she breathes, voice shaking.

I pause… just for a second. I know she said that. Know it's fast and stupid and reckless, but I can't lie—disappointment slices through me like a hot blade. I school it down, shake it off, and lean close, licking her bottom lip as I grind my fingers deeper.

"Then we're practicing."

Her eyes go wide, breath catching hard.

I add a third finger, just to hear her whimper.

"You don't get it yet," I whisper against her lips. "I'm not just tryin' to fuck you. I'm tryin' to ruin you. Want you walkin' around with me dripping out of you every single day. Want you so full of me, you don't remember what it felt like to not be mine."

She shudders violently, another moan tearing from her throat. "You're gonna kill me."

"Nah, baby. I'm gonna make you beg for more."

And I do.

Until her body's trembling, her voice gone hoarse from moaning my name. Until she's spent and soaked, sticky with sweat and honey and every drop I've poured into her. Until there's nothing left of her but blissed-out whimpers and the way she curls into me like I'm home.

By the time I pull the blankets around us, her lashes are fluttering shut, cheek pressed to my chest, breath warm and steady against my skin.

And as my eyes finally drift closed with Georgia wrapped in my arms, skin still humming from everything we just shared, only one thought cuts through the quiet.

If this is all I ever have…

If this is the only kind of peace I ever get from the demons still chasing me… It'll be enough.

Chapter Thirty Seven

Trading Stars for Ashes and Tears

The first thing I notice is her.

Not the stars still falling from the sky or the bite of cool air brushing over my bare shoulders—but *her*. Georgia, warm and soft, curled up against me beneath the thick pile of blankets in the bed of my truck. One of her legs is tangled with mine, her face tucked under my chin, palm resting just above my heart.

It's quiet as hell, except for our breathing.

So still that, for a second, I think I might be dreaming.

But then her fingers twitch against my chest, and I blink up at the sky, eyes adjusting to the streaks of light slicing through the dark. Shooting stars, dozens of them, maybe more, all at once. The meteor shower must be at its peak, which means it's around two or three. We haven't been asleep for long.

I pull her in closer, my heart thudding with something wild and full in my chest.

Peace.

It's the only word I can think of.

Not the lazy, passive kind—but the bone-deep, soul-shattering kind that settles in when something fits so right, it stops feeling fleeting and starts feeling like home.

We went twice more before we passed out, her just as insatiable as I am.

Once with her riding me, the stars catching in her curls like the wildfire in her soul—like the freckles I'm in love with, and once bent over the stack of pillows, her bare back arched, body slick and trembling beneath me.

We ate every damn thing I packed. Drank until the thermoses, waters and cider were empty. Took pee breaks wrapped in blankets and teased each other over how weird but comfortable it all was.

And she made wishes.

God, did she make wishes.

Every time a star streaked overhead, her lashes fell, her lips moved, and I watched her whisper them like prayers. I didn't ask what they were—I didn't have to. The way she looked at the sky told me enough.

When Georgia Walked wishes, she wishes for more. Something bigger, greater, and deeper. Something that'll soothe the ragged, worn parts of her lonely soul.

Don't need to know the exact words to know it's not fleeting. And for one night, I'm grateful I could give her a chance to sink into that hope. Into the magic of wishes.

Everything was perfect.

Not just the sex—even though I'll be riding that high for the rest of my life. Not even the laughter or dancing naked under the stars or the way her hands never stopped touching me, like she was trying to memorize me in the dark.

No, it was the trust.

The way she let go, gave me all of her—mind, body, heart, and fuck, when we connected, my girl gave me her soul. The way she let me take care of her, again and again. And the way I gave myself back in return.

I've never felt like this before. Never had something like this. Even with Marlee, it wasn't like this. We were young and dumb, and I thought it was love. Over the years, especially recently, I'm starting to realize it was something much darker. Ugly and rotten at its core.

With Georgia, everything feels… just *more*.

I brush her hair from her cheek when she shifts, snuggling closer in her sleep, and my chest cracks wide open, a quiet voice inside me whispering words on a loop. Words that make my stomach clench and flip, heart hammering beneath her.

This is it.

This is everything.

You could love this woman for the rest of your life.

She smiles as my lips brush her forehead. "Again already? Abby was right. Cowboys are insatiable."

The words, *it's you I'm insatiable for*, sit on my tongue, but before I can say them, a breeze cuts through the air, and it's all wrong.

I inhale deeply—and freeze.

Beneath the scent of honey and sweat and Georgia... There's smoke. Deep and thick, and gaining by the damn second.

My heart slams into my ribs.

Gently, I roll her off me, easing her onto the pile of pillows, and sit up, scanning the darkness ahead. The truck bed sits at the edge of a drop-off, a steep hill that rolls down toward the river, and beyond that, the end of our property.

Everything's still and quiet so I grab my boxers and jump out.

"Where are you going?" Georgia mumbles, burrowing deeper into the blankets.

"Stay there, darlin'."

"Oookay..."

I quickly step into my boxers and snag my jeans, tugging them up as I circle the truck, searching the direction we came from only to stop dead in my tracks.

To the far left, past the tree line and fencing, a haze of orange light pulses against the sky, smoke rising thick and high.

Too much for a simple bonfire. Too much for a controlled burn.

Something's on fire.

And it's bad.

Alive and hungry—eating through something big.

It's not a field. There aren't any in that direction.

All that's off to the east are buildings.

Barns. Animals. Houses. People.

"Fuck."

I sprint to the cab, yanking open the door and grabbing my phone off the charger I hooked up when the playlist drained the battery earlier.

"No missed fuckin' calls," I snap, tugging at my hair as my mind spins. No one knows. They'd call if they did. "Shit."

Who's on night watch? Who's even running point while Ridge and Hazy are out of town?

Should have fuckin' asked, but I was too caught up in Aurora. In Georgia. In trying to find my footing in this new life while it merges with the one I left behind a long damn time ago.

Hazy never came to me with plans for her absence. No one did.

Phone in hand, I step back, eyes on the fire. I swallow hard, panic clawing at my chest.

My whole world is where that fire is.

Shaking the anxiety away before it can take over, I call my mom. No answer. I call again. Still nothing.

I don't stop hitting numbers, trying to reach out for anyone who might be close, who might pick up, and circle back to the truck bed. Phone on speaker, I dig through the piles of blankets until I find our clothes, quickly sorting them.

"Baby, wake up," I call, gently shaking her. "We gotta go."

"Huh?" she asks, bleary-eyed.

I shake harder. Not enough to scare her—but fuck, *I'm terrified*. "Georgia, darlin', you need to get up. There's a fire at the ranch."

That does it. She shoots upright so fast the blankets tumble off her body, revealing every inch of smooth, naked skin—breasts rising and falling with each panicked breath. I stare for all of two seconds, my brain short-circuiting at the sight, before reality slaps me in the face and I shake it off.

"What the hell?" she gasps, still half-asleep, voice thick with confusion. "What do you mean? Is Aurora okay?"

Christ. My heart caves in on itself and twists sideways.

This woman—bare, vulnerable, and worried about a kid who's not even hers by blood—is damn perfect.

"I don't know." I toss her clothes across the truck bed. "Can you get dressed? I'm trying to get a hold of my mom."

"Of course," she chokes out, already moving, pulling on her sweatshirt with shaking hands as I ram my boots on. She stands, balancing like a pro as the truck sways slightly under her weight, completely unconcerned about her body being on full display. My eyes flick between her and the faint glow across the hill, adrenaline crackling under my skin.

I'm calling anyone I can think of—Mom, the twins, Ridge, Hazel—but no one's picking up. My jaw's locked so tight, I think I'll crack a tooth.

Finally, Hazel answers, panting like she's out of breath. "What the fuck do you—?"

"There's a fire!" I bark, helping Georgia step down from the bed of the truck. "A building's lit. I'm at Archer Hill with Georgia. We're heading back now. I can't get a hold of anyone else."

"Ridge!" she snaps, her voice cutting through the phone like a whip. "Ridge! Get up! We gotta go!"

"Hazy!" I bark, slamming the tailgate shut. "Don't need you home. Won't make it in time. I need to know who's managing right now. And do we have anyone on fire duty?"

She sucks in a sharp breath. "No. We had to let them go. Couldn't afford the fire crew anymore."

Fuck.

I yank the passenger door open and Georgia climbs in silently, her fingers already flying over her phone. She's pale, lips pressed into a tight line, but she's with me, ready for fuckin' battle.

Ridge's voice explodes in the background of Hazel's line—loud, angry, commanding. It's oddly comforting. That prickly bastard might be impossible to deal with, but he knows how to run this place.

"Who's on night watch?" I ask again, throwing myself behind the wheel.

"Ridge called Vander. We left him and Nev in charge tonight," Hazel says, voice tight. "But they were at Saddle with everyone else."

Of course they were. Drinking and dancing and well on their ways to fuckin' instead of watching the damn property.

Swearing up a storm, I toss my hat into the back and rake a hand through my hair.

"I'm calling Summit Rural Fire," I decide, mind already racing. "We need help."

"Do it," my sister barks, breathless. "We're heading out now. Call the second you know more."

"I will."

Then I slam my phone into the cup holder, my foot hitting the gas so hard the tires spin before we launch forward down the hill, back toward the farm, back toward whatever the fuck is waiting for us.

"I got ahold of your mom," Georgia rushes out, hand squeezing mine. "Everyone is safe. Aurora and your sisters are with her. She went outside to check and said the fire is…" She pauses, glancing at her phone. "She thinks it's somewhere near the north ridge. She couldn't see clearly, but it looked close to the livestock paddock."

"Fuck!" I shout, fingers tightening around the wheel. The truck slides in the mud, and I fight it, forcing myself to slow down. My pulse is thunder, but I keep my grip steady. "Baby, grab my phone. Need you to call for backup."

By the time we pull onto the gravel road leading toward the heart of the property, I'm more collected than I was before. Maybe it's knowing that no one I love is in danger. Maybe it's the training or sheer survival instinct. Years in the Rangers taught me how to compartmentalize when shit hits the fan. Right now, my family needs that guy.

I park the truck a hundred or so feet from the blaze, the fire lighting up the night sky like a second sun. The equipment barn is a full inferno—red, orange, and violent. It's roaring, feeding on fuel and dry timber, and the wind is pushing those flames toward the horse barn.

Turning to Georgia, I pull her into me and kiss her hard, grounding myself in her even as the fire crackles in my periphery. She trembles against me, and my heart damn near shatters.

"Need you to go find my mom, darlin'. Need you to be with my family. Take care of Aurora. Can you do that for me?"

She pulls back, blinking fast, eyes flitting between the blaze and my face. "What? No. You c-can't go in there. Absolutely not, Kade!"

I cup her face, forcing her to meet my eyes. "I can, baby. I'm trained. Volunteer for Summit County Fire Watch. Certified for rural wildfire containment. I've done this before. I have to."

She sobs, low and guttural, fingers white-knuckled around mine. "Please don't. Don't go. I just… I just got you." She sucks in a harsh breath that cracks something deep inside me. "D-don't *leave me.*"

I press my forehead to hers, forcing back the flood of emotion threatening to take me under. Her fear isn't just about fire. It's about abandonment. Loss. Being left behind.

Know that fear well. I've lived it too.

"I'm coming back," I whisper. "You hear me? I'm not going anywhere. Not now. Not ever."

I kiss her one more time and then nod toward the blaze.

"The equipment barn's gone," I say quietly. "But the horse barn's only a few hundred feet away. And with the wind? The grass? That fire will leap in minutes if we don't stop it. The others'll be here soon. Ten, maybe less. But until then, it's just me."

She nods, eyes wide and glassy. "What do I do?"

"Go to the house. Find my mom. Get to Aurora. That's your job. Our girl needs you."

"Our…" she breathes, voice catching before she shakes herself hard. "Okay. I can do that. You can do this. We're going to be fine."

"Yes we are," I vow, pulling her close one last time, then I force myself from the truck before I convince myself to stay with her. "Now go."

She hesitates just a second longer, then climbs over the stick shift and drops into my seat. Our eyes lock—something raw and unspoken passes between us. Words neither of us are ready to say sit on my tongue like a loaded gun.

Instead, I rough out, "Go, Georgia."

That lower lip of hers is locked between her teeth, but she nods. And then she's gone, wheels spinning through gravel and smoke, racing toward safety, toward our girl.

Leaving me behind and taking my heart with her.

CHAPTER THIRTY EIGHT

GIDDY FUCKIN' UP, COOPER CUNTS

I PRACTICALLY FALL FROM the truck, slamming the door behind me and stumbling toward the farmhouse. My legs are shaking, lungs tight and brittle, and it feels like every nerve in my body is short-circuiting with panic. Bea's outside with the twins, her arms wrapped around Aurora like a shield.

Colby is sobbing, shoulders hunched, her dark brown curls bouncing as she paces in tiny, frantic circles. Clementine stands beside her mom, pale and wide-eyed behind thick glasses, her hoodie pulled up tight like it might protect her from the sight of fire licking the sky.

But Bea… Bea is still. Too still. Stoic, almost.

Her arms are soft as she bounces Aurora gently, whispering something too low for me to hear, but her eyes are locked on the flames, a storm of worry behind them that she clearly doesn't want her daughters to see.

I see it, though.

I *feel* it.

Don't even realize I'm running until Colby throws herself into my arms with a wild sob. "It's bad, Georgia," she cries, fists clinging to my jacket. "The barn—there was so much smoke. I thought it was the house. I thought—I thought—"

"I know," I whisper, wrapping my arms around her and pulling Clem in too, surprised by the fierceness of my protectiveness for these sweet girls. "It's okay. You're safe. We've got you."

Clementine presses her face into my side, whispering, "Kade'll fix it. He always does."

And that's like a sucker punch to my damn gut.

But I nod, because how can I not? "He fixes everything for me too. He's a *really* good fixer."

Bea lets out a breath of relief and crosses the short distance to us, giving me a one-armed hug that speaks volumes. It's tight and full of unspoken things she probably won't let out in front of the girls.

"Glad you made it home okay," she says, kissing my cheek. "Hope you had a wonderful date, before… all this."

"I'm so sorry, Bea," I choke out, hugging her back just as tightly, careful not to hurt Aurora. "Kade said the equipment barn is completely gone. I can't even imagine."

She pulls back, eyes flicking to her daughters. A forced smile curves her lips like muscle memory. "It's not the first fire we've had here, and it won't be the last."

Before I can reply, she passes me Aurora, her expression gentling. "Missed her, no doubt."

"Hard not to," I admit, scooping her up without hesitation, cuddling her close to my chest.

Aurora blinks up at me with those huge brown eyes and lets out a quiet sniffle before digging her fingers into my hair. My throat constricts, emotions overwhelming me.

"Kade is coming," I whisper, pressing a kiss to her curls. "Our guy will be back soon."

And like she was waiting for me to say just that, her eyes flutter closed and she nuzzles into my neck, breath warming my skin.

Something inside me settles, then shifts.

I did miss her. More than I probably should. More than is probably safe.

But it's too late for my heart where this family is concerned.

Just then, a pair of trucks come into view. The first is large and red, with bold white letters reading *Summit County Rural Fire Protection*, followed closely by a second, even larger truck bearing the same markings. A minute later, a black SUV rolls in behind them, headlights slicing through the early morning dark. Wildwood Sheriff's Department is stenciled along the side.

I blink. "Why is the sheriff's department from a town over here? Wouldn't Heart Springs send someone?"

Bea shakes her head, tucking the girls against her sides. "That'll be Memphis Calloway. He's the sheriff in Wildwood, but he and his brothers are all volunteer firefighters with the rural district."

"Like Kade," I murmur, turning back to watch the trucks curve around the drive like they know exactly where they're headed.

As I drove here, I passed a steady stream of trucks and headlights headed toward the fire. Some faces I recognized from mudding and around the farm, others I didn't. But every one of them jumped in without hesitation, throwing themselves into the fray.

The five of us stand there, watching from a safe distance. The fire's still burning, but it's not raging anymore. The chaos has begun to ebb, but my heart hasn't caught up.

Eventually, Bea breaks the silence. "Looks like they've got it under control. No point standing around here doing nothing. Let's do what Archers do best and take care of the people around us."

"I don't wanna," Colby whines, shivering. "Can't Archers have a better hobby? Napping, perhaps?"

Clementine bobs her head, tugging her hoodie higher. "Or eating. I love food."

"Same," her sister says. "Can we have breakfast?"

Bea clicks her tongue. "Lucky for you, breakfast for the crew is exactly what I was suggesting, you rotten little toads."

"Thank fuck," Colby mutters, peeling away from us. "I'm freezing and starving."

"Colby Mildred!" Bea hisses, eyebrows shooting up as she sighs. "What am I going to do with you?"

She shoots me a tired smile. "Only seventeen, but they've got mouths like they're twenty-five."

Clementine giggles and presses a kiss to her mom's cheek. "At least we're still virgins, Ma."

With that, she chases after Colby, cackling at Bea's groan.

I laugh, the sound shaky in my throat, but it quickly fades. I hesitate, torn—unsure if I'm meant to follow them into the house or maybe head back to Kade's.

Before I can decide, Bea tucks her arm around me and presses a kiss to my cheek. "Soon-to-be Archers are included in that, dear," she says with a wink that knocks the wind out of me.

I stumble, heart in my throat.

Bea chuckles, ignoring my panic, brushing her hand over Aurora's hair as she guides us toward the Big House. "And tiny, new little Archers, too."

My throat is so tight, I can barely swallow around it, but I let Bea lead us up the wide porch steps and through the front door of the house Kade grew up in.

The moment I cross the threshold, I feel it—love, history, home.

Their house is old but well cared for, the kind of place that wears time like a badge of honor instead of trying to erase it.

The floors creak, the floral wallpapered walls are lined with photos in mismatched frames, and there are scuff marks in the hallway that probably have stories attached to every single one.

There's a sitting room off to the left and a long hallway straight ahead that opens into a big, warm kitchen. Two wings branch off the main living space, and a staircase curves up from the middle of the foyer like an old spine.

"How big is this house?" I ask, hugging Aurora a little tighter against my chest when she whimpers in her sleep.

Bea chuckles softly and shrugs. "Ten bedrooms."

At my gasp, she winks and pats my back.

"Get your head out of the gutter, sweetheart. I've always loved to entertain." Her smile falls and she looks away. "Not that we have a use for most of them now."

I barely have time to process her words before my mind flashes to Kade—to that morning we walked around his nearly finished house and he told me his plans to fill every room.

His filthy, dirty, breeding-kink plans that sent shivers down my spine.

Then to tonight—his mouth pressed to my ear, his voice low and rough as he shoved his cum back into me and whispered promises about *practice*, about *filling me up again and again*, like we've been together for years.

Not months. Not weeks. Not a single weekend that cracked open my chest and shoved everything familiar aside.

The problem is, I liked it. Probably too much. I love kids, always have. Always wanted a whole house full of them, but after a while, I just figured it wouldn't happen for me. That I'm too broken—too scared to reach out and take what I want for fear of eventually losing it.

But Kade...

Kade is feral about making babies, and it's fucking with my phobias.

I shake the thought off before I combust, dragging myself back to the present as Bea pushes open a swinging door into the kitchen.

"It's beautiful," I breathe, and I mean it.

The space is soft and golden, full of warmth and the scent of cinnamon and smoke—the latter from an open window Clem quickly closes.

Wooden beams stretch across the ceiling, and the farmhouse table in the center looks big enough to seat a small army. Cabinets are painted a muted sage green, and the counters are cluttered with both cooking essentials and well-loved extras—a stand mixer, three coffee pots, and a stack of well-used baking sheets leaning against the backsplash.

"Holy shit, this is huge," I choke out.

Colby snorts. "That's what she said."

Clementine offers her a fist bump as she crosses to the fridge and starts pulling out eggs, butter, and what looks like enough supplies to feed a battalion.

"How many guys do you think are out there, Mom?" she asks, rolling up her sleeves.

Bea glances toward a large wall of windows over the sink, her brows pulling together. "Maybe thirty? If all the hands are back, and Dallas's crew showed up."

Clem nods, completely unfazed, and starts washing her hands. I can only gape, watching her move through the kitchen like she's done this a thousand times.

Colby elbows me and grins. "She wants to be a chef. Practically lives for this shit." Her expression softens as she watches her twin crack eggs into a giant bowl. "This is basically her Kentucky Derby."

I smile, tightening my arms around Aurora as her breath puffs soft and warm against my collarbone.

I don't want to put her down—not yet. Maybe never.

Swallowing hard, I bury the fear that rises along with the love in my chest.

"If she fusses," Bea says gently, nodding toward the living room, "the bag Kade packed is by the portable crib near the couch. Should have everything she needs."

I nod, glancing down at Aurora's peaceful face.

She's completely out—little lips puckered, lashes fluttering, hands tucked under her chin. My heart clenches. I missed her more than I realized. And I already dread the thought of going back to work Monday. I don't want to leave her. I don't want to leave either of them.

It's a problem.

A big, huge freaking problem.

I need to call Abby, ASAP. This is a code-red.

"How have you been, Georgia?" Bea calls across the kitchen, peeling potatoes while looking at me like it's second nature. It makes my whole body flinch. "Last time we talked, you weren't feeling too well. Kade said you had another flare-up."

She gives me a look that's full of honest sympathy, not pity or questions. Like she believes my illness is real.

I shift Aurora in my arms and lean my hip against the counter across from her. "I'm doing better," I say, cheeks warming. "Thank you so much for everything you sent over with Kade. I really appreciate it."

Bea waves me off. "Least I could do."

"The salts were amazing," I admit, ducking my head a little. "Seriously. Magic."

She blinks. "Salts?"

"Yeah—the bath salts. Kade said they were your recipe." I shrug, pushing Aurora's hair back. "They were on his window ledge."

Her face lights up. "Oh! Yes. I didn't realize he had any left. Gemma and I used to make them pretty often for the farmers market. They were quite popular, actually, but…" She sighs. "After she moved, I wasn't able to dedicate the time it took for the salts, candles, and teas. I spend most of my time with the bees since we cut back on staff."

Something about her tone makes me pause. I hesitate, then step closer, lowering my voice so the girls don't hear.

"You said you needed help with the Honey Bea Bash," I say carefully. "Hazel mentioned that the farm's struggling…"

Bea flinches.

Shit.

"I'm so sorry," I blurt, heat rising to my cheeks. "That was out of line. I didn't mean to pry. I just—" I exhale sharply. "It's probably the social worker in me. I want to help."

Her expression softens, the sharpness melting away. I ramble on before I can stop myself.

"When you asked me to help, I agreed because I wanted to. Because I think your family is wonderful, and what you're doing out here is amazing. There's so much love and community. I just…" I tip my shoulders, helpless. "Wanted to be involved, I guess."

In something.

In everything.

Oh, and I also wanted to get to know you well enough to ask if you know anything about my family.

I don't say any of that, though, because I'm a coward.

And because Bea Archer, standing a foot away with her kind, motherly eyes and that calm presence, makes it so hard to breathe through the feelings I can't seem to hold back anymore.

"Well," she finally says, her voice thick but steady, "aren't you just a surprise."

My mouth opens to respond, but she cuts me off with a soft shake of her head and turns her attention back to the potatoes she's now chopping.

"Honey Bea has been my dream since I was eighteen years old and falling in love. Not the land or the wheat or the big production of it—but a home, a family, bees and flowers." Her lips twitch like she's holding something back, but her eyes gloss over anyway. "It was our dream—my William's and mine. And we had it, for a long time. We grew it, expanded it. We lived on this land. Loved on it. Loved hard."

Her gaze flicks to her daughters, who are still bustling around the kitchen, and she blinks fast to clear her eyes. "Still do."

I don't say a word. I just bounce Aurora gently against my chest and let the lump in my throat burn while this wonderful, resilient woman lays her soul bare in a kitchen that smells like breakfast and safety.

"Anyway," she murmurs with a sigh, wiping her hands on a towel. "Things were already shifting before William passed. People want quick and cheap now. They want things packaged and shipped and on their doorstep in twenty-four hours. They don't want to drive out to the country for wildflower honey or cut their own bouquets. They don't care if the meat's fresh or the produce local. They care about convenience. And convenience is killing places like ours."

Her voice tightens. "Then William passed, and not long after, Cooper Ridge moved into Summit, and everything I thought I could handle just… fell apart."

Cooper Ridge.

My brows pinch. That name sounds familiar.

"Those Ridge Ranch people are all assholes," she mutters, chopping more aggressively now, the knife hitting the board with a little more force. "Insufferable fuckin' pricks. Every last one of them."

And then it clicks.

The asshole from the bar.

The guy Kade nearly went full Hulk on.

"Would it make you feel better," I murmur, trying not to smirk, "to know your son beat the shit out of their leader the other night?"

Bea freezes mid-chop, brows shooting up. "Clint the Cunt Cooper?"

A loud, unfiltered laugh bursts from me before I can stop it. Aurora stirs, and I quickly clamp my mouth shut, but I nod as Bea grins. "Yep."

"That's my boy," she says proudly, resuming her chopping with a little more pep.

When the laughter fades, I press gently, "So what does Cooper Cunt Ridge have to do with everything happening here? Hazel mentioned them trying to destroy Heart Springs."

"Nice one," Bea says with a dry chuckle, but her smile doesn't last. "Cooper Ridge is big. Corporate-level big. They started buying up land about five years ago—first on the outskirts, then moving in closer. They've got backing, infrastructure, investors. They undercut pricing to push out the smaller farms, then sweep in and buy what's left for pennies."

She pauses, brushing a strand of hair from her face. "They've offered to buy Honey Bea a few times. Said we were wasting prime acreage. I turned them down every time. The last time... they weren't so happy about it."

The way her voice goes quiet has a chill crawling down my spine.

"What do we do?" I ask, heat rising in my chest. "How do we stop them from ruining this place? From running over people like you and your family?"

Bea gives me a tired smile. "What *can* we do? We're small. They're big and rich. I don't have the funds to fight, as much as I wish I did."

"Maybe not a court fight," I say, voice low, eyes narrowing. "But this is the country, Bea. Don't you all do things a little differently out here?"

She huffs a laugh and squeezes my hand. "It's a rural farming town, sweetheart. Not the Wild West."

"Fuck that." My eyes widen and I wince. "Sorry—"

"Don't be. 'Fuck' is one of my favorite words," she says, grinning. "Don't censor yourself on my account."

That earns a giggle from me, and then I shrug, adjusting Aurora on my hip.

"There's gotta be something we can do. You have a town full of people who'd do anything for the Archers."

My mind kicks into gear.

I've done this before.

Not like this, not against a corporate farm with deep pockets and dirty tactics—but I've organized in crisis.

It was one of my favorite parts of working at Safe Haven, the non-profit I worked for in New York. We helped women and children get out of dangerous situations and rebuild from nothing. My role was boots-on-the-ground: coordinating shelter placements, hosting community fundraisers, securing grant funding, and mobilizing people fast when everything was on the line.

Yes, I used to work in social work back in New York, but the field is broad, and this is the first time I've ever been a caseworker. When I moved to Summit, DCFS was the only opening. I transferred my license, took the required state modules, and jumped in.

It's harder than I expected. More red tape. More impossible choices I'm not sure I was quite prepared for.

But this? Saving Honey Bea from Cooper Ridge before they buy this farm's soul?

That I can fight.

"What are you thinking?" Bea asks quietly.

"We fight smart. We tell your story. We host events on the farm—open markets, honey tastings, kids' days, fall festivals, whatever it takes to get people here and keep them invested. We rally support from the town, hit social media, and use your community ties. Make the farm a symbol of what's worth protecting in Summit."

Her brows lift. "And Cooper Ridge?"

"We expose them. Public records, labor practices, land zoning violations, anything we can find. We use their size against them—make it personal. Make it public. If we can't outspend them, we out-heart them. People fight harder for things they love."

Bea stares at me for a long second, then nods slowly. "Well damn, Georgia Walker. Remind me not to get on your bad side."

I smile, but it's sharp. "You're not the one who should be worried."

"Country justice," she murmurs, eyes flicking toward the window. "Now that might just be the kind of fight we can win."

"Time to cowgirl up, Archers," I say with a grin, my heart thudding with adrenaline.

Because when everything else feels like it's spinning—too fast, too big, too scary...

Too good.

This?

This feels right.

This is something I can do.

Bea turns to me with a wide, hopefully smile. "Giddy fuckin' up, Cooper Cunts."

Chapter Thirty Nine

A Public Claiming

"Thanks again for coming out, guys," I rasp, voice wrecked from smoke and shouting.

My body's exhausted, hands raw, thighs burning, throat coated in ash, but I can still feel the adrenaline buzzing in my blood. The air around us is thick and acrid, wet from the hoses and still too hot in places—but the worst of it's over.

The equipment barn is gone.

Everything inside—tools, fuel, irrigation systems, even the newer harvester we managed to finance two seasons ago, is now a steaming pile of blackened metal and ash.

And the small shed my mom uses for event prep—the one she sets up with decor and flower buckets every time the Honey Bea Bash rolls around? Gone. Collapsed in on itself, smoldering quietly near the tree line.

But no animals were hurt. The crops are untouched. No one was injured fighting the fire, thank fuck.

The guys from Summit County Rural Fire showed up fast, efficient, and ready to get to work. We hit the worst of it before it reached the horse barn, and with their help, we pushed the line back just in time.

"No problem," Memphis Calloway says, shaking my hand with a strong grip. "You did damn good work before we even got here. Miss havin' you out on calls."

After I came home from the military, I needed an outlet. Needed to feel needed. That's how I fell in with Iron Shield. The guys felt the same, so they followed me, but I needed more.

Working for JP was fine—but it was just that: work.

Some jobs I took were high adrenaline, and I actually got to help people, protect them from bad shit.

But a lot of times, it was just rich businessmen wanting to feel powerful with personal security for events or driving them around.

Hated that shit. One of the reasons I took less and less jobs away.

Also one of the reasons I ended up volunteering for Summit County Emergency Services. Spent many days with these guys, fighting wildfires, out on search and rescues, or responding to emergencies in rural areas where help is needed.

I have the training, the time, and fuck, got a hell of a lot more fulfillment from those un-paid jobs than I even have with Iron Sheild.

Good thing I quit.

"Know it's been a while," I say, glancing toward the dark shape of the big house in the distance. "But since I'm currently out of a job, you'll probably be seeing more of me."

"No shit," Dallas, the Wildwood fire chief and youngest of the three Calloway brothers here tonight, claps me hard on the back. "Why don't you join the department? You're good with a hose."

Memphis and Nash bark out identical laughs that echo through the steam and early dawn air.

I snort. "Nah, man. I'm living here full-time now." My gaze drifts to the house again, jaw tightening, anxiety clawing at my veins. Wanna get back to them. "Got a little girl to watch out for now. Can't be signing up for anything that dangerous on the regular."

Nash, who teaches engineering over at the college and volunteers whenever he can, frowns. "When the fuck did you find the time to make a kid, Archer?"

My smile drops, throat tightening. "Actually, I adopted her."

There's a beat of silence, then Nash shakes my hand again, clapping my shoulder. "Well, fuck. Congrats, man."

"Yeah," Dallas says, tipping his chin. "Hell of a thing, Kade. Good for you."

I nod, grateful for the simplicity of it. No questions. No pity. Just respect.

Dallas glances over his shoulder at the smoking ruin behind us. "Once it cools, we can do a full inspection for you. But first impressions?"

I step forward. "You three are the professionals. I'll take your thoughts."

Memphis gestures for me to follow, and I do, the four of us trudging across scorched earth, the mud sucking at our boots. The smoke stings my eyes, and steam rises in gentle plumes off what used to be the most valuable building on the back half of our land.

This is fucked and so bad.

Dallas crouches low near the barn's side, running a gloved hand along the frame. "See this?"

I follow his finger. There's a patch along the metal siding that looks… *off*. Warped in a way that doesn't match the rest of the structure. Almost like it melted from the inside out.

"Burned hot, real fast," Dallas says, frowning. "Too hot, too fast for a standard equipment fire. Especially one that started after midnight, when no one was working."

He nods toward another spot where the earth's scorched in a weird semicircle.

"That's accelerant."

Nausea hits me in the gut. "The fuck?"

"Sorry it's not better news, man," he says, standing and brushing ash off his pants with a pained look. Dallas has a small farm of his own. Knows the hit we're about to take.

"We'll get you something solid in a few days," Memphis adds. "But first take? This wasn't an accident."

My blood runs ice-cold.

It's one thing to lose a barn. One thing to face an act of God, or bad luck, or faulty wiring. But arson?

That's someone declaring war.

"Hey, guys!" a voice calls.

We turn as Vander jogs up the hill, winded but grinning. Anger pulses through me at the sight of his smug, likely-drunk, ass.

"Your mom sent me to grab everyone for breakfast at the big house. Said she's not takin' no for an answer."

My fists clench at my sides.

The fire's still warm, ash still floating in the damn air, and this little shit has the audacity to show up with a smile like it's just another day on the job. Like he's not at fault for this gettin' so bad, so damn fast.

"You good, Kade?" Dallas asks under his breath, clearly picking up on the shift in my posture.

"I'm fine," I grit out, eyes locked on Van's smug face.

The fact that Hazel put Vander and his brother in charge while Ridge was gone—and they spent the night drinking at the *Saddle* instead of checking on the animals or walking the fields—makes me want to put my fist through a wall. Or his teeth.

The fact that he doesn't even seem to realize he screwed up?

Infuriating.

I jerk a nod and shove past him, calling over my shoulder, "Round up your crews, Calloways. My mom'll lose her shit if you don't stop by."

I swallow hard, rolling my neck to relieve the tension, but it's no use. I'm too pissed.

And it gets the best of me.

Stopping mid-step, I spin, damn near colliding with Dallas. He jerks his hands up and steps aside, blue eyes wide.

"And Van?" I bark, dragging his smirk from his phone. He glances up at me and pales. "Since you weren't here to do your fuckin' job, you and your brother can skip breakfast and sober up. On watch." Growling, I point a shaking finger at his stupid face. "Y'all move a damn muscle away from your posts, swear to fuck, you'll be on your asses before the whiskey leaves your blood."

With that, I spin on my heel and stomp toward the Big House, the sound of the Calloway's whistling and chuckling behind me.

"Hazel needs to fire every last one of these assholes," I hiss.

Or maybe I do.

The guys laugh, clapping my back, but veer off, probably to collect the rest of the volunteers.

I kick off my boots and strip out of my jacket at the front door, the fabric soaked in smoke and sweat. The air inside the house is warm, the strong scent of coffee, breakfast, and home, permitting my frazzled senses.

Laughter echoes down the hallway. The sound of dishes clinking, of overlapping conversations and squeaky chairs on the old hardwood, rises up like a smothering blanket around me.

But I tune it all out and charge forward like a man possessed.

I washed off the worst of the fire outside with the hose, my hands still raw, my skin chilled, but I need a real shower. A full scrub. I need the heat to burn away what I saw out there—what I felt. The fear, the loss, the flashbacks that inevitably came.

But first?

First, I need to see my girls.

I round the corner into the kitchen and stop cold in the doorway.

The room is full. The long table's packed tight with ranch hands, volunteers, and my family. My mom's at the stove, flipping something in a pan while barking orders at Colby and Clementine. The twins are laughing, faces pink, hair a mess. There's a whole crew of guys I don't even recognize hovering near the back door, plates in hand, boots muddy, eyes heavy.

But all of that fades.

Because at the head of the table, tucked into the biggest chair we've got, Georgia is feeding Aurora.

She's got the baby cradled in her arm like she was born to do it, one hand gently tilting the bottle while her mouth moves in a soft laugh at something my mom must've said. Her curls are falling down around her face, cheeks flushed, and her eyes—

Christ, her eyes.

They're tired. But they're alive. Brighter than I've ever seen them. She doesn't even notice the way she kisses Aurora's hair between sentences, or how she adjusts the blanket wrapped around her little legs every few seconds like she can't stop checking to make sure she's warm.

I lean against the archway and just stare. My body's tired, my lungs ache, but in this moment… I've never felt more awake.

There's a plate of untouched food in front of her.

My first thought is: Is it not safe for her? My mom's careful, she always is, but Georgia's system is tricky. It doesn't take much. Then again, maybe she hasn't eaten because she's been feeding Aurora.

And that—fuck, that guts me.

That she'd put herself second so easily. That she already does it without thinking. That she's already here, like this, like *mine*.

And that little girl in her arms?

She's got me.

Tied me up in knots. Bundled my heart in her tiny little fists and squeezed until it started beating again.

The ache in my chest grows sharp. I rub at it, trying to breathe past the heat that rises up my throat.

Tonight, when I saw that fire, when I realized how fast it was moving, how bad it could've gotten, I couldn't think past them. Yeah, my mom, my sisters, my friends—they were at the top of the list.

But Georgia and Aurora?

They *were* the list.

I fought harder, ran faster, because the thought of losing either of them made my whole damn chest cave in. It scared the shit out of me. I couldn't breathe. Couldn't think.

Still can't.

I run a hand through my beard, shake my head, try to pull myself together. I'm in. I'm all the way the fuck in. And it scares me half to death.

But I've never wanted anything more.

Like she can hear my thoughts, Georgia's eyes find mine.

And those big eyes—all rolling green hills and emeralds dancing in the sun—immediately turn glassy. Her mouth parts, and she pushes to her feet like she's been waiting for this exact second, like her body needs to get to mine.

The bottle slips from her hand, clattering onto the table and Aurora makes a whimpering sound that stabs me in the gut.

I'm coming, baby, I think, not even sure if I mean Georgia or the both of them.

Probably both.

I push off the doorframe and start toward them, the noise of the room dimming until all I can hear is the pounding of my heart, and the tiny, perfect breaths of the girl in her arms.

We collide.

My arms wrap around both of them. Georgia sniffles. Aurora fusses. And my heart? It tumbles right out of my chest and explodes in their laps like it's been waiting for this moment to be claimed.

"I was so worried," Georgia whispers, pressing frantic kisses to my jaw, one after the other like she can't get close enough. "I thought—"

"I know," I rasp, cutting her off. I lean back just enough to look at them—really see them—and Aurora's already staring up at me with those big brown eyes like I hung the damn moon. "Hi, baby girl."

She babbles something incoherent, squeals, then screeches in the way only babies can get away with. Her chubby hands shoot up toward me, desperate to be held.

Georgia chokes out a sound that's part sob, part laugh. "God, that's adorable. She already loves you, Kade. We—"

Her voice cracks, and she shakes her head, lips parting like she might finish the thought, but doesn't. I watch the long line of her throat move as she swallows.

What were you gonna say, darlin'? We what?

Instead, I say the only thing I know to be true.

"Feeling's mutual," I murmur, my voice rough with ash and emotion and too many sleepless nights as I hold her gaze.

Georgia gasps, eyes widening before she blinks and shakes her head like she's reading too much into my double-meaning.

She's not.

Aurora bats at my beard with a frustrated line of incoherent babbles I assume means she's cussing me out and I chuckle, stepping back, tension broken.

"I need to go home and shower. Don't wanna get either of you covered in soot."

She nods, her hand rubbing slow circles on Aurora's back. "You should eat something first."

I jerk my chin at the full plate she left behind. "You didn't eat."

"I did," she murmurs. "That one's for you."

My brows lift in surprise, and maybe doubt, because Georgia doesn't eat when she's nervous. Something I've learned since I met her.

She scoffs, eyes still glassy. "You're so worried about my food consumption."

"Just lookin' out for you, darlin'." I lean in and press a kiss to her mouth, not giving a single damn who sees.

She jolts back. "Kade! Your mother will see!"

"So the fuck what."

"But…" Her free hand flaps helplessly, Aurora bouncing on her hip. "Then she'll know—"

"That we're together?" I shrug, stepping into her side and facing the whole room. "Good."

She mutters a string of hissed curses under her breath, but I ignore them.

"Listen up, everyone!" I bark, loud enough to shut the room down. Every fork pauses mid-bite. Every chair stops creaking. Every mouth shuts.

I smirk to myself.

Still got it.

"This is Georgia," I say, gesturing to my girl before dropping to point at Aurora. "And this is Aurora." Finger up. "My woman." Finger down. "My daughter. Any questions?"

The silence lasts three whole beats.

Then—

"Oh my God!" Colby shrieks, clapping like a lunatic.

Clem sniffles beside her, dabbing at her eyes like I just proposed marriage instead of claimed my whole damn life in two sentences.

My mom? Full-on tears.

Emmy hollers.

The kitchen explodes in cheers.

Georgia, though?

She just turns her head and glares at me. Side-eye so sharp it could kill a man twice my size. I grin, unrepentant and waggle my brows. "Now I don't have to hide it when I kiss you. Problem solved."

"You'll be lucky if you ever kiss me again, sunshine," she mutters, but her tone's soft, eyes full of something that looks a hell of a lot like hope.

"You claimed her as your daughter," she whispers.

I look down at the baby in her arms—*my baby*—and smooth a hand over her soft curls. It's new, it's fast, but I don't give a fuck. She's mine.

"I know."

"I'm so happy for you," Georgia breathes. "So damn proud."

My throat goes tight again. I kiss her, then press my lips to the top of Aurora's head, inhaling her soft, baby scent.

"Let's go home. I'll pack some food to go, but we're beat. And she needs her bed."

Georgia hesitates, worry flashing in her eyes. "But what about the fire? What happened?"

My eyes flick to the corner, where Memphis, Dallas, and Nash are now talking in low tones with my mom. Dallas says something, and Ma's face crumples—but she doesn't let it drop. Shoulders straight. Chin up. Always.

Like an Archer.

"The Calloway brothers have some ideas."

"Which ones are the Calloways?" she murmurs.

I gesture to the three hulking men surrounding my mom like blue-eyed, tanned storm-clouds. "Them."

Her eyes widen, and she stares for a long moment, throat bobbing, damn near drooling.

I gape, pinching her side and she gasps, spinning to face me. "Sorry. Did you say something?"

"Christ," I mutter, shooting the assholes a glare for existing in her proximity. "I know they're attractive fuckers, but can you please pretend I'm still the hottest guy the room? My pride can't take it, baby. I literally *just* publicly claimed you."

Georgia giggles, reaching up to kiss me. I glare at her through it, but eventually soften when she tugs on my hair.

"Sorry," she whispers, biting her lip when she falls back. "I'll make it up to you later."

Groaning, I shake my head and release her to make to-go boxes. "Now that's inappropriate, freckles. Can't be hard this close to my family. It's wrong."

She rolls her eyes, stepping up to my side to watch me plate food. After a minute she finally murmurs, "So how did it happen?"

"Arson," I whisper, careful not to let the twins hear.

Georgia's breath catches. "Who the hell would do something like that? And why?"

I shake my head, jaw tight. "I don't know. But I'll sure as fuck be finding out."

A little while later, after Aurora's been changed and tucked into bed, I strip Georgia naked and drag her into the shower with me, the monitor sitting on the vanity across from us.

Dead on my feet or not, I'm still desperate for her. Still want her in every damn way—more now than ever before.

Her skin is chilled from the night air, her fingers trembling where they curl around my arm, but her eyes? They're soft, raw, and full of everything I'm too much of a coward to say.

The second the hot water hits her, she flinches with a gasp, then melts, muscles going loose against me.

"I was so scared," she whispers, lips brushing the scar that cuts across my chest. "I thought you weren't going to come back to me."

My hands tighten around her waist as I guide her fully beneath the spray, letting it pour over both of us in a curtain of steam and heat. My forehead drops to hers, and I breathe her in.

"Not a damn thing in this world that would keep me from you, freckles."

She tucks her face into the hollow of my throat, her breath warm against my skin. Her fingers slide up my back, curling against the muscle like she's trying to fuse us together.

And for a long stretch of time, I just hold her. Let the water do the talking. Let it rinse away the ash and pain and fear that clung to both of us like that smoke.

But then I remember it's also washing away my cum, and the honey, and the perfect night we had before it all went to shit.

I tug her face up to mine and cradle her jaw, eyes asking her a silent question.

One she pushes onto her tiptoes to answer.

The kiss is soft, deep and a conversation without words. A promise sealed with every drag of her lips against mine, every sweep of my tongue along hers. She tastes like safety and sugar and salvation, and I don't even realize I've pressed her back against the shower wall until she's whimpering against my mouth.

I lift her like she weighs nothing, because to me, she's everything, and she wraps her legs around my waist like she belongs there.

Because she does.

We make love in the steam and water, my hips moving slow and deep, her hands in my hair, her eyes locked on mine. No frantic rhythm like earlier. No wild thrusts. Just us, breathing each other in, chasing something more than pleasure.

Chasing something real and permanent.

Her soft moans echo off the tile, mingling with the hiss of the shower and the rasp of her name on my lips. I watch every emotion cross her face, the joy, the ache, the vulnerability, and I swear I feel each one like it's etched into my ribs.

And when she comes, shivering and whispering my name, I hold her even tighter, chasing her over the edge and falling right with her, filling her like I swore I would.

Afterward, I keep her in my arms, her body slick and warm, both of us trembling for different reasons.

Gently, I reach for the soap and wash every inch of her, starting with her shoulders, down her arms, the dips of her waist. She tries to protest, but I hush her with a kiss to the curve of her belly. Then she returns the favor, fingers trailing across my chest, careful around the scars as if they're fresh, until the water runs clear between us.

Once we're dry—her in one of my shirts that swallows her whole, me in boxers, we crawl into bed, quiet and spent.

She curls into me like it's her favorite place to be, her cheek against my chest, her fingers tracing slow circles over my chest.

And I hold her.

Hold her like I'll never let her go.

Words press against my ribs, aching to be spoken. Words I've never said, not to anyone, not since I was too young and stupid to know better. Words that sit heavy in my throat, too scared to fall out... because *this*?

All of this?

It feels a hell of a lot like the happily ever after I told myself I'd never get a second chance at.

CHAPTER FORTY

SHEETS OF GLORY

"Kade!" I shout, hands shaking as I slam another drawer shut. "Kade William Archer!"

Footsteps slam down the hallway, echoing my chaotic heartbeat.

"What?" he barks, careening into the kitchen, eyes wild. "What's wrong? Is it Aurora?"

I soften.

For two seconds.

Then I'm stabbing an accusing, trembling finger at the open drawer labeled *Georgia's GF Snacks*. "What the hell is this?"

My voice is high pitched and thready, and it only gets worse when I open the next drawer, this one labeled similarly, and packed full of my favorite granola bars.

Panic twists in my chest. I slam it shut, yanking open the next one. My favorite gluten-free crackers, boxed and organized next to jars and jars of the stupid nut butter he saw me having a meltdown over.

Months ago.

When we still hated each other.

But it's the cabinet labeled *Baking Stuff For G* filled with new, still-packaged baking supplies that has my knees giving out.

I catch myself on the counter just as Kade shoots forward, wrapping his arms around me from behind.

"What…" I trail off, voice cracking as I blink back tears. *I think I'm in shock.* "Why?"

He presses his lips to the side of my face. "Because I could."

"Kade…" Spinning in his arms, I force my knees to stay upright and shake my head. "You didn't have to do any of this. I… I have baking stuff and food at my place."

"Then bring it here."

My brows furrow. "Then what will I use when I'm at home?"

His jaw ticks, stormy eyes narrowing down at me. "Don't want you there. I want you here. With me." He flicks his gaze to Aurora who's happily babbling in her playpen. "With *us*."

Oh, God.

Oh, fuck.

This sounds a hell of a long like permanence and forevers and big, *big*, commitments. It sounds like he's asking me to move in.

My heart tries to break through my ribs and nausea swells, fast and hard.

I want him. I want them both. But this is all happening at warp-speed, and yet, it's been a slow, dragging burn of hate, and anger, soft moments, and me *falling*.

Falling hopelessly, desperately in love with this man. This life.

Abby's right.

My heart does live in my vagina.

Shaking my head, I rub my temples and sigh. "You still didn't need—"

"I wanted to," he murmurs, dragging my face up and sliding his mouth against mine. "So I did."

My hands find his chest, fingers curling into his shirt as I sink into the kiss. It's soft and reverent. He tastes like warmth and safety, and the barest hint of coffee. He smells like sweat, and ash, and *my* Kade.

He's spent the last few days helping clear what the fire left behind, showing up for everyone while quietly carrying the weight of it all. I'd only had one appointment this morning, which meant I was able to get back to the farm early to help.

Bea's beside herself.

Everyone is.

They lost a lot in that fire. Equipment that insurance will replace, but not soon enough. Irrigation stuff I don't understand—but that sounds like a major loss.

It's the Honey Bea event shed that hurts Bea the most, though.

What it represents.

The night of the fire, over breakfast with the crew, she explained that it was something she started over twenty years ago, with her late husband at her side.

It was a way to celebrate what they created here, but also, a way to bring the town together. And for years, it did.

After William passed, she struggled to keep the big event going all on her own. And with times changing, her children growing, it's become more of a difficult task than a celebration.

But I saw the ache in her eyes. The heartbreak on her face.

The Honey Bea Bash is more than a simple summer kick off—it's an Archer tradition. And I vowed then and there to make it happen for her.

No matter what it takes.

Fighting Cooper Ridge, rallying the community—that'll take time, people, and a hell of a lot of resources. But the Honey Bea Bash? That's something we can do. Something I can do.

For them.

Kade groans softly into my mouth, pulling me back to the present before breaking the kiss with a reluctant sigh. "Can't kiss you like that with Aurora in the room."

I giggle, peeking over my shoulder. She's chewing on her teether now, absolutely enraptured by whatever cartoon animal is dancing on the screen of her new baby-safe tablet.

"Rory is busy, but I get it." My nose wrinkles and I force a few feet between us. "It does feel weird to touch when she's around."

"Rory?" he asks, voice rough.

My cheeks heat and I shrug, turning away to close all the cabinets I still haven't processed. Probably never will. "Suits her."

"Rory Grace," he mutters, running his fingers over the adoption application we filled out last night. I need to send it off when I leave for work tomorrow. "Rory Grace Archer."

Swooning, I nod, squeezing his hand. "It's beautiful."

"So are you."

I swat at him with a tea towel. "Don't flirt with me."

"Why the hell not?" He crosses his arms and leans against the counter, looking truly put out. "Flirting with you's my favorite thing."

"Because," I huff, hanging the towel. "It leads to your mouth on me, or your…" My brows waggle knowingly as I gesture to his obviously hard dick. "*That* winds up in my…"

"Your what, baby?" he asks huskily, stepping toward me like a predator. "Your sweet, honey-flavored pussy? Your deliciously soaked pussy? Your greedy, insatiable, cum-filled pussy. Say it."

"You're…" My mouth opens and closes in shock, blood heating and pussy clenching at nothing but his filthy mouth. "You're incredibly inappropriate!"

"Been a while since you called me that." He chuckles. "Haven't called me inappropriate since before I started eating your pretty pussy. In fact, lemme do it now and see what else you can call me."

I squeal when he makes a dive for me and run around the kitchen, putting the island between us. "Don't say that! She'll hear you!"

"She's not paying a lick of attention to you or your pussy," he taunts, biting his lip as he closes in on me with his massive strides. "But *I* love your *pussy*. Love to taste your *pussy*. Touch your *pussy*. Fuck it with my fingers and mouth and—"

"Poo–poo–seeeee," a tiny voice screams with an adorable laugh.

We both freeze, heads whipping toward Aurora who's waving her teether around above her head like a cowboy hat as she repeats the babbled word again and again.

"Oh my God," Kade drawls, mouth hanging open, face pale. "Did she just…"

"Yep," I breathe, nodding. "She did."

"*Pooooo–seeeeeee!*"

We stare at her, stunned into silence, as if the air's been sucked clean out of the room.

Aurora, completely oblivious to the absolute chaos she's unleashed, erupts into another round of delighted giggles. Her cheeks are flushed, her dimples on full display, and she's so damn proud of herself it makes something in my chest go soft—and unhinged—all at once.

Kade breaks first, a choked sound bursting from him as he claps a hand over his mouth, eyes wide with horrified amusement.

I don't even try to hold it in—I throw my head back and lose it. The full-body-shaking, face-wet, can't-breathe kind of laughter.

Kade follows suit, wheezing, bent over, actually crying as he mutters, "We're so screwed," between gasps.

We.

My laugh dies, but my smile sticks, as I press a kiss to Aurora's head and smooth her hair back. "You're perfect, you sassy little genius."

Today, she's in an adorable yellow romper, and I've squeezed her short curls into a tiny half-up ponytail—the rest still as chaotic as ever.

My heart squeezes as she giggles up at me, giant brown eyes rimmed with lashes I'm jealous of, and I can't help but wonder if she looks like Marlee.

If so, Kade's ex was stunning.

Throat tight, I flick my gaze to him and find him already staring at her, an adoring but... sort of sad, expression on his face.

Does he think of her mom every time he looks at her? Does he miss her and wonder what it would be like if Aurora were *theirs*?

Is he thinking of her now?

Shaking my head, I step back and grab my cardigan.

"Where are you going, freckles?" Kade asks, closing the distance between us.

Stomach twisting painfully, mind a mess, I move toward the door, needing a minute to get my head right. "Your mom asked me to help her with laundry day."

He watches me slip into my tennis-shoes, brows high. "You do know what that means, right? It's not just a load in the wash at the Big House."

I scoff, rolling my eyes and adjusting the part in my long, yellow sundress that matches Aurora's. I'm an idiot. Dressing like her. Like we're... like we're...

Stupid fool. Stupid hopeful, head in the clouds, heart in your vagina, fool.

"I know," I say, voice harsher than intended as I move toward the door. "She explained it. It's hanging sheets on the clotheslines. I've done it before. How hard can it be, Kade?"

I can feel my blank mask slipping into place and I hate it. Hate that I'm like this.

He stares at me for a long moment, jaw ticking before shaking his head and dragging me into him, planting a lingering, delicious kiss on my lips that has my toes curling and my mind momentarily forgetting to panic over...

Nothing?

Everything?

I don't know anymore, and that's the problem.

"Good luck. Don't say I didn't warn you."

Turns out, hanging sheets is a lot harder than it looks.

For one, they're heavy as hell.

Second, the wind is a menace.

And third, Bea Archer has what I'm convinced is the largest clothesline system in the entire state.

By the time I'm halfway through my fifth row, I'm sweating like crazy, my hair's fallen out of its clip, and the clean sheets keep slapping me in the face like Abby when she's had too much Vodka.

Still, it's weirdly calming.

There's something about the repetition, the clothespins, the fluttering fabric, the golden sun above, that soothes the part of me still trying to find my footing in this town, this farm.

With Kade.

After an hour, my mind is more collected than before, and I've had multiple full-blown arguments with myself about letting go of this weird jealousy I have about Marlee.

The woman is dead, and being jealous of a ghost is only going to destroy what's growing—and make me miserable.

Not to mention… an awful human being.

She passed. She's not here to raise her daughter. Aurora will never see her mom again.

Being jealous of that is awful.

But, simply telling myself to stop is impossible. Only time will make the ache and life's worth of insecurity stop.

I'm reaching for another sheet, arms stretched high, when a low whistle cuts through the air.

"Damn, baby," a familiar voice drawls. "Sun behind your back, pretty tits heaving in that dress… Even your shadow's tryin' to kill me."

My eyes widen, and I search the field for him, but with all the sheets, I can't see a damn thing.

I glance at the one I'm hanging, and the sun at my back and smile, though. My shadow casts an outline on the sheets around me, distorted but sexy in a way. I wonder what I look like to him? Can he really see my boobs or is he just fucking with me?

Giggling, I lift my arms, tugging my heavy hair up off my neck, and arch my back.

A masculine groan comes from somewhere in the maze of sheets, sending shivers down my spine.

God, he can really see me?

"This is like porn," he mutters, his words catching on the breeze.

Giggling, I turn in place. "Where are you?"

A pause, then a deep rumbling sound that goes straight to my clit. "Can't see me, darlin'?"

Brows furrowed, I shade the sun from my eyes and move through the lines of sheets. They're all still wet and heavy, making them hard to navigate through. After a minute, I still haven't found him, but in the distance, I can hear the soft crunch of his boots against the grass.

My heart skips a beat, stomach swooping.

"Kade," I breathe, spinning in a circle. "Where the hell are you?"

"You were upset earlier," he drawls and I try to chase his voice, but when I dip under a sheet, there's nothing but more fucking sheets.

Swallowing, I shake my head. "I don't know what you're talking about."

"Don't lie to me, Georgia. I know you. Know your smiles and tears, your screams for more and harder. Know what you like to eat for breakfast and how it feels to have you curled into my side. I know you."

I chase every word with my bare feet, moving through the cool, prickly grass quietly, long dress tugged up above my knees, chest pounding.

"Just because you know me doesn't mean I was lying," I say just as another crunch lands a few feet to my left. Smiling, I dart under another line and run toward it.

But when I get there, he's gone.

"How the hell are you doing this?"

"I trained for this," comes a quiet, sultry purr that ghosts across my neck a second before hands grip my hips.

My mouth opens to scream, but Kade claps a hand over it, silencing me as he drags me into his chest. Behind me, his cock is hard and thick, digging into my back. I whimper, shivering and hot and aching.

"You wanna play with me, freckles?"

He releases my mouth, hand sliding lower to curl around my throat, tipping my jaw up to face him, upside down.

"Out here?" I breathe, licking my suddenly dry lips. "What if someone sees?"

"Mom took Aurora and the twins to the grocery store," he murmurs, eyes tracking my every breath. "Won't be back for an hour."

"But..." My nails dig into his arm, breaths sawing in and out. "What if someone *else* sees?"

He smirks, hand flexing around my throat. "Guess you'll have to be quiet and hide real good then."

"Hide?"

Kade nods, releasing me. I nearly collapse, my legs are so wobbly, but I catch myself, spinning to face him as he steps back, ripping off his t-shirt with one hand behind his neck. The move is masculine, so sexy and primal, a shudder runs through me.

"Are we playing naked hide-and-seek?" I ask breathily, fingers tightening in the hem of my dress as my eyes slide over his thick, ripped body greedily. "In the sheets?"

I'm not opposed to the idea.

In fact, it sounds like the hottest thing I'll likely ever experience.

"If you want to," he murmurs, kicking out of his boots, eyes blazing. "Unless you're scared you'll lose."

My jaw ticks and I glare at him, shoulders back, chin high, pussy regrettably empty. This man has my libido trained. "Fine, I'm in."

"Terms?"

"Well…" I start, shaky fingers digging into the buttons on my dress, but I get distracted by the sight of Kade in nothing but boxer briefs. "Winner gets to do whatever they want to the loser."

His eyes widen. "Whatever they want?"

"Don't be weird, Archer."

Smirking, he rakes his eyes down my body just as I let my sundress pool on the ground, leaving me in nothing but boyshorts.

"No bra," he mutters, shaking his head with a groan as he adjusts himself. "Never gonna get used to that."

I tuck my lips between my teeth and bend, dragging my underwear down my thighs before stepping out of them. "How about no panties? Can you get used to that?"

His throat bobs, jaw ticking. "What are you doing, baby?"

"You said naked hide-and-seek," I murmur breathily as I step behind a sheet and arch my back, hands cupping my breasts in a way I hope looks sexy instead of distorted.

By the sound of his choked, desperate, *"Fuck me,"* I'd say I'm already winning.

"Game on. May the best woman win."

And I plan to.

CHAPTER FORTY ONE

NAKED HIDE AND SEEK.... MY CUM?

SHOULD BE HIDING.

Should be waiting in the shadows for the right moment to strike.

But I can't.

Not when she's out here—naked and flushed, chasing the warm spring sunlight with bare skin and bouncing golden red curls like a goddamn dream.

Not when she moves and teases like she wants me to lose fuckin' control.

And I am. Quickly and happily.

Her silhouette dances behind the sheets, all soft curves and long legs. Every few feet, she stops and arches her back or cups her tits, lifts her hair and plays with herself like she knows I'm watching. Like she knows this isn't a fuckin' game of hide-and-seek, but a hunt, and she's my damn prey.

I pause on the edge of a line and catch sight of her from the back. She doesn't see me or hear me—I'm careful to keep my steps silent. Her eyes flutter closed and she bites that thick bottom lip, slipping her hand between her thighs, shuddering at what she finds.

Goddamn, she's just as keyed up as I am. Just as lost to the madness… the freedom.

I palm my throbbing cock and stroke myself slowly, catching precum on my fingers and using it to soften the ache. Doesn't work. Not a damn thing will but her.

My Georgia. My sunlight and freckles and everything in between.

She pinches her nipple and for a breath, pretty sure she loses herself to pleasure, palm moving with purpose between her thighs.

Holy fuck—she's so hot.

When I can't stifle the groan lodged in my throat, she whimpers breathily and takes off like a shot again.

I smile, heart thudding for a whole new reason, starting the slow prowl of a hunt all over.

I'm losin' and I don't even give a fuck.

"Are you hidin' from me, darlin'?" I taunt, voice thick with lust and excitement. "Or are you tryin' to make yourself come?"

Georgia laughs, quiet and breathy, the kind of sound that lives under a man's skin.

My eyes slide over the mess of sheets, most of them finally drying enough to whip in the soft breeze. It distracts me so I pause, waiting for the wind to die down.

Then I hear it—the whisper of her feet against the sun-warmed grass, the slight intake of breath she's trying to choke back.

There.

Her shadow pulses behind a panel of white cotton, and I stop breathing.

Her body is outlined by the slowly sinking sun—breasts full, back arched, hand slipping between her thighs as she rocks gently against her own palm.

From behind, all fair skin and freckles, perfect ass bouncing with her movements, she was stunning and perfect, a memory etched in my fuckin' brain.

But this…

This is somethin' you never forget. Not for a second. This is something that lives and dies with a person.

A singular moment of pure, unforgettable bliss.

My girl outside, running wild and free in the country, on the land where I was raised. Land that means more to me than I think I ever realized.

She's here, with me, not complaining about the smell or the dirt. Not telling me she has dreams of places far away, bigger and better. She's happy here. She's glowing under the South Dakota sun like it's part of her DNA, too.

And for a few minutes, I just let the weight of it sink in.

Georgia may be terrified to give me more than one day at a time, but every day that she lays between us, she chooses *this*. She chooses m—and Aurora, honey, and wildflowers.

She chooses *me*.

And God, I choose her right back.

"Come find me," she calls, running from sheet to sheet, hair flying around her as she searches for me. "Come claim your prize, Archer."

She's perfect. Fresh air and this moment. A fucking fever dream I never wanna wake up from.

Love that she wants me to catch her.

Love that this is a game I already know I'll lose just to see *her win*.

My grip tightens around my cock, precum slicking my palm as I imagine sinking into her, fucking her into the grass while the sheets whip around us like ghosts. Out here where anyone could see, anyone could catch us. It's the adrenaline I've been desperate for—for years. The kind you could get high on and never come back down from.

I stalk through the sheets, over the game, needing her like I need to breathe, but when I round the line where she just was, there's nothing.

Freezing, I close my eyes, and just listen.

Nothing.

No breath, no gentle but loud footsteps, no whimpers or moans. Just the wind and sheets and the thundering of my heartbeat.

"Georgia?" I call, voice low and warning. The smile slips from my face, and I release myself, fist clenching at my side.

But before I can spiral, she crashes into me from behind, arms around my waist, laughter bright and triumphant.

I whip around, grabbing her and lifting her with a playful growl. "You little brat."

She grins up at me, breathless and pink-cheeked, body slick and soft as she wraps her legs around my waist. "A brat who won."

My cock throbs between us, digging into her thigh. All I'd have to do is shift her a few inches and I could slip inside, fuck her hard right here for anyone to see.

"Can I have my prize now?" she asks breathily, trailing her lips across my throat.

My fingers tighten on her ass and unable to help myself, I grind against her, committing her responding moans to memory.

"What do you want me to do, darlin'? Want me to get on my knees and worship the pretty pussy that's leaking all over my dick? Or do you want me on my back so you can ride me? Just say the word, I'll do it."

Anything.

Everything.

"I wanna explore you, Kade Archer," she whispers, fingers trailing over my chest as she drops her legs, sliding down my body. "Explore the man who claims I'm his."

"You are," I growl, hands tightening around her hips.

She steps closer, lips brushing my peck. "That makes you mine, right?"

There's vulnerability in her hazy eyes as she blinks up at me.

"All fuckin' yours, freckles," I promise, tone soft but sure. "All of me." *For always.*

"Then that's what I want," she breathes, hands skimming my ribs. "To learn every inch of you."

And she does.

Taking her time torturing me slowly, softly, reverently.

She circles me like prey she's finally caught, like she's gonna savor every inch.

Her hands glide over my back, mapping me, committing me to memory. Her lips follow, brushing over every muscle, every dip and scar. When she reaches my chest, her mouth pauses at the thick shrapnel scar slicing across my shoulder, and like she does every time she sees it, her finger trails the ridges and slopes, following the path with her lips and tongue.

Like she's apologizing and thanking me all at once.

Makes no damn sense, but it cracks and twists something inside me anyway.

My eyes flutter shut, a groan catching in my throat.

Georgia whispers quiet words across my skin, too soft for me to hear, and continues her exploration until I'm vibrating, barely standing upright and seconds from snapping.

"Baby," I murmur, shaking my head with a thick swallow. "I'm losin' my mind here."

"Lose it," she whispers, biting down on my nipple. Ecstasy shoots through me, fast and hard. "You won't need it."

And then she drops to her knees before me.

She doesn't touch my cock. Doesn't rush.

She cups my scarred thigh—the one with the worst of the damage—and runs her hands over it slowly, carefully, massaging gently. Kissing the puckered skin like it doesn't ruin me. Like it doesn't still burn on bad days.

"What are you doin'?" I rasp, threading a hand into her hair, cupping her and drawing her closer.

"You've been working too hard," she murmurs, lips sliding over my knee, my calf, and thigh along with her hands. It feels so damn good, I nearly cry out. "I know it hurts."

"How do you know?"

"You limp when it flares. And sometimes… your face gets that look. Like you need to stop but you'd rather die than say it out loud."

Fuck.

Didn't realize she'd notice. Didn't think anyone would.

"Baby," I try again. "You won. You don't have to—"

"I said whatever I want," she cuts in, fierce and tender. "And what I want… is to take care of what's mine. You take care of me so much, Kade. Me and Aurora." A soft shrug. "Now it's my turn."

I can't speak. Can't breathe.

So I let her.

She massages the tension from my thigh, her touch both clinical and deeply intimate, like she's not on her knees in dirt and grass, naked and soaked from the game. When she's satisfied, she moves, kissing her way upward—first along the inside of my leg, then my hip, then my lower stomach.

My cock is leaking, twitching, begging for her, but I don't dare touch it or ask for more than what she's willing to give.

I nearly collapse when Georgia finally puts me out of my misery, licking a long, languid path across the head.

"Jesus," I gasp, fingers flexing against her scalp on instinct.

She does it again, tongue swirling, soft and exploratory—learning me, teasing me, torturing me.

And when my legs are shaking, balls throbbing, I watch my cock disappear between those perfect lips, the tension in my spine turning to fire. Her tongue presses to the underside of my shaft and she moans around me. After a few seconds, she pulls back, letting me slip free, but her hand follows, stroking hard and fast, then soft and slow, only for her mouth to come right back.

Again.

And again.

And fuckin' again.

"Baby, I can't," I pant, sweat dripping down my brow, entire body trembling. "You're killin' me here. I…" Swallowing hard, I shake my head and push her hair back with a shaking hand. "I c-can't."

She pops off me, smiling like sin, and gathers her hair into a ponytail.

"I cheated," she breathes. "You win. Do whatever you want to me, Archer."

Then she sticks out her tongue, eyes locked to mine and waits.

Just... *waits*.

I snap.

"You wanna be a cock-drunk little tease for me?" I growl, fisting her ponytail. "Wanna choke on it till your eyes water?"

She moans, nodding as I slide back into her mouth.

"Good girl," I hiss. "Take it. You look so perfect with your mouth full, baby. Like you were made for this. On your knees, hands covered in dirt and precum, pussy dripping all over your pretty freckled thighs..."

"More," she mumbles around me, tongue lashing out. "*Deeper.*"

I groan, head falling back and thrust in harder, hitting the back of her throat. "You're a dream come true, Georgia Walker. My dream come to life."

I fuck her mouth, slow at first, my hips flexing as she whimpers, her hands gripping my thighs. But it's not enough. With her, it never is.

"Spread your thighs," I demand roughly, cupping her jaw to force her eyes up. "Show me how wet sucking my cock made you."

She doesn't even hesitate, fingernails digging in her legs, tits heaving with every strangled breath.

"Wanna come with me?" I rasp, picking up pace. "Wanna play with that pretty little cunt while I fuck your throat like a good girl?"

Her head bobs in jerky movements, fingers already slipping between her thighs.

"I'm close," I grunt, fingers tightening around her jaw and in her hair. "Better get yourself there fast."

Her fingers work harder, quicker, her body writhing against her hand and the dirt like she's just as lost in the madness as I am.

My spine tingles, the tell-tale sign of an orgasm barreling down on me.

"Georgia." I tug my pulsing cock from her swollen lips, breath stuttering from my chest. "I'm there, baby."

"Do it," she pants, fingers still circling her clit, shivers wracking her frame. "I wanna swallow your cum."

Shaking my head, I drop to my knees, and flip her over with the kind of growl that shouldn't be humanly possible. Her body bounces on the grass and I spank her ass, hard, delighting in the red bloom across her skin.

"Hands and knees."

"What—what?" she gasps, scrambling for purchase. "But—"

"I told you where my cum goes, darlin'," I cut her off by saying with another slap to her ass. "Now get on your fuckin' hands and knees and let me remind you."

She does.

And I do.

I pound into her like I'm trying to erase every man who ever came before me. Like I'm trying to brand her from the inside out. She screams my name, clutches the grass, and when she comes around me, it's a full-body quake that drags me with her.

After, I collapse at her side, chest heaving and drag her into me, kissing her slow and sweet like I didn't just fuck her throat and pussy like a man possessed.

"You okay?" I murmur, tucking her curls behind her flushed ears. "Was I too rough?"

She swallows hard, smiling. "You were perfect. That was..." A sweet giggle she buries in my throat. "That was incredible."

I nod, though she can't see it, mind racing with what we just did. It was reckless and wild and she's right... incredible.

From the day she walked into my life, it's been like this. We fought instead of played, argued and threw insults like an old married couple, but it was fire and adrenaline and I felt alive.

God, that's what she fuckin' does to me.

"It's been a long damn time since I played or laughed or had fun like I do with you," I murmur, kissing her hair. "You brought me back to life, Georgia Walker."

She lifts and meets my eyes, brushing my hair off my forehead, eyes shining. "And I'm not done yet, sunshine. Not even close."

Fuck, I hope not.

CHAPTER FORTY TWO

HEALING IN MOTION

THE CLANG OF THE post driver rings through the empty pasture as I drive the steel down hard, grip tight, sweat running down my spine beneath my shirt.

It's quiet out here—just the wind rustling through the grass, the occasional groan of wood settling under strain, and the sound of our horses grazing. Dusty's tail flicks at a fly. Pudding—the mare Georgia's claimed as her baby, huffs and stomps the ground.

Behind me, my girl pushes a strand of hair out of her face, hands on her hips, squinting down at the broken section of fence. The split in the post is too clean to be from a cow. No splinters or crush marks. Just a sharp crack near the base and a bent rail that was definitely pried out on purpose.

"Don't think it's cattle pressure," I grunt, shaking my head. "No way."

She kneels down, fingers trailing the jagged break. "Not unless they've figured out how to use tools."

"Hazel said she thought it was just leanin'. Said it's been happenin' for a while."

"Yeah?" Georgia looks up. "Because this looks like someone kicked the damn thing in."

"Exactly," I mutter, yanking another post out of the truck bed and dragging it over. "And this section runs the boundary where we lease land to the Stevens ranch. But if their cows get loose and tear up someone's land or make it onto the road, the liability falls back on us. Lease says we maintain the perimeter."

Her eyebrows lift. "So you could get sued."

"We could lose the whole lease," I say flatly. "It's one of the only steady income streams Ma's got since wheat sales dropped last season."

All the little shit I've learned since moving back has thrown me for a loop. Even worse, I feel awful that I've been away, avoiding my family, avoiding responsibility, while they've suffered and struggled.

Grief where my dad's concerned might be healing, but this all just adds another layer of guilt to the never ending pile.

Georgia watches as I line up the new post and slam the first strike down with the driver. The sound vibrates through my arms and chest.

"Thinking of putting in cameras," I add into the comfortable silence. "Good ones. Night vision, motion triggers. Friends of mine could rig them up."

"That's a good idea," she says softly. "Honestly? I'm surprised you haven't already."

"My parents never had the money before. And after Dad died, I wasn't around to notice how bad it got." My jaw flexes. "But I'm here now."

She doesn't say anything, but I feel her eyes on me while I hammer. When the post's set, I step back and wipe the sweat from my brow with my shoulder, breathing hard.

"Still don't make sense though," I finally say, mind racking for answers. "Who the hell would have it out for us?"

Georgia walks up beside me, her gaze scanning the field like it might hold answers. "Could be someone trying to rattle you. Or your mom. Or maybe it's not about you at all—it's about the land."

"Yeah," I mutter. "Been thinkin' the same."

"Cooper Ridge?"

"Don't know, baby. Doesn't make sense for a big fuckin' company like them to mess with us in such…" I trail off searching for the word.

"Immature way?" She scoffs, using her hand to cover her eyes and glare up at me. "Did you forget the reckless, irrational behavior of the leader at the bar?"

Anger swirls through me, fast and hot. "Fuck no."

And I haven't. Probably never will. And now that I know who he is—Clint Cooper, son of multi-millionaire Jett Cooper, I'm even more pissed.

Wealthy, spoiled rich fucks like him don't know how to take *no* for an answer. Explains why he thought putting hands on my woman was okay.

But he's in my town now.

Not in a big city, with big lawyers.

We handle shit differently here.

Money and power aside—I see him near her again, I'll probably kill him, consequences be damned.

"Still don't think it could be them?"

With a long, tired exhale, I shrug. "Don't know, to be honest. Seems like they'd use money instead of fear tactics and fucking with our little operation, but if it's not them, I have no idea who or why it's happening."

Dropping my head back to stretch my aching shoulders, I stare at the blue sky, not a cloud in sight. The constant random showers of early spring have passed, and now that it's nearly June, the sun is bright and hot.

Winter crops are blooming strong, and wildflowers are poking up in long rows of bright colors. The wheat's about a month and half out from being harvested, and I make a mental note to talk to Georgia about what she wants to do when it happens.

"And the fire?" she asks, drawing my attention back to her. "Did you get the final word from the Calloways?"

I nod, pulling my hat off and dragging a hand through my hair. The sweat at my temples is drying sticky in the breeze.

"Definitely arson. Ridge found a gas canister about a mile out past the south pasture. Right next to fresh tire tracks in the mud. But nothing we can track 'em by. Whoever it was, they knew how to cover their trail."

Which pisses me the fuck off.

Some insurance money came through and we've been replacing what we lost, but it's not fast enough, and we're losing valuable time that could make or break things on a farm like this.

Georgia steps closer, placing a gentle kiss on my cheek like she doesn't give a damn about how filthy I am. "I'm sorry. I know how much this land means to your family,—your dad."

My throat tightens. I look out across the field, my heart stuck somewhere between anger and memory.

"Every post I drive, I hear him," I say after a minute. "Not his voice exactly. Just... that look he used to give me. Quiet pride when I got something right. When I followed his lessons without reminders."

Georgia doesn't move. Just waits and listens. Like she always does.

"I messed it up," I admit. "He wanted me home years ago. Told me to stop runnin', to let it hurt, to heal here. I didn't listen. And then..."

"You didn't know he'd go," she says gently. "You didn't know he'd pass. No one thinks their loved ones' time with them is temporary."

"No, but I stayed gone a hell of a lot longer than I should have." I pause, swallowing hard, the truth of it sinking in deep. "I was pissed. At him. At myself. At everything."

She wraps her arms around my waist. I fold mine over her shoulders and drop my chin to the top of her head. She smells like flowers and sunlight, and home.

"You're here now," she whispers. "You're back, and you're helping out the best you can. You're breaking yourself, Kade. Running ragged."

"Yeah," I murmur. "Doesn't feel like enough."

"It is." She kisses my throat. "You're enough for them. I promise."

Her phone buzzes, breaking the moment. She pulls back, checks the screen, then lights up.

"Oh my God. Thank fuck!" she says, grinning wide.

"What's up, darlin'?" I ask, smiling already just from her joy.

She bounces on the balls of her feet. "Okay, don't laugh—but I've been working on something in secret."

My heart pounds but I lean on the fresh post and gesture for her to continue.

"Okay, so… you know how your mom doesn't think the Honey Bea Bash can happen this year? She thinks there's not enough money, not enough time, not enough help. Especially with everything you guys lost." Georgia waves her phone, curls bouncing around her. "Well, I've been messaging local vendors, business owners, friends of friends—seeing if they'd be willing to donate food, time, services. Like a full-town collaboration."

My brows rise, stomach flipping with…

Fuck, I don't know.

Excitement? Not at what she's planning, not really.

But her commitment to help my family, my mom, like she's already a part of this place. Like she's finally digging in roots of her own. All I can do is pray like hell they're deep and the permanent kind and she doesn't rip them out and run, taking my whole world with her.

"That's awesome, baby," I murmur, voice thick. "Tell me more."

She beams. "I've got almost twenty vendors confirmed. Two food trucks. Three bands and someone who can set up a little stage here. Craft booths. The works. If I can keep pulling it together, we can make the Bash happen without your mom spending a dime, and it'll be bigger and better than ever."

I blink, stunned. "You serious?"

"Dead serious. This town needs something to celebrate after everything that's happened. And your mom needs to see that she's not alone."

My heart kicks, and for a second, I forget how to breathe. I just stare at her—this woman who walked into my life with fire in her chest and hope in her hands, and decided we were worth saving.

She grins, snatches my hat straight off my head, and turns on her heel, sprinting toward Pudding.

"Hey—" I call after her.

She swings into the saddle with ease, adjusting the reins like she's done it a hundred times. Her new Lucchese boots flash in the sun, buttery tan and stitched with delicate turquoise. I bought them for her last week on a whim, and she wore them like they were made for her—like she was always meant to belong out here.

From the saddle, she winks, dropping her voice to a low imitation of mine. "You know the rule, *darlin'*."

I shake my head, smiling despite myself. "I'm countin' on it, sunshine."

She kicks her heel gently, and Pudding takes off at a steady lope, her laughter trailing behind her as she waves my hat in the air, hair flying behind her.

Wild. Free. Mine.

Chapter Forty Three

Bake Me Up Before You Go-Go

I WAKE UP TO silence.

The kind that settles over a house that's been well-loved lately—blankets kicked off, sunlight slanting through the open windows, and the faint scent of something sweet and sex still clinging to my sheets.

Rolling over, I snag the camera monitor we have for the nursery and stare at my girl.

Aurora's on her stomach, diapered butt high in the air, face tilted toward the camera like she knows I'm watching. Her chubby cheeks are rosy and one hand is clenched around the ear of her bear, the other tucked between her puckered lips.

I stare for a while, just watching her chest rise and fall, the sound of her soft little sighs echoing through my too-quiet room.

Heart full and aching, I snag the monitor and get up, dragging on sweats as I head for the door. Second I open it, the soft sound of a song I now know by heart, drifting through the warm, oven-scented air.

Smiling, I quietly head toward the kitchen, where I can hear Georgia softly singing.

She's baking and listening to her playlist. The one I made from memory—every female voice she's ever played through her phone, humming under her breath while working through case files or washing dishes or brushing her hair. It started as a note in my phone. Became a playlist for our date night under the stars.

She's had it on repeat ever since.

That night, I asked her why she loves female singers so much. Never hear her listen to anything else but ballads and anthems, strong, powerful voices. She shrugged, cheeks burning red hot, but simply said, "I just do."

I stop short at the kitchen threshold, spotting her like I'm programmed to find her in any room.

She's standing barefoot in front of the island, wearing nothing but one of my flannels that can't be all that buttoned judging by the way it's falling off her small frame. The hem barely skims the curve of her ass, and the sleeves are rolled up, hair clipped up in some messy twist. There's flour on her fingers, cinnamon in the air, and sunlight pouring over her like a fuckin' dream.

She's stunning.

I've found her this way too many times to count since I filled my cabinets with food she can eat, and baking shit she can safely use. To me, it was a no brainer, but to Georgia, it was stress relief in the form of soft dough, and early mornings gettin' her head right before she heads off to a hard day of work. Work that seems to be tugging on her soul, more and more, every day.

We spend every morning in this kitchen. Her humming, us dancing, coffee on her tongue, her body wrapped around mine, soft and sleepy and pliant.

And when I'm done lovin' on her, we eat whatever she cooked out on the porch in the wicker rockers I bought, just for that purpose.

The mornings are still cold, and sometimes, it's so early, steam rises off our coffee like fog from the ground, but in those quiet moments, I've never felt so damn whole.

Georgia tips her head back, a smile tugging on her lips and softly sings the soulful words of "A Case Of You" by Joni Mitchell like she means every damn word.

My heart fumbles in my chest, and my cock throbs painfully, pressing thick and hot against the inside of my sweats.

I move before I can think, stepping up behind her and wrapping my arms around her waist, my face dipping into her neck.

"Morning, freckles," I rasp, voice still rough with sleep and need.

She leans back into me instantly, a soft sigh escaping her. "Morning, sunshine."

My hands roam over her hips, her belly, slipping under the warm cotton to cup her bare skin.

My fingers meet nothing but heat and smooth flesh.

"No panties?" I groan, rolling my hips into her. My cock glides between the swell of her ass cheeks and my spine prickles, my balls tightening. "Always tryin' to kill me, aren't you?"

She giggles, but it cuts off with a moan as my hand slides up and cups her breast, thumb brushing over her hard nipple.

"Kade," she gasps, hands still planted in the dough. "I can't stop. The dough will go bad."

"Then don't," I murmur against her neck, my fingers teasing the flannel's buttons. "But I can't stop either. You—lookin' like this? Sunlight in your hair, wearin' my shirt, settled and comfortable like you never wanna leave this place…" I swallow hard, lips ghosting her throat. "Like you never wanna leave me."

Her breath catches and she whimpers, melting against me. "Maybe I don't."

"Baby," I choke out. "Say it again. Say you wanna stay."

"I do," she's quick to breathe, her heart racing under my hands.

"Fuck. Could come just from hearin' you say that."

"That sounds like a personal problem," she pants, her eyes fixed on where the flannel slips open, revealing soft, freckled skin and the tight peaks of her nipples.

"No," I groan, sliding my hands down her body, pushing the shirt so it falls, catching on the crooks of her elbows. "Sounds like my favorite kinda good morning."

"Sounds like every morning with you."

"Like I said. My favorite." My hands drift over the counter, brushing cinnamon-dusted bowls and a mixing spoon, but I pause on a bowl full of something white and sticky that looks sweet. "What're you makin', darlin'?"

"Cinnamon rolls."

"So," I mutter, smiling in her hair. "This is icing?"

Georgia nods, voice cracking as she whispers, "Vanilla. It's so good."

She shifts her hips back, grinding against me deliberately, and I groan in actual pain.

I drop a hand between her thighs, sliding my fingers along her lower lips, already wet and slick, teasing her clit as I rock my hips forward. My cock catches between her ass cheeks, pressure building with every stroke.

Her head drops back, breath catching. "Oh god… that feels so good."

"Can you come like this, baby?" I whisper against her ear, sliding my fingers deeper, my cock throbbing against her. "Can you come on my hand with my fingers buried in your pretty cunt, my cock rollin' against your ass?"

"Yes," she chokes out, no hesitation.

"Don't stop what you're doin', then," I murmur, curling my fingers inside her, my other hand spreading over her lower belly. "Don't make a sound. Just keep your hands on the counter, fingers in that dough, and let me feel you. Can you do that, Georgia? Can you let me taste what's mine?"

"T-taste?" she stutters, voice wrecked.

"Yeah, baby." I bite down gently on her shoulder, licking where I leave the mark. "Come all over my hand, and I'll eat you for breakfast while you make yours."

Her whole body tenses, trembling hands kneading the dough in ragged, uneven strokes.

"That's it," I murmur, rolling my hips harder, grinding against her with every motion. "You're soaked. You love this. Love makin' a mess in our kitchen, moanin' my name while you pretend you're busy."

"I'm not—pretending," she says with a sharp gasp.

"No? Then why're your hands barely workin', baby? Why's that pretty little pussy of yours clenching around my fingers like it knows what's comin'?"

She bites her lip, hips jerking, breath catching. "Because you're insatiable."

"So are you," I murmur, fingers barely moving, just letting the pressure against her clit and g-spot be guided by the slow, torturous grind of my hips.

"I-I'm not."

"But you are, baby. Think I haven't noticed your body's never satisfied with just one orgasm or two? Your pussy clenches and begs again and again until I've wrung you dry and you're passed out."

Georgia tenses, but I shake my head, sucking hard on her throat. "Don't you dare apologize. Getting you off isn't work for me, it's a fuckin' gift. And I'll do it as many times as it takes for you to feel good."

"I always feel good with you." She whimpers, little fingers digging holes into the poor dough. "I can't… Kade… I'm gonna—"

Her thighs quake, her body locking around me, and I tilt her head back just in time, catching her loud moan with a deep kiss. My hips never stop, hand never slipping free. She's dripping all over my palm, pussy squeezing the hell out of my fingers.

It's hot as hell.

When our mouths separate, I don't move, don't stop or release her. Instead, I reach to the icing bowl and dip two fingers into the thick, sugary glaze.

She pants, watching me in the sunlight, dazed.

"What are you doing?"

"Shh," I whisper. "Just watch."

I trail the icing down her throat, letting it drip slow and thick. Down her chest. Around her nipple. Over the curve of her belly, circling her navel. Down, lower still—following the same path I took with honey the first time I ever touched her like this.

She shudders violently, breath stuttering as I pull my fingers from her and suck them clean, moaning around the taste that is solely *her*.

Then I flip her around, kneel, and lick every drop off her skin. From collarbone to breast, to stomach and between her thighs. I lift one of her legs over my shoulder and bury my tongue inside her pussy, groaning at the taste of her and sugar and morning sun.

She cries out again, one hand gripping my hair, the other flattening against the counter for balance.

While I work her with my mouth, I reach down, grip my cock, and stroke myself slow, matching the pace of her moans.

As soon as her second orgasm hits, I rise, flip her around again, and bend her over the counter.

"Cover your fuckin' mouth, darlin'," I grit out, on edge. "I'm not coming on my hand."

She bites her own fist just as I slam into her, burying myself to the hilt in one rough, deep thrust. Her body bows, little whimpers and moans slipping free around her flesh, and I grip her hips, fucking her hard, fast, relentless.

When I feel the edge start to crash over me, I press her tighter to the counter, hips locked to hers, and come hard, filling her with everything I've got. She shudders under me, breath catching again.

I rub her clit in slow, tight circles, still rocking my hips.

"I can't," she cries. "Not again."

I drop my lips to her ear, low and dark. "Want my cum as deep as it can get, baby. Need you to come before I pull out."

"Kade," she pleads, shaking her head. "God, it's so good."

She clenches around me with a broken whimper, her body giving in before her mind can fight it.

"I told you," she pants. "I'm on birth control. Your efforts are a waste."

"Making love to my woman could never be a waste," I murmur, kissing down her spine, still buried deep inside her. "Never."

Sighing, she melts into the counter with a quiet giggle. "I take it you want more kids, then."

Only if they have your smile.

Choking back the words is harder than it should be, but I nod against her, peppering her back and neck with soft kisses. "Yeah, darlin'. I really fuckin' do. Want a big family with laughter and chaos and messes."

And I want it all with you.

"That sounds really nice," she whispers, eyes meeting mine, all soft and glazed. "I think I'd love a life like that. A home filled with so much love."

Fuck.

"Then lemme give it to you," I whisper, kissing her slowly. "Let me give you a home, Georgia Walker."

And it's the words she breathes against my lip that change this thing between us from earth shatteringly *big*, to unshakable *forever.*

"You already have."

CHAPTER FORTY FOUR

GUILT GROWS LIKE WEEDS

IT'S BEEN JUST OVER a month since the fire, and the farm's finally starting to feel like it's breathing again.

After the cameras went up, rigged top to bottom by the best guys I know, the vandalism stopped cold. Not a single gate left open. Not one damn fence knocked down. No tools missing. Nothing.

And maybe it's just my gut. Maybe it's the years I spent hunting patterns in places most people couldn't survive, but the sudden silence is too clean. Too deliberate.

If it was just bad luck, bad timing, or animals leaning too hard, it wouldn't have stopped just because we rolled in with surveillance, intentionally loud and obvious.

Which means someone out there saw the cavalry roll in, and they decided to back the hell off.

It wasn't random. It wasn't chance. Somebody's targeting Honey Bea.

And I've got no idea who.

The farm's been busy as hell ever since.

Between Aurora, Georgia, and the everyday grind, I've been spending most of my time working the land again. Fencing, irrigation checks, helping Ridge rotate feed, brushing down Dusty and easing him back into saddle work. There's something honest about the labor. Forgot how much I missed it—the blisters, the ache in my shoulders at the end of the day, the smell of dirt and sun and sweat clinging to my skin like proof I'm still alive.

Didn't see it for years, but I was rotting away in that tiny crap-studio. Wasting my life in a ten-by-ten box with no connection to the outside world beyond small bits of town, my family, and work.

I missed this. Missed them. More than I ever let myself admit.

It's not perfect yet, but the anger between Hazy and me has started to soften.

Every Sunday, Georgia and I bring Aurora to dinner at the big house, and little by little, I've stopped flinching when I walk through the door. The chair at the head of the table still stays empty—Mom won't let anyone touch it—but I've learned how to look at it without the guilt wrapping around my throat like barbed wire.

The grief's still there. Always will be.

But being here, *staying here*, has made it quieter. More manageable. Avoiding this place for so long made it grow teeth. Made it bigger, meaner than it had to be.

But facing it? Sitting across from Hazel while she passes the mashed potatoes and teases me like no time passed? Listening to the twins never ending thoughts about their upcoming senior year while Mom stares at everyone with love and a little sadness in her eyes.

And doing it all with Georgia at my side, holding Aurora while she smashes honey-glazed carrots into her hair...

It's made things surprisingly easier.

I sigh as I pull into an empty parking spot downtown, my eyes drifting to the vacant building before me.

Griff's already here—leaning against his truck like a fuckin' ad for the feed store. Carhartt jacket stretched over his barrel chest, worn jeans slung low on his hips, boots still covered in Tennessee horseshit. The only thing he's missing is a cowboy hat to tip and a *"ma'am"* to go with that thick drawl I love to talk shit about.

And emulate.

Only with Georgia.

Wilder's still out in Washington on a long solo detail he picked up, running protection for a senator's daughter with a stalker. Job he took on his own, freelance, after he walked from Iron Shield—something I still can't wrap my head around.

True to his word, Griff sold off his land in Tennessee to chase this new dream.

A dream far away from the demons he left back home.

I haven't seen him much lately. He's been bouncing back and forth, tying up loose ends out east. And me? I've been buried in this new life I didn't see coming.

I climb out of my truck, slamming the door behind me.

"Jesus," I mutter, walking over. "You ever think about shrinking?"

Griff smirks. "You ever think about growing?"

"You've got three inches on me, asshole. Relax."

We clap hands and pull into what Colby claims is *bro-hug.*

"You good?" I ask.

"Better now that I'm here," he says roughly, eyes trailing downtown. "Tennessee's a mess. Final papers are signed though. I'm all in now."

"Never doubted you." I glance around the lot, then up at the building that sits on the corner of two main streets. "Where's the realtor?"

Griff chuckles, pulling a ring of keys from his pocket. "Didn't need one."

I blink, jaw unhinging. "You *bought* the fuckin' thing? Christ, Sarge."

"Rented," he grunts, bearded face tipping with a smirk. "Long-term lease. But yeah. It's ours, man."

I gape at him as he unlocks the front door and pushes it open. Sunlight spills into a wide, open space that smells like old paint and drywall dust. It's dated, sure—but it's got good bones. Room for desks and a few private offices. Even space for the tech setup we'll need."

"Damn. You did good." I shoot him a look. "Hope you kept all the shit I gave you from working remotely. Just sprung for a surveillance system at the farm."

He waves me away. "I've got it all. No worries."

Gratitude washes through me. "Can't believe you really pulled this shit off, man. And fast."

"Yeah, well... now I just need a place to live."

"You can crash at the farm," I offer, leaning against a wall, arms and ankles crossed. "Mom loved having you and Wild in the big, empty house."

He scoffs. "I'll be damned if I move in with Mrs. A, Kade. I'm forty fuckin' years old."

I laugh, and he just shakes his head, dragging his fingers through his long, messy hair.

"So how are you?" he asks. "How are your girls?"

I smile before I can stop it, everything in me soaring. "Good. They're really fuckin' good."

Griff studies me. "You gonna marry her?"

My heart skips a beat. There's a lot I haven't said—not out loud, not even to myself. But I meet his eyes and grin, because yeah, if she lets me, I'm gonna marry the fuck out of that woman.

"I didn't want to love again," I say, voice thick. "Then she stormed into my life, all fire and fight, and suddenly…" My hands flail helplessly. It's exactly how I feel. "I couldn't help myself."

Griff's face softens. He closes the distance between us and claps a heavy hand on my shoulder, squeezing hard. "She's damn good for you."

I nod, throat thick. "You never said that about Marlee."

"Yeah, man. I didn't." His expression darkens. "She wasn't good for you. You deserved a hell of a lot better."

"You knew something I didn't," I say quietly, staring out the window so I don't have to see the look in his eyes. "Saw through all the charm, the golden blonde hair, and fake smiles. All the lies. I was too young and too damn stupid to notice what she was hiding."

"What're you talking about?"

I sigh, running a hand through my beard. Need to clean it up again, but Georgia and Aurora like tugging on it too much and I'm weak where they're concerned.

"Kade?" he prompts, voice and expression serious.

"The day the social worker brought Aurora…" I swallow thickly, heart twisting along with my insides. "Ethel told me things. About Marlee. Her husband. The accident. Stuff I didn't know. Stuff I wish I didn't know now."

And for the first time, I let it all out.

Tried to bury it. Pretend the past didn't matter.

Told myself the things I wasn't there to see or stop aren't on me—and logically, I know that. Had no idea Aurora even existed.

And still, I don't know exactly what happened to her. If the abuse was done by Marlee or Travis, or both. Fuck, maybe neither, but the asshole's record would suggest otherwise.

And Marlee…

I know not all abuse is cyclical. I know people can stop it if they want to. Know that just because her grandma Kim and her mom were awful and solved shit with open hands and closed fists, doesn't mean Marlee followed the pattern with her own kid.

But then I think back to the fights we'd get in when we were young. I think about the way she didn't shy away from hitting me or slapping me when she was pissed.

She'd be crying and raging and burning, and I'd see those tears and soften, every damn time. I'd grab her up, ignoring the sting of her hands, and hug her tight, telling myself it was just the trauma, just the hurt she was working through. I'd comfort and love on her, and she'd cry some more, tell me she was sorry and she wouldn't do it again.

That never stuck either.

But, we were young, and I had myself convinced it was passion, not...

Not something *ugly*.

When I'm done rambling, sharing more than I meant to, Griff is still as a statue, eyes burning, jaw ticking. "You learn anything else?"

"Nah. But... does it really matter anymore? Aurora's adjusting. We even caught her trying to walk the other day. She's sleeping better now, too." My throat constricts, and I mutter, "Thought it was just her teeth, but I think maybe it was nightmares. The trauma of all the shit she's been through."

Griff doesn't say anything for a long time, but when he speaks, it's soft and measured like he's worried I'll get mad. "You tell Georgia all this?"

I shake my head, stomach twisting with the amount of shit I'm keeping from my girl right now. Wasn't intentional, I'm just... delicate with her.

"She's got a lot going on. And she's finally settling in. Working her ass off at her day job, and on this thing for my mom. Been over a month since that night in the field. Since I told her she was mine. She hasn't tried to run."

"But?" he asks.

"But sometimes, I can still see her fingers twitch and her eyes dart to the door when things get heavy, like she's checking for an escape plan."

He frowns. "She alright?"

I nod, pulling my phone from my pocket, more guilt and sadness eating at me.

"Yeah. Just... scared, I think. She's like Aurora. Been through a lot." I bring up the file and hand it over. "Remember how I told you her mom was born here?"

He nods, gaze flicking to the screen.

"I've been digging. Trying to help her find her family."

He scrolls, brows drawing together. "Fuck. They're all dead?"

"Every single fuckin' Walker," I say, voice low. "Mom. Grandparents. Even a brother. All buried out in Serenity Falls."

"What about her dad?"

"Don't know who he is, and trust me, I looked deep." I shrug, grimacing as my mind flits through all the connections I reached out to for information. "Lorna had a rough upbringing. Parents were religious, but the kind of religious where they lean on God and use it as an excuse for the bad shit they did."

He scoffs, nodding, no doubt thinking about his late father who was the same.

"Anyway, from what I could dig up," I continue, referring to the locals in Heart Springs and Serenity I regrettably talked to. "Lorna escaped from home the only way she could, lookin' for love or happiness or whatever, in all the wrong places. Had a lot of boyfriends—a lot of them were older men, too. When she got pregnant, I assume it went badly at home, so she ran."

Though, I can't prove any of that. At this point, it's speculation.

From what gossip suggested, Lorna was a promiscuous young girl from a bad home. When she ran away, her parents wrote her off as no longer being their child—a pregnant, unmarried seventeen-year-old high school dropout.

They went on with their lives, never looked or asked for help, and Lorna…

Lorna died alone a few states over.

And Georgia… my Georgia, paid the price of everyone's mistakes.

"Damn," he breathes, handing my phone back. "That's gonna kill her."

I nod, slipping it into my pocket. "She wanted roots. Answers. Now there's no one left to ask. No one to tie her to this place. And when her contract's up in a few months… I don't know, Sarge. I'm terrified she might go if she knows what she came here for is all dead and buried."

"You think she will?"

"I hope not." I glance at the empty room around us. "All I can do is keep building something here that feels like home. Something worth staying for."

And pray like hell it's enough.

That Aurora and I are enough.

CHAPTER FORTY FIVE

Kade

DADA'S DON'T CRY

GEORGIA'S BEEN KNEE-DEEP IN Honey Bea Bash prep all weekend—clip-boards, spreadsheets, flower crates, and more color-coded sticky notes than should be legal.

And I've helped where I can, hauling tables, lifting bins, making trips into town for extra sunshade tents and extension cords.

But this? This thing is hers. She's taken it on with both arms and her whole damn heart.

And the thing is… watching her bring life back into this farm with nothing but determination and her wide-open soul? It's doing something to me I don't know how to name.

I lean against the fence, arms folded, just… *watching*.

Aurora toddles through the rows of tulips, her tiny sandals kicking up dust with every unsteady, supported step. Georgia crouches beside her, curls tumbling loose around her face, one arm around her waist while she guides Aurora's hands to a bloom, talking her through how to trim it.

Our girl giggles, snipping the stem with blunt little scissors, then drops the flower into the basket with dramatic flair. She claps like she's just won a damn award, and inside, I feel like she should.

Georgia looks up at her, laughing softly, her whole face lit from within and presses a soft kiss to her chubby cheek.

My heart ricochets so hard I nearly stagger.

Christ.

I love them.

I love them so damn much it hurts.

It hits me with no warning—like everything I've been holding back just decided to crash through my ribcage at once. It's not just affection. It's not even just love. It's everything. The future I didn't think I deserved anymore. The quiet joy I didn't know I needed. The sense of home I stopped believing in.

Georgia must feel it, because she glances over and catches me staring just as Aurora drops to her butt and digs her fingers into the blooms with a giggle.

My woman flushes, a slow pink creeping across her freckled, rosy cheeks. "What are you looking at, sunshine?"

I shake my head, throat thick. "Everything."

"Everything?" she asks, barely above a whisper.

I nod, pushing off the fence and walking toward her. Her eyes stay locked on mine as I reach down and help her stand, her fingers curling instinctively into my shirt. I pull her in, soft and slow, and brush my mouth against hers.

"*My everything*," I murmur against her lips.

The kiss deepens, lazy and warm, like the sun overhead. Her hands slip up around my neck, mine settling on her waist. It's the kind of kiss that says I'm not going anywhere. I'm yours. The kind that hums low in your chest and steals time.

Just like always.

Months in, and I'm still not over the feel of her against me. Still rattled every single time our lips touch. Will it always be like this? Will every moment with her, with them, always feel like more?

"*AHHHHHHH!*"

A tiny squeal slices through the moment, followed by a sharp tug on my jeans.

We break apart, both of us laughing as Aurora stares up at us with scandalized eyes and dirt-covered fingers gripping my boot.

"She pulled herself up," Georgia breathes, grinning wildly. "You did it, big girl!"

"Yeah," I scoff, smiling as I mutter, "To cock block."

Aurora shoots me a glare like she knows exactly what I just said and beats her little fist against my shin.

"Well, excuse me, ma'am," I drawl, scooping her up under her arms and hoisting her into the air. "Didn't know we had a chaperone."

She shrieks in delight, legs kicking wildly as I spin her in a lazy circle. Her curls, now a little bit past her ears, bounce, and she claps her hands so hard, dirt falls in my eyes. A never ending stream of babbles leaves her gummy little mouth.

I swing her twice more, then pull her tight against my chest. She grabs a fistful of my beard like she always does, squealing with delight as her fingers tug.

"Easy, wild thing," I mutter, tickling her belly.

"Yeah, sweetheart," Georgia adds, stepping into my side and poking Aurora's dimple. "I love your dada's beard. Please don't rip it out."

My stomach flips at the casual words, but I'm getting used to it. Georgia refers to me as dada all the time in an effort to encourage Aurora to say it as her first word.

Well, first word besides pussy.

Thank fuck that one didn't stick.

Aurora screeches and tugs on Georgia's hair instead.

"Don't yank her curls out either," I say with a laugh, unwrapping her tiny fist.

It's on my tongue to call Georgia mama, but like always, I'm careful, knowing too much will send her for the hills. But I've been practicing with our girl in private, and maybe hearing the word from a tiny mouth instead of mine will hit different.

"*Dada!*"

Everything in me goes still.

Georgia gasps.

I just… freeze. Like my soul just slammed on the brakes and flipped the emergency lights.

"Oh my God," Georgia chokes out, sniffling as she coos, "Say it again. Say dada, baby."

Aurora blinks up at me, entirely unfazed, then grins wide.

"Dada," she says again, confident now, hands slapping against my cheeks.

My knees almost give out.

Georgia claps a hand over her mouth and starts sobbing—ugly, beautiful tears spilling down her face as she watches us. My own eyes blur, and

I bury my face in Aurora's neck, breathing her in and whispering, "Say it again."

"Dadadadadada!"

I laugh through the tears, peppering her chubby cheeks with kisses. "That's right, baby girl. I'm your Dada. I'm your Dada."

And I am.

Somewhere between pain and farm chores and Georgia's quiet love, I've become a dad. Unlikely as fuck, but it happened and I...

It's everything.

She squeals, wrapping her arms around my neck and squeezing. Her whole body hugs me like she's been waiting for this moment just as much as I have. And right then, everything else disappears.

Georgia steps in, still crying, and wraps herself around both of us.

We stay like that for a long time. A family, held together by dirt-stained hands, wildflowers, and a single, life-altering word.

CHAPTER FORTY SIX

Georgia

COWGIRL IN CRISIS

I DON'T REMEMBER TURNING off the ignition. Don't remember kicking off my heels or unlocking the front door. But I must've done all three, because I'm inside now, still fully dressed, work bag clutched to my chest like it'll help me breathe.

Kade's house smells like home and the reality of that's like a sucker punch to my already aching chest.

Ignoring the pain, I walk straight into the living room and collapse onto the comfy couch I've spent weeks—longer, even, cuddling on with the two people who feel a hell of a lot like my family.

My bag clatters to the floor along with my sanity. Holding my breath, I listen to the sounds of the house, waiting for Aurora's adorable squeals or heartbreaking cries. I wait for Kade's heavy steps or his rough voice calling out to see if I'm home.

When nothing but silence greets me, I crumble. The tears start before I even register the sob that rips out of me. I clutch one of the throw pillows to my chest, the rough linen scraping my cheek, and I finally release the sob that's been building all day.

My chest heaves. My throat aches. My hands shake so hard I have to dig them into the seams of the pillow just to keep from unraveling further.

It wasn't supposed to go this way.

I fought.

God, I fought.

Tessa's case landed on my desk three months ago—a fifteen-year-old with chronic truancy reports and red flags all over her file.

But the first time I met her… when I stood in that filthy living room with its dim lights and fridge humming like a dying animal, I knew the truth didn't live in the papers. It lived in her eyes. In the way she stood in front of her much younger siblings, protecting them from a threat like she'd been doing it her whole life.

She wasn't skipping school to party or get high. She was *working*.

A baby herself, babysitting and waitressing. Scrubbing houses for neighbors just to keep the power on. Their mom, recently divorced and drowning in bills, was barely holding on. Three jobs, no support or family, an MIA ex.

But she was trying.

That's why I did all I could to keep them together. They weren't eating out at fancy restaurants, but they were fed. Weren't thriving, but not cold or injured or abused.

They were loved, just struggling.

They were getting by *together*.

And now they're not.

Today, I went to do a wellness check and the door creaked open like it hadn't been locked in days. The kids were in the living room, curled up together on the couch, eating crackers straight from a box because it was the only thing left.

The cabinets and fridge were empty. The power was off.

And Tessa… beautiful, brave Tessa, ran into my arms and sobbed against my chest, all her prickly walls and protective instincts drained dry. I did all I could to soothe her, and when she could finally breathe again, she admitted hadn't seen her mom in almost a week.

I stayed calm and professional and kind the whole way through. I didn't break. Not even when the smallest one, the six-year-old, Morgan, asked me if I knew when Mommy was coming back.

And then I called the cops, because I had to.

By the time the cruiser pulled up, all three kids were crying, clinging to each other like they already knew what was coming. Tessa begged me not to let them go. She held onto her brother and sister so tight I thought her arms might snap.

I told her I was sorry, because what else can you say?

They ignored me, too busy screaming while strapped into an SUV by another social worker. Strapped into a system I know too well. One that chews up kids like them and spits them out in pieces.

Just like me.

When I climbed into my car, it was with my finger hovering over Abby's number and my car pointed toward home—*my home.*

I don't remember driving to Kade's, or if I ever called my best friend.

I just remember Dean's tiny voice asking if his mom had sent me to get them. I remember Morgan asking if I brought more groceries. I remember Tessa's eyes, broken and resigned.

And now…

Now I can't *breathe.*

A sob punches its way out of my chest again, sharper this time.

In the distance, a door creaks and then boots are thudding across the wood floor, picking up speed as they near.

"Freckles—hey—hey, baby," Kade says, crouching down in front of me, voice tight with panic. "What's wrong? Are you hurt? Are you sick? Talk to me—please, Georgia, what happened?"

I can't.

I just shake my head, shoulders jerking as I try to swallow the sound that won't stay down.

His hands hover for a second, then land on my face, warm and steady. One brushes back my hair gently, thumb skimming along my cheek where tears have already soaked in.

He drops to his knees fully, sitting back on his heels, like he's trying to get smaller for me. Trying to make room for me to fall apart.

"C'mere," he says softly, and I fold, unable to hold myself up anymore.

I fall forward, into his chest, into his arms, into *him,* and he catches me like he always does.

His arms wrap tight around me, one hand cradling the back of my head as he pulls me close. He doesn't rush me for answers, just rocks me gently, grounding me with his body and scent and soft coos to *breathe.*

"I've got you, baby," he murmurs. "Whatever it is, I've got you."

I only sob harder.

He doesn't flinch. Just keeps holding me. One hand rubs slow circles over my spine. The other threads through my hair, soothing without pressure. I feel him press a kiss to my temple, then one to my forehead, my cheek, my jaw, my tears.

Eventually, my breathing evens out enough to whisper, "Sorry. Really bad day at work."

"Don't apologize," he roughs out. "Wanna talk about it?"

"No," I choke out. "Really don't."

"That's okay, too." He leans back to look at me, brows drawn. "What can I do? How can I help?"

I shake my head, chest hollow, vision blurry.

There's no fixing this. No solution I can come up with. Not just for Tessa and her family, but for this… this… *ache* inside me. No miracle cure for the pain that comes from knowing I wasn't enough today. That something was bigger than what I could control with my two hands.

I just stare at him. At his wide shoulders and steady care. At the quiet strength I want to crawl into and live inside. The safety I don't know what I'd do without.

Somewhere along the way, Kade has become my home. It's as terrifying as it is real.

"Just…" I swallow, shrugging helplessly. "Help me forget." Licking my dry lips, I rasp, "*Please.*"

His brow furrows. "Baby…"

"I don't want to think about it anymore," I whisper, voice raw and desperate. "Please, Kade."

He hesitates, but he doesn't leave or judge me. Doesn't tell me it's a fucked-up way to cope. And maybe it is. Maybe I should be doing yoga or… I don't know, praying for healing.

But neither of those things are me, and neither of them will make my brain turn off or my body stop bending under the pressure sinking in around me.

Being with him, though… Losing myself in all that is Kade Archer… Losing myself in his *love*—love he hasn't spoken out loud but shows me quietly every day with his mouth and body and unspoken promises…

That heals me.

So I kiss him, laying all the things I can't say in the space between us.

I slam my lips to his and climb into his lap in the same breath, straddling his thighs and grabbing handfuls of his hair like he's the only thing keeping me tethered. I feel his hands catch my waist on instinct, steadying me.

"Georgia—" he murmurs against my lips, but he doesn't stop kissing me.

"Please," I beg, pulling back just long enough to breathe the words into his mouth. "I need to feel something else. Anything but this. I need to feel you."

Need you to love me the only way you can.

He nods against my mouth, breath ragged, then slips one arm under my thighs and the other behind my back, lifting me with ease. I bury my face in his neck as he carries me toward his bedroom, each step silent except for the pounding in my chest.

"Where's Rory?"

He passes the nursery door, shifting me enough to tug it closed. "Asleep. So you'll have to be quiet," he murmurs. "Can you do that? Can you be my good girl and stay quiet?"

I nod fast, heart thudding, throat dry.

He steps into the bedroom and shuts the door with a quiet click before lowering me slowly to the floor, letting my body slide down his. I can feel every muscle, every ridge, every inch of him against me.

His eyes rake over my body as I steady myself, and his throat bobs with a heavy swallow. "God, you're beautiful, baby."

My chest rises and falls too fast and I clench my hands in front of me, suddenly nervous under his watchful gaze. "What… what do you want me to do?"

He doesn't move, just stares for a long time before finally murmuring, "Strip."

A shiver races down my spine. I swallow hard and slip the blazer off my shoulders, letting it drop to the floor. My hands tremble as I yank my tank top over my head and reach behind me for the clasp of my bra. It falls next.

I go to kick off my heels.

"Uh-uh." He shakes his head, voice like gravel. "Keep those heels on. I want you just like this. Wrecked. Wild-eyed. Covered in freckles."

He drags his tongue over his bottom lip, pupils blown.

"*Mine.*"

I whimper, knees weak, and slide my wide-legged pants down my hips. My thong follows, pooling at my feet until I'm left in nothing but heels and the racing beat of my heart.

Kade's jaw flexes. He adjusts himself through the front of his sweats, eyes locked on my body like he's starving.

"Just missing one thing."

He turns, crossing to the closet.

I don't know what I expect, but when he comes back, my breath catches.

He's holding one of his cowboy hats, a black Stetson saved for fancy occasions. The one he wore the day of the mediation hearing.

God, that feels like forever ago.

My throat works around a painful swallow, but I stay still, letting him lead this. *Needing* him to lead this.

He steps close, drops the hat gently onto my head, then steps back again, groaning deep in his chest.

"Fuckin' hell, darlin'. Look at you. Wearin' nothin' but my hat and those sky-high heels I've fantasized about since the day I met you."

"You have?" I breathe, shivering.

He nods slowly, slipping his sweats down until he's in nothing but his boxer briefs. His cock strains against the fabric.

"Couldn't stop thinkin' about bendin' you over that shitty couch and eatin' your sweet cunt from behind while you looked just like this..."

"In your hat?" I ask, throat tight, pussy clenching around nothing.

"My hat, your heels. Little of my country, poured all over your sexy city girl ass" he mutters, palming himself, lips wet. "Sit on the bed. Feet up. Spread those pretty legs for me."

My body obeys before I can think. I climb onto the mattress, spine brushing the headboard, and part my thighs.

He closes the distance, standing just to my right and peers between my legs, catching sight of something I'm sure is truly indecent.

"Soaked," he breathes. "Wanna watch you touch yourself."

Heat floods my cheeks as I trail my fingers down and swirl them between my legs, already trembling.

"That's it. Rub slow. Wanna see how pretty you fall apart for me."

I moan softly, hips rolling and slip a finger inside myself, then two, already shivering at the pleasure that rockets through my system.

"Goddamn," he rasps, his heavy cock twitching against the fabric. "That's sexy as hell."

"Can I watch you, too?" I whimper, throat dry. "Please, Kade?"

He curses but yanks his boxers down and wraps a hand around his cock, stroking slowly.

It's long and thick, the tip already a deep shade of red. I know there's a vein just beneath his shaft that throbs and pulses when he's this hard and the thought makes me even more turned on.

"Fuck, Georgia. Look what you do to me." He fists himself harder, pre-cum glistening at the tip. I rub tight circles on my clit, my body rocking with need, watching him unravel for me.

"Keep goin'. That's it, baby. Fuck that pretty pussy till you come. I wanna see it. Wanna hear you cry out for me."

I whimper, wetness coating my fingers, hips twitching, thighs shaking. Biting my lip hard, I reach up and cup my breast, playing with my nipples while I watch his strokes pick up pace.

The sinful sound of our movements, our heavy breaths, fills the air, and I shiver at how hot it is. I've never done the things I've done with Kade. Never stepped outside the tiny box I put sex inside of.

With him, everything is new, and sexy, and fun. Maybe that's why I'm always so ready for him, always wanting more.

But this…

There's something so utterly erotic about watching your partner masturbate while they watch you.

"You close?" he growls, reaching out to squeeze his balls roughly.

I nod rapidly, throat bobbing. "Are you?"

"Don't worry about me, darlin'."

"But…"

"Come, Georgia," he demands, cutting me off. "Come for me."

My body bows, and I cry out as the orgasm slams into me so hard and fast, I gasp his name with a loud, accidental shout.

I've barely taken a breath before he drops to his knees on the bed and grabs my thighs. "Kade—"

"Shh," he murmurs, licking a long, slow stripe over me. I twitch hard, oversensitive.

"Gotta stay quiet, baby," he warns, peering up at me from between my trembling thighs. "Or I'll stop."

When I bob my head in agreement, he does something wild and intense with his tongue and I cry out again.

"Cover your mouth, Georgia," he quietly barks, pausing until I obey. "That's my girl," he praises, slipping a finger inside me. "Fuckin' soaked. Like always. Soaked and filthy and beggin'. Perfect."

And then he's eating me like he's just as starved as I am. His fingers are thick and perfect, his mouth every woman's dream, and it undoes me faster than should be possible.

On the verge of another orgasm, I drop my hand and arch my back, scrambling for his hair, his shoulders, anything. "Kade! Please, ple—"

He pulls away.

"No," I gasp, eyes snapping open, head shaking in outrage. "No, no, I'm so—"

"I told you," he grunts, glaring up at me. "Told you I'd stop if you couldn't behave."

"I hate you," I hiss, smacking the bed in frustration.

He just laughs darkly and climbs from the bed, leaving me spread open, dripping and empty. When he returns a second later, there's something balled up in his hands but it's not until he's squeezing my jaw and dangling the scrap of lace that I understand his intentions.

"Open up, baby."

Eyes narrowed, pussy too angry and keyed up to care, I do what he says, sticking out my tongue.

He groans, stuffing the panties between my lips.

"Can't have you wakin' Aurora while you're screamin' for the man you claim to hate to fuck you harder." He kisses my nose. "Be a good girl and bite down for me, baby."

I do.

He rewards me instantly—mouth on my skin, worshipping his way down my body. Then I'm tossed further up the bed, breathless and wild. His hat tumbles off, but we both ignore it.

"You wanna forget?" he drawls, pinching my nipples. "Hands on the headboard. Don't let go."

I do as I'm told, and he devours me.

Again and again.

By the time he's done, my body's shaking, coated in sweat, spent and ruined.

He climbs up next to me, pulls the panties from my mouth, and cups my cheek with a smirk.

"Ride me, cowgirl. Swing that fuckin' hat around and make me come."

I giggle, breath hitching, and crawl onto his lap, snagging his discarded hat and tugging it on. My thighs burn as I lower myself onto him slowly, and we both shiver at the contact.

His head falls back with a groan. "Jesus Christ."

"Be quiet, or I'll have to stop," I breathlessly threaten as I grind down. "Don't make me stuff panties in your mouth, sunshine."

"Do it," he whispers, hands tightening around my hips.

I smile slowly, shaking my head. "Can't. Love your dirty mouth too much. Makes me come every time."

"Fuck, baby," he groans, dragging me down and sucking my nipple into his mouth. "You're gonna kill me."

"Well," I pant, rolling my hips, playfulness and lust replacing the chasm of sadness from before, "don't die before you fill me up."

He freezes—eyes going molten—and bites down gently on my nipple.

"You like that?" he rasps. "Like being filled up and leaking with my cum?"

I shrug, shameless. "I shouldn't. But I do. I love it. It's so hot."

"*Fuck*, Georgia." He flips me beneath him like he's lost control, slamming inside with one hard thrust. "Shouldn't have fuckin' told me that."

"Why?" I cry out against my palm.

"Because now you'll never get rid of me."

Good, because I don't want to.

His thumb finds my clit, and my body arches off the bed, my climax ripping through me, a scream trapped in my throat.

Two more thrusts and he follows, groaning my name as he spills deep, pressing his hips flush to mine.

I collapse, limp and boneless.

He slips out with a groan but doesn't stop—fingers replacing his cock, holding everything inside.

"What are you doing?" I pant. "I'm done."

"Fuck no you're not. He grins, eyes full of fire. "You wanted to forget, darlin'. I'm not stoppin' till you've lost your damn mind."

Chapter Forty Seven

Georgia

His Name, Her Words, My Undoing

I'm practically running across the pasture, heels in hand, wind knotting my curls, the final Honey Bea Bash meeting still buzzing in my chest.

We're two weeks out from the event and everything's falling into place—no, *soaring* into place.

Everyone's locked in. Vendors are confirmed. The Honey Bea products we'll be selling are labeled and ready to go. Kade, Ridge, Hazel, and all the farm hands managed to keep the fields gorgeous despite everything that's happened, and the west meadow is a rainbow right now.

This week alone, we finished organizing flower cutting stations for guests, scheduled back-to-back meet-the-animal tours, and set up a tasting tent near the front gate where Bea will personally walk people through every single variation of Archer honey—wildflower, alfalfa, orange blossom, clover.

There'll be food trucks from Wildwood, music from that Langley bluegrass band everyone loves, pop-up booths from just about every local shop I could talk into showing up.

The twins are running a face painting booth and Hazel's organized horse rides. And tucked into the middle of it all, the *real surprise*—Aurora's first birthday bash, built into the main event.

I ordered her a confetti cake, decorations, and the sweetest little crown I could find on Etsy. Everything's bee themed, including our matching dresses, which is insanely stupid on my part, but I can't find it in me to care anymore. Of course, she has no idea, but it'll mean something big to Kade.

Sort of hope he cries.

Grinning, I skid up the porch steps, already unbuttoning my blazer. My cheeks are flushed from the run and the fact that, for once, things feel... *good*.

Like mine. Like I belong here.

The moment I hit the bedroom; I head straight for the dresser, his dresser, and open the second drawer without thinking. My clothes are folded neatly inside. A mix of farm gear, soft tees, and a few pairs of my favorite jeans.

I slip into a tank and one of the Archer Farm tees Bea gave me, then pull on jeans and boots before tucking my work clothes into the hamper. It's weird. I don't even pause anymore. I sleep here every single night. Between Bash planning and life with Kade and Aurora, it's just easier to crash at his place.

Besides, being here feels as easy as breathing.

Bea's expecting me at the main house to show me how to harvest honey—something I've been weirdly excited about for weeks. There's a whole art to it. The frames, the uncapping, the spinner. I've watched countless videos so I can impress her, but really, I'm just happy to spend time with Kade's mom.

But first, I need my checklist.

I jog into the kitchen, scanning the counter, the table, the messy coffee table. No sign of it, so I start opening drawers.

"Where did I put you?" I murmur, tugging through the silverware tray, a pile of notepads, rubber bands, and tiny Post-its that say things like *"Georgia's gluten-free"* and *"DO NOT FEED HER THIS OR SHE'LL DIE"* in Kade's handwriting.

The corner of my mouth tips up and a chuckle slips free.

Sweet, over the top, wonderful man.

God, I love him so much.

Spinning, brows furrowed, I move to the living room.

My cardigan's draped across the back of the couch next to Aurora's. My sneakers are by the front door, between one of Aurora's sandals and Kade's mud-crusted boots. Gluten-free flour is still on the counter from the waffles I made this morning beside her sippy cup and a plate I forgot to rinse.

My chest tightens and I freeze.

There's a mug beside the sink—*mine*. A scrunchy on the doorknob. Robin's quilt I brought from my place is tossed over the arm of the couch, now part of our nightly movie routine.

Signs of me are… *everywhere*.

My heart skips, then twists. And not in a sweet way.

In a spinning room, can't catch your breath, you've let it happen again kind of way.

Day by day, he said.

And day by day, I fell. Deeper and further into the kind of life I never believed was meant for me.

I haven't told him I love him.

And he hasn't told me, either.

For all his *you're mine* and *stay with me*. His *this is our home*, and *I hope you get knocked up*…he hasn't said *I love you*.

Not once.

And maybe I didn't realize how much I needed that until now. Until I'm standing in the middle of this kitchen that feels more like mine than my actual apartment and realizing we skipped a few steps.

We got lost in kisses and laughter and Sunday breakfasts and sex so good it makes me forget my name—but I don't know what any of it means if the one thing that proves he's different never made it out of his mouth.

I squeeze my eyes shut and shake my head, forcing the thoughts out.

No. That's old wiring talking. Old pain. Old patterns.

But still… it simmers.

I walk toward the entry table, needing to find that list, needing anything to anchor myself again instead of the emotions clawing at my insides.

The stack of mail is thick and untouched, most of it ads or junk.

I sigh, grimacing. Damn, we really have been swamped, haven't we?

A large manila envelope slips free from the pile and lands on the floor with a soft thud.

I lean down and pick it up, flipping it over—and my heart stutters.

Kade Archer

Regarding: Aurora Grace Vernal-Parker

Holy shit.

It has to be about the adoption. We've been waiting for this for weeks. Kade's been lowkey panicking, trying to hide it behind his usual gruff, steady front, but I know him. He's been bracing himself for bad news. I tried to reassure him. These things take time. Processing backlogs, courthouse delays. It's normal. But this…

Bet it's been sitting here this whole time.

I drop my phone and keys on the table and rip open the seal, already picturing how I'll tell him. I bought Aurora a tiny T-shirt that says *Officially an Archer* the day we submitted the paperwork, but it might be too snug now—she's grown so fast.

The Honey Bea Bash will be perfect. I'll announce it there. A family surprise. He'll cry. I'll cry. It'll be beautiful.

I pull the papers out of the envelope, smile stretching wide—

Then faltering.

It's not from the court. It's from the Vernal's probate attorney. A sticky note is slapped to the top in the same messy handwriting I sifted through those first few weeks.

Sorry, I was out of state. This got lost in the chaos and I found it in my paperwork when I returned. Hope it clears things up. Good luck.

My mouth pulls tight. Fuck this guy.

He's been a disaster since day one—late emails, missed forms and a vacation that dragged on way too damn long.

I peel off the note and start flipping through the paperwork, confusion bubbling.

It's not a ruling. It's a copy of the will. And a letter. A letter addressed to Kade.

I skim the heading, the first few lines, my pulse rising. Then I see the signature and my heart drops. My gaze flies to the door, hands shaking, eyes blurring. I know I shouldn't read it. Know this isn't mine.

But… how can I not?

It's from *her.*

My stomach churns, fingers curling tightly around the page.

My legs barely hold me as I move to the couch and drop into the cushions, the letter trembling in my grip. I swallow hard and tell myself whatever's in here won't change anything.

But I've always been a great liar.

Especially to myself.

Chapter Forty Eight

My sweet Kade,

If you're reading this, then I'm gone, either by my own hand, or his. Maybe both.

He and I have always been a tragedy waiting to happen.

And I wish I could say I'm sorry in a way that matters. But we both know I was never good at saying the right things. Never good at doing the right things either.

Especially when it came to you.

You were always the good one. The safe one. The one who held steady when I spun out.

And I did spin out, didn't I? God, I was such a mess. So young. So loud. So desperate for more. Such a fuck-up.

But you loved me anyway. You held on when anyone else would've let go. You believed in me, even when I made it impossible. Sometimes I hated you for that. Because no one had ever looked at me like I was worth saving... not until you.

And still, I ran.

See? A fuck-up.

Not because I stopped loving you. I did love you. Maybe too much. But I wasn't built for the life you offered. The porch swing and the picket fence. The promises and a house full of babies.

God, I never even wanted kids. How messed up is that?

I tried to be that girl. Really, I did. But the storm inside me never went quiet. And you... you craved peace.

I wanted anything but stillness. I thought I could outrun the wreckage in my chest. Thought someone like me could start over clean.

Then I met him.

Jonathan didn't ask me to be soft, or good, or whole. He didn't expect anything at all... just control. And it didn't start that way, of course. It never does. At first, he made me feel seen without needing to be better.

But that kind of love... it has teeth.

He was cruel, Kade. Not just to me. But when he was, I let it happen. Because by then, I was already drinking to cope. Already screaming to be heard. Already too broken to come back to you, even if I wanted to.

It got dark. And I wasn't just surviving him. I was surviving me.

There were nights I'd look in the mirror and barely recognize myself. Nights I couldn't control my anger. Nights I scared myself. But he pushed me there. He made me that way. He chipped away until all that was left was the worst in me... and even then, he told me that was my fault, too.

And I believed him.

Maybe that's the worst part.

When the baby came, I thought I'd be different. But I wasn't. There were days I couldn't look at her without thinking of everything I lost. Everything I gave up. And there were nights I heard her crying and couldn't move. Couldn't feel anything but regret and rage and exhaustion.

I hated her, and then I hated him for making me, and myself for letting it happen.

And sometimes, I hated you.

She deserved more, and more is all you ever gave me. So I'm giving you her.

Because even after everything, you were still the only man I trusted to love without demanding I be someone I couldn't. You were the only one who ever stayed.

And I need you to stay again.

You gave me everything once. Your heart. Your faith. Your money.

And I gave you lies.

But I never meant to hurt you. I just didn't know how to be loved the way you loved me. I didn't know how to receive something I was never taught to give.

If I had more time... maybe I could've figured it out. But I don't. So I'm giving you the only thing I have left that matters.

Our daughter.

And yes, I'll call her that, even if I didn't carry her with you. Because I will never claim that man as her father. She was never his. She was always meant to be yours.

We were soulmates, remember?

I was your one and only. The girl you swore forever to under that old tree behind your parents' house... the one you carved our initials into like it made us indestructible.

You made big promises, Kade.

You used to look at me like I was your whole damn future. Said you'd never stop loving me. Even if I ran. Even if I broke things. Even if I hurt you. You said I'd always be it for you.

And maybe... maybe I always believed that. Even when I walked away. Even when I married someone else. Because deep down, I thought that if things ever really fell apart... you'd come.

You always came for me before.

Why didn't you come for me this time?

When I found out I was pregnant, I was angry. I didn't want her. Didn't want to be trapped again. I felt caged and used and tired. But then I thought of you. Your loyalty. Your steadiness. The way you love with your whole chest, your whole heart, no questions asked.

And I knew... there was no one else I could hand her to.

You were supposed to be the constant. You always were for me. So I figured... maybe you still meant every word you said. That no matter how messy it got, you'd still see me.

Still choose us.

Because no matter how it ended... no matter how many lies or bruises or years came between us... I was yours. And you were mine. Four years in. Together forever.

You owed me forever, Kade Archer. And all I got was a happily never after.

So take her. Love her like you loved me. Give her the life I never could. And maybe one day, when she's old enough, you'll tell her that her mother wasn't always broken.

That people made her this way.

That once upon a time, she loved a boy so much she gave him everything she had...

Love always,
Your Marlee May

CHAPTER FORTY NINE

THE SILENCE BETWEEN I LOVE YOU

AURORA BABBLES AGAINST MY chest, her cheek sticky with sweat and sun-shine, and I hum the next verse of her favorite song while adjusting her carrier like it's all second nature.

We've just finished feeding the goats, and her little body is heavy against my tired muscles, but she smells like hay and applesauce, and the lotion Georgia rubs on her after every bath, so I don't give a damn.

"Don't tell your mama," I murmur into the top of her head, "but you're my favorite helper."

She lets out a squeal and thumps a tiny palm against my sternum like she knows she's hilarious.

I chuckle and keep walking toward the house, the gravel crunching beneath my boots.

"Think Mama's gonna love this weekend?" I ask her, already picturing Georgia's face when we pull up to the cabin by the lake. "It's quiet out there. Real quiet. Just the trees and the water. No work. No phones. Just us."

Aurora gurgles something close to "Mmm-hmm," and I grin.

"She's been workin' herself to the bone for this Bash. Wanna give her a reason to exhale. She deserves, don't you think, baby girl?"

The wind kicks up, brushing the sweat from my neck, and I pull Aurora in tighter.

"I've been thinkin' about finally telling her," I murmur, using my daughter as my sounding board like always. Everything I read says it'll help her language skills. "About her family. The stuff I found out. Thought about holdin' onto it a while longer, but… she deserves to know. She deserves the choice, at the very least."

She shifts against my chest, eyes fluttering sleepily, and I rub her back gently.

"But more than that, I need to tell her I love her." I swallow hard. "It's killin' me to keep it in. I almost say it a hundred times a day. I'm scared to scare her, but damn, sweetheart, how can I not when you two take up my whole heart?"

Aurora tangles her dirty hands in my beard and suckles on air so I slip her pacifier from the pocket of my vest and plop it in her mouth. She latches on and stares up at me with wide, alert eyes, suddenly catching a second wind.

"I love your mama," I whisper. "So fuckin' much it hurts. And I know I should've told her sooner, but I didn't wanna scare her off. She's got this way of runnin' when things get real. But lately… things have been right. She's ours. We're hers. This is it."

The house comes into view in the distance, warm and familiar in the late afternoon light. I catch sight of Georgia's jeep and feel my chest expand.

"Harvest season's nearly here," I mutter, mind flicking through chores I need to take care of. "Already called a guy to price out an outdoor decontamination station so I don't track wheat into the house. Don't want her breathing any of that in."

Aurora smacks my cheek and screams, the sound barely muffled by the paci, and I chuckle.

"I agree. It's not good for her. Been thinking about booking her a hotel for a week or two just to be safe." Another scream and I nod, patting her back. "I know she still has her place, but after we went to grab stuff a few weeks back…"

I shake my head.

"Nah. I hate it. That place is too far out. Feels like a ghost town. She didn't say it, but I could see it in her eyes. She's scared out there in the middle of nowhere. Used it as an excuse to tell her she should just move in."

Aurora babbles again and I grimace.

"I know, I should have gone about it differently, but I can't help it."

Another hard yank.

"Yeah, baby girl." I sigh. "But I love your mama, and there's not a damn thing I wouldn't do for her."

I pull my phone out of my pocket and tap the screen, lifting it so Aurora can see the lock screen photo—Georgia holding Rory in the flower field, grinning up at me with that sun-bright smile and wild curls spilling in every direction.

I tug the pacifier free and pause mid-step.

"Can you say it, sweetheart? Say *Mama*. Mama."

"Mmmmmmm," she tries, drooling all over herself while smashing a fist against my phone.

I laugh and tickle her side, kissing her dimpled cheek. "That's right. Mama."

Gravel crunches beneath my boots as I hit my long driveway, and I start mentally cataloguing all the things I still need to do this week before we leave.

The flower harvest is nearly wrapped. Sales are lookin' solid this year—bouquet orders from Serenity Falls and even a few wedding clients lined up. The honey's almost gone already, even with Mom stashing boxes for the Bash. The wheat'll be ready in a few weeks, and I've got extra hands lined up for the heavy lifting, but it's gonna be tight.

When I reach the house, my brows furrow. Georgia's Jeep is parked in the drive like always, but the passenger door's open. I jog the last few steps and shake my head, smiling.

"Frazzled little tornado," I mutter, moving to close it.

But when I reach it, I go still.

Piled inside are clothes. Not just a bag or some spare laundry, but all her shit.

Shoes. Her laptop. That green dress she wore to Sunday dinner last week. The one that had me damn near feral all night.

I grip the side of the car as my stomach flips violently.

"Comin' or goin'?" I rasp, mind spinning violently.

But I already know.

The front door creaks open behind me, and a suitcase hits the ground behind her. A pained groan catches in my throat, knees going weak.

Her head jerks up and she freezes.

Georgia's hair's a mess. Face blotchy and red. Shoulders hunched like she's carrying the weight of the world and losing. And even like this, wrecked and breaking, she's the most beautiful thing I've ever seen.

And I can't fucking *breathe.*

"No." The word snaps from my throat like it's been lit on fire. "*No.*"

She startles like I've struck her and tears her eyes away, bolting down the steps. Her hand grips the suitcase handle like it's the only thing holding her together, but she doesn't speak or pause or fuckin' look at me.

"Georgia," I bark, heart hammering so hard, Aurora stirs. "Stop. What the hell are you doing?"

Why won't she look at me?

"Please," she finally chokes. "Please just let me go."

"No," I snap again, louder, and my voice cracks. "You don't get to just walk out on us."

Aurora shifts against me, confused, and my hands are trembling so badly I can barely comfort her.

"I never should've stayed so long," she says, voice high and shaking. "I knew better. I knew better. *I knew better.*"

"Stop," I beg, chasing after her. "Talk to me. What the fuck is going on?"

She's trying to pull away from me now, but I reach out, gripping her shoulders, desperate and breaking alongside her.

"Please," she sobs, whipping her head back and forth. "Just let me—"

"*I said no!*"

The sharpness of it slices through the air like thunder.

Aurora startles in the carrier, letting out a terrified whimper. I look down and she's staring up at me with wide, scared eyes, her mouth puckered and trembling.

My stomach drops to the fucking ground.

"No," I whisper, breaking instantly. "No, no, baby girl. I'm sorry." I press my lips to her forehead, heart shattering. "I'm so sorry. I'm not mad. I'm not mad, sweetheart."

Georgia makes a noise between a sob and a pained moan. Her hand twitches like she wants to reach for Aurora but can't.

"She was right," she chokes out. "You're so good for her."

"Georgia," I rasp, bouncing Aurora, hand rubbing her back gently. "Baby. What happened? What are you talkin' about? Who?"

She shakes her head, eyes locked on Aurora like she's drowning in her own guilt.

"I fucked up," she says, voice cracking. "I read the letter. And I shouldn't have. I shouldn't have. Because all it did was prove me right."

My heart goes still. "What letter?"

"The letter from Marlee," she whispers, tipping her chin at our daughter. "Her mom."

What the fuck is she talking about?

My vision tunnels then sways before zeroing back in on her. It's always on her. On them. My world.

And right now, it's shattering.

"You're her mama," I finally force out. Swallowing hard, I grab her hand and place it against Aurora's cheek. "You, freckles. You are her mama now. It's us. You, me, Rory. We're a family."

"But we're not," she says, smoothing Aurora's curls like she's memorizing them. "I want it so bad, but it'll never be me. Every time you look at her, you'll see her real mom. You'll see the woman who came first. The one you built this house for. The one with her eyes and her smile and her laugh. The one with the initials in a tree. Your forever and always."

She yanks her hand away and steps back, voice breaking.

"And I'll just be the shadow who tried to take her place."

"Georgia…"

How did I fuck this up so badly? And how the hell did Marlee get to her from the fuckin' grave?

"I would've stayed, you know," she whispers, meeting my gaze with tears so heavy, she doesn't bother erasing them. "I would've stayed forever. But you never said it. Not once. Not when I was sick. Not when I crawled into your bed. Not when I was holding your daughter. Not even when I told you I wanted to stay."

She laughs bitterly, breath hitching.

"All this time, I thought I was the one too scared to love. But it was you. It's always been you because you've—" Her voice catches on a sob I feel right down to my fucking bones. "Because you've always been *hers*."

"No," I grunt, body trembling, head shaking rapidly. "No, baby. I'm not. Never was. Not like this. Not like you."

But she's already turning, dragging the suitcase, climbing into her car and panic turns to something cold and sharp and burning all at once. I throw myself forward, legs damn near buckling beneath me.

"I do love you," I choke out, blinking through tears. "God, Georgia, I've loved you since the moment you stole my fuckin' hat and rode into the sunset. Baby, I've loved you this whole damn time. I was just… scared you'd run the second I said it. But I love you. I do. I love you. *I love you.*"

She's sobbing, yanking on her hair, but her Jeep starts anyway. She looks fuckin' terrified and broken and so small in big SUV and my panic about her leaving me bleeds into something else.

"Darlin', stop!" I shout. "Stop! Stay! Don't you dare drive right now!"

Georgia pauses for a minute, hands tight around the wheel, and for a few breaths, I think she might stay. Think she might choose me. Us.

But then she exhales roughly and glances at me through the window, eyes soaked with tears, expression so cold, it guts me.

The mask is back. The one I painstakingly disassembled, brick by fucking brick. It's back, and she's running. Just like I knew she would.

"Day by day, Kade. That's what you said…" Her brows tighten in pain. "That's all you said."

I stagger.

She swallows hard, her eyes locked on our daughter.

"The days are up. And the dream?" She closes her eyes and puts the Jeep in drive. "It was never meant to be mine."

And then she's gone.

And so is the sun.

"Mama," Aurora whimpers, ripping the air right from my fuckin' lungs.

My knees hit the ground a second later, and when my daughter's first tear falls, I break right along with her.

And this time? I don't think I'll ever get back up.

CHAPTER FIFTY

THE DOWNPOUR KNEW HER NAME

IT'S BEEN A WEEK.

A full fuckin' week since she walked away from me, suitcase in hand, tears down her face, and my daughter between us—blinking up at the two people who were supposed to make her feel safe.

Now, I sit on the back porch, boots planted on the creaking wood, the monitor balanced beside me like some kind of leash I can't let go of. Aurora's out for the night after a long day with my sisters and Mom, while I finished up maintenance on the east irrigation line and pretended I was fine.

I'm not.

I'm not fuckin' fine.

Don't think I ever will be again.

My beard's grown wild. My clothes haven't matched in days. I haven't shaved, haven't eaten a full meal that didn't involve one of her protein bars or something left over from Rory's tray. I look like hell and feel worse.

The sky's gone dark, swollen clouds pushing low, heavy with rain. A storm's coming. I can feel it in my bones—every old break and scar aching under the pressure of it.

And still, none of that hurts half as much as missing her.

I haven't heard a word. Not a call. Not a text. Not even a *"go to hell."*

Just silence.

I've called her. Left messages. A dozen voicemails where I start to say something and end up muttering nothing. I've sat on this porch every night since, watching the horizon like she might come back on foot, dust in her wake, suitcase in one hand and forgiveness in the other.

But she hasn't.

And I don't blame her.

Because I read the letter.

And fuck me, but God, *fuck Marlee* for writing it.

That woman always did know how to twist the knife and make it look like love. That damn thing was wrapped in guilt and tied in ribbons of nostalgia. It was her voice, sweet and aching, but I know better now. Every word was soaked in manipulation.

She made herself the martyr. Made me the boy who could've been enough if only he'd been bigger, richer, better. She tried to rewrite history like I hadn't sent her every paycheck while she played house with a man who raised his hand to her and let Aurora suffer in silence.

But no, Marlee always wanted tragedy. It made her feel important.

And now Georgia's gone because of her.

Because of that letter.

Because of the bullshit Marlee wrote from the grave, where she gets to play the victim one more time and leave me to clean up the wreckage.

Worst part was the way she talked about her own flesh and blood. Not once did she say Aurora's name or speak about her like she was more than a burden or pawn.

After the first time I read it, I threw up in the sink.

Then I forced myself to read it again and again until I could see what Georgia saw. See past what I know to be the truth and picture shit from her eyes.

Eyes that don't know reality because I never opened my goddamn mouth and gave it to her.

All I wanted was to protect her from something ugly when she's already lived enough of it, but by doing so, I kept her in the dark, the last place she ever should have been.

The screen door creaks and closes behind me, and I don't look up until a cold beer lands in my palm.

"Thought you could use that," Griffin says, dropping down into the chair beside mine.

He's quiet for a minute. Just lets the silence wrap around us like he knows how close to the edge I am.

"I get it now," I murmur when the quiet starts to grate at my nerves.

"Get what?"

I tip the bottle to my lips, swallow hard. "Why my dad didn't start dreamin' big until after he met my mom."

He nods once, brow furrowing. "What do you mean?"

I stare out at the land stretching wide in front of me. "What's the point of buildin' all this if you're doin' it alone?"

Griff doesn't answer right away. He just watches me for a long beat before quietly saying, "You're not alone, though."

I scoff. "I know I've got my family."

"And a daughter," he adds.

I nod, my eyes flicking to the monitor. She's peaceful. Curled up in her crib, arms around that little bear I got her months ago that she won't sleep without. She's safe and home and mine, but still missing a piece she doesn't understand yet.

"And your friends," Griff tacks on, reaching over to squeeze my shoulder. "But that's not who I meant."

I swallow hard, my throat raw.

I can't cry anymore.

Can't break anymore.

There's nothin' left in me that hasn't already been shattered.

"She's in town," I whisper. "Somewhere close. But I've never felt so far from someone in my life."

Only know she didn't pack up and move back to New York because she's still quietly putting finishing touches on the Honey Bea Bash. From what I've gathered around town, she's doing it all from home, telling people she's really sick, but not letting up on the event.

Whole thing pisses me off and makes me want to cry all over again.

"She loves you," Griff says plainly.

"Then why'd she leave?"

"Because she's scared."

I shake my head. "We're all scared. Love is fuckin' terrifying."

He gives me a long, hard look. "Did you tell her that?"

"What?" I snap. "That love is hard? That it's messy and unfair and asks too much of you? I think she knows, man."

He tilts his head. "That you love her."

My jaw locks. I drop my gaze and chug half the beer in one go. "Too fuckin' late."

"Thought so," he mutters.

"Don't you start with the guilt trip," I grit out. "You weren't here. You didn't see her face."

"No," he says. "But I saw yours. And I've known that look on you for years. When you got that final letter from Marlee. When you lost your dad. And now."

He turns to face me, deadly serious. "You fought harder battles than this. Did you learn nothin' in the Rangers?"

"And nearly died," I snap, fingers so tight, the bottle creaks.

He shrugs, nursing his drink. "But you didn't. You lived. And for what? To bury yourself in grief, guilt, and a shitty life for years?"

"I got out of the hole I was in."

"Did you?" he asks, one brow arched.

I hate how sure he sounds.

"Are you really out of it? Because, brother, healing ain't linear. It ain't fast. It's not some checkbox on a fuckin' form. You think you're fine because the outside looks better. Because you ain't drinkin' yourself into a coma or bleedin' on foreign soil. But inside?" He taps his chest. "That takes longer. That takes work. And love? Love's part of the work."

I close my eyes, pain slicing down my spine like a blade.

"Go get your fuckin' girl."

"I can't," I croak. "She doesn't want me to."

Griff stands and yanks me to my feet for a back slapping hug.

"Then take my advice. When she comes back to you, because she will, forgive her. Remember, you ran from your problems for years, but Georgia didn't inherit her trauma. She was born into hers. It's gonna take her a minute to believe she deserves the dream."

"What dream?"

Griff smiles, slapping my back hard. "The happily ever after, man. The thing that makes all the pain worth it."

I close my eyes and pull him in again, grip tight. "When will you be back?"

"Shouldn't take more than a couple weeks to wrap up everything back in Tennessee." He passes me his still-full beer. "Then I'll be back in your business for good."

He turns for the steps, flashing a cocky wink. "Make sure she's by your side next time I see you. I miss lookin' at her perky ti—"

"Get the fuck out!" I bark, hurling my empty bottle toward him but intentionally missing by a mile. It lands on the lawn with a thud. "Get on a plane and don't come back, asshole."

He laughs all the way to his truck, flipping me off without looking back.

And then I'm alone with dark clouds that match my mood again. Minutes later, the first raindrop hits the roof. Then another.

Within seconds, the sky cracks open and the downpour starts, cool and hard and relentless.

Throat tight, I drop my beer bottle onto the railing and make my way down the steps, into the downpour. It seeps into my clothes, soaking me instantly, but I don't move, just tip my head back and breathe.

Don't know what I'm hoping for—peace, maybe closure or answers, but all I feel is the absence where she's supposed to be.

Georgia.

The woman who stole every part of me worth keeping. The woman who brought me back to life with fire and fight and freckles. The woman who made this house a home and helped me become a dad. Who laughed in the rain and told me it made the world feel new.

I remember that day—months ago, just the two of us on the back of Dusty, her body against mine, her heart in my hands.

The day I knew I loved her. Was too afraid to acknowledge it then, to realize what it all meant. The gravity of it.

"I love the rain."

"Why's that, darlin'?"

"Love the way it makes me feel."

"Wet?"

She giggled, elbowing me. "No."

"Then what?"

"I love when everything goes still, and the air smells new. When the light starts to change and, if you're lucky, a rainbow stretches across the sky like a quiet little promise. A reminder that something beautiful always shows up after the worst of it."

I stare into the dark, hoping to feel what she felt. Hoping for that promise.

But all I see is her.

All I feel is her.

And when my tears get lost in the rain streaking down my cheeks, the only person I want to kiss them away is her.

CHAPTER FIFTY ONE

WARNING: TRAUMA MAY CAUSE REGRET AND OTHER SIDE EFFECTS

THE SILENCE IS THE worst part.

Not the cold floors, or the drafty windows, or even the shower that wheezes and gasps like an asthmatic dragon just to get lukewarm.

No.

The quiet is what gets me.

For a while, this place felt like a little country sanctuary. Old, but mine. A place I'd carved out of the chaos I dove into headfirst.

I learned the quirks of it like muscle memory—the way the light switches are reversed in the hallway, the constant buzz of the old fridge, how the second drawer in the kitchen sticks if you pull too hard. Learned how to make the shitty oven work in my favor.

Now, it just feels empty and cold.

And not because I left my favorite blanket back… *there*.

I'm wrapped in the same cardigan I've been wearing for three days, half a sleeve tucked under my cheek, the rest balled up in my lap. There's a crusted-over bowl of soup I never touched on the floor, and the TV is playing reruns I've seen a hundred times but couldn't describe to anyone if they asked.

I haven't been able to eat. Not really. I tried toast from bread I'd made a while back, frozen and thawed yesterday and ended up gagging over the sink, a migraine splitting my skull wide open.

Food tastes like nothing. Coffee tastes like nothing. Everything tastes like nothing.

I feel like nothing.

I miss him.

God, I miss him.

His hands. His voice. The way he looks at me like I matter more than the air in his lungs.

But more than anything—I miss her.

Aurora.

The way she clutches her bear when she's tired. The way she says Dada like it's her favorite word in the world. The way she used to reach for me, like maybe... just maybe... I belonged to her, too.

I let my past destroy everything. Let one letter from a dead woman tear through all the progress I'd made. Through everything we build together.

A letter that at first glance, was heartbreaking.

She was everything I always thought she would be.

Loving, and tragic, and *his*.

And in that moment, I saw what I wanted to see all because I was already hanging on by threads, too terrified by the realization that Kade's home had somehow become my home. That the three of us became a family. And that the future I'd always dreamt of, the wishes I'd spent my life making, had all come true.

For months, I was living the dream. I was knee-deep in those wishes.

And I wasted it. Didn't see it. Was too scared to grab hold and never let go.

But as the days stretch into a week, and the ugly cloud of fear has dissolved into regret, I see that letter for something else entirely.

Marlee's words, syrupy and bitter, equal parts hurt and poison, have been echoing through my head all week.

And like the idiot I am, I listened to them. Let them get under my skin. Let them poke all the places I've tried to stitch closed. The old scars.

The ones that whisper, *You're not good enough. You're just a placeholder. You're always second best.*

I didn't even give Kade a chance to explain. Didn't trust the man who's done nothing but show up for me, day after day, without fail. I ran. He said he loved me, finally gave me the words on a broken rasp, and I still ran.

And now, I'm stuck in this hell of my own making.

Wrapped in the quiet and loneliness and hell I deserve.

Until a sharp knock shatters it.

I jolt upright, tissues and blankets tumbling off me in a cascade. My heart slams against my ribs.

Kade?

Oh, God.

No one else knows where I live. I never told the Archers because no one ever asked. Like they all assumed that Kade's home was my home.

I stumble to my feet, adrenaline roaring through me. In my haste, I trip over a pillow, kick an empty mug, all in an effort to shove my way toward the bathroom mirror.

Soon as I catch sight of myself, I wince and want to cry all over again.

My curls are flat and tangled, pulled back in some limp half-knot. My eyes are red and swollen, my cheeks blotchy. I'm wearing an oversized tee with a random stain on the hem and sweatpants I may have also slept in last night. Or the night before.

Probably all week.

They're both Kades, because even while running for my emotional life, I was still greedy and lovesick and obsessed. A few days ago, when I spilled on his stolen shirt, I sobbed even harder.

My eyes snag on that stain.

And I promptly start crying again.

"Open up, ginger tits! Or I'll find the nearest cowboy and break the fucking door down!"

My mouth falls open, and a fresh sob punches up my throat.

Abby.

I sprint to the door, tripping over a pair of my suitcase and a half-folded laundry basket I gave up on three days ago. I unlock the bolt with shaking hands and yank it open.

And there she is.

All five-foot-two inches of smoky-eyed, curvy perfection. Black leggings, a hoodie that says *Hex the Patriarchy,* combat boots, and an armful of chaos. In one hand, she holds a bottle of tequila. In the other—a fresh box of tissues.

Grinning, she steps aside.

Behind her sits a suitcase.

"I packed the essentials," she says with a wink. "Enough to perform either a love spell, a hate spell, or a moving-on spell." Waving the alcohol, she adds, "And the courage to pick one."

I throw myself into her arms, sobbing.

"Abby," I cry, collapsing against her like the wreck I am. "I fucked up."

She sighs, hugging me tight, her familiar perfume hitting my nose like a wrecking ball.

"I know, babe," she whispers, her chin on my shoulder. "Let's fix it."

The tequila bottle's half-empty and my heart feels the same.

I'm curled into the far corner of my sagging couch, wrapped in the softest blanket I've ever felt, wearing the new pajama set Abby brought me. It's navy with moons and stars and says *Manifest That Shit* across the chest. The irony is not lost on me. The blanket matches. So do the slippers.

I have the best friend in the world.

Abby's got her feet in my lap, her green satin robe slipping off one shoulder. Her toenails are painted black and chipped to hell, her eyeliner smudged like she's in a rock band, and her mouth is full of gluten-free tortilla chips that she's shoveling in with tequila-shot timing in mind.

"You've got crumbs in your cleavage," I mutter, voice raw from crying and drinking.

She shrugs. "Built-in snack tray."

I laugh. It's wet and pathetic, but it still counts.

She tops off both our glasses, squinting one eye shut like that helps her aim.

"When I didn't hear from you for a while, I figured you were off somewhere finally hooking up with the cowboy."

I snort but it turns into a drunken sob.

"I'm not that obvious," I cry. "Maybe I found someone else to fuck."

Abby scoffs. "Georgia, you talked about him like he was some combination of John Wayne and Jason Momoa. Of course it was obvious."

"I hate John Wayne."

She rolls her eyes and sips her drink. "No one hates John Wayne, but that's not the point."

"Then what is the point, Abby?" Sniffling hard, I give her a desperate look. "Because I don't understand it anymore. Don't understand any of this. How did I get here?"

"You fell in love, Georgia. That's how."

I nod slowly. "I really did."

She shifts her feet, drawing her knees up, voice gentler now. "And the baby? His little girl?"

"Aurora." I swallow thickly, tears pressing behind my eyes again. "She's mine."

"Wow." Abby lets out a quiet breath, smiling around the rim of her glass. "Then let's get your family back, babe."

"Oh, yeah?" I blink at her but she's all blurry. "Just like that?"

"Yeah. Just like that. I mean, we might have to sacrifice a goat and ask the stars for help, but yeah, basically."

"Don't touch the goats. They're adorable." I shake my head, a choked laugh escaping. "I don't even know what I'd say to him. I ran. I didn't trust him. I read a letter that wasn't mine and let it break me. I don't deserve to go back."

She's already heard the whole sordid tale multiple times, but I can't get past the letter. How did I get it so wrong? How could I have been so stupid? So selfish?

So blind.

Abby leans forward, pointing her lime wedge at me. "Okay first, don't ever say you don't deserve love again or I will hex your ovaries."

"Is that… a thing?"

"I'll make it a thing."

My brows furrow. "Hex them in what way? Like never have kids, because that's awful, Abigail. Even for you."

"I would never," she snaps, pressing a hand to her chest. "I may not want a little spawn of my own, but I would never take that from someone."

"Then what are you threatening?"

She waggles her brows. "Octuplets."

I throw a pillow at her face with a cry of outrage. "My poor vagina!"

"Exactly. Don't cross me, ginger tits." She snags the pillow and hugs it to her chest with a sigh. "Look. Did you fuck up? Yeah. But he loves you. You're not the only trauma-ridden mess in this relationship, Georgia. You both deserve forgiveness. Especially from yourselves."

I suck in a breath, trying not to dissolve again. "I just… I miss them so much."

Her eyes go soft. "I know, babe. I know."

We sit in silence for a minute, the kind only best friends can share without it being awkward. The only sound is a storm raging outside and the faint clink of ice in our glasses.

Then Abby tips over sideways on the couch with a groan.

"You're not the only one who fucked up," she says, flopping dramatically onto her back.

I arch a brow, the room spinning just enough to make it feel like the couch is floating. "Care to elaborate?"

She winces. "Would've been here days ago, but I sort of…"

"*Abigail.*"

She takes a deep breath and lets it out in a rush.

"Met a hot guy in a bar, went to a hotel with him, had the best sex of my entire life—like, fall-in-love-during-it kind of sex—and then…"

I jolt upright, gripping the back of the couch when the room spins hard. "And then? Don't leave me on a cliffhanger, witchling! I know where you're sleeping tonight!"

"And then," she drawls, sniffling discreetly, "I answered his phone the next morning thinking it was mine and do you know who was calling him?"

I stare.

She finishes on a whisper. "His fucking *wife.*"

I gasp so hard I nearly choke on my shock. "What?! Oh my god. I swear to everything, Abby, give me his name and I will track him down. I will throw salt circles around his house and unleash your witchy ancestors on his balls."

"I already hexed his penis to shrink an inch every time he lies."

My head tilts, brows high. "Inches? Not like…" Hands flapping, I hedge, "Centimeters?"

"*Inches.*"

"So… he had a lot of, um… length to lose?"

She nods solemnly.

I bite my lip, stomach flipping as memories of Kade's impressive dick assault my senses. That man could lose five inches and still hit my g-spot.

"How much?"

Abby shrugs. "At least ten."

"Ten inches!?" I screech, spilling my drink all over the floor as I shoot to my knees. "But.. But.. *Abby*! You're so tiny! How did you even accommodate a ten-inch dick without dying?"

She snorts tequila and coughs into her sleeve, wagging her fingers in my face. "Really good foreplay and giant fingers to stretch me out."

"You swear?" I ask, still in shock. "Ten?"

"Ten."

I suck in a breath so sharp I might've dislodged a lung. "Not like... combined total from multiple sessions?"

She shakes her head. "Single session. Single source. Single soul-destroying cock."

"Jesus, Abbs. That's not a penis, that's a bodily hazard."

Abby sniffs. "The man not only caused emotional damage but also pelvic bruising."

"You lucky little slut," I mutter, shaking my head. "One for the bucket list?"

"Yep."

"Did you really hex him yet?"

She tips her head back and wails. "No! I couldn't bring myself to do it. Cheater or not, the man fucks like a god!"

We fall apart, both of us cackling so hard it turns into a wheeze. My face is soaked with tears again, but at least these are from laughter.

Eventually, the quiet creeps back in and we both slump, legs tangled, tequila forgotten.

I wipe my cheek and whisper, "I'm so happy you're here, Abby."

"Me too, ginger tits. Me too."

CHAPTER FIFTY TWO

THE TOWN THAT KEEPS ME

IT TAKES EVERYTHING IN me to leave the house.

The air feels too sharp, the sunlight too loud, and I keep tugging at my cardigan like it's armor instead of cotton. Abby hands me a to-go cup from Snug as a Mug and starts prattling about the barista being cute, but my brain's still fogged with the weight of everything that's happened.

We stroll past the bookstore, the hardware store with Holt's signature red flyers in the window, and the corner where the honey stand will go back up next month. This is my first time downtown since the break-up.

Since I left him.

Since I shattered myself.

I've burned through a week of sick time and my only vacation day, hiding out in my house like heartbreak is contagious. But I have to go back to work Monday. The world keeps moving, even when your heart's in pieces.

Abby loops her arm through mine. "This town is disgustingly cute."

I nod, sipping my coffee. "It grows on you."

We cross the street, and I'm just starting to feel normal again when Abby stops so abruptly I nearly slam into her.

"Abbs?" I murmur, frowning. She's staring at a two-story white-shiplap storefront with wide windows and an old hand-painted sign that reads *Mabel's Candles*. There's a smaller sign taped crookedly to the door: *For Sale. Entire Shop. Contents Included.*

Abby's nails dig into my wrist.

"Hey, are you okay?"

She blinks, chokes out a breath. "Holy shit. This... this is it."

"What's it?" My eyes dart around the sidewalk like the ten-inch God, or, fuck...*Kade*, might jump out. "What the hell are you—"

"I have to go in."

And then she's moving, practically jogging toward the door. I scurry after her, my heart racing for reasons I don't understand.

Inside, the candle shop smells like heaven. Like vanilla, wax, and lavender. Sunlight pours in through the front windows, catching on shelves of handmade candles, jars of bath salts, and little wrapped soaps that look like candy. The displays are charming but a little outdated. Doesn't seem to bother my bestie in the least.

In the center of the shop sits a thick wooden counter, carved and nicked with age. Behind it, in an antique-looking chair, is a woman who has to be at least eighty. She's hunched slightly, glasses low on her nose, eyes closed.

Abby approaches slowly. "Excuse me, ma'am? Are you okay?"

The woman jerks, startled, blinking behind thick lenses. "Oh! Goodness. Yes, yes, I'm fine. Just resting my eyes."

They fall into easy conversation while I browse, but I catch the highlights.

The woman's name is Mabel. She's owned this place for over twenty years, but her kids live out of state and they're putting her into assisted living. Right now, she lives in a converted two-bedroom upstairs, but she can't manage to get up there anymore, so she's sleeping on the couch in the breakroom.

It's devastating, and I rub my chest, but the ache only grows.

"So, it's time," Mabel croaks, eyes misty but resigned. "I'm selling it. Everything inside too. I just want it to go to someone who loves it like I did."

My heart skips a few beats, and I turn to my best friend, watching her with wide eyes. Abby listens intently, but her gaze keeps drifting around the shop, reverent, like she's not seeing it—she's *dreaming* it.

I've seen that face before.

Goosebumps erupt across my skin.

When we finally leave, Abby has Mabel's personal number scribbled on the back of a receipt, tucked into her pocket like a secret.

We walk for a few blocks in silence, and I can tell she's thinking hard, planning maybe.

"You okay?" I ask finally.

"Not even a little," she breathes with a big smile. "But in the best way."

I laugh softly and look around. This town. This stupid, magical, heart-breaking town.

"I really do love it here."

She nods. "Yeah, I get it."

"Heart Springs is a place I never wanted to fall in love with." I pause, heart thudding. "But Kade? There was no fighting that. Loving him feels... inevitable, Abbs. And loving them both feels like forever."

She squeezes my hand and lets out a slow breath. "Sounds like a done deal to me, babes."

"What would it even look like, me staying here and you back in New York?"

She smirks, shaking her head. "For one, I knew you weren't coming back the second you left."

I gape. "How?"

She bumps her shoulder into mine. "Georgia, you've been chasing a family since you were little. You just thought it had to be the one that gave you your name. But you didn't want answers out here. You wanted to be loved. Cherished. No strings. No conditions. It's what we all want."

"Abby..."

She turns to me, eyes serious. "I love you. And I'm so damn proud of you. For everything. For coming here. For trying. Even if it didn't look like you imagined, you still found what you were looking for. A big, messy, honey-covered family. A cowboy. A baby."

My chest aches.

"So what are you gonna do about it?"

I look out over the town that's slowly become my home.

Every instinct I've ever had tells me to run. But for the first time in my life... I want to run *toward* something, not away.

Love. Home. Them.

The only question is... am I brave enough to do it?

CHAPTER FIFTY THREE

FOUR DIGITS AND A CHANCE

> *Beatrice Archer: Meet me at Snug as a Mug today at three. Please, sweetheart. I know you're scared, just… try.*

EVERY INCH OF ME is shaking. My palms are clammy around the cup I'm not drinking from, and my heart is thundering so loud I'm surprised no one else in this coffee shop can hear it.

But I'm here, waiting not so patiently for the lecture I'm sure I'm about to get. One I deserve.

Right on time, Bea walks through the door already scanning the busy coffee shop. As soon as her eyes find mine, her whole expression crumples. She doesn't hesitate—just crosses the room and pulls me into a hug so tight I can barely breathe.

"Georgia," she whispers. "I've missed you so much, sweetheart."

My broken heart finds a way to break a little more at that.

"I've missed you too," I choke out, meaning it with everything in me.

When she pulls back, my breath catches in shock.

She's crying.

And not the silent kind of misty-eyed tears people dab away with a tissue. These are real tears, heartbreak and grief and worry etched across her face, and I realize… Bea really cares for me.

Like a mom would.

The kind of mom who squeezes your hand too tight. The one who shows up, even when you're the one who left. The one who loves loud and doesn't let go.

I hold my breath, waiting for her to order a drink and return to the table. Then I hold it until she's finally settled and staring at me with a soft, patient expression that hits me right in all my messy feelings.

"How are they?" I blurt.

She gives a soft smile, but it wobbles, and she shakes her head. "Not good, sweetheart."

My chest caves in, eyes squeezing shut as pain assaults me. "Oh."

"Kade's been… lost. He was doing so well, coming back to life, spending time with the family again. But now? He hasn't run, but he's not himself. He's just… a shell of who he was becoming."

"And Aurora?" I whisper, my throat closing.

Bea reaches across the table, squeezes my shaking hand. "She misses her mama, Georgia. She misses you."

"I'm not—" The words catch in my throat. "I'm not her mother."

"You are," Bea cuts in, firm and sharp. "You are that girl's mother. The one who feeds her, holds her, bathes her, and sings her to sleep. The only one who knows her lullabies. The one she looks for first thing in the morning. You're the one who calms her nightmares and dries her tears. That makes you her mama."

"But Marlee…"

"Marlee," Bea says gently, "is gone. And you? You're still here. You have a choice, Georgia. You can let the ghost of a woman scare you away, or you can cowboy up and be there for your child the way you wish someone had been there for you."

My lungs seize.

"Wh—what?" I gasp.

Bea smiles sadly. "I knew your family, sweetheart. Your mama, Lorna Walker? She and I were in the same grade."

My heart stops.

"You've known who I am this whole time?"

"I'm sorry. I didn't want to deceive you. But yes, I knew. The day I met you, I recognized her in you." She clicks her tongue, smiling softly as her eyes trail over me. "You're her spitting image."

"Then…" I wipe away tears. "Why didn't—"

"Because you weren't ready," she interrupts, nodding gently. "I didn't want to weigh you down with a past before you had a chance to build your own future. And I knew you'd ask when you were ready."

My breath catches and I look away, sorting through her words.

"Did I make a mistake, sweetheart?" Her brows furrow, and she looks truly worried. "I'm so sorry. It wasn't my call to make."

"No," I whisper, clearing my throat. "Thank you. I'm glad I got this time. To explore. To fall in love with Heart Springs."

Her brows arch. "And did you? Fall in love, that is."

I nod, a shaky breath leaving me. "So much."

Another sob slips from her, but she stifles it and grabs my hand. "So did he."

"I haven't heard from him. Not since…"

"Sweetheart, you ran. You needed space. He knew that. He gave it to you."

Guilt clogs my throat, making it hard to breathe.

"Did he talk to you?" I choke out. "Did he… is he talking to you about what happened?"

As much as I hate the idea of her knowing how epically I fucked up, all the ways I failed her son, he deserves to talk it out with his mother. To lay his burdens at her feet. For so long, he kept everything bottled up. I don't want that for Kade. I don't want him to lose his family, or go back on all the progress he's made.

She reaches into her bag and pulls out an old phone, the screen scratched, the case worn down with time. She lays it on the table and taps a yellow Post-it stuck to the back. A four-digit code is written in neat, slanted handwriting.

"This was William's phone," she whispers, swallowing repeatedly like the words hurt. "Not sure why I kept it in service. At first, it was because all the business contacts would reach out to his number. Took over a year to get them all sorted. And for a while, I used to call just to hear his voicemail." Bea bats at relentless tears that match my own. "But then, one day, *it rang*."

My chest constricts, and it only gets worse with the meaningful look she gives me, wordlessly begging me to understand.

Oh.

Oh, *God*.

"Kade called his dad?" I choke out through a pained sob.

She nods. "He does. Often."

My hand presses to my chest, but the ache just grows and grows, the room spinning with every throbbing, twisting breath.

I stare at the phone for a long time like if I look hard enough or from the right angle, I'll be able to see Kade staring back at me, telling me what to do.

"Did you…" I wet my dry lips, hands shaking. "Did you listen to them?"

"Just the first few," she murmurs, face contorted. "Just to make sure he was okay. I was scared. So scared, Georgia." Her head shakes. "Kade was so adamant about never talking to his dad. Never finding a way to connect. It's all I wanted for him. To find a way to just forgive himself. And when the phone rang and his name popped up, he was in such a dark place, so distant."

Tears stream freely now from both of us and she stifles a sob with her hand.

"I… I thought he was saying *goodbye*."

"Oh my God," I croak, entire body revolting even the mere idea of Kade not existing. "Bea."

She wipes her tears with a napkin and pats my hand. "He's okay, and that's not why he called."

"Then… why?"

"For you, sweetheart." Bea slides the phone across to me. "Call when you're ready. Listen. They're his love letters to you."

Silence fills the space between us, both of our attention and thoughts riveted to the phone, to the men it represents. The loves of our lives, both gone, but in different ways.

She can't have her love anymore, and I…

I hope like hell it's not too late for me to get mine.

To get my one chance at a family. The only chance I want.

The thought batters against something inside me, knocking loose all the ideals I'd hung my hopes and dreams on. Abby was right. I came to Heart Springs looking for answers, for roots and a family, and I found it. Just not in the way I'd planned.

And as the weeks turned to months, and my six-month contract and leases were ending, I stopped wondering about where I came from and started dreaming about where I'd end up.

I'm still curious. I think I always will be, but… for now, maybe I just need enough to lay it to rest.

"Bea," I whisper. "My family. Was it… was it bad?"

Her lips purse. "Your mama was beautiful. Kind. Just a girl had a hard life who ran as far as her feet could take her. It was a tragedy. A quiet one."

"It always is," I murmur.

She cocks her head. "Would you like to hear the rest?"

"Maybe someday. But for now, I'm okay."

Bea stands and kisses the top of my head. Her hand smooths my hair, the gesture achingly maternal.

"You are," she says. "And you will be. I promise."

"Bea," I blurt, pointing to the phone. "Does he hate me?"

She sighs softly. "I didn't listen to more than a few, Georgia, and he hasn't said much. But I know my son. The only person he's ever hated is himself."

"I don't want that for him," I cry. "He's so amazing. A wonderful man. The best father. Aurora loves him so much." My voice breaks. "I love him so much."

"Then go to him. Go to your family."

My family.

I'm still processing the weight of that, the way it finally feels like something I can actually have, when she gasps, eyes on her watch. "Oh, shoot. Book club."

I blink. "You joined a book club? When the hell do you have time for that?"

"You know my knitting club?" she asks, grinning devilishly.

I nod slowly and she leans in, dropping her voice to a conspiratorial whisper. "It's really a smutty book club. You should join. We even have a dick chart."

My jaw drops.

"Biggest book boyfriend wins the Hole-A-Fame every month," she says, eyes twinkling. "Think about it."

And with that, Beatrice Archer walks out, leaving me raw, reeling, and… desperately wanting to join book club.

The house still smells like tequila, incense, and Abby.

But it doesn't smell like honey or wildflowers. No cedar, sweat, or leather. No lavender and baby powder.

It doesn't smell like home.

I sit curled up on the couch, knees hugged to my chest, and the blanket Abby bought and left me draped over my shoulders, but I'm still freezing.

William's phone is clutched in my trembling hands, the weight of it heavier than anything so small has a right to be. The passcode loops through my brain like a dare I'm not sure I have the courage to take.

My heart is racing, my mouth dry.

My anxiety creeps in with sharp claws, whispering every doubt I've been trying to suppress. *What if he hates me? What if I hear something I can't un-hear? What if these voicemails make it worse?*

What if I was wrong to leave, and worse—what if it's too late to come back?

I close my eyes and suck in a shaky breath. I know one thing: whatever's on this phone is going to break me, heal me, and ruin me, all at once.

But I need that.

And I need to hear his voice.

My fingers hover, then finally move with determination. I wake the screen, type in the four digits from the sticky note, and the phone unlocks with a soft click.

I go to the voicemail app.

A long list appears instantly. Dozens of entries. All from the same name. All from him.

The first call came in just a few days after the mediation hearing.

It's been five months.

And the last… the last was only a few days ago.

My breath snags in my throat. My vision blurs.

With a trembling finger, I press *play* and bring the phone to my ear.

Chapter Fifty Four

Georgia

Break Me

"I don't even know why I'm calling. Some uptight social worker showed up a week ago, all fire and fight and freckles. Told me Marlee's dead. That she left her daughter—her daughter—to me. I didn't ask for this. Didn't sign up for this. And I wish you were here to tell me what the hell I'm supposed to do. But you're not. You're not because you're dead. And that's my fault, isn't it? It's all my—fuck."

Click.

"I met her. The baby. Aurora. She's... God, she's beautiful. Big brown eyes. Sweet little curls. She looked up at me like I was someone she could trust. Like I mattered. And Georgia? The social worker? She was there too. Smiling at me like she thought I could actually do this. Her smile... it made me forget, for a second, that I'm not a good man. And her laugh? Her laugh could heal a man. But... I don't deserve to be healed. Not yet. Maybe never."

Click.

"I can't do this. I can't. I'm not built for this kind of responsibility. Aurora deserves someone better. Someone who knows what the hell they're doing. I can barely function, Dad. What kind of man thinks he can raise someone else's kid when he can't even fix himself?"
Click.

"Fuck, Dad. I can't stop thinking about Georgia. She got reassigned. Haven't seen her in a week and... I miss her. I miss the way she argued with me. It's stupid. She's everything I shouldn't want. A city girl who'll leave. Someone just passing through on her way to bigger shit. I can't do that again, but I miss her. And I hate that I do. I hate her. I... fuck. I'm a liar."
Click.

"Found her on the ground at Wildwood Market today. Thought she was hurt. Turns out she has celiac. Couldn't even stand. And there I was, ready to burn the place down. Of course it's the city girl with a gluten allergy who gets stuck in my head when no other woman has held my attention for over a fuckin' decade. But you should see her, Dad. She's got this perfect red hair that's all wild curls and a smile that makes my heart twist. But her freckles... they're like little starbursts of distraction. She's dangerous. I'm fucked, aren't I? Christ."
Click.

"Aurora is mine. Not officially. Have to apply for adoption, but she's here in my house. And Georgia? I think she might be mine, too."
Click.

"Georgia and I were harvesting honey today. She got stung and still didn't complain. Just smiled. And a while ago, when I was checking her sting, she told Aurora bees only sting when they're scared...like she really gives a damn about all this—the farm, Aurora, me. She's teaching me patience, Dad. She's teaching me how to be more than I am. Think you'd love her. Think I might, too."
Click.

"Caught her listening to Fleetwood Mac. One of yours and Mom's songs. My heart stopped. Then she smiled, and I smiled back. It was.... It was nice. Good. She's so damn good, Pops."

Click.

"*I took her to see the stars, Dad. Spread a blanket, laid under the sky, made love to her with the whole damn universe watching. And I fell. I fell so hard, I'll never recover. She's my one. My forever.*"
Click.

"*There was a fire. Lost a lot of equipment. And the fence got cut again. I don't know who's fucking with us, but I swear, I'll protect the farm. I'll protect our land. Our family. I'll do right by you. I, uh… I won't let you down, Dad.*"
Click.

"*Aurora tried to walk today. Just let go of the couch and took a step like she trusted the world to catch her. Like she trusted me. I don't deserve that trust, Dad. But I want to earn it. I want to be someone she can count on.*"
Click.

"*I'm sorry. For not coming home sooner. For letting my anger keep me away. I blamed myself for your death, but I think you just… missed me. And I missed you too. I miss you every damn day. But I'm letting go of the guilt. I have to. I can't be a good dad to Aurora if I'm still stuck in the past. I love you, and I forgive myself. Finally.*"
Click.

"*She kissed me after we picked wildflowers together. Said the smell reminded her of belonging. That was the first time I realized she saw this place as home. And maybe… maybe that means I'm doing something right.*"
Click.

"*She left, Dad. Georgia left. And it broke me. I fucked it all up. I love her so goddamn much, and she left. Aurora keeps looking around for her, calling out for Mama. And I… I feel like I'm missing the other half of my soul. Is this how Mom feels without you? Because if it is, if it's even an ounce of what I'm feeling right now… then come back, Pops. Defy reality. Come back for her, because I can't breathe.*"
Click.

"*I will never stop loving Georgia. I'll wait for her until she's ready to let me love her the way she deserves. Because Dad, she deserves it all. And I'm gonna find a way to give it to her. I promise. I won't let you down. I'll do right by her. Love you, Pops. Miss you."*

Click*.*

I don't know how long I sit there. I don't know how many times I replay them. His voice, rough and ragged, laughing sometimes, breaking others. Whispering my name like a prayer.

Like a plea.

The sheer emotion in his words shatters something deep inside me I didn't think was left to break.

And when the last voicemail ends, the one where he promises to love me until I'm ready, I collapse forward with a sob so violent it rips out of my chest and echoes through the empty house.

God, what have I done?

I ran.

I let fear win.

I let the past take something that belonged to my future. And for what? A letter written in grief? A ghost who no longer exists? The ugly words of a woman who broke him once upon a time?

Kade isn't just some man I slept with. He's not just the guardian of a little girl I was assigned to.

He's the man who cleared out every inch of gluten in his house without ever being asked. Who learned how to do my hair from YouTube tutorials because I was too sick to move. Who held me like I was precious, and called me freckles like it meant something. Because to him, it did.

I did.

Do I still?

And Aurora...

Aurora is mine.

She was mine the moment she reached for me, the moment she smiled when I sang. When she wrapped her little arms around my neck and laid her head on my shoulder with so much trust, it rewrote some of the ugly memories I try to forget.

I belong with them.

I've spent my whole life wishing. On stars. On eyelashes. On birthday candles and dandelions and every silly, impossible thing that carried even a sliver of hope.

But maybe it's time I stop wishing.

Maybe it's time I fight.

For Kade. For Aurora. For the family I've always dreamed of and the future I was too scared to believe I could have.

I wipe my tears, set the phone down gently beside me, and press a hand to my heart. It's still beating, fragile, bruised, but steady.

I love them.

I love them both.

And it's time I go home.

CHAPTER FIFTY FIVE

SO SWEET TO BEE ONE

THE AIR SMELLS LIKE sugar and sunshine, like honey and hay. The turnout is the biggest I've ever seen. Cars line the road all the way down to the river bend. People are spilling into every corner of the property, laughing and tasting and spinning through flower fields like a Hallmark special exploded on our land.

It's beautiful.

It's chaos.

And it's everything Georgia built.

I should be happy, but all I can find in me to be is silently proud because I'm hanging on by a thread here.

Aurora's toddling around with my sisters, dressed in that tiny yellow romper Georgia ordered weeks ago, the one that says *So Sweet To Bee One* across her chest.

It's the cutest thing I've ever seen, but all I can think is she's not here to see it.

I keep catching myself scanning the crowd, stupidly hopeful I'll see those freckles and that fire again. Every damn smile I fake is a crack in the dam, and when Mrs. Widdleston from the bakery downtown waves me over, I paste another one on.

"I just had to tell you, Kade," she gushes, clutching a honey-sampler cone in one hand. "This event is stunning. One of the best community gatherings I've ever been to."

"Appreciate that, ma'am."

"And that Georgia girl?" Her eyes twinkle. "What a gem. Organized everything so beautifully. You're lucky to have someone like that."

My smile tightens, heart cracking.

I don't have shit.

"Yes, ma'am. I am."

She leans in, brows tight. "I haven't seen her around today, though."

My chest hollows out. "She's around," I lie. "Probably putting out a fire or helping someone settle in."

Mrs. Widdleston nods, satisfied. "That sounds like our Georgia."

Our Georgia.

God.

It hits like a gut punch.

Can't stand to be here, in the middle of something covered and dripping in the one woman I'd literally kill to fuckin' see right now. Even if it's just so she can yell at me.

Sighing, I head back toward my house, leaving the happy chaos behind me. Aurora is with my sisters, probably with the goats. It's her favorite thing these days, spending time with the animals. I shoot off a quick text, letting them know where I am just in case.

Hands in my pockets, eyes on the ground, I make my way up the new walkway. I've been throwing myself into finishing the house, the front yard. It's kept my brain busy—at least I'm pretending it has.

"You planted lilies," a soft voice chokes out.

My head snaps up, heart racing.

"My favorite flower. You filled the yard with them."

My neck burns, and I stumble, but quickly catch myself before I can trip.

Georgia.

My Georgia.

A long yellow dress that matches Aurora's ghosts across her body, following the flow of her curves. Her hair is a wild mess, falling around her shoulders. The sun is spilling around her, making her skin glow.

She looks... Stunning.

Perfect.

I shake my head and step closer, slowly, like I'm worried she'll run off.

When I get close enough my shadow blocks out the sun and I can finally make out all her features.

Dark circles are under her eyes, and her face is thinner, her collarbone more pronounced. Her freckles are standing out stark against her paler than usual skin, and something about the sight of it twists my gut.

She's beautiful, but God, she looks *so sad*.

"Hi," she breathes, meadow eyes glossy as she blinks up at me.

"Hi," I choke out, throat tight. I blink again and again, but the mirage doesn't change. She doesn't disappear. "You're really here."

Why are you here, baby?

"I…" she nods, swallowing hard. "I couldn't miss the event. I promised your mom."

My jaw tightens, but I breathe through the hurt. "Yeah." My voice cracks and I clear my throat, taking a step back. "Well, she's, uh…" I rip off my Stetson and yank on my hair, looking away. "Mom's around here somewhere."

"I know," she whispers, stepping into me. "I already talked to her. I came here looking for you."

Tell me, freckles. Tell me why. Be honest with me.

"Why?" I hate that my voice is sharp. Laced with so much fuckin' pain. She flinches and I kick myself mentally, but she doesn't run, doesn't back down, and pride fills me.

That's my girl.

"I deserve your anger. I deserve for you to hate me like you used to. I ruined…" She chokes out a sob that has my shoulders tensing, body aching to wrap her up. "I ruined this."

Oh, darlin'. It's me who fucked up.

"Georgia—" I start, shaking my head. "No. Absolutely not. You—"

Before I can finish, a scream pierces the air.

"Kade!"

We both spin and I find Colby sprinting toward us, Aurora wrapped in her arms, eyes wide and face coated in tears.

I charge forward, Georgia hot on my heels.

"What the fuck happened?" I bark, eyes sliding over both of them. "Are you okay?"

"It's Rory!" Colby gasps around a broken sob as she thrusts my daughter into my arms. "We were picking flowers and…and sh-she go–got—"

"Colby!" I snap above Aurora's screams.

But it's Georgia who gently pushes me aside and grips my little sister's face, calmly saying "Sweetheart, breathe."

They breathe together for a beat and then Colby finally nods, letting Georgia wipe her tears. "We were picking flowers and Aurora got stung. I was bringing her home to check on the sting, but she started turning red and breathing funny and…" She swallows hard. "I think she's allergic."

My body locks up, and I lift Aurora, frantically searching for signs of reactions, finding them immediately. The world spins and my knees buckle.

I know how fast bee stings can go south and for a baby…

"Call an ambulance," I choke out, shaking as bad as my daughter.

Georgia kisses Colby's head. "You did good. Now listen, I need you to run inside and go get Kade's truck keys. Right now."

Colby runs off and Georgia calmly turns to me. "Her seat is in your truck, so we're going to take that. Can you strap her in or do I need to do it?"

"W-what?" My head shakes along with my limbs. "Ambu–"

"Will not get here in time." She steps up, brushing Aurora's cheeks, but she's too busy screaming and gasping, every breath wheezing more than the last, to see her. "We need to go. Right now."

Colby comes flying out with my keys and throws them at Georgia, who catches them like a fuckin' baseball player.

"Good job, sweetheart. We're leaving. Go tell your mom what happened and that we're headed to the Heart Springs Clinic. And that she needs to call ahead for us and let them know what's happening. If you don't get to your mom in five minutes, call me. Got it?"

Colby disappears in a blur of frantic limbs, and Georgia doesn't waste a second. She grabs my forearm, her grip steady but urgent, and pulls me toward the truck.

"Come on, Kade. We don't have time."

My feet move, but my mind doesn't. I follow her like I'm underwater, ears ringing, heart punching the inside of my chest like it's trying to break free. Aurora's tiny body shakes against mine with every sob, her skin flushed, her lips starting to swell.

This can't be happening.

Georgia wrenches open the back passenger door and holds it for me. "Strap her in," she says gently but firmly. "I'll drive."

My hands tremble so badly I nearly fumble the buckles. "I—I can do it, I can—"

"I know you can, baby," she soothes. "If you can't, I can. It's okay. I've got you both."

I nod, or I think I do.

My fingers somehow manage the harness, clicking it into place as Aurora's cries weaken into gasping whimpers. Georgia's already in the driver's seat, adjusting mirrors, sliding her phone onto the mount, starting the truck. She's a blur of motion, calm and composed and fucking heroic.

I slam the door shut and run to the other side, climbing in next to Aurora so I can keep an eye on her. Georgia reverses the truck and catches my gaze, giving me a wobbly nod. I think I nod back, but my vision tunnels.

All I can hear is the slightly wheezing cry from next to me. All I can see is a little girl I'd kill for, hurting and helpless.

My daughter.

God, please don't take her from me.

I can't lose anyone else.

Georgia peels out of the gravel drive, tires spinning as we take the winding road like a bat out of hell. I don't take my eyes off Aurora, don't take my hand from her chest, as I monitor the swelling and her breathing. It's fast, but full and not closed off. Her lips are slightly puffy, cheeks red, but her airway's open.

I don't think I breath or focus on a damn thing except Aurora until I feel Georgia's touch.

She reaches back and squeezes my hand hard enough to drag me back to the present.

"Everything's going to be okay," she says softly, not even looking at me. Her voice is barely above a whisper, like it's meant for someone else entirely.

And then it hits me… she's not just talking to me, she's talking to Aurora too.

"I've got you, baby girl," she murmurs, voice cracking with love. "You're safe. We're almost there. I love you. I love you so much. Nothing's going to take you away from me ever again. Nothing."

Tears hit my face before I realize I'm crying. Her words slide under my ribs like a balm, pushing through the fear and chaos and cracking something open. She's soothing both of us. And I didn't even know how much I needed to be soothed until I heard it.

She's here, strong and brave and not running.

And I never want to live a single damn second without her again.

I squeeze her hand back, tight and desperate, just as she turns into the clinic.

Georgia parks in the tiny emergency bay and throws the truck in park, exhaling like it's the first breath she's taken in miles. Her knuckles are white on the steering wheel. And her eyes… her eyes are locked on the building's sign like it's a ghost.

The realization slices through me.

This is where her mom was born. The last link to a past she's never made peace with. She once told me this building haunted her. That every time she drove by, she thought about stepping inside and asking if the doctors knew Lorna or the Walkers. But she was too scared. Too terrified of what they'd say.

Or what they wouldn't.

And now… she's here, fighting for her own daughter. Not by blood but loved more than her family ever loved her.

More than Marlee ever loved Aurora.

She did it because it was the fastest route to saving the little girl she's come to love like her own. She did it without hesitation, even knowing what it would cost her.

I stare at her in awe, the air punched from my lungs.

"You said you love us," I choke out, her words trickling in like honey.

She turns to me, eyes glassy but sure, and nods. "You're my family. Of course I love you."

And right then, it hits me like a freight train.

This woman… this fierce, soft, wildfire of a woman… is mine.

Ours.

And we're never letting her go again.

Chapter Fifty Six

Georgia

Mama

The moment we step through the door, the nurse bustles toward us. Her eyes widen at the sight of Aurora, red-faced and softly wheezing in Kade's arms, but she doesn't panic. Her hands are steady. Her voice is calm.

I'm jealous.

"Let me take her, please," she says gently.

Kade hesitates for half a second before handing our daughter over, his arms shaking. I don't think he realizes how close he is to collapsing.

The nurse smiles, kind but firm. "Just give us a minute to assess. This clinic is small, tiny rooms, tight spaces. I promise we'll get your family back together soon."

And then she's gone, our daughter disappearing through the swinging doors.

My heart pounds in my chest, my ears, my throat.

I thought coming here would be unbearable. That the second I stepped through the doors I'd be haunted by the images of a family I've never met.

But all I can think about is Aurora.

Her little body pressed against Kade's. Her frantic gasps, her swollen lip, the angry red patch spreading over her soft skin. How she screamed until her voice cracked.

She looked at me like I could make it better, and I couldn't. Not fast enough. Not this time.

I don't even realize I'm crying until Kade's in front of me, his calloused hands cradling my face. He tips my chin up, those stormy-gray eyes locked on mine.

"She's going to be okay, darlin'," he says, throat bobbing. "We're all going to be okay."

And it's the sound of that nickname on his rasping voice that makes my knees give out. Kade catches me around the waist and picks me up, before sitting in a chair with me in his lap.

All the pain from the last few weeks comes tumbling out. All the hurt and fear and longing. He holds me, rocking me softly, whispering reassurances only loud enough for me to hear.

When I finally pull myself together enough to meet his eyes, I'm shocked to see him crying too.

"I'm so sorry," I choke out.

He shakes his head, brushing my tears away with his thumb. "Nothing to be sorry for, baby."

"Yes," I argue, gripping his forearm for all I'm worth. "I fucked up. I left when I should have listened."

"Maybe," he murmurs, brows tight. "But there's so much I should have told you. So much about my past with Marlee. It wasn't good, Georgia. I'm so sorry you thought I was still…" Exhales roughly, jaw ticking, and I want to interrupt, but I need this, and I think he does too.

With a sigh, he grips my neck, fingers tangling in my hair and hugs me tight to his chest.

"Marlee used me for a long fuckin' time. Used me to feel like she had a family. Used me to fulfill some fantasy she had. Convinced me to join the military–something I never wanted till she came along. And when I was away, she was using my checks to fund her escape plan. Thought she was paying for college, or fuck, I don't know, preparing for our life together. But she was paying for a life far away from me."

He sucks in a shuddering breath.

"And yeah, when I got her letter, it fucked me up. I lost my head. Couldn't see through the shit raining down around me. I was young and stupid and stubborn. And no, it's not all her fault, but I need you to know that the love I felt for her was nothing compared to what I feel for you. *Nothing.*"

He swallows hard, a choked, broken sound that has me wrapping my arms around him and tugging him into me.

He left his Stetson in the truck, so I smooth his dark wild hair out of his eyes—hair that reminds me so much of our daughter's.

"There's something else…something I should have told you months ago, but fuck, I didn't know how. Wanted to forget it all, but…"

"It's okay," I whisper, kissing his cheek, his jaw, his temple. "It's okay, Kade."

"It's not, though."

I wipe away his tears as he blinks up at me.

"Aurora…she…Ethel said someone hurt her, baby. Hurt her before she was ours."

My breath catches, and the room spins.

"What?"

He nods sadly. "Few broken bones, some scars, but only one hospital visit."

I pull back, eyes narrowed and shake my head. "That wasn't… that… when I did the intake… when I talked to the hospital…"

He pulls me in and kisses my forehead. "I know. Ethel had to dig. But it's more. Marlee and Travis, they were drunk the day of the accident. No signs of swerving or anything. They… they did it on purpose. And they could have…"

"Could have killed Aurora," I hiss, anger and venom splitting me open. "Jesus, Kade. That's…."

I run a shaking hand through my hair and shove off his lap, pacing through the waiting room. "How dare they!"

"I know," he murmurs, watching me process, watching me fall the fuck apart. "How fucking dare they do that to her! To our daughter!"

I'm spiraling. My words are a mess. I'm crying and cursing and shaking.

After a few minutes, Kade steps into my path and blocks my even strides.

"What the hell, you brooding tree!" I half-sob, half-shout, swatting at him.

He drags me into him and chuckles softly, but it's full of tears. "You called Aurora our daughter."

"Well, she is!" I snap, meaning it with my whole heart. My shoulders fall as I stare up at him, the weight of everything pressing in on me. "She is. Right?"

He nods slowly. "Yeah, baby. That's your little girl in there."

"And you?" I whisper, throat tight. "Are you…"

"Yours? Yeah, Georgia. I'm yours." Bending down, he ghosts his lips over mine. "For the rest of your life, so you better get used to planting roots. I've got a whole farm waiting for you to grow."

"But only Archers grow on Honey Bea," I breathe against his mouth, shivering violently, heart battering between us.

"*Exactly.*" And then he's kissing me.

God, does he kiss me.

It's fierce and tender, desperate and healing. My hands bury in his hair as he presses me into the clinic wall, pouring every unsaid word into my mouth. It's a kiss that steals my breath, that strips away every doubt I've ever had. His body is solid and warm and home.

My soul sings and my heart shatters and remakes itself with every brush of his lips.

Someone clears their throat, and we reluctantly break apart, breathless, dazed.

"Good to see you again, Kade," an older woman says kindly, wearing a white lab coat and a knowing smile.

He straightens, keeping one arm around me. "Nice to see you, Glenda."

"Aurora's fine," she assures us quickly, like she knows we can't stand another second without news. "It's a mild bee allergy. We treated her with epinephrine and an oral antihistamine, and she responded well. Given where you live, I'd recommend keeping an EpiPen on hand, just in case."

Relief makes my knees weak.

She glances between us, then rests her eyes on me. "Sorry, Kade. I haven't met your wife yet."

I open my mouth to correct her, but Kade beats me to it.

"Glenda, this is Georgia," he says softly. "My everything."

She visibly melts, and I get it. Kade has that effect.

"Well then," she smiles. "Come on, Archers. Let's go see your girl. Saw her outfit. Seems like she had a hell of a first birthday."

My breath catches at the reminder, and Kade squeezes my hand, smiling down at me. "We've got a lifetime to make it up to her."

My heart is still in my throat as I step into the room and lock eyes with our now much more aware daughter, who thrusts her tiny, chubby arms up at me with a drowsy, pained sob.

"*Mama!*"

And just like that... I know.

Every wish I've ever made has come true.

Epilogue One

My Ruination

Aurora's fast asleep, her cheeks still rosy from the antihistamine and exhaustion. I check the monitor one more time, watch the steady rise and fall of her chest, and close her bedroom door with a soft click.

Then I just… stand there.

My hand's clenched around the monitor, and I'm staring at our bedroom door like it's a cliff I'm about to fall off.

She's in there.

My girl.

My Georgia.

I take a breath I don't really feel and step into the room. The light is dim, just the soft glow of the bedside lamp spilling across the walls, but it still makes her shine.

She hasn't changed out of her yellow dress from the Bash—the one that makes her look like sunlight dipped in honey. She's standing dead center, arms loose at her sides, curls falling like wildfire around her shoulders.

Georgia's not crying, or fidgeting, and for once, she doesn't seem seconds from bolting. Her face is nervous, but sure, like she's ready for whatever's about to happen.

Like she's ready to fight… for us.

Swallowing thickly, I take a step inside our room and close the door behind me.

"I'm sorry," we both say at the same time.

I shake my head slowly and take another step.

"Why are you sorry?" My voice is soft, but my heart's pounding like I just ran here. "I already told you, Georgia. You don't have anything to be sorry for."

Her lip trembles, and her hands lift and fall at her sides like she doesn't know what to do with them. "Maybe you're right. Maybe I do ruin things."

That stops me cold.

My stomach drops and I quickly close the distance between us.

"What are you talking about, darlin'?"

"You've been saying it from the beginning," she chokes out, eyes shining. "That I ruin things. Your shirts. Your shoes. Your days. I didn't want to ruin this too—us. It's the best thing that's ever happened to me."

God.

Fuck.

I've been a goddamn idiot. Thought I was being funny, flirting. Didn't realize she was taking every word and twisting it in her trauma.

I cup her jaw in my hands, my thumb stroking her cheek as I tilt her face up to mine.

"No," I whisper. "No, baby. There is not a single part of you capable of ruining a damn thing. I'm the one who's ruined."

She blinks, and her fingers curl around my hips like she's afraid I'll vanish.

"I was a shell," I tell her. "Walking around pretending to be a man when all I was doing was surviving. Drinking too much. Hurting too quiet. Hating myself for not being the son my father raised."

I move closer, so close I feel her breath on my lips.

"Then you walked in. All fire and fight. Lit the damn match. And now?"

My hand slides down, over the soft curve of her hip, my fingers dragging slowly up the slit in her dress until I find bare skin.

I trace the curve of her hip then slip between her thighs, letting her feel the weight of my words. "Now I'm the one who's gonna ruin you."

She gasps, lips parting. "You are?"

"Yes. Ruin you for all other men. Ruin your pretty little birthday outfit. Ruin your vocal cords as you scream out my name, begging me again and again for more. Ruin your makeup when I fuck your mouth, and hit the back of your throat."

Georgia whimpers, shuddering against me.

"But mostly, baby? I'm about to ruin this." I slide under her panties and cup her pussy possessively. "I'm gonna destroy this right here. With my mouth and fingers and cock. And then? Then I'm gonna make a mess out of your sweet little cunt with my cum."

We're both panting hard, gripping each other like we're afraid of falling.

"See? It's me who ruins things."

"Oh," she whispers, eyes flicking to my lips where they stay.

"Tell me I can make you come, Georgia. Tell me I can slip my fingers into this tight little pussy and listen to you beg and moan and whimper for more." I bite down on her neck, licking away the sting and she cries out, hips thrusting forward. "You gotta tell me. You gotta ask me to touch you, ask you to make you come so hard, I'll be able to lick your sweet taste from my hand when I'm done."

She melts into me, fingers clawing at every part of me she can reach.

"Yes," she breathes, "I want…"

Her throat bobs, but she doesn't finish so I grip her throat and tug her closer.

"I'm right here, darlin'," I coo. "Be brave. Gimme that wildfire and sass I love so much. Tell me what you need."

Her gaze flicks to my lips, and her shoulders straighten.

"I want you to fuck me like you love me, Kade Archer."

I don't even let her breathe before I'm on her, slamming my lips to hers.

She tastes like summer and honey, like fear and forgiveness and *forever*.

My girl moans into my mouth, and just like I knew it would, it wrecks me. I lift her with one arm under her thighs and carry her to the bed, laying her down like she's the most precious thing I've ever held.

Because she is.

She's mine.

And tonight, I'm going to remind her exactly what that means.

She lies beneath me, wild curls fanned out across her pillow. The one I slept with every night she was gone. That damn yellow dress is wrinkled and hitched high around her thighs, her chest rising and falling like she's trying to catch up to her heart.

I'm not doing much better.

My hands tremble as I slide them up her ribs, across her waist, like I'm memorizing her shape in case I wake up and this was all a dream.

She looks up at me, lashes damp, lips parted, and whispers, "I love you."

Three words, but they're everything.

"Baby," I rasp, shaking my head with a smile. "Georgia, I fell in love with you slowly, like honey sliding down warm skin. That love healed parts of me I didn't even know were broken. And now I can't stop craving the taste of you. Sweet on my tongue, wild under my hands. Mine in every way."

"Yours," she chokes out, tugging me forward. "Say it again."

"I love you."

"I love you, too."

Unable to wait a second longer, I dip down and kiss her like I need her mouth to breathe. Her fingers lace behind my neck, dragging me closer, deeper, until there's no space left between us and nothing holding us back.

We undress each other slowly, reverently.

Nothing but warmth and skin and soft, shaky laughter when I can't get one of the buttons undone and she rolls her eyes, helping me. I kiss every new inch of her as it's revealed—her shoulder, her collarbone, the dip of her waist. Her freckles glow like stars across her skin, and I swear I've never seen anything so beautiful.

When I finally settle between her thighs, I pause.

Her legs curl around my hips, and she strokes her thumb across my cheek.

"Make love to me, sunshine," she whispers. "Make it slow and sweet, like we've got forever."

"We do, darlin'," I breathe, dropping my forehead to hers as I push inside her sweet warmth. "I'm never leavin' you."

As I rock into her, I murmur against her lips that I love her, that I'm hers, that there's nothing broken in her I wouldn't spend my whole damn life cherishing.

And when she comes apart beneath me, whispering my name like a prayer, dragging me with her, *I know.*

This is it.

This is what my grandparents and parents meant when they talked about soul mates. This is what they said was worth dreaming for. Fighting for.

Living for.

Later, we're lying in bed, the moonlight pooling through the windows and casting our skin in soft silver. Georgia's tucked against my side, her fingers drawing lazy circles on my chest, her breath still a little uneven.

I brush my lips to her forehead and murmur, "How was that? Did I ruin you?"

She lets out a shaky laugh, then lifts my hand and presses it to the center of her chest.

"The only thing you've ruined is this," she whispers, eyes locked on mine. "It used to beat a restless song. A running song."

I freeze, watching her, the weight of those words already coiling tight in my chest.

"You once asked me why I love the music I do," she goes on. "It's because they're strong women singing about surviving on their own. About never needing anyone—especially not a man. And when they sing about love? It's always after the heartbreak. After the leaving. They sing about how to pick up the pieces, not how to keep them whole."

She traces the line of my forearm, down to my wrist, her fingers featherlight but sure.

"I didn't have a mom to teach me how to break or heal. Those women did. Their voices raised me. That's the beat my heart lived by for a long time." She swallows, her eyes shimmering in the low light. "But then you walked in. And now... now it beats for you."

"Baby," I whisper, the word catching in my throat.

She starts to shake her head, like she's said too much, but I cover her hand with mine and hold it still—hold her still.

"I'm serious," she breathes, blinking up at me. "You ruined every rule I had. Every guard I put up. And I'd let you do it again."

I slide closer, wrapping her up in my arms like I never want to let her go—because I don't.

"Then let me be just as clear," I rasp. "I lived my life in numbness. On autopilot. I survived off duty and guilt and whiskey, not because I was strong, but because I didn't know how to feel anymore. I forgot what light even looked like."

My thumb brushes over her cheekbone, catching a stray tear.

"And then you walked in—loud and stubborn and wild as hell—and you lit a match inside me I didn't think could ever burn again."

She sniffles, burrows in, and I tighten my hold.

"My life used to be a long road, no destination. But now it's broken into moments. Moments of you. You smiling. You laughing. You whispering things to Aurora like she's your whole world. You in the kitchen with flour on your face. You asleep beside me with your hand curled on my chest. Every moment, Georgia... it's you. It's always been you."

She lets out a sound between a sob and a sigh and kisses my throat. "You mean it?"

I cradle her face and tilt her chin so there's no doubt when I say, "I love you, Georgia Soon-to-Be Archer. You're it for me. You're my best friend, my heart, my family. You gave me a reason to come home and someone to come home to."

Her lips tremble. "I love you too, Kade. So much it terrifies me."

"Don't be scared anymore," I whisper, voice low and thick. "I've got you. And I'm not lettin' go."

She nods, pressing a kiss to my jaw and settling into my chest like she belongs there.

And hell, maybe she always did.

Because in this moment, in our bed, in our home, with our daughter asleep in the next room, I know one thing for sure.

This is forever.

My happily ever after.

Epilogue Two

Somewhere Over The Rainbow Is An HEA

It's my thirtieth birthday.

And I'm surrounded by more love than I've ever known.

Our house is buzzing with life—laughter, music, chaos. Kade's family… *my family.* Our friends from town. The people who've built a home around me without ever asking me to change.

Aurora is walking now, babbling her way through conversations like she belongs in every single one. Kade's doing everything he can to get Honey Bea fully back up and running. We never figured out who was vandalizing the farm, but after he installed the cameras, the incidents stopped. He thinks it might've been kids, some dumb prank taken too far.

I don't know. But for now, it's quiet, and I'm thankful for it.

My man needs rest.

I glance up and spot Colby, Clementine, Hazel, and Gemma all huddled in a corner of the living room, laughing over something that has Colby cackling and Clem hiding behind her hands in shock. Hazel looks far too pleased with herself. Bea sits behind them with a cup of sweet tea, her eyes soft and misty as she watches her daughters reunited.

She glances up and shoots a smile at me like she knows what's on my mind. Like I'm every bit as one of her girls as they are.

The weight of it hits me, but it's not a wrecking ball that sends me running anymore. It's soft, and sweet, and warm. Addicting. I'm not the outsider anymore. I'm not the girl passing through, testing the waters.

I belong here with them.

With Kade and Aurora.

Everyone is here today to celebrate me in the biggest, best birthday party I've ever had. Everyone except for my best friend.

My chest tightens at the thought of Abby. A little over a month ago, she shocked me by buying Mabel's candle shop downtown—the whole building and everything inside it. She said it was a gut feeling. *A calling.*

Her dream apothecary is finally within reach.

She has a few loose ends to wrap up in New York before the move becomes permanent, so she couldn't swing a visit for my birthday. But I'm too excited to be upset. Too proud of her for taking the leap to care about my birthday.

She deserves this.

A taste of happiness.

Who knows? Maybe she'll find her own Heart Springs happily ever after.

I refill the pitcher of sun tea and wipe my hands on a towel, half listening to Kade's friends talk about their new company—Last Out Security.

Griffin, Wilder, and even Ridge—our elusive, salt-and-pepper mustached foreman with a jawline cut from stone, are all grinning over beer and paperwork.

Everything feels settled, peaceful.

Right.

Except... Kade and Aurora have been missing for ten minutes, and I'm starting to get worried. Those two alone means trouble or messes, every single time.

"Hey," I call, and all three men turn to me with soft smiles. I blush. "Have you guys seen—?"

"*Happy birthday to you...*"

I spin at the chorus of voices and find them. Kade is hunched beside Aurora, helping her walk as they make their way toward me—her tiny hands clutched around his fingers, her curls bouncing with every wobbly step.

In his other hand is a cake. It's lopsided and adorably chaotic with a rainbow painted in frosting across the top. The sides are covered in glitter that look like...

Like shooting stars.

My heart shatters in the best possible way.

"Say happy birthday, Mama," Kade prompts gently, guiding her toward my legs.

She takes a few solo steps that are getting stronger every day and collides with my dress.

"Ha–p bird, Mama!" Rory squeals, clapping wildly.

Tears blur my vision as I scoop her into my arms and bury a kiss against her cheek. "Thank you, baby."

Kade lifts the cake and flashes me a sexy grin. "She helped. Everything's gluten-free. Even the decorations."

"It's perfect," I say, choking on a laugh-sob combo. "Completely perfect."

He leans in and kisses my temple. "Make a wish, darlin'."

I stare at him, my daughter in my arms, the family around us, and my chest swells so big I'm surprised I can breathe. "What if I already have everything I want?"

He grins with a shrug. "Wish anyway."

Aurora pats my cheek. "Wih, Mama!"

With a chuckle, I close my eyes and make the simplest, truest wish I've ever made—

Let this last.

Let it always be *this.*

When I open them... the cake and Kade are gone.

But only for a second—because when I blink again, he's on one knee.

Time stops.

"I've been waiting for this moment since the first time you wished on a damn eyelash," he says, voice thick, ring box trembling in his hand. "Georgia Walker... you walked into my life like a wildfire and burned down every wall I had. You made yourself a home in my heart without even trying."

He opens the box, revealing a ring with a storm-gray stone that looks just like his eyes, circled by smaller gems—each a different color of the rainbow.

"You told me once that storms mean something beautiful is coming. That rainbows are a promise. I want to be that promise for you. Wanna give you rainbows every damn day of your life. Marry me, freckles. Fill our big house with brothers and sisters for our daughter. Be blissfully happy at my side for the rest of our lives." He chokes on his breath and inches closer, dropping his voice. "Be my forever."

I'm crying before he even finishes.

I nod furiously, throwing myself into his arms, clutching his shirt like it's the only thing holding me up. "Yes," I whisper. "Yes. Yes, yes, yes."

Applause breaks out as I sink into him, the ring between us, our mouths tangling with one another like we're alone. I lose myself in Kade, my fiancé, my forever, and I don't give a damn who sees it.

"Oh my God, that was so sweet!"

We freeze.

Staticky clapping breaks out, and I pull myself away enough to hunt it down. My eyes dart to the corner where my phone's propped up against the sugar jar and find…

Abby's wide-eyed face staring back at me from FaceTime.

"I made him promise!" she squeals, wiping tears. "Had to see it live if I couldn't be there!"

"Oh my God!"

"Show me the ring, Mrs. Ginger Tits!"

I bust out laughing and hold up my ring to the camera. She coos and cries, and I lean in close, dropping my voice.

"I'm so fucking happy, Abbs." I sniffle.

She grins through her own tears. "I can't wait to see you."

"Can't wait to see you, witchling."

Behind me, a commotion breaks out. Voices rise and I turn just in time to see Wilder flailing at his best friend, Griffin, who's whisper-yelling while pointing vaguely in my direction.

"What's going on?" Abby hisses, leaning closer to the camera like it'll help.

"I don't know," I mutter, spinning to Kade, whose smile has dropped. He shrugs at me, just as confused. "Drama, I think."

"Point me! I wanna see the drama!"

Laughing, I turn the phone just as Griffin finally seems to break loose, shoving past Wilder and storming toward me like a man on a mission.

Kade moves to intercept, body rigid. "What the fuck are you doing, Sarge?"

Griffin ignores him. Eyes locked on the phone in my hand, jaw clenched. He stops an inch from me, boots nearly smashing my toes and growls, "*Pixie.*"

Abby gasps.

"What the hell is he doing there?" she snaps.

"Who?" I croak, blinking in confusion.

Her face hardens, and she crosses her arms, sitting up straight.

"That's him," she bites out. "The married asshole I slept with."
Oh. Fuck.

More!!

Gimmie More!

OMG! Who saw that coming? AH!
Wanna know more about the fire and who's behind the sabotage at Honey Bea?
Preorder Griffin and Abby's book, **Magic Never Ends,** a roommates, second-chance-at-love, age-gap romance!

Want more Happily Never After? Make sure you've subscribed to my newsletter for bonus content and deleted scenes! (Coming soon!)

And what about a special edition of your new favorite book, or a limited book box to celebrate the release of HNA??
Check out my site
www.authorpaisleynash.com

ACKNOWLEDGEMENTS

THAT STILL MAKE ME CRY

First and foremost, to my best friends—Jamie and Katelin.

Y'all have been my lifeline through this book. From the very first spark of an idea to the final comma, you've listened to me rant, ramble, spiral, sob, and second-guess myself more times than I can count. You've seen the unfiltered version of this journey: me ugly crying into my pillow, convinced I wasn't cut out for any of this.

You never once let me believe that lie.

Your love, your patience, your relentless belief in me, even when I couldn't find a shred of it for myself, is the reason this book exists. You plotted scenes with me, edited pages at midnight, and celebrated every tiny win like it was the Super Bowl. I don't know what I did to deserve best friends like you, but I'm so fucking grateful I get to do life and smutty books with you both.

To my husband, Johnny, thank you for loving me through every high and low of this writing rollercoaster. Thank you for listening to me ramble about fictional people like they were real (because to me, they are), for letting me cry when things didn't click, and for putting up with the full range of unhinged threats I've made toward my own characters. You've held space for me in the chaos, cheered me on, and never once made me feel silly for chasing this dream. I love you.

To my beta team, including my incredible sensitivity readers for celiac and social work:
Megan Stitzer
Elise Galvez
Devon Hughes
Alisha O'Toole
Katelin Stephenson
Maureen Cook
Emma Brown
Rose DeVault
Nina Harris
Kennedy Lambert
Cori Hamm
Courtney Roth

You got me through the home stretch. Your feedback, your joy, your notes and chaos-laced messages filled with tears, screaming, and kicking feet gave me the energy to push through when I was running on empty. You helped me make this story better. More real, more accurate, more heart-wrenching, more healing. Thank you for helping me take care—with every detail and every page.

To my editor, Victoria at Cruel Ink Editing—thank you for jumping in with both feet and tackling this project with so much compassion, clarity, and hustle. You were a lighthouse in the storm, and I truly don't know how I would've finished this book without you. You've got a lifetime client, whether you want me or not.

To the over fifteen hundred of you who applied to ARC Happily Never After—are you kidding me?! Fifteen HUNDRED people wanted to read this book before it even released. As a debut small-town romance author, that number still makes me want to sit down and cry in the best possible way. You showed up for me. You keep showing up. And that? That means the world. Thank you for spreading the word, for giving new authors a chance, and for making this dream possible.

And finally—to the readers.

Thank you for picking up this book. For highlighting your favorite lines. For reviewing, sharing, messaging me, following my pretty pink journey across social media and newsletters. For loving the stories I build out of late nights, loud playlists, and too many cups of coffee.

Whether you found me through Bex Dawn, Phoenyx Saint, or now Paisley Nash… you've changed my life. I mean that. Your support has shaped this wild dream into something real, and I'm still trying to wrap my head around it.

Here's to the next chapter. To finding family in unexpected places. To second chances, slow burns, and so many more sticky, happily ever afters. 'Till next time, Nashland!

With all my love,
Paisley

About Author

Paisley Nash

Paisley Nash writes swoon-worthy small-town romance with flirty banter, angsty plots, and plenty of heart. Her stories are filled with feral-for-their-woman guys, cozy hometown vibes, and just enough spice to melt more than your heart. When she's not writing, you can find her sipping sun tea, dreaming up her next book, or belting out T-Swift songs in the kitchen.

For updates and new releases, follow Paisley on socials, and her newsletter.

www.authorpaisleynash.com

Interior Formatting

Bexley Co. Luxury Author Services and

The Witching Hour Publishing LLC

Cover Creation

The Witching Hour Publishing LLC

Proofreading

Katelin Stephensen

Editing

CruelInk Editing Services